GOLLANCZ

LONDON

Copyright © Hannu Rajaniemi 2010
All rights reserved

The right of Hannu Rajaniemi to be identified as the author
of this work has been asserted by him in accordance with the
Copyright, Designs and Patents Act 1988.

First published in Great Britain in 2010 by Gollancz
An imprint of the Orion Publishing Group
Orion House, 5 Upper St Martin's Lane, London WC2H 9EA
An Hachette UK Company

A CIP catalogue record for this book is
available from the British Library

ISBN 978 0 575 08887 0 (Cased)
ISBN 978 0 575 08888 7 (Trade Paperback)

7 9 10 8

Typeset by Deltatype Ltd, Birkenhead, Merseyside

Printed by Clays Ltd, St Ives plc

The Orion Publishing Group's policy is to use papers that are natural,
renewable and recyclable products and made from wood grown in sustainable
forests. The logging and manufacturing processes are expected to conform to
the environmental regulations of the country of origin.

www.orionbooks.co.uk

This is for Nana

'… there comes a time when you cease to know yourself amid all these changes, and that is very sad. I feel at present as the man must have felt who lost his shadow …'

Maurice Leblanc, *The Escape of Arsène Lupin*

1

THE THIEF AND THE PRISONER'S DILEMMA

As always, before the warmind and I shoot each other, I try to make small talk.

'Prisons are always the same, don't you think?'

I don't even know if it can hear me. It has no visible auditory organs, just eyes, human eyes, hundreds of them, in the ends of stalks that radiate from its body like some exotic fruit. It hovers on the other side of the glowing line that separates our cells. The huge silver Colt would look ridiculous in the grip of its twiglike manipulator limbs if it hadn't already shot me with it fourteen thousand times.

'Prisons are like airports used to be on Earth. No one wants to be here. No one really *lives* here. We're just passing through.'

Today, the Prison's walls are glass. There is a sun far above, almost like the real one but not quite right, paler. Millions of glass-walled, glass-floored cells stretch to infinity around me. The light filters through the transparent surfaces and makes rainbow colours on the floor. Apart from them, my cell is bare, and so am I: birth-naked, except for the gun. Sometimes, when you win, they let you change the little things. The warmind has been successful. It has zero-g flowers floating in its cell, red and purple and green bulbs growing out of bubbles of water, like cartoon versions of itself. Narcissistic bastard.

'If we had toilets, the doors would open inwards. Nothing ever changes.'

All right, so I *am* starting to run out of material.

The warmind raises its weapon slowly. A ripple passes through its eyestalks. I wish it had a face: the stare of its moist forest of orbs is unnerving. *Never mind. It's going to work this time.* I tilt the gun upwards slightly, my body language and wrist movement suggesting the motion I would make if I was going to put up my gun. My every muscle screams *cooperation. Come on. Fall for it. Honest. This time, we are going to be friends—*

A fiery wink: the black pupil of its gun, flashing. My trigger finger jerks. There are two thunderclaps. And a bullet in my head.

You never get used to the feeling of hot metal, entering your skull and exiting through the back of your head. It's simulated in glorious detail. A burning train through your forehead, a warm spray of blood and brain on your shoulders and back, the sudden chill – and finally, the black, when things *stop*. The Archons of the Dilemma Prison want you to feel it. It's educational.

The Prison is all about education. And game theory: the mathematics of rational decision-making. When you are an immortal mind like the Archons, you have time to be obsessed with such things. And it is just like the Sobornost – the upload collective that rules the Inner Solar System – to put them in charge of their prisons.

We play the same game over and over again, in different forms. An archetypal game beloved by economists and mathematicians. Sometimes it's chicken: we are racers on an endless highway, driving at each other at high speeds, deciding whether or not to turn away at the last minute. Sometimes we are soldiers trapped in trench warfare, facing each other across no-man's-land. And sometimes they go back to basics and make us prisoners – old-fashioned prisoners, questioned by hard-eyed men – who have to choose between betrayal and the code of silence. Guns are the flavour of today. I'm not looking forward to tomorrow.

I snap back to life like a rubber band, blinking. There is a discontinuity in my mind, a rough edge. The Archons change your neural makeup a little bit every time you come back. They claim that eventually Darwin's whetstone will hone any prisoner into a rehabilitated cooperator.

If they shoot and I don't, I'm screwed. If we both shoot, it hurts a little. If we cooperate, it's Christmas for both of us. Except that there is always an incentive to pull the trigger. The theory is that as we meet again and again, cooperative behaviour will emerge.

A few million rounds more and I'll be a Boy Scout.

Right.

My score after the last game is an ache in my bones. The warmind and I both defected. Two games to go, in this round. *Not enough. Damn it.*

You capture territory by playing against your neighbours. If, at the end of each round, your score is higher than that of your neighbours, you win, and are rewarded with duplicates of yourself that replace – and erase – the losers around you. I'm not doing very well today – two double defections so far, both with the warmind – and if I don't turn this around, it's oblivion for real.

I weigh my options. Two of the squares around mine – left and back – contain copies of the warmind. The one on the right has a woman in it: when I turn to face it, the wall between us vanishes, replaced by the blue line of death.

Her cell is as bare as mine. She is sitting in the middle, hugging her knees, wrapped in a black toga-like garment. I look at her curiously: I haven't seen her before. She has a deeply tanned skin that makes me think of Oort, an almond Asian face and a compact, powerful body. I smile at her and wave. She ignores me. Apparently, the Prison thinks that counts as mutual cooperation: I feel my point score go up a little, warm like a shot of whisky. The glass wall is back between us. *Well, that was easy.* But still not enough against the warmind.

'Hey, loser,' someone says. 'She's not interested. Better options around.'

There is another me in the remaining cell. He is wearing a white tennis shirt, shorts and oversized mirrorshades, lounging in a deck chair by a swimming pool. He has a book in his lap: *Le Bouchon de cristal.* One of my favorites, too.

'It got you again,' he says, not bothering to look up. 'Again. What is that, three times in a row now? You should know by now that it always goes for tit-for-tat.'

'I *almost* got it this time.'

'That whole false memory of cooperation thing is a good idea,' he says. 'Except, you know, it will never work. The warminds have non-standard occipital lobes, non-sequential dorsal stream. You can't fool it with visual illusions. Too bad the Archons don't give points for effort.'

I blink.

4

'Wait a minute. How do you know that, but I don't?'

'Did you think you are the *only* le Flambeur in here? I've been around. Anyway, you need ten more points to beat it, so get over here and let me help you out.'

'Rub it in, smartass.' I walk to the blue line, taking my first relieved breath of this round. He gets up as well, pulling his sleek automatic from beneath the book.

I point a forefinger at him. 'Boom boom,' I say. 'I co-operate.'

'Very funny,' he says and raises his gun, grinning.

My double reflection in his shades looks small and naked. 'Hey. Hey. We're in this together, right?' *And this is me thinking I had a sense of humor.*

'Gamblers and high rollers, isn't that who we are?'

Something clicks. Compelling smile, elaborate cell, putting me at ease, reminding me of myself but somehow not quite right—

'Oh fuck.'

Every prison has its rumours and monsters and this place is no different. I heard this one from a zoku renegade I co-operated with for a while: the legend of the anomaly. The All-Defector. The *thing* that *never* cooperates and gets away with it. It found a glitch in the system so that it always appears as *you*. And if you can't trust yourself, who can you trust?

'Oh yes,' says the All-Defector, and pulls the trigger.

At least it's not the warmind, I think when the bright thunder comes.

And then things stop making sense.

In the dream, Mieli is eating a peach, on Venus. The flesh is sweet and juicy, slightly bitter. It mingles with Sydän's taste in a delicious way.

'You bastard', she says, breathing heavily.

They are in a q-dot bubble fourteen klicks above the Cleopatra Crater, a little pocket of humanity, sweat and sex on a rough precipice of Maxwell Montes. Sulphuric acid winds roar outside. The amber light of the cloud cover filtering through the adamantine pseudomatter shell makes Sydän's skin run copper. Her palm fits the contours of Mieli's mons Veneris exactly, resting just above her still moist sex. Soft wings flutter lazily in her belly.

'What did I do?'

'Lots of things. Is that what they taught you in the *guberniya*?'

Sydän smiles her pixie smile, little crow's feet in the corners of her eyes. 'It's kind of been a while for me, actually,' she says.

'My ass.'

'What about it? It's very nice.'

The fingers of Sydän's free hand trace the silvery lines of the butterfly tattoo on Mieli's chest.

'Don't do that,' Mieli says. Suddenly, she feels cold.

Sydän pulls her hand away and touches Mieli's cheek.

'What's wrong?'

All the flesh of the fruit is gone, and only the stone remains. She holds it in her mouth before spitting it out, a rough little thing, surface engraved with memory.

'You are not really here. You're not real. Just here to keep me sane, in the Prison.'

'Is it working?'

Mieli pulls her close, kissing her neck, tasting sweat. 'Not really. I don't want to leave.'

'You were always the strong one,' Sydän says. She caresses Mieli's hair. 'It is almost time.'

Mieli clings onto her, the familiar feel of her body. The jewelled serpent on Sydän's leg presses hard against her.

Mieli. The pellegrini's voice in her head is like a cold wind.

'Just a little while longer—'

Mieli!

The transition is hard and painful, like biting down on the peach-stone, the hard kernel of reality almost cracking her teeth. A prison cell, fake, pale sunlight. A glass wall, and beyond it, two thieves, talking.

The mission. Long months of preparation and execution. Suddenly, she is wide awake, the plan running through her head.

It was a mistake to give you that memory, says the pellegrini in her head. *It is almost too late. Now let me out: it is getting cramped in here.*

Mieli spits the peach-stone at the glass wall. It shatters like ice.

First, time slows down.

The bullet is an ice-cream headache, burrowing into my skull. I am falling, yet not falling, suspended. The All-Defector is a frozen statue beyond the blue line, still holding his gun.

The glass wall to my right shatters. The shards float around me, glinting in the sun, a galaxy of glass.

The woman from the cell walks up to me briskly. There is a deliberation in her step that makes it look like something she has rehearsed for a long time, like an actor who has received a cue.

She looks at me, up and down. She has short-cropped dark hair, and a scar on her left cheekbone: just a line of black against her deep tan, precise and geometrical. Her eyes are pale green. 'It's your lucky day,' she says. 'There is something for you to steal.' She offers me her hand.

The bullet headache intensifies. There are patterns in the glass galaxy around us, almost like a familiar face—

I smile. *Of course. It is a dying dream. Some glitch in the system: it's just taking a while. Broken prison. Toilet doors. Nothing ever changes.*

'No,' I say.

The dream-woman blinks.

'I am Jean le Flambeur,' I say. 'I steal what I choose, when I choose. And I will leave this place when I choose, not a second before. As a matter of fact, I quite like it here—' The pain makes the world go white, and I can no longer see. I start laughing.

Somewhere in my dream, someone laughs with me. *My Jean,* says another voice, so familiar. *Oh yes. We'll take this one.*

A hand made from glass brushes my cheek, just as my simulated brain finally decides it is time to die.

Mieli holds the dead thief in her arms: he weighs nothing. The pellegrini is flowing into the Prison from the peachstone, like a heat ripple. She coalesces into a tall woman in a white dress, diamonds around her neck, hair carefully arranged in auburn waves, young and old at the same time.

That feels better, she says. *There is not enough room inside your head.* She stretches her arms luxuriously. *Now, let's get you out of here, before my brother's children notice. I have things to do here.*

Mieli feels borrowed strength growing within her, and leaps into the air. They rise up higher and higher, air rushing past, and for a moment she feels like she lived in Grandmother Brihane's house and had wings again. Soon, the Prison is a grid of tiny squares beneath them. The squares change colour, like pixels, forming infinitely complex patterns of cooperation and defection, like pictures—

Just before Mieli and the thief pass through the sky, the Prison becomes the pellegrini's smiling face.

Dying is like walking across a

desert, thinking about stealing. The boy is lying in the hot sand with the sun beating down on his back, watching the robot on the edge of the solar panel fields. The robot looks like a camouflage-coloured crab, a plastic toy: but there are valuable things inside it, and One-Eyed Ijja will pay well for them. And perhaps, just perhaps Tafalkayt will call him son again if he is like a man of the family—

I never wanted to die in a

prison, a dirty place of concrete and metal and bitter stale smells and beatings. The young man's split lip aches. He is reading a book about a man who is like a god. A man who can do anything he wants, who steals the secrets of kings and emperors, who laughs at rules, who can change his face, who only has to reach out his hand to take diamonds and women. A man with the name of a flower.

I hate it so much when they catch you.

pull him up from the sand, roughly. The soldier backhands him across his face, and then the others raise their rifles—

not at all as much fun as

stealing from a mind made of diamond. The god of thieves hides inside thinking dust threaded together by quantum entanglements. He tells the diamond mind lies until it believes he is one of its thoughts and lets him in. up—

9

The people who are many have made worlds that shine and glitter, as if just for him, and he just has to reach out his hand and pick them up

It's like dying. And getting out is like

a key turning in a lock. The metal bars slide aside. A goddess walks in and tells him he is free.

being born.

The pages of the book turn.

Deep breath. Everything hurts. The scale of things is wrong. I cover my eyes with vast hands. Lightning flashes at the touch. Muscles are a network of steel cables. Mucus in my nose. A hole in my stomach, burning, churning.

Focus. I make the sensory noise into a rock, like those on Argyre Planitia, large and clumsy and smooth. In my mind, I lie down on a fine mesh, pouring through it, crumbling into fine red sand, falling through. The rock cannot follow.

Suddenly it is quiet again. I listen to my pulse. There is something impossibly *regular* about it: every beat like a tick of a perfect mechanism.

Faint scent of flowers. Air currents tickling the hairs of my forearms, and other places – I am still naked. Weightlessness. The inaudible but palpable presence of smartmatter, all around. And another human being, not far away.

Something tickles my nose. I brush it aside and open my eyes. A white butterfly flutters away, into bright light.

I blink. I'm aboard a ship, an Oortian spidership by the looks of it, in a cylindrical space perhaps ten metres long, five in diameter. The walls are transparent, the dirty hue of comet ice. There are strange tribal sculptures suspended inside them, like runic characters. Spherical bonsai trees and many-angled zero-g furniture float along the central axis of the cylinder. There is starry darkness beyond the walls. And small white butterflies, everywhere.

My rescuer floats nearby. I smile at her.

'Young lady,' I say. 'I believe you are the most beautiful thing I have ever seen.' My voice sounds distant, but mine. I wonder if they got my face right.

Up close, she looks awfully young, genuinely so: her clear green eyes lack that rejuvenated, seen-it-all look. She wears the same simple garment as in the Prison. She floats in a deceptively comfortable angle, smooth bare legs outstretched, relaxed but ready, like a martial artist. A chain made from multicoloured jewels snakes around her left ankle and up her leg.

'Congratulations, thief,' she says. Her voice is low and controlled, but betrays a hint of contempt. 'You have escaped.'

'I hope so. For all I know this could be some new Dilemma variation. The Archons have been pretty consistent so far, but you are not paranoid if they *really* have you imprisoned in a virtual hell.'

Something stirs between my legs and banishes at least some of my doubts.

'Sorry. It's been a while,' I say, studying my erection with detached interest.

'Evidently,' she says, frowning. There is an odd expression on her face, a mixture of disgust and arousal: I realise she must be listening to this body's biot feed, a part of her feeling what I'm feeling. Another jailer, then.

'Trust me, you are out. It required considerable expense. Of course, there are still several million of you in the Prison, so consider yourself lucky.'

I grab one of the handles of the central axis and move behind a bonsai tree, covering my nudity like Adam. A cloud of butterflies alights from the foliage. The exertion feels strange as well: the muscles of my new body are still waking up.

'Young lady, I have a name.' I offer her my hand across the bonsai tree. She takes it, dubiously, and squeezes. I return the grip as hard as I can. Her expression does not change. 'Jean le Flambeur, at your service. Although you are absolutely right.' I hold up her ankle chain. It squirms in my cupped hand as if alive, a jewelled serpent. 'I am a thief.'

Her eyes widen. The scar on her cheek goes black. And suddenly, I'm in hell.

I am a bodiless viewpoint in blackness, unable to form a coherent thought. My mind is trapped in a vice. Something *squeezes* from all sides, not allowing me to think or remember or feel. It is a thousand times worse than the Prison. It lasts for an eternity.

Then I am back, gasping, stomach heaving, vomiting bile in floating gobbets, but infinitely grateful for every sensation.

'You will not do that again,' she says. 'Your body and mind are on loan, do you understand? Steal what you are told to steal, and you may be allowed to keep them.' The jewelled chain is back around her ankle. Her cheek muscles twitch.

My Prison-honed instincts tell me to shut up and stop throwing up, but the flower man in me has to speak, and I cannot stop him.

'It's too late,' I gasp.

'What?' There is something beautiful about the wrinkle that appears on her smooth forehead, like a brushstroke.

'I am reformed. You got me out too late. I'm an evolved altruist now, mademoiselle, a being filled with goodwill and neighbourly love. I could not possibly dream of taking part in any sort of criminal activity, even at the behest of my lovely rescuer.'

She stares at me blankly.

'Very well.'

'Very well?'

'If you're no good for me, I'll just have to go back for another one. *Perhonen*, please bubble this one up and throw it out.'

We stare at each other for a moment. I feel stupid. Too long on the train of defection and cooperation. Time to jump off. I'm the first one to look away.

'Wait,' I say slowly. 'Now that you mention it, perhaps I do retain some selfish impulses after all. I can feel them coming back as we speak.'

'I thought they might,' she says. 'You are supposed to be irredeemable, after all.'

'So, what's going to happen now?'

'You'll find out,' she says. 'My name is Mieli. This is *Perhonen*: she is my ship.' She makes a sweeping gesture with one hand. 'As long as you are here, we are your gods.'

'Kuutar and Ilmatar?' I ask, naming the Oortian deities.

'Perhaps. Or the Dark Man, if you prefer.' She smiles. The thought of the place she put me in before does make her look a little like the Oortian dark god of the void. '*Perhonen* will show you your quarters.'

When the thief is gone, Mieli lies down in the pilot's crèche. She feels exhausted, even though the biot feed of her body – that has been waiting for her with *Perhonen*, for months – tells her she is perfectly rested. But the cognitive dissonance is worse.

Was it me who was in the Prison? Or another?

She remembers the long weeks of preparation, days of subjective slowtime in a q-suit, getting ready to commit a crime just so she could be caught by the Archons and enter the Prison: the eternity in her cell, mind wrapped in an old memory. The violent escape, hurled through the sky by the pellegrini, waking up in a new body, shaking and raw.

All because of the thief.

And now there is the quantum umbilical that connects her to the body the pellegrini made for him, a constant dull awareness of his thoughts. It feels like lying next to a stranger, feeling them moving, shifting in their sleep. Trust the Sobornost goddess to make her do something guaranteed to drive her crazy.

He touched Sydän's jewel. The anger helps, a little. *And no, it's not just because of him, it's for her as well.*

'I've put the thief away,' says *Perhonen*. Its warm voice in her head is something that belongs to *her* at least, not something that was tainted by the Prison. She takes one of its tiny white avatars and cups it in her palm: it flutters, tickling, like a pulse.

'Feeling amorous?' asks the ship, jokingly.

'No,' says Mieli. 'I just missed you.'

'I missed you too,' says the ship. The butterfly takes flight from her hand, fluttering around her head. 'It was terrible, waiting for you, all alone.'

'I know,' says Mieli. 'I'm sorry.' Suddenly, there is a throbbing sensation inside her skull. There is an edge in her mind, like something has been cut and pasted in place. *Did I come back the same?* She could speak to her Sobornost metacortex, she knows: ask it to find the feeling and wrap it up and put it away. But that's not what an Oortian warrior would do.

'You are not well. I should not have let you go,' *Perhonen* says. 'It was not good for you to go there. She should not have made you to do that.'

'Ssh,' says Mieli. 'She's going to hear.' But it is too late.

Little ship, says the pellegrini. *You should know that I take care of my children, always.*

The pellegrini is there, standing above Mieli.

Naughty girl, she says. *Not using my gifts properly. Let me see.* She sits down next to Mieli gracefully, as if in Earthlike gravity, crossing her legs. Then she touches Mieli's cheek, her deep brown eyes seeking hers. Her fingers feel warm, apart from the cold line of one of her rings, exactly where Mieli's scar is. She breathes in her perfume. Something *rotates*, clockwork gears turning, until they click into place. And suddenly her mind is smooth as silk.

There, is that not better? One day you will understand that our way works. Not worrying about who is who, and realising that they are all you.

The dissonance being gone is like cold water on a burn. The sudden relief is so raw that she almost bursts into tears. But that would not do in front of *her*. So she merely opens her eyes and waits, ready to obey.

No thank you? says the pellegrini. *Very well.* She opens her purse and takes out a small white cylinder, putting it in her mouth: one end of it lights up, emitting a foul smell. *So tell me: what do you make of my thief?*

'It is not my place to say,' says Mieli quietly. 'I live to serve.'

Good answer, if a little boring. Is he not handsome? Come now, be honest. Can you really pine after your little lost amour with somebody like him around?

'Do we need him? I can do this. Let me serve you, like I've served you before—'

The pellegrini smiles, her rouge lips perfect like cherries. *Not this time. You are, if not the most powerful of my servants, the most faithful. Do as I tell you, and faith will be rewarded.*

Then she is gone, and Mieli is alone in the pilot's crèche, butterflies dancing around her head.

My cabin that is not much bigger than a cleaning cupboard. I try to ingest a protein milkshake from the fabber in the wall, but my new body is not taking to food too well. I have to spend some time on the space-bog: a tiny autonomously moving sack that comes out of the wall and attaches itself onto your ass. Apparently Oortian ships are not big on comfort.

One of the curving walls has a mirrored surface, and I look at my face in it while going through the undignified if necessary bodily functions. It looks *wrong*. In theory, everything is exactly right: the lips, the Peter Lorre eyes (as a lover said, centuries ago), the dimpled temples, the short hair, slightly grey and thinning, the way I like to wear it: the skinny, unremarkable body, in reasonable shape, with its tuft of chest hair. But I can't help looking at it and blinking, as if it was out of focus slightly.

What's worse, I have a similar feeling *inside* my head. Trying to remember feels like poking at a loose tooth with my tongue.

It feels like something has been *stolen*. Ha.

I distract myself by looking at the view. My wall has enough magnification to show the Dilemma Prison in the distance. It's a diamonoid torus almost a thousand kilometers in diameter, but from this angle it looks like a glistening slit-pupilled eye among the stars, staring straight at me. I swallow and blink it away.

'Glad to be out?' asks the voice of the ship. It's a feminine voice, a little like Mieli's, but younger, sounding like some-body I'd quite like to meet under happier circumstances.

'You can't possibly imagine. It's not a happy place.' I sigh. 'Your captain has my gratitude, even if she appears to be somewhat on the edge at the moment.'

'Listen,' says *Perhonen*. 'You don't know what she went through to get you out. I'm keeping an eye on you.'

It's an interesting point, which I file away for future inves-tigation. How *did* she get me out? And who is she working for? But it's too early for that, so I simply smile.

'Well, whatever job she wants me to do *has* to be better than shooting myself in the head every hour or so. Are you sure your boss would be all right with you talking to me? I mean, I am a manipulative master criminal and all that.'

'I think I can handle you. Besides, it's not like she is my *boss*, exactly.'

'Oh,' I say. I'm old-fashioned, but the whole human-gogol sexuality thing always bothered me in my youth, and old habits die hard.

'It's not like *that*,' the ship says. 'Just friends! Besides, she made me. Well, not *me*, but the ship. I'm older than I look, you know.' I wonder if that accent in its voice is real. 'I heard about you, you know. Back then. Before the Collapse.'

'I would have said that you don't look a day over three hundred. Were you a fan?'

'I liked the sunlifter theft. That was classy.'

'Class,' I say, 'is what I've always aimed for. By the way, you don't look a day over three hundred.'

'Do you really think so?'

'Mm-hm. Based on the evidence so far.'

'Would you like me to show you around? Mieli won't mind, she's busy.'

'I'd love that.' *Definitely female – maybe some of my charm survived the Prison.* I suddenly feel the need to get dressed: talking to a female entity of any kind without even a fig leaf makes me feel vulnerable. 'Sounds like we'll have plenty of time to get to know each other better. Maybe after you get me some clothes?'

First, *Perhonen* fabs me a suit. The fabric is too smooth – I don't like wearing smartmatter – but looking at myself in a white shirt, black trousers and a deep purple jacket helps with the sense of unself a little.

Then she shows me the spimescape. Suddenly, the world has a new direction. I step into it, out of my body, moving my viewpoint into space so that I can look at the ship.

I was right: *Perhonen* is an Oortian spidership. It consists of separate modules, tethered together by nanofibres, living quarters spinning around a central axis like an amusement park ride to create a semblance of gravity. The tethers form a network in which the modules can move, like spiders in a web. The q-dot sails – concentric soap-bubble-thin rings made from artificial atoms that spread out several kilometres around the ship and can catch sunlight, Highway meso-particles and lightmill beams equally well – look spectacular.

I steal a glance at my own body as well, and that's when I'm *really* impressed. The spimescape view is seething with detail. A network of q-dots under the skin, proteomic computers in every cell, dense computronium in the bones. Something like that could only have been made in the *guberniya* worlds close to the sun. It seems my rescuers are working for the Sobornost. Interesting.

'I thought you wanted to get to know *me*,' *Perhonen* says, offended.

'Of course,' I say. 'Just, you know, making sure I'm present-able. You don't spend much time in the company of ladies in the Prison.'

'Why were you there, anyway?'

Suddenly, it feels amazing that I haven't thought about it for so long. I have been too preoccupied with guns, defection and cooperation.

Why was I in the Prison?

'A nice girl like you should not worry about such things.'

Perhonen sighs. 'Maybe you're right. Maybe I should not be talking to you. Mieli would not like it if she knew. But it's been so long since we had anyone *interesting* onboard.'

'This certainly does not seem like a lively neighbourhood.' I indicate the starry field around us. 'Where are we?'

'The Neptunian Trojan belt. Arse-end of nowhere. I waited here for a long time, when she went to get you.'

'You have a lot to learn about being a criminal. It's all about the waiting. Boredom punctuated by flashes of sheer terror. Sort of like war.'

'Oh, war was much better,' she says, excitedly. 'We were in the Protocol War. I loved it. You get to think so *fast*. Some of the things we did – we stole a moon, you know. It was amazing. Metis, just before the Spike: Mieli put a strangelet bomb in to push it out of orbit, like fireworks, you would not believe—'

Suddenly, the ship is silent. I wonder if it realised it has said too much. But no: its attention is focused elsewhere.

In the distance, amidst the spiderweb of *Perhonen*'s sails and the spimescape vectors and labels of habitats far away, there is a jewel of bright dots, a six-pointed star. I zoom in in the scape view. Dark ships, jagged and fang-like, a cluster of seven faces sculpted in their prows, the same faces that adorn every Sobornost structure, the Founders: god-kings with a trillion subjects. I used to go drinking with them.

The Archons are coming.

'Whatever it was that you did,' *Perhonen* says, 'looks like they want you back.'

2

THE THIEF AND THE ARCHONS

What did I do?

Mieli's heart pounds as the pilot's crèche embraces her. *Something went wrong in the Prison. But it was just like the sims. Why are they after us?* She summons the combat autism the pellegrini built into her. It enfolds her like a cool blanket, turns the world into vectors and gravity wells. Her mind enmeshes with *Perhonen*'s, thinking fast thoughts.

Objects: *Perhonen.*

Scattered Trojan asteroids, clustered around 2006RJ103, a two-hundred k nugget of rock, inhabited by slow-brained synthlife.

The Prison, a diamond doughnut thirty lightseconds behind them, the origin of *Perhonen*'s current vector, dense, dark and cold.

The Archon bladeships, coming in fast at a .5g, much more delta-v than the gentle tug of *Perhonen*'s lightsail. The torches of their antimatter engines are fiery pillars of backscattered mesons and gamma rays in the spimescape.

The Highway, twenty lightseconds away, their next way-point. A constant torrent of ships, one of the few rare ideal invariant surfaces in the N-body Newton's nightmare of the Solar System, a gravitational artery that lets you travel fast and easy with the gentlest of pushes. A safe haven, too far away.

All right, breathes Mieli. *Combat mode.*

The hidden Sobornost tech beneath the Oortian sapphire coral wakes up. The spidership reconfigures itself. The scattered modules pull themselves together along their tethers and fuse together into a tight, hard cone. The q-dot winglets transform from a perfectly reflective material into a diamond-hard firewall.

Just in time, before the Archons' nanomissiles hit.

The first volley is just a series of thistledown impacts that fail to penetrate. But the next batch will adapt and optimise, and so will the ones after that, over and over and over until either the software or the hardware of the firewall collapses. And after that—

We need to get to the Highway.

The engines in her mind prune the game-theoretic branches like diamond-bladed chainsaws. There are many paths through this, like meanings in an Oortian song, and she only needs to find one—

Another barrage, innumerable needles of light in the spimescape. And this time, something gets through. One of the storage modules blossoms into a misshapen sapphire growth. Calmly, she ejects it, watches it drift away, still mutating and shifting in slow motion like a malignant tumour, forming strange organs that fire molecule-sized spores at *Perhonen*'s firewall until she burns it with the anti-meteorite lasers.

'That hurt,' *Perhonen* says.

'I'm afraid that this will hurt a lot more.'

22

She burns all the delta-v in their emergency antimatter in one burst, swinging the ship into the shallow gravity well of 2006RJ103. *Perhonen*'s flesh groans as the antiprotons from the magnetic storage ring turn into hot jets of plasma. She diverts some of the power to pumping up the binding energies of the programmable matter rods in the hull. The Archons follow without effort, approaching, firing again.

Perhonen screams around Mieli, but the autism keeps her mind on the task at hand. She thinks a q-dot torpedo around the strangelet in *Perhonen*'s tiny weapons bay and fires it at the asteroid.

There is a brief flash in the spimescape, gamma rays and exotic baryons. Then the rocky lump becomes a fountain of light, a lightning flash that does not end. The scape struggles to keep up, turns into white noise and goes down. Flying blind, Mieli spreads *Perhonen*'s wings again. The particle wind from the strange death of the asteroid grabs them and hurls them towards the Highway. The acceleration makes her heavy, suddenly, and the sapphire structure of the ship sings around her.

It takes a moment for the scape to come back up and to filter out the particle noise and the madness. Mieli holds her breath: but no black fang-like ships emerge from the slowly expanding incandescence behind them. Either they were consumed, or lost track of their target in the subatomic madness. She lifts the autism to let herself feel a moment of triumph.

'We made it,' she says.

'Mieli? I don't feel so good.'

There is a black stain spreading in the ship's hull. And in the centre of it, is a tiny black shard, cold and dark. An Archon nanomissile.

'Get it out.' The fear and disgust taste like bile after the combat autism, raw and foul.

'I can't. I can't touch it anymore. It tastes like the Prison.'

Mieli shouts a prayer in her head, at the part of her mind that the Sobornost goddess has touched. But the pellegrini does not answer.

Around me, the ship is dying.

I don't know what Mieli did, but, judging by the miniature nova that lit in space minutes ago, she is putting up a good fight. But now there is a spiderweb of blackness spreading into the sapphire in the walls. That's what the Archons do: they inject themselves into you and turn *you* into a Prison. There is a burning sawdust smell as the nanites work, faster and faster, overcoming whatever immune systems the ship is throwing at it. There is a noise, too, the roar of a forest fire.

It was too good to last, I suppose. Fair cop, guv. I try to remember the thrill of stealing Mieli's jewel. Maybe I can take it with me. Or maybe it's all another dying dream. I never left. This was just a prison within a prison, all along.

Then I hear a mocking voice in my head.

Jean le Flambeur, giving up. The Prison broke you. You deserve to go back. No different from the broken warminds and mad Sobornost toys and the forgotten dead. You don't even remember the exploits, the adventures. You are not him, just a memory that thinks it is—

Hell no. There is always a way out. You are never in a prison unless you *think* you are. A goddess told me that.

And suddenly, I know exactly what I need to do.

'Ship.'

There is no answer. *Damn it.*

'Ship! I need to talk to Mieli!' Still nothing.

The cabin is getting hot. I need to move. Outside, *Perhonen*'s wings are ablaze, like trapped aurora borealis, burning in space around us. The ship has so much acceleration that it actually has gravity now, at least half a g. But the directions are all wrong: *below* is somewhere towards the rear end of the central chamber. I scramble out of my cabin, grasp the axis handles and start hauling myself towards the pilot's crèche.

There is a blast of heat and a searing light: an entire segment of the cylinder spins out to the void below. The only thing separating me from the vacuum is a soap-bubble wall of q-dots that flashes into being. But it is too late to cut the infection out. Hot sapphire fragments swirl in the air around me: one leaves a painful bloody brushstroke on my forearm, razor-sharp.

It is hot now, and the sawdust stench is everywhere. The blackness in the walls is spreading: the ship is burning, burning into something else. Heart beating in my chest like there was a Notre Dame hunchback making it ring, I climb upwards.

I can see into the pilot's crèche through the sapphire: madly swirling utility fog like heat haze in the air, with Mieli suspended inside, eyes closed. I pound the door with my fist. 'Let me in!'

I don't know if her brain has been compromised yet. For all I know, she could already be in the Prison. But if not, I need her to get out of this. I try to get leverage from the pole and kick at the door with my heel. But it's no use – unless either her or the ship tells the smart sapphire to open.

Sapphire. I remember her expression when I woke up with a hard-on. She is reading this body's biot feed, but must be filtering it out. Unless there is a threshold—

Oh crap. Not hesitating makes it easier. I grab a long, sharp sapphire shard from the air and push the point through my left palm, between the metacarpal bones, as hard as I can. I almost black out. The shard scrapes the bones as it goes in, tearing tendons and veins. The pain is like shaking hands with Satan, red and black and unrelenting. I smell blood: it is pumping out of the wound, all over me and falling down into the void below, slowly, in large misshapen droplets.

It is the first time I feel real pain since the Prison, and there is something glorious about it. I look at the blue shard sticking out of my hand and start laughing, until the pain gets to be too much and I have to scream.

Someone slaps me, hard.

'What the hell do you think you are doing?'

Mieli is looking at me in the doorway of the pilot's crèche, eyes wide. *Well, at least she felt that.* Inert utility foglets swirl around us, grey dust adding to the chaos: it makes me think of falling ash, in a burning city.

'Trust me,' I tell her, grinning madly, bleeding. 'I have a plan.'

'You have ten seconds.'

'I can get it out. I can fool it. I know how. I know how it thinks. I was there for a *long* time.'

'And why should I trust you?'

I hold up my bleeding hand and pull out the sapphire. There is more blinding pain, and a squelching sound.

'Because,' I hiss through gritted teeth, 'I will rather put this through my eye than go back.'

She holds my eyes for a moment. And then she actually smiles.

'What do you need?'

'Root access to this body. I know what it can do. I need computing power, way more than baseline.'

26

Mieli takes a deep breath. 'All right. Get that bastard off my ship.'

Then she closes her eyes, and something inside my head goes *click*.

I am *root*, and the body is a world-tree, an Yggdrasil. There are diamond machines in its bones, proteomic tech in its cells. And the brain, a true Sobornost raion-scale brain, able to run whole worlds. My own human psyche inside it is less than one page in a library of Babel. A part of me, the smiling part, thinks of escape immediately, using this wonderful machine to launch a part of it into space, to leave my liberators to my jailers. Another part surprises me by saying *no*.

I move through the dying ship, looking for the nanomissile, no longer a clumsy monkey but gliding smoothly in the air under my own power, like a miniature spaceship. *There*, my enhanced senses tell me: burrowing into a fabrication module in the other end of the cylinder, a point from which the Prison-matter spreads.

With one thought, I reach out and make a local copy of *Perhonen*'s spimescape. I tell the ship's sapphire flesh to open. It becomes a soft wet gel. I push my hand deep into it, reach for the missile and pull it out. It is tiny, not much larger than a cell, but shaped like a black tooth with sharp roots. My body grasps it with q-dot tendrils. I hold it up: such a tiny thing, but with at least one Archon mind inside, looking for things to turn into Prisons.

I put it into my mouth, bite down hard and swallow.

The Archon is happy.

For a moment, there was an imperfection, when it tasted

the thief, a sense of dissonance, like there were two Thieves, in one.

But things are strange outside the Mother Prison: out here, the games are not pure. The old ugly physics is not perfect like the game of the Archons, perfect in its simplicity, yet capturing all of mathematics in its undecidability. That's why its task is to turn this matter into another Prison, to increase the purity of the Universe. This is what their Father the Engineer-of-Souls thought them to love. This is the way the world is made right.

And this is good matter to turn into a Prison. Its mouth waters in anticipation of the taste of the patterns that the iterated Dilemmas will make. Its copyfather discovered a defector pattern that tastes like pecan ice cream: a replicating strategy family like a flyer in a Game of Life. Perhaps it, too, will find something new here, on this little gameboard of its own.

Far far far away, its copybrothers whisper to it through their quptlink, still complaining about the gut-wrenching *wrongness* of finding out about the escape of the thief, and the *other one*, the anomaly. It tells them all is made well, that they will join the Mother Prison soon, that it will bring back something new.

It looks down upon the grid of cells where the little thieves and butterflies and Oort women live when it finds them in the sweet matter. And soon the Game will begin again, any moment now.

It will taste like lemon sherbet, the Archon thinks.

'Magic,' I tell her. 'You know how magic tricks work?'

I am back to my human self again. The memory of the extended senses and computational power is fading, but still

28

feels like a phantom ache of a lost limb. And of course, I have an Archon running inside me now, locked inside my bones, in computational deep freeze.

We are sitting in one of the cramped storage modules, spinning on a tether for gravity, while the ship repairs itself. But there is a sparkling river of spaceships all around us, scattered over thousands of cubic kilometres but magnified by *Perhonen*'s skin: overclocked fast zoku generation ships that dump waste heat madly, every day of a journey like a thousand years for them; whalelike calmships with green and miniature suns inside, Sobornost thoughtwisps everywhere like fireflies.

'It's quite simple, really – it's all about neuroscience. Misdirected attention.'

Mieli ignores me. She is setting up a small table between us. There are Oortian dishes on it: odd purple transparent cubes and squirming synthlife and neatly cut sections of multicolored fruits – expertly fabbed – and two small glasses. Her movements in setting it up are formal and composed, ritual-like. Ignoring me, she produces a bottle from a wall compartment.

'What are you doing?' I ask her.

She looks at me, expressionless. 'We're celebrating,' she says.

'Well, we should.' I grin at her. 'Anyway, it took me a long time to discover that: you can still induce inattentional blindness in Sobornost minds, would you believe? Nothing ever changes. So I swapped its sensory inputs, hooked it up to a sim based on *Perhonen*'s spimescape. It still thinks it's making a Prison. Very, very slowly.'

'I see.' She frowns at the bottle, apparently trying to figure out how to open it. The lack of interest she displays in my master plan irritates me.

'See? It works like this. Look.'

I touch a spoon, grab it gently, make a motion like closing my hand around it, whereas in fact it's already falling into my lap. Then I hold up both of my hands, opening them. 'Gone.' She blinks in astonishment. I close my left fist again. 'Or, perhaps, transformed.' I open it, and her ankle ringlet is there, squirming. I hold it out to her, an offering. Her eyes flash, but she reaches out, slowly, and takes it from my hand.

'You will not touch that,' she says. 'Ever again.'

'I promise,' I tell her, meaning it. 'Professionals from now on. Deal?'

'Agreed,' she says, with an edge to her voice.

I take a deep breath.

'The ship told me what you did. You went to hell to get me out,' I say. 'What is it that you want so badly to do that?'

She says nothing, opening the bottle's seal with a sudden twist.

'Listen,' I say. 'About that offer. I have reconsidered. Whatever it is that you need stolen, I will steal. No matter who you work for. I'll even do it your way. I owe you that. Call it a debt of honour.'

She pours the wine. The golden liquid is sluggish, so it takes time. When she's done, I raise my glass. 'Shall we drink to that?'

Our glasses clink together: toasting in low-g is a skill. We drink. *Thanisch–Erben Thanisch, 2343. A faint matchstick smell the older bottles of the stuff have: sometimes called Thaddeusatem, Thaddeus's breath.*

How do I know that?

'It's not *you* I need, thief,' Mieli says. 'It's who you *were*. And that's the first thing we have to steal.'

30

I stare at her, breathing in Thaddeus's breath. And with the smell comes a memory, years and years and years of being someone else, being poured into me

like wine into a glass. 'Medium full-bodied, robust, with a trace of eagerness', he says, looking at her through the Riesling that is like liquid light, smiling. 'Who are you calling full-bodied?' she asks, laughing, and in his mind she is his.

But it is he who is hers for many years, years of love and wine, in the Oubliette.

He – I – hid it. Mind steganography. The Proust effect. Somewhere the Archons would not find it, an associative memory unlocked by smell that you would never come across in a prison where you never eat or drink.

'I am a genius,' I tell Mieli.

She does not smile, but her eyes narrow, a little. 'Mars, then,' she says. 'The Oubliette.'

I feel a chill. Clearly, I have little privacy in this body, or in my mind. Another panopticon, another prison. But as prisons go, it is a lot better than the last one: a beautiful woman, secrets and a good meal, and a sea of ships carrying us to adventure.

I smile.

'The place of forgetting,' I say, and raise my glass. 'To new beginnings.'

Quietly, she drinks with me. Around us, *Perhonen*'s sails are bright cuts in space, carrying us down the Highway.

3

THE DETECTIVE AND THE CHOCOLATE DRESS

It surprises Isidore that the chocolate factory smells of leather. The conching machines fill the place with noise, echoing from the high red-brick walls. Cream-coloured tubes gurgle. Rollers move back and forth in stainless-steel vats, massaging aromas from the chocolate mass inside with each gloopy, steady heartbeat.

There is a dead man lying on the floor, in a pool of chocolate. A beam of pale Martian morning light from a high window illuminates him, turning him into a chocolate sculpture of suffering: a wiry pietá with hollow temples and a sparse moustache. His eyes are open, whites showing, but the rest of him is covered in a sticky layer of brown and black, spilled from the vat he is clutching, as if he tried to drown himself in it. His white apron and clothes are a Rorschach test of dark stains.

Isidore 'blinks, accessing the Oubliette exomemory. It lets him recognise the man's face like it belonged to an old friend. *Marc Deveraux. Third Noble incarnation. Chocolatier. Married. One daughter.* It is the first fact, and it makes his spine tingle. As always in the beginning of a mystery, he feels like a child unwrapping a present. There is something that makes sense here, hiding beneath chocolate and death.

'Ugly business,' says a raspy, chorus-like voice, making him jump. It is the Gentleman, of course, standing on the other side of the body, leaning on his cane. The smooth metal ovoid of his face catches the sun in a bright wink, a stark contrast against the black of his long velvet coat and top hat.

'When you called me,' Isidore says, 'I didn't think it was just another gogol pirate case.' He tries to sound casual: but it would be rude to completely mask his emotions with gevulot, so he can't stop a note of enthusiasm escaping. This is only the third time he has met the tzaddik in person. Working with one of the Oubliette's honoured vigilantes still feels like a boyhood dream come true. Still, he would not have expected the Gentleman to call him to work on mind theft. Copying of leading Oubliette minds by Sobornost agents and third parties is what the tzaddiks have sworn to prevent.

'My apologies,' the Gentleman says. 'I will endeavour to arrange something *more* bizarre next time. Look closer.'

Isidore takes out his zoku-made magnifying glass – a gift from Pixil, a smooth disc of smartmatter atop a brass handle – and peers at the body through it. Veins and brain tissue and cellular scans flash into being around him, archeology of a dead metabolism floating past like exotic sea creatures. He 'blinks again, at the unfamiliar medical information this time, and winces at the mild headache as the facts entrench themselves in his short-term memory.

'Some sort of . . . viral infection,' he says, frowning. 'A retrovirus. The glass says there is an anomalous genetic sequence in his brain cells, something from an archeon bacterium. How long before we can talk to him?' Isidore never looks forward to interrogating resurrected crime victims: their memories are always fragmented, and some are unwilling to overcome the traditional Oubliette obsession with privacy, even to help solve their own murder or a gogol piracy case.

'Perhaps never,' the Gentleman says.

'What?'

'This was an optogenetic black box upload. Very crude: it must have been agony. It's an old trick, pre-Collapse. They used to do it with rats. You infect the target with a virus that makes their neurons sensitive to yellow light. Then you stimulate the brain with lasers for hours, capture the firing patterns and train a black box function to emulate them. That's where those little holes in his skull are from. Optic fibres. Upload tendrils.' The tzaddik brushes the chocolatier's thinning hair carefully with a gloved hand: there are tiny black dots in the scalp beneath, a few centimetres apart.

'Produces enormous amounts of redundant data, but gets around gevulot. And of course completely scrambles his exomemory. Kills him, if you like. This body eventually died of tacyarrhythmia. The Resurrection Men are working on his next one, but there is not much hope. Unless we can find out where the data went.'

'I see,' Isidore says. 'You are right, it *is* interesting, for a gogol pirate case.' Isidore can't suppress a note of distaste in his voice at the word *gogol*: a dead soul, the uploaded mind of a human being, enslaved to carry out tasks, anathema to anyone from the Oubliette.

Usually, gogol piracy – upload without the victim's knowledge, stealing their mind – is based on social engineering. The pirates worm their way into the victim's confidence, chipping away at their gevulot until they have enough to do a brute-force attack on their mind. But this – 'A Gordian knot approach. Simple and elegant.'

34

'*Elegant* is not the word I would use, my boy.' There is a trace of anger in the tzaddik's voice. 'Would you like to see what happened to him?'

'See?'

'I visited him earlier. The Resurrection Men are working on him. It's not pretty.'

'Oh.' Isidore swallows. Death is much less gruesome than what happens *after*, and thinking about it makes his palms sweat. But if he ever wants to be a tzaddik, he can't afford to be afraid of the underworld. 'Of course, if you think it's useful.'

'Good.' The Gentleman passes the co-memory to him, opening both hands. Isidore accepts it, momentarily tickled by the intimacy of the gesture. And suddenly he remembers being in a room with the dark-robed Resurrection Men, in the underground spaces where they restore minds from the exomemory into freshly printed bodies. The remade chocolatier lay in the synthbio vat as if taking a bath. Dr Ferreira touched the still form's forehead with the ornate brass Decanter. The sudden flash of eye whites, the reverbrating scream, the flailing limbs, the *pop* of a dislocating jaw—

The leather smell makes Isidore nauseous. 'That's ... monstrous.'

'Unfortunately, it is very human,' the Gentleman says. 'But there is some hope. If we can find the data, Dr Ferreira thinks they can cut the noise from his exomemory and restore him properly.'

Isidore takes a deep breath. He lets the anger dissolve into the calm pool of mystery.

'But can you guess why you are here?'

Isidore feels around with his gevulot sense – an Oubliette citizen's acute awareness of privacy settings in the intelligent matter all around. The factory feels *slippery*. Trying to reach into exomemory for things that happened here is like trying to clutch air.

'This was a very private place for him,' Isidore says. 'I don't think he would have shared the gevulot even with his close family.'

Three little synthbio drones come in – large, dextrous spiders, bright green and purple – and adjust levers and dials of the conching machine. The heartbeat sound goes up a notch. One of them stops to examine the Gentleman, spindly limbs brushing its coat. The tzaddik gives it a sharp poke with his cane, and the creature scutters away.

'Correct,' the Gentleman says. He takes a step forward, standing so close to Isidore that he can see his own reflection in the tzaddik's silver oval face, distorted. His curly hair is in disarray, and his cheeks are burning.

'We have no way to reconstruct anything that happened here, except the old-fashioned way. And, as much as it pains me to admit it, you do seem to have the talent for it.'

Up close, the tzaddik has a strange, sweet smell, like spices, and it feels like the metal mask radiates heat. Isidore takes a step back and clears his throat. 'I will do what I can, of course,' he says, pretending to look at his Watch – a simple copper disc on his wrist, with a single hand, ticking down to his time as a Quiet. 'I expect it to be quick,' he says, nonchalance spoiled by the quiver in his voice. 'I have a party to go to tonight.'

The Gentleman says nothing, but Isidore can imagine the cynical smile beneath the mask.

Another factory machine sputters into life. This one looks much more sophisticated than the stainless steel conching machines. The ornate brass lines hint at a Kingdom-era design: a fabber. An intricate clockwork arm dances above a metal tray, painting a neat row of *macarone* into being with a series of neat atom beam brushstrokes. The drones pack the sweets into small boxes and carry them away.

Isidore raises his eyebrows disapprovingly: a traditional Oubliette craftsman is not really expected to rely on technology. But something about the device does fit in the nascent shape that he can feel forming in his mind. He examines it more closely. The tray is covered in thin strips of chocolate residue.

'I will need whatever else you have, of course, to begin with,' he says.

'His assistant says she found the body.' With a flick of a white-gloved hand, the Gentleman passes Isidore a small co-memory: a face and a name. He recalls her like a passing acquaintance. *Siv Lindström. Dusky skin and a pretty face, dark hair arranged in a swirl of dark cocoa.* 'And the family has agreed to speak to us – what are you doing?'

Isidore puts a piece of the chocolate from the fabber tray in his mouth, 'blinking as fast as he can, cringing at the headache of alien memories. They let him recognise the faint red berry taste and bitterness, and the strange *terroir* of the soil in Nanedi Valley. There is something *wrong* about it, about the fragility. He walks over to the chocolatier's body and tries some of the chocolate from the vat he is holding. And that, of course, tastes exactly right.

Unbidden, the shape of the chocolatier's story emerges in his mind, brushstroke by brushstroke, like the *macarone* a moment before.

'Detecting,' Isidore says. 'I want to see the assistant first.'

The walk back to town leads Isidore and the Gentleman across the Tortoise Park.

That, in itself, is a testament to the chocolatier's success. The red-brick building with a huge mural depicting cocoa beans sits in one of the most desirable locations of the city. A green space with low, rolling hills perhaps three hundred metres across, like all the interlocking parts of the City, the park is carried by a walking robotic platform. The green fields are dotted with tall, graceful, Kingdom-era villas that the young Time-rich of the Oubliette restore and incorporate into the city. Isidore has never understood the need of some of his generation to burn their Time fast on material goods and services, spending their Noble lives in brief opulence before the long, back-breaking labour as a Quiet. Especially when there are mysteries to solve.

Even though the park is an open space, it is not an agora, and walking down the sandy pathways, they pass several gevulot-obscured people, their privacy fog shimmering like the morning dew of the grassy fields around them.

Wanting to be alone with his thoughts for a moment, Isidore walks fast, holding his hands inside his overcoat sleeves against the chill: with his long legs, he usually manages to keep a distance between himself and others. But the Gentleman stays with him, seemingly without effort.

You are bored, aren't you? Pixil's qupt is abrupt. Along with her voice, it brings a tangle of sensations: a taste of espresso, the odd too-clean smell of the zoku colony.

Isidore massages the entanglement ring he wears on the index finger of his right hand: a silver band with a tiny blue stone, speaking directly to his brain. He has yet to get used to the zoku method of qupting. Sending brain-to-brain messages directly through a quantum teleportation channel seems like a dirty, invasive way to communicate compared to Oubliette co-remembering. The latter is much more subtle: embedding messages in the recipient's exomemory so that information is *recalled* rather than received. But as with everything else with Pixil and her people, it is all about compromises.

I can't believe it. Your tzaddik friend snaps its fingers and you leave me behind, to get ready for the party, all by myself. And now you are bored.

I'm not bored, he protests, too quickly, and realises that it is the wrong answer.

I'm glad. Because you will never hear from me again if you don't make it here in time. The qupt comes with an unmistakably erotic sensation of smooth fabric on skin, like a caress. **I'm deciding what to wear. Putting clothes on, taking them off again. I'm thinking of turning it into a game. I could use some help. But, your loss.**

Last night was one of their better nights, in Isidore's small Maze apartment; no distractions, just the two of them. He cooked; afterwards, she showed him a new bedroom game she had designed, which was both intellectually and physically stimulating. Still, he lay awake while she slept, the wheels of his mind turning without traction, looking for patterns in her hair, falling across her pale back.

He tries to think of the right thing to say, but he is still caught in the shape of the dead chocolatier. **It's just gogol pirates,** he qupts back, attaching a careless shrug. **It won't take long. I'll be back in no time.**

The response comes with a sigh. **This. Is. Important. My whole zoku is going to be there. The whole zoku. Coming to see me, the rebel. And to see my stupid primitive Oubliette boyfried. You have two hours.**

I'm making real progress here—

Two. Hours.

Pixil—

I could spoil your game, you know. I could tell you exactly who your tzaddik is. How would you like that?

He is *almost* certain that the threat is a bluff. Her zoku's q-tech does give her abilities far beyond the Oubliette's old calmtech, but the tzaddikim guard their identities well. But even the thought of *not finding out if he could*, not putting the final piece in place on his own, makes him afraid. Before he can stop it, his terror goes down the qupt as a heartbeat, quick and thick.

See? That's what really matters, isn't it? Have fun. Bastard. And then she is gone.

'And how is young Pixil?' asks the Gentleman.

Isidore does not reply and tries to walk faster.

The chocolate shop is in one of the wide shopping streets of the Edge, a gently curving avenue that follows the southern rim of the city. The platforms here are relatively large, and the layout stable, so maps exist. Hence, it is where many offworlders come to catch a glimpse of the Oubliette. The restaurants and cafés are just opening, lighting heaters to make the chilly Martian air palatable to early customers. Purple and green biodrones cluster around them, holding their spindly limbs out for warmth.

The Gentleman stops in front of a narrow shop window. Remarkable objects are on display: a football-sized sphere that looks like a scale model of Kingdom-era Deimos, dotted with multicoloured candy, and an intricate chandelier hanging from the ceiling, both made from chocolate. But a large object next to them is the one that draws Isidore's attention. It is a dress: a sober, high-collared affair with a sash at the waist and a flowing skirt, frozen in a swirly chocolate snapshot.

The tzaddik opens the door, and a brass bell rings. 'Here we are. As your lady friend might put it – the game is afoot. I'll be nearby: but I'll let you do the talking.' He fades out of sight, suddenly, a ghost in the pale morning sun.

The shop is a narrow space with a long glass counter on the left and display shelves on the right, brightly lit. There is a pleasant, sweet smell of chocolate and caramel, not at all like the raw leather of the factory. Beneath the counter, moulded pralines glitter, like bright-carapaced insects. The showpieces are on the right, ornate chocolate sculptures. There is an arching butterfly wing as tall as a man, with an etching of a woman's face, and what looks like a death mask, impossibly thin, made out of chocolate the colour of terra-cotta.

For a moment, Isidore is captivated by a pair of red shoes with flowing chocolate ribbons. He files them away for future reference: Pixil's current mood may require some offerings on his part.

'Looking for something special?' asks a voice, familiar from exomemory. *Siv Lindström*. She looks more tired than the memory, lines in her pretty face. But her blue shop uniform is smooth, and her hair carefully arranged. Their Watches exchange a brief burst of standard shop gevulot, enough for her to know that he does not really know much about chocolate but has Time enough to afford it – and for him to glimpse public exomemories about her and the shop. Her gevulot must be hiding an emotional reaction of some kind, but to Isidore she presents a perfect facade of good service.

'We have a very nice range of *macarone*, fresh from the factory.' She motions towards a counter, busily restocked by a synthbio drone Isidore saw earlier, placing the colourful chocolate discs in neat rows.

'I was thinking,' says Isidore, 'about something … more substantial.' He points at the chocolate dress in the window. 'Like this one. Could I have a closer look at this?'

The assistant walks around the counter and opens the glass panel that separates the window from the shop. She walks in with that abrupt, shuffling step of old Martians, flinching in the absence of Earth's gravity: like a dog that has been beaten too many times, expecting a blow when receiving a caress. Up close, Isidore can see the intricate details of the dress, how the fabric seemingly flows, how vivid the colours are. *Maybe I'm wrong about this.* But then he can feel her gevulot shifting, just a little. *Or not.*

'Well,' she says, tone unchanged. 'This is certainly something very special. It is modelled after a Noblewoman dress from the Olympian Court, made from Trudelle-style chocolate: we had to try the mixture four times. Six hundred aromatic constituents, and you have to get them just right. Chocolate is fickle, it keeps you on your toes.'

'How interesting,' says Isidore, trying to affect the world-weary tone of a Time-rich young man. He takes out his magnifying glass and studies the hem of the dress. The swirly shape becomes a crystalline grid of sugars and molecules. He probes deeper into his fresh chocolate memories. But then the shop gevulot interferes, detecting an unwanted invasion of privacy, and turns the image into a blur.

'What are you doing?' asks Lindström, staring at him as if seeing him for the first time.

Isidore frowns, looking at the white noise.

'Damn. I almost had it,' he says. He gives Lindström his best smile, the one Pixil says turns older women's bones to water. 'Could you please taste it? The dress?'

The assistant looks at him incredulously.

'What?'

'My apologies,' he says. 'I should have told you. I am investigating what happened to your employer.' He opens his gevulot just enough for her to know his name. Her clear green eyes glaze over for a moment as she 'blinks him. Then she takes a deep breath.

'So, you are the wonderboy they keep talking about. Who sees things the tzaddikim don't.' She walks back to the counter. 'Unless you are going to buy something, I'd appreciate it if you left. I'm trying to keep the shop open. It's what he would have wanted. Why should I talk to you? I already told them everything I know.'

'Because,' says Isidore, 'they are going to think you had something to do with it.'

'Why? Because I found him? I barely had enough of his gevulot to know his last name.'

'Because it fits. You are of the First Generation, I can see it in the way you walk. That means you spent almost a century as a Quiet. That can do strange things to a person's mind. Sometimes enough to make them *want* to be a machine again. The gogol pirates could make that happen, for a price. If you did them a favour. Like helped them to steal the mind of a world-famous chocolatier—'

Her gevulot closes completely, and she becomes a blurry placeholder for a person, wrapped in privacy: at the same time, Isidore knows he is a non-entity for her. But it only lasts for a moment. Then she is back, eyes closed, fists pressed against her chest as if she's holding something in, knuckles hard and white against her dark skin.

'It was not like that,' she says quietly.

'No,' Isidore says. 'Because you had an affair with him.'

His Watch tickles at his mind. She offers him a gevulot

contract, like a cautious handshake. He accepts: the conversation over the next five minutes will not go into his exomemory.

'You really are not like them, are you? The tzaddikim.'

'No,' Isidore says. 'I am not.'

She holds up a praline. 'Do you know how hard it is to make chocolate? How long it takes? He showed me that it wasn't just candy, that you could put yourself into it, make something with your hands. Something real.' She cradles the candy, as if it were a talisman.

'I was in the Quiet for a long time. You are too young, you don't know what it's like. You are yourself, but not yourself: the part of you that *speaks* is doing other things, machine things. And after a while, that is the way things should be. Even after. You feel wrong. Unless someone helps you find yourself again.'

She puts the half-melted praline away. 'The Resurrection Men say they can't bring him back.'

'Miss Lindström, they might be able to, if you help me.'

She looks at the dress. 'We made it together, you know. I wore one like it once, in the Kingdom.' Her eyes are far away.

'Why not?' she says. 'Let's have a taste. In his memory, if nothing else.'

Lindström takes a small metal instrument from behind the counter and opens the glass door hesitantly. With infinite care, she carves a small chip from the hem and puts it in her mouth. She stands still for almost a minute, expression unreadable.

'It's not right,' she says, eyes widening. 'It's not right at all. The crystal structure is not right. And the taste ... This is not the chocolate we made. Almost, but not quite.' She hands another small piece to Isidore: it dissolves on his tongue almost instantly, leaving a bitter, faintly nutty taste.

Isidore smiles. The feeling of triumph is almost enough to wipe the lingering tension of Pixil's qupts from his mind.

'Can I ask what the difference is, from a technical point of view?'

Her eyes brighten. She licks her lips. 'It's the crystals. In the last stage, you reheat and cool the chocolate, many times; you get something that does not melt in the room temperature. There are crystals in chocolate: there is a symmetry there, that's what keeps it together, made from hot and cold. We always try to make type V, but there is too much type IV here, you can tell from the texture.' Suddenly, all the hesitation and fragility seems to be gone from her. 'How did you know? What happened to my dress?'

'That's not important. What matters is that you *must not* sell this one. Keep it safe. Also, please give me a small piece of that? Yes, that's good – a wrapping will do. Don't lose hope: you may still have him back.'

Her laugh is bitter and dark. 'I never had him in the first place. I tried hard. I was nice to his wife. His daughter and I were friends. But it was never real. You know, for a moment, it was almost easier, like this. Just the memories and the chocolate.' She opens and closes her hands, slowly, many times. Her fingernails are painted white. 'Please find him,' she says quietly.

'I'll do my best.' Isidore says. He swallows, somehow relieved that the conversation is not etched in the diamond of exomemory, just in the mortal neurons of his mind.

'By the way, I was not lying. I really do need something special.'

'Oh?'

'Yes. I am going to be late for a party.'

The door opens, suddenly. It is a teenage boy, blond and remarkably handsome, with regular Slavic features, maybe eight Martian years old.

'Hi,' he says.

'Sebastian,' Lindström says. 'I'm with a customer.'

'It's all right; I don't mind,' Isidore says, making a polite offer of gevulot to unhear the conversation.

'I was just wondering if you had seen Élodie?' The boy gives the assistant a radiant smile. 'I can't seem to reach her.'

'She is at home, with her mother,' she says. 'You should give her some space now. Be respectful.'

The boy nods eagerly. 'Of course, I will. It's just that I thought I could help—'

'No, you can't. Now, would you please let me finish here? It is what Élodie's dad would have wanted.'

The boy looks a little pale, turns and flees the shop.

'Who was that?' Isidore asks.

'Élodie's boyfriend. A little sleaze.'

'You don't like him?'

'I don't like *anyone*,' Lindström says. 'Except chocolate, of course. Now, what is this party you are going to?'

When Isidore leaves the shop, the Gentleman is nowhere to be seen. But as he walks along the Clockwise Avenue, he can hear its footsteps, stepping from one shade to another, away from the bright sunlight.

'I must say,' the tzaddik says, 'I am interested to see where this is going. But have you considered that the theory you presented to her might actually be correct? That she could, in fact, be responsible for stealing her employer's mind? I assume that it's not her pretty smile that makes you think otherwise.'

'No,' says Isidore. 'But I want to talk to the family next.'

'Trust me, it will be the assistant.'

'We'll see.'

'As you wish. I just received another lead from my brothers. There have been traces of a vasilev operation nearby. I'm going to investigate.' Then the tzaddik is gone again.

The exomemory guides Isidore to the chocolatier's home. It is in one of the high white buildings that overhang from the Edge, providing a glorious view of the Hellas Basin's rolling desert, patched with green. Isidore descends one of the stairways that connect the outwards-facing facades to a green door, feeling a mild vertigo glimpsing the City's legs through the dust cloud they raise far below.

He waits in front of the red door of the apartment for a moment. A small Chinese woman in a dressing gown opens it. She has a plain, ageless face and black silky hair.

'Yes?'

Isidore offers his hand. 'My name is Isidore Beautrelet,' he says, opening his gevulot to let her know who he is. 'I think you can guess why I am here. I would appreciate it if you had time for a few questions.'

She gives him a strange, hopeful look, but her gevulot remains closed: Isidore does not even get her name. 'Please come in,' she says.

The apartment is small but bright, a fabber and a few floating q-dot displays the only nods to modernity, with a stairway leading to a second floor. The woman leads him in to a cosy living room and sits down by one of the large windows on a child-sized wooden chair. She takes out a Xanthean cigarette and removes its cap: it lights, filling the room with a bitter smell. Isidore sits on a low green couch, hunched, and waits. There is someone else in the room, obscured by privacy fog: the daughter, Isidore guesses.

'I should really get you – a coffee or something,' she says finally, but makes no effort to get up.

'I'll do it,' says a girl, startling Isidore with the sudden opening of her gevulot, appearing next to him as if out of nowhere. She is between six and seven Mars years old: a pale and willowy teen with curious brown eyes, wearing a new Xanthean dress, a tubelike affair that vaguely reminds Isidore of zoku fashion.

'No, thank you,' Isidore says. 'I'm fine.'

'I didn't even have to 'blink you,' the girl says. 'I read *Ares Herald*. You help the tzaddiks. You found the missing city. Have you met the Silence?' She seems unable to stay still, hopping up and down on the couch pillows.

'Élodie,' the woman says threateningly. 'Don't mind my daughter: she has no manners.'

'I'm just *asking*.'

'It's the nice young man who is here to ask the questions, not you.'

'Don't believe everything you read, Élodie,' Isidore says. He gives her a serious look. 'I am very sorry about your father.'

The girl looks down. 'They will fix him, right?'

'I hope so,' Isidore says. 'I'm trying to help them.'

The chocolatier's wife gives Isidore a weary smile, excluding her words from her daughter's gevulot.

'She cost us so much. Foolish child.' She sighs. 'Do you have children?'

'No,' says Isidore.

'They are more trouble than they are worth. It is his fault.

He spoiled Élodie.' The chocolatier's wife runs her hands through her hair, one hand clutching the cigarette, and for a moment Isidore is afraid that the silky hair is going to catch on fire. 'I'm sorry, I'm saying terrible things when he is … somewhere. Not even a Quiet.'

Isidore looks at her, calmly. It is always fascinating to watch what people do when they feel they can talk to you: he briefly wonders if he would lose that as a tzaddik. But then there would be other ways to find things out.

'Were you aware of any new friends that M. Deveraux might have made recently?'

'No. Why?'

Élodie gives her mother a tired look. 'That's how they operate, Mom. The pirates. Social engineering. They gather bits of your gevulot so they can decrypt your mind.'

'Why would they want *him*? He was nothing special. He could make chocolate. I don't even *like* chocolate.'

'I think your husband was exactly the kind of person the gogol pirates would be interested in, a specialised mind,' Isidore says. 'The Sobornost have an endless appetite for deep learning models, and they are obsessed with human sensory modalities, especially taste and smell.'

He takes care to include Élodie in the conversation's gevulot. 'And his chocolate certainly is special. His assistant was kind enough to let me try some when I visited the shop: freshly made, a sliver of that dress that arrived from the factory this morning. Absolutely incredible.'

Disgust twists Élodie's face into a mask, like an echo of the chocolatier's death. Then she vanishes behind the blur of a full privacy screen, jumps up and runs up the stairs with three hasty, low-gravity leaps.

'My apologies,' says Isidore. 'I didn't mean to upset her.'

'Don't worry. She has been putting on a brave face, but this is very difficult for us.' She puts out her cigarette and wipes her eyes. 'I suspect she will run off and see her boyfriend and then she'll come back and not talk to me. Children.'

'I understand,' Isidore says, getting up. 'You have been very helpful.'

She looks disappointed. 'I thought ... that you would ask more questions. My daughter said you always do, that you always ask something the tzaddiks never think of.' There is a strange eagerness on her face.

'It is not always about the questions,' Isidore says. 'My condolences again.' He tears a page from his notebook and scrawls a signature on it, attaching a small co-memory. Then he hands it to the woman. 'Please give it to Élodie, as a form of apology. Although I'm not sure if she is a fan anymore.'

As he leaves, he can't help whistling: he has the full shape of the mystery now. He runs a finger along it in his mind, and it makes a clear sound, like a half-full glass of wine.

Isidore eats octopus risotto for lunch in a small restaurant on the edge of the park. The ink leaves interesting patterns in the napkin when he dabs his lips. He sits and watches the people in the park for half an hour, scribbling in his notebook, making observations. Then he gets up and goes back to the chocolate factory to spring his trap.

The biodrones let him in. At some point the Resurrection Men have come and taken the body away. Its outline and the chocolate stain remain on the floor, but obscured by privacy fog now, like the discarded skin of a snake, made of light. Isidore sits on a rickety metal chair in a corner and waits. The sound of the machines is strangely soothing.

'I know you are here, you know,' he says after a while.

Élodie steps out from behind one of the machines, unblurred by gevulot. She looks older, showing more of her true self: her eyes are hard.

'How did you know?'

'Footprints,' Isidore says, pointing at the chocolate stains on the floor. 'Not as careful as last time. Also, you are late.'

'The co-memory you left with your note was crap,' she says. 'It took me a while to figure out you wanted to meet here.'

'I thought you were interested in detecting. But then, first impressions can be deceiving.'

'If this is about my father again,' Élodie says, 'I'm just going to leave. I'm supposed to meet my boyfriend.'

'I'm sure you are. But it's not about your father, it's about you.' He wraps his words in gevulot so tight that only the two of them will hear them, or will ever remember them being spoken. 'What I'm wondering about is if it really was that easy for you.'

'What?'

'Not thinking about consequences. Giving your father's private gevulot keys to a stranger.'

She says nothing, but she is staring at him now, every muscle tense.

'What did they promise you? Going to the stars? A paradise, all for you, like a Kingdom princess, only better? It doesn't work that way, you know.'

Élodie takes a step towards him, spreading her hands slowly. Isidore rocks back and forth on his chair.

'So the keys did not work. And Sebastian – vasilev boy-friend, one of *them* – was not happy. He does not really care about you, by the way: it is just someone else's emotion they put in him, a mashup.

'But it seemed real enough. He got angry. Maybe he threatened to leave you. You wanted to please him. And you knew that your father had a place with gevulot, where one could do things undisturbed. Maybe he came with you to do it.

'I have to say you were very clever. The chocolate tasted subtly wrong. He is in the dress, isn't he? His mind. You used the fabber to put it there. They had just finished the original: you melted it and made a copy. The drones delivered it to the shop.

'All that data, encoded in chocolate crystals, ready to be bought and shipped away to the Sobornost, no questions asked, not like trying to set up a pirate radio to transmit it, a mind all wrapped up in a nice chocolate shell, like an Easter egg.'

Élodie stares at him, blank-faced.

'What I don't understand is how you could bring yourself to do it,' he says.

'It didn't matter,' she hisses. 'He didn't make a sound. There was no pain. He wasn't even dead when I left. No one lost anything. They will bring him back. They bring us all back. And then they make us Quiet.

'It's unfair. *We* didn't fuck up their fucking Kingdom. *We* didn't make the phoboi. It's not our fault. We should live forever properly, like *they* do. We should have the right.'

Élodie opens her fingers, slowly. Hair-thin rainbows of nanofilament shoot out from underneath her fingernails, stretching out like a fan of cobras.

'Ah,' says Isidore. 'Upload tendrils. I was wondering where those were.'

Élodie walks towards him in odd, jerky steps. The tips of the tendrils glow. For the first time, it occurs to Isidore that he might indeed be very late for the party.

'You should not have done this in a private place,' she says. 'You should have brought your tzaddik. Seb's friends will pay for you as well. Maybe even more than for *him*.'

The upload filaments snap forward, whips of light, towards his face. There are ten pinpricks in his skull, and then an odd dullness. He loses control of his limbs, finds himself getting up from the chair, muscles responding involuntarily. Élodie stands in front of him, arms outspread, like a puppeteer.

'Is that what he said? That it wouldn't matter? That they would fix your father no matter what?' His words come out in a stutter. 'Have a look.'

Isidore opens his gevulot to her, giving her the co-memory from the underworld, the chocolatier screaming and fighting and dying again and again in the room below the ground.

She stares at him, open-eyed. The tendrils drop. Isidore's knees give way. The concrete floor is hard.

'I didn't know,' she says. 'He never—' She stares at her hands. 'What did I—' Her fingers clench into claws, and the tendrils follow, flashing towards her head, vanishing into her hair. She falls to the ground, limbs spasming. He does not want to watch, but he has no strength to move, not even to close his eyes.

'That was one of the most spectacular displays of stupidity I have ever seen,' says the Gentleman.

Isidore smiles weakly. The medfoam working on his head feels like wearing a helmet made of ice. He is lying on a stretcher, outside the factory. Dark-robed Resurrection Men and sleek underworld biodrones move past them. 'I've never aimed for mediocrity,' he says. 'Did you get the vasilev?'

'Of course. The boy, Sebastian. He came and tried to buy

the dress, claimed it was going to be a surprise for Élodie, to cheer her up. Self-destructed upon capture, like they all do, spewing Fedorovist propaganda. Almost got me with a weaponised meme. His gevulot network will take some rooting out: I don't think Élodie was the only one.'

'How is she doing?'

'The Resurrection Men are good. They will fix her, if they can. And then it will be early Quiet for her, I suspect, depending on what the Voice says. But giving her that memory – it was not a good thing to do. It hurt her.'

'I did what I had to do. She deserved it,' Isidore says. 'She is a criminal.' The memory of the chocolatier's death is still in his belly, cold and hard.

The Gentleman has removed his hat. Beneath, whatever material the mask is made from follows the contours of his head: it makes him look younger, somehow.

'And you are criminally stupid. You should have shared gevulot with me, or met with her somewhere else. And as for deserving—' The Gentleman pauses.

'You knew it was her,' Isidore says.

The Gentleman is silent.

'I think you knew from the beginning. It was not about her, it was about me. What were you trying to test?'

'It must have occurred to you that there is a reason that I haven't made you one of us.'

'Why?'

'For one thing,' the Gentleman says, 'In the old days, on Earth, what they used to call tzaddikim were often *healers*.'

'I don't see what that has to do with anything,' Isidore says.

'I know you don't.'

'What? Was I supposed to let her go? Show mercy?' Isidore

bites her lip. 'That's not how mysteries get solved.'

'No,' says the Gentleman.

There is a shape in the one word, Isidore can feel it: not solid, not certain, but unmistakably there. Anger makes him reach out and grasp it.

'I think you are lying,' says Isidore. 'I'm not a tzaddik because I'm not a healer. The Silence is not a healer. It's because you don't trust someone. You want a detective who has not Resurrected. You want a detective who can keep secrets.

'You want a detective who can go after the cryptarchs.'

'That word,' the Gentleman says, 'does not exist.' He puts on his hat and gets up. 'Thank you for your help.' The tzaddik touches Isidore's face. The touch of the velvet is strangely light and gentle.

'And by the way,' the Gentleman says, 'she will not like the chocolate shoes. I got you something with truffles instead.'

Then he is gone. There is a box of chocolates in the grass, neatly tied with a red ribbon.

Interlude

THE KING

The King of Mars can see everything, but there are places where he chooses not to look. Usually, the spaceport is one of them. But today, he is there in person, to kill an old friend.

The arrival hall is built in the old Kingdom style, a vast, grand space with a high dome. It is barely filled by the colourful crowd of visitors from other worlds, walking gingerly in the unfamiliar Martian gravity, trying to get used to the feel of guest gevulot on their skin.

Invisible and inaudible to all, the King walks through the throng of aliens: Realm avatars, scrawny Belt people in their medusa-like exoskeletons, flittering Quick Ones, Saturnian zoku folk in baseline bodies. He stops by a statue of the Duke of Ophir and looks up past the cracked features, defiled by the Revolutionaries. He can see the beanstalk through the dome high above, an impossible line shooting up at the rust-coloured sky, a pit of vertigo if you try to follow it with your gaze. Nausea assaults him: the compulsion implanted in him by rough hands centuries ago is still there.

You belong to Mars, it says. *You will never leave.*

Fists clenched, the King makes himself look as long as he

can bear it, rattling the chain in his mind. Then he closes his eyes and starts looking for the other invisible man.

He lets his mind wander through the crowd, looking through other eyes, looking for traces of manipulation in fresh memories like disturbed leaves in a forest. He should have done this before. There is something pure about being here in person. For the King, memories and actions have almost become one over the years, and the sharp taste of reality is exhilarating.

The memory trap is subtle, hidden in the fresh exomemory of a Realm flesh-avatar whose eyes the King looks through. It is recursive: a memory of a memory itself, almost swallowing the King in an infinite tunnel of *déjà vu*, like the vertigo of the beanstalk, pulling him inwards.

But the memory game is the King's game. With an effort of will, he anchors himself back in the present, isolates the toxic memory, follows it back to its source, peels back the layers of exomemory until only the kernel of reality is left: a thin, bald man with hollow temples and an ill-fitting Revolutionary uniform, standing a few metres away from him and staring at him with dark eyes.

'André,' the King says chidingly. 'What do you think you are doing?'

The man gives him a defiant look, and for a moment there is an older memory that comes from deep within the King, a real memory: of the hell that they went through together. *Such a pity.*

'I come here sometimes,' André says. 'To look out from our goldfish bowl. It's good to see the air and giants beyond, you know.'

'But that is not why you are here,' the King says softly. His tone is gentle, fatherly. 'I don't understand. I thought we agreed. No more deals with them. And here you are. Did you really think I would not find out?'

André sighs. 'A change is coming,' he says. 'We can't survive much longer. The Founders have been weak, but that won't last. They are going to eat us, my friend. Even you can't stop it.'

'There is always a way out,' the King says. 'But not for you.'

Out of courtesy, the King grants him a quick truedeath. A flash of a zoku q-gun, a breeze through exomemory eradicating all traces of the person once called André, his friend. He absorbs all of André that he needs. Passersby flinch at the sudden heat and then forget it.

The King turns to leave. Then he sees the man and the woman, the first in a dark suit and blue-tinted glasses, the second hunched in the gravity like a crone. And for the first time in the spaceport, the King smiles.

4

THE THIEF AND THE BEGGAR

The Moving City of the Oubliette, the Persistent Avenue on a bright morning, hunting for memories.

The streets here shift and change as walking platforms join or leave the city's flow, but the wide Avenue always comes back, no matter what. It is lined with cherry trees, with streets and alleyways leading off it to the Maze, where the secrets are. The shops that you find only once, selling Kingdom toys or old tin robots from old Earth, or dead zoku jewels that fell from the sky. Or doors that only show themselves if you speak the right word or have eaten the right food the day before, or are in love.

'Thank you,' says Mieli, 'for bringing me to hell.'

I lift my blue-tinted shades and smile at her. She is suffering visibly in the gravity, moving like an old woman: she has to keep her enhancements down while we are temporary citizens.

I have been to few places that look less infernal. The deep indigo of the Hellas Basin sky above, and clouds of white gliders, huge wingspans clinging to thin Martian air. The tall, intricate buildings, like *belle époque* Paris without the burden

59

of gravity, spires of red-tinted stone, wearing walkways and balconies. Spidercabs scampering up their sides, leaping across rooftops. The shining dome of the zoku colony near the Dust District where the red cloud raised by the city's feet billows upwards like a cloak. The gentle swaying, if you stand very still: a reminder that this is a city that travels, carried on the backs of Titans.

'Hell,' I tell her, 'is where all the interesting people are.'

She squints at me. Earlier, in the beanstalk, she had that bored *déjà vu* look that told me she was running virs, preparing. 'We are not here to sightsee,' she says.

'Actually, we are. There is another associative memory here somewhere, and I need to find it.' I wink at her. 'It could take a while. So try to keep up.'

Muscle memory is back, at least, so I put distance between us, easing into the low, gliding John Carter lope of the tall Martians all around.

Fashions have changed while I've been away. Fewer people now wear the nondescript white shirts and trousers, based on the old Revolutionary uniform. Instead, there are Kingdom frills and hats and flowing dresses, alongside abstract zoku smartmatter creations, not so much clothing as geometry. Almost no one hides beneath a full gevulot privacy screen here. This is the Avenue: you are supposed to flaunt it.

The one constant, of course, are the Watches – in all shapes and forms, in wristbands and belt buckles and necklaces and rings. All measuring Time, Noble Time, time as a human being – time that you have to earn back through back-breaking labour as a Quiet. I have to suppress pickpocket instincts.

I stop at the Revolution Agora to wait for Mieli. It is a square where one of the Revolution monuments stands, a low slab of volcanic rock, sculpted by the Quiet. It is engraved with the billions of names of the gogols who were brought here from Earth, in microscopic script. Small fountains play against its sides. I remember being here, many times before.

But who was I? And what was I doing?

The Martian wine brought memories, but in no discernible patterns: just dashed them across my brain like spatters of paint. There was a girl called Raymonde; there was something called Thibermesnil. Perhaps Mieli is right: I should not rely on my old self to magically reveal where to go next, and to approach things in a more systematic fashion. I have a debt to pay to her and her mysterious employer, and the sooner I can get that sorted out, the better.

I sit down on a wrought-iron bench on the edge of the agora, just short of the boundary of the public sphere. The Oubliette is a society of perfect privacy, except in the agoras: here, you have to show yourself to the public. The people change their behaviour instinctively as they move from the avenue to the agora: backs straighten, and it is as if everyone walks with exaggerated care, greeting people with curt nods. What happens there is remembered by everybody, accessible to everyone. Places of public discussion and democracy, where you can try to influence the Voice, the Oubliette's e-democracy system. Also good for the cryptoarchitects: publicly available data, to help shape the evolution of the city—

How do I know all that? I could have gotten all that from the little exomemory that came with the temporary citizenship and the Watch that Mieli bought for us. But I didn't: I didn't 'blink – consciously focus on retrieving information from the Oubliette's collective data bank. That means I must have been an Oubliette citizen, before, at least for some time.

That means I had a Watch: and here, having a Watch also means having an exomemory, a repository for your thoughts and dreams, where they keep *you* as you flip between being a Noble and a Quiet. Maybe that's what I should be looking for: the Watch of whoever I was here.

I roll the thought around in my head. It seems too *simple*, somehow, too inelegant, too fragile. Would the old me have done that? Stored secrets in the exomemory of an Oubliette identity? It chills me to realise that I have no idea.

Feeling the need to do something that makes me feel like myself again, I get up and walk the edge of the agora until I find a beautiful girl. She is sitting on another bench next to a public fabber, putting on parkrouller skates with huge round smartwheels she has just printed. She is wearing a white top and shorts. Her bare legs are like sculpted gold, long and perfect.

'Hi,' I say, giving her my best smile. 'I'm looking for the Revolution Library, but they tell me there aren't any maps. Any chance you could point me in the right direction?'

She wrinkles her tanned nub of a nose at me and disappears, a grey gevulot placeholder popping into being in her place. And then she is gone, the blur in the air, moving down the Avenue.

'I see you are sightseeing,' Mieli says.

'Twenty years ago, she would have smiled back.'

'This close to an agora? I don't think so. And you botched the gevulot exchange: you should have made that ridiculous line private. Are you sure you used to live here?'

'Somebody has been doing their homework.'

'Yes,' she says. I'm sure she has: going through virs and sims, sending out little slave-minds to dig up whatever our temporary gevulot allows us to get from public exomemories. 'It is surprisingly little. If you did live here during the past two decades, you either looked very different, or never visited agoras or public events.' She holds my gaze. There is a sheen of sweat on her forehead. 'If you somehow forged that memory – if this is an escape attempt, you will find me ready. And you will not like the outcome.'

I sit down on the bench again, looking across the agora. Mieli sits next to me in an uncomfortable-looking position, her back arrow-straight. The gravity must be hurting her, but she'll be damned before she shows it.

'It's not an escape attempt,' I say. 'I owe you a debt. And everything is so familiar – this is where we are supposed to be. But I don't know what the next step is. There is nothing on this Thibermesnil thing, and that's not surprising; it's layers and layers of secrets here.' I grin. 'I'm sure, somewhere, the old me is enjoying this. Honestly, he might have been too clever for us by half.'

'The old you,' she says, 'got caught.'

'Touché.' I squirt some Time from my temporary Watch (a little silver circle on a transparent strap around my wrist; the hair-thin dial moves a millimetre) into the fabber next to the bench. It spits out a pair of dark sunglasses. I hand them to Mieli. 'Here. Try these.'

'Why?'

'To hide that Gulliver look of yours. You don't do planets well.'

She frowns, but puts them on, slowly. They accentuate her scar.

'You know,' she says, 'my original idea was to keep you in suspension on *Perhonen*, come here to gather sensory data and feed it into your brain until your memories came out. You are right. I don't like this place. There is too much noise, too much space, too much everything.' She leans back on the bench, spreading her arms, lifting her legs up into a lotus position.

'But their sun is warm.'

That is when I see the barefoot boy, maybe five years old, waving at me from across the agora. And his face is familiar.

You know, when this is over, I'm going to kill him, Mieli tells *Perhonen,* smiling at the thief.

Without torturing him first? the ship says. *You are getting soft.*

The ship is in high orbit, and their neutrino link – strictly hidden from the Oubliette's paranoid technology sniffers – allows barely more than a normal conversation.

Another little frustration of this place, but not nearly as bad as the constant heaviness, and the stubborn refusal of objects to stay in mid-air when she lets go. As ashamed as she is of her Sobornost enhancements, she has come to rely on them.

But secrecy is one of the mission parameters. So she wears the temporary gevulot shell the black-carapaced customs official Quiet in the beanstalk station gave them (*no imported nanotech, q-tech, sobortech; no data storage devices capable of storing a baseline mind; no—*), keeps her metacortex and q-stone bones and the ghostguns and everything else in camouflage mode, and suffers.

Anything on the public exomemory data yet? she asks. *Or our mysterious contact who never showed up?*

No, says *Perhonen. The gogols are going through it, but there is a lot: no Thibermesnil, no Flambeur lookalikes yet. So I would make our boy work harder for his freedom, if I were you.*

64

Mieli sighs. *That's not what I wanted to hear,* she says.

The only good thing so far is the artificial sunlight, from the bright pinpoint in the sky that used to be Phobos. *At least I'll have my Venusian tan back in no time.*

'To hide that Gulliver look of yours,' the thief says again.

Suddenly, Mieli feels disoriented: an overwhelming sense of *déjà vu* pulses in her temples. *Damn the biot feed, trust the pellegrini to know exactly what would drive me insane.* In her koto, back in Oort, she lived in an ice cave with two dozen other people, a hollowed-out comet with living space not much bigger than *Perhonen*. But it was nothing like this, a constant awareness of another's thoughts and actions through a quantum umbilical. She filters most of it out, but every now and then, thoughts and sensations tunnel through.

She shakes her head. 'All right,' she says. '*Perhonen* tells me we are going to have to do this the old-fashioned way. We are going to keep walking until—'

She is talking to empty air. The thief is nowhere to be seen. She takes off the sunglasses and stares at them, looking for some trick, for some augmented reality function that allowed the thief to slip away. But they are just plastic. *Perhonen! Where the hell is he?*

I don't know. You are the one with the biot link. She can almost hear the amusement in the ship's voice.

'Vittu. Perkele. Saatana. The Dark Man's balls,' Mieli swears aloud. 'He's going to pay for this.' A passing couple in Revolutionary white, with a child in tow gives her a strange look. Clumsily, she tries to think at her visitor's gevulot interface. *Private.* An odd, stifled sensation tells her that she is now a placeholder to those around her.

Gevulot. Of course. I am an idiot. There is a *boundary* in her memories, between those which are *local* and *exo*. The thief passed her a co-memory of them talking, from seconds before, and her primitive gevulot accepted it. *I was talking to a memory.*

Mieli's self-loathing is sudden and sharp. It reminds her of the smartcoral infection she had as a child, sharp spikes growing from her teeth and pressing painfully into the gums. Karhu cured her with a song, but it was impossible not to poke the protrusions with her tongue. She swallows the feeling, and focuses on the biot feed.

It is difficult to work without resorting to the metacortex and revealing it to the sniffers. So she just tries to focus on the part of her mind that is connected to the thief's. It feels like trying to reconnect with a phantom limb. She closes her eyes and focuses—

'Lady, have pity,' says a voice, coarse and ragged. There is a naked man standing in front of her, intimate areas tastefully censored by a grey gevulot blur. His skin is pale, and he has no hair. His eyes are red-rimmed, and he looks like he has been crying. The only object on his body is a Watch, a thick metallic band with a clear crystal disc, dangling from one scrawny arm.

'Have pity,' he says. 'You come from the stars; you will spend a few luxurious moments here and then go back to plenty, to immortality. Have pity on someone who only has a few moments of this life left, before being forced to atone for my sins, before they come and take my soul and cast it into the maw of a tongueless machine so I cannot even cry out in pain—'

Are you okay? Perhonen asks. *What is happening?*

Mieli tries the same basic gevulot trick as before – complete privacy – to exclude the madman from her horizon and vice versa – but the gevulot layer simply informs her that she

66

has entered into a gevulot contract with another individual guaranteeing mutual superficial observation for the next fifteen minutes.

There is a naked madman in front of me, she tells the ship, helpless.

I thought he escaped.

'If I could only beg you to share a few worthless seconds, insignificant slivers of your time, I would reveal all my secrets to you. I was a Count in the King's Court, no less, a Noble, not as you see me now, but with a robotic castle of my own and a million gogols to do my bidding. And in the Revolution, I fought in the troops of the Duke of Tharsis. You should see the true Mars, the old Mars, I will give you all that for only a few seconds—' Tears are streaming down the long, pale face now. 'I have only dekaseconds, have pity—' Cursing, Mieli gets up and starts walking, just to get away from the man, and notices a sudden hush. She is standing right in the middle of the agora.

Here, the Martians walk with exaggerated care. No one acknowledges anyone else. Tourists – a few Quick Ones, like fireflies, a delicate-limbed polymorph from Ganymede-zoku, and a few others, turn from inspecting the engraved names on the Revolution monument through floating smartmatter lenses to look at her.

The man is clinging to the hem of her toga. 'One minute, even, a few seconds, for all the secrets of old Mars—' He is completely naked now, unprotected by gevulot in the agora. She brushes his arm aside, with mere human strength instead of tearing it from its socket. But he lets out a high-pitched yelp, and collapses to the ground at her feet, still clinging to her garment and moaning. Suddenly, she is certain that everybody is looking at them, although it seems that no one is.

'All right,' she says, lifting her Watch, a crystalline model she chose because it looked like Oortian jewellery. 'Ten minutes. It will take me longer than that to get rid of you.' She thinks at the device, and the golden dial moves a fraction. The beggar leaps up, licking his lips.

'The ghost of the King bless you, lady,' he says. 'The stranger said you were generous.'

'The stranger?' asks Mieli, even though she already knows the answer.

'The stranger in the blue-tinted glasses, bless him, and bless you.' A wide grin spreads across his face. 'A word of warning,' he says in a businesslike tone. 'I would get out of this agora right now.' Around Mieli, everybody, except the tourists are leaving. 'Blood, water. I'm sure you understand.' Then he springs into a naked run, scrawny legs carrying him away from the agora.

I am going to torture the thief, Mieli says. *Blood and water? What did he mean by that?*

On Earth, says *Perhonen, there was this type of fish called sharks. I think the time beggars watch the public exomemory feeds, like from the agoras, no privacy there, so they would have seen you giving Time to a—*

Suddenly, the agora is full of the sound of running bare feet, and Mieli finds herself face to face with an army of beggars.

I chase the boy through the Avenue crowd. He stays ahead of me, navigating the forest of legs with ease, his bare feet a blur, like the needle of a fabber. I elbow people aside, shouting apologies, leaving a trail of angry grey gevulot blurs in my wake.

I almost catch him at a spidercab stop, where the Avenue

breaks into a hundred different alleys into the Maze. He stands in front of the long-legged machines, ornate horseless carriages with brass legs, curled up beneath them as they wait for passengers, looking at them in fascination.

I approach him slowly, in the crowd. He has different *texture* from everything else around me, sharper. Maybe it is the dirt on his face or the ragged brown garment he is wearing, or the dark brown eyes so different from those of the Martians. Only metres away—

But he is just taunting me. He lets out a faint peal of laughter as I lunge forward and slips under the long-legged cab carriages. I'm too big to follow and am left negotiating the crowd to get around the vehicles and their waiting passengers.

The boy is me. I remember being him, in my dream. The memories are pressed flat like a butterfly beneath the centuries, fragile, and fall apart when I touch them. There was a desert, and a soldier. And a woman in a tent. Maybe the boy is in my head. Maybe he is some construct that my old self left behind. Either way, I need to know. I shout his name, not Jean le Flambeur, but the older one.

A part of me is counting seconds to when Mieli manages to deal with her little distraction and shuts me down, or sends me to some new hell. I may only have minutes to find out what he has to tell me, without my minder looking over my shoulder. I catch a glimpse of him vanishing down an alley, into the Maze. I curse and keep running.

The Maze is where the larger platforms and components of the city collide, leaving spaces in between for hundreds of smaller jigsaw pieces that constantly move, forming occasional hills and winding alleyways that can slowly shift direction as you walk down them, so smoothly that the only way to tell is to see the horizon moving. There are no maps of the place, just firefly guides that brave tourists follow around.

I run a rough-cobbled steep slope downwards, lengthening my steps. Running on Mars is an art that I've never properly mastered, and as the street beneath lurches, I land badly after a particularly high leap, skidding down several metres.

'Are you all right?' There is a woman on a balcony above, leaning over the railing, clutching a newspaper.

'I'm fine,' I groan, fairly certain that the Sobornost body Mieli gave me is not going to break easily. But the simulated pain from the bruised tailbone is still pain. 'Did you see a little boy go past?'

'Do you mean that little boy?'

The rascal is less than a hundred metres away, doubled over with laughter. I scramble up and keep running.

Deep, deep into the Maze we go, the boy always ahead, always rounding a corner, never getting too far ahead, running across cobblestones and marble and smartgrass and wood.

We run through little Chinese squares with their elongated Buddhist temples, red and gold dragons flashing in their facades; through temporary marketplaces full of a synthfish smell, past a group of black-robed Resurrection Men with newly born Quiet in tow.

We race down whole streets – red lights districts, perhaps – blurred with gevulot, and empty streets where slow-moving builder Quiet – larger than elephants, with yellow carapaces – are printing new houses in pastel colours. I almost lose the boy there, lost in the loud hum and the odd seaweed smell of the huge creatures, only to see him wave at me from the back of one of them and then leap down.

For a time, a group of parkroullers follows us, mistaking our race for some urban game, young Martian girls and boys in faux-Kingdom wear of corsets and umbrella skirts and powdered wigs, smartmatter-laced so they know to stay out of the way and flex as the kids bounce off walls and make somersaults across gaps between rooftops, the oversized wheels sticking to every surface. They encourage me with shouts, and for a moment I consider spending some Time and buying a pair of skates from one of them: but the fading imaginary pain in my backside keeps me on foot.

Every second, I wait for my body to shut down, to wait for Mieli to come and give me whatever punishment she has thought up. Still, I wish I could have seen her face.

I finally run out of breath when we reach the old robot garden. I curse the fact that I can't override the strictly base-line human parameters of the body as I lean on my knees, wheezing, the sweat stinging my eyes.

'Look,' I say. 'Let's be reasonable. If you are a part of my brain, I'd expect you to be reasonable.' Then again, I probably was anything but reasonable at that age. Or at any other age.

The garden looks strangely familiar. It is some piece of the old Kingdom that the city picked up and swallowed somewhere during its passage through the Martian desert, and its strange urban metabolism has brought it here. It is an open space within the Maze, protected by a cluster of tall synagogues around it, made from black and white tiles of marble perhaps five metres square, forming a ten-by-ten grid. Someone has planted trees here, and flowers: green and red and white and violet spill over the neat monochrome borders on the ground. The boy is nowhere in sight.

'I don't have a lot of time. The scar-faced lady is going to come for us both soon, and she's not going to be happy.'

In each square stands a giant machine: medieval knights

and samurai and legionnaires, with intricately carved armour, yawning helmets and fearsome, spiked weapons. The plates are rusty and weather-beaten, and the empty helmets of some have been turned into flower-pots, with clusters of begonias and pale-hued Martian roses peeking out of them. Some of them are to be frozen in mid-combat – except that, as I catch my breath, they appear to be slowly moving. Something tells me that if I stayed and watched, they would play out a slow game set in motion by players long dead.

The laughter again. I turn around. The boy dangles from the arm of a red robot apart from the others, frozen with its scythelike weapon raised up. I jump forward, trying to catch him in a bear grip, but he is no longer there. I fall down a second time during the chase, right into a bed of roses.

Still out of breath, I roll over slowly. The thorns tear at my clothes and skin.

'Little bastard,' I say. 'You win.'

A ray from bright Phobos – on its eight-hour passage through the sky – hits the robot's open helmet. Something glints inside, something silver. I get back to my feet, reach up and climb up the robot's armour; that, at least, is easier in Martian gravity. I dig in the dirt in the helmet and uncover a metal object. It is a Watch, with a heavy silver wristband and a brass face. The dial rests solidly at zero. I quickly put it in my pocket for a later, thorough inspection.

There are footsteps, along with a sharp gevulot request. I don't bother trying to hide. 'All right, Mieli,' I say. 'I can't run anymore. Please don't send me to hell, I'll come nicely.'

'Hell?' says a gruff voice. 'Hell is other people.' I look down. A man with a carelessy aged face and a shock of white hair, in blue coveralls, is staring at me, leaning on a rake. 'It's not an apple tree, you know,' he says.

Then he frowns.

'I'll be damned. Is that you?'

'Uh, have we met?'

'Aren't you Paul Sernine?'

5

THE DETECTIVE AND
THE ZOKU

Isidore almost makes it in time.

The spidercab races across the rooftops of the city. It costs a hundred kiloseconds, but it is the only option to get even close. He holds on tight to his safety belt. The carriage lurches back and forth as the vehicle – the bastard child of a spider, a H. G. Wells war machine and a taxi – leaps over rooftops and clings to walls.

He drops the box of chocolates and curses as it bounces back and forth in the cabin.

'Are you okay back there?' asks the driver, a young woman in the traditional red, webbed domino mask of the cabbies. In a shifting city where many places are permanently hidden by gevulot, their job is to figure out how to get you from point A to point B. There is a certain amount of pride that comes with that. 'Don't worry, I'll get you there.'

'I'm fine,' says Isidore. 'Just go faster.'

The zoku colony is near the prow of the city, in the Dust District, just above where the Atlas Quiet prepare Martian sand to bear the weight of the city. It is easy to see where the colony's boundary lies: beneath the red dust clouds the wide avenues with their *belle époque* fronts and cherry trees give way to fairy-tale castles of diamond, like mathematics given physical form. Evening light refracts and bounces among the buildings' glossy surfaces, prismatic and dazzling. The zoku colony has been here for more than twenty years, since they requested asylum during the Protocol War; but rumour has it it was grown from a nanoseed in a single night. A shard of the quantum tech empire that rules the outer planets, here on Mars. Ever since he started dating Pixil, Isidore has made attempts to understand the odd non-hierarchy of the zokus, but without much success.

After several more stomach-churning leaps, the spider-cab comes to a stop. They are in front of a cathedral-like building made from glass and light, with towers and spires and organic-looking Gothic arches jutting from its sides at random intervals.

'Well, here we are,' the driver says. 'Friends in high places, eh? Don't let them quantum your brain.'

Isidore pays, watching the dial of his Watch lurch downwards in dismay. Then he picks up the box of chocolates and assesses the damage. It is slightly dented, but otherwise intact. *She won't be able to tell the difference anyway.* He jumps out, slams the door of the cab harder than necessary and starts walking up the stairway to the massive pair of doors. His bow tie is choking him, and he adjusts it nervously, hands shaking.

'Invitation only,' says a voice that sounds like it is coming from underground.

A monster steps through the door. The material behaves like the surface of a vertical pond, rippling around the creature's massive form. It is wearing a blue doorman's uniform and a cap. It is almost three metres tall, with green skin, a face like a dried prune, tiny eyes and two massive yellow tusks. One of them has a clear, tiny zoku jewel embedded in it. Its voice is deep and unnaturally resonant, but human.

The creature holds out a massive hand. There are horned ridges running along its forearms, black and sharp, glistening with a liquid of some sort. It smells of liquorice. Isidore swallows.

'I have an invitation,' he says. He holds out his entanglement ring. The monster bends down and studies it.

'The party has already started,' the monster says. 'Guest tokens expire.'

'Look,' he says. 'I am a little late, but Lady Pixil is waiting for me.'

'Sure she is.'

I'm at the door, he qupts at Pixil desperately. **I'm running late, I know, but I'm here. Please come let me in.** There is no reply.

'That's not going to work,' says the monster. It clears its throat. 'The Tangleparty is an important tradition representing the unity and cohesiveness of the zoku, dating back to the days of the ancestral metaverse guilds. On this day of celebration, we are as our ancestors were. They are not going to interrupt it to let a latecomer in.'

'If it's so important,' says Isidore, 'what are you doing here?'

The monster looks oddly sheepish. 'Resource optimisation,' it mutters. 'Somebody has to do the door.'

'Look, what is the worst that can happen if you let me in?'

'Could get thrown out of the zoku, unentangled. On my own on an alien planet. Not good.'

'Is there any way to,' Isidore hesitates. 'you know, to bribe you?'

The monster studies him. *Damn. Have I offended it now?*

'Any gems? Jewels? Gold?'

'No.' **Come on, Pixil, this is absurd!** 'Chocolate?'

'What is that?'

'Cocoa beans, processed in a very particular way. Delicious. For, ah, baselines anyway. This was meant as a present for Lady Pixil herself. Try one.' He struggles to get the box open, then loses his patience and tears the lid. He tosses a beautifully crafted chocolate nugget to the monster: it snatches it from mid-air.

'Delicious,' it says. Then it tears the box from Isidore's hands. It disappears down its throat with a shredder-like sound. 'Absolutely delicious. Could I have the spime as well, please? They are going to love these in the Realm.'

'That was it.'

'What?'

'I don't have any more. It was just a physical object, one of a kind.'

'Oh crap,' the monster says. 'Oh man. That's way too much. I'm really sorry. I didn't mean to – look, I think I can regurgitate it and we can put it back together again—'

'Really, it's fine.'

'You know, it was a reflex, this body just has to conform to all kinds of narrative stereotypes. I'm sure I can come up with some sort of replica at least—' The monster opens its mouth wide and starts pushing one of its arms in, at an impossible angle.

'Can I just go in?'

The monster makes a gurgling sound. 'Sure. Sure. We'll

say no more about it. I didn't mean to be an asshole, okay? Have fun.'

The two doors swing open. The world clicks into *something else* when Isidore walks through. The constant tinkering with reality is something that he really hates about the Dust District. The zokus do not have the decency to hide their secrets under the surface of the mundane, but plaster them all over your visual cortex, in layers and layers of spimes and augmented reality, making it impossible to see what truly lies beneath. And the sudden feeling of *openness*, no boundaries of gevulot, makes him feel something akin to vertigo.

There is no diamond cathedral inside. He is standing at the entrance of a large open space, with pipes and wires in the walls and the high ceiling. The air is hot and smells of ozone and stale sweat. The floor is unpleasantly sticky. There are dim neon lights, and ancient-looking, clunky flatscreens on low tables, showing either rough animated characters or abstract dancing shapes. Loud music with a headache-inducing beat fills the space.

The party crowd is moving between the tables, talking to each other. They all look surprisingly … *human*. They wear homemade chainmail bikinis over pale bodies. Some carry padded swords. Others are clad in cardboard boxes. But all carry boxes with wires, or have circuit boards strapped to their belts.

'Hey. Want to entangle?'

The girl looks like a plump, pink-haired elf. She is wearing large cat ears, far too much makeup and an uncomfortably tight T-shirt in which a large-eyed female is doing something obscene with *something*. She is also carrying twin phallic silvery rockets in a backpack, connected to a touchscreen phone in her hand with a thick umbilical cable.

'Uh, I would love to, but—' He loosens his bow tie again. 'I'm actually looking for Pixil.'

The girl stares at him, eyes wide. 'Ooooh.'

'Yes, I know, I'm late, but—'

'It's all right, it's not really even started yet, people are just starting to entangle. You are Isidore, right? That is so cool!' She waves her arms and almost jumps up and down. 'Pixil talks about you all the time! Everybody knows about you!'

'You know Pixil?'

'Silly boy, of course I do! I'm Cyndra. I'm her Epic Mount!' She squeezes her tiny left boob through the pink fabric. 'Great avatar, huh? Sue Yi, from the original Qclan! I bought her old lifestream off a – hang on, I shouldn't tell you that, you play that "detective" game, right? Sorry.'

Isidore 'blinks at the words 'Epic Mount', but here in the zoku colony, the Oubliette exomemory system is silent. *I really hope it's a metaphor.*

'So, uh, could you tell me where to find Pixil?'

'No.'

'Why not?'

'Silly boy, can't you tell – it's a costume party! We'll have to go and figure out what she is wearing.' And before Isidore knows it, Cyndra's sweaty hand is squeezing his and pulling him into the thick of the crowd.

'You have no idea how many people want to meet you.' She winks at him. 'You know, we are all in awe. An Oubliette boy! The things you do with your bodies. Bad, bad, bad.'

'She told you about—'

'Oh, she tells me *everything*. Here, *they'll* know where she is.' Cyndra steers them to a cluster of old computers that hum and radiate heat, surrounded by bean-bags.

There are three people huddled around the machines. To Isidore's eye they don't look very much like he would expect Pixil to look. Two of them have beards, to begin with. One of the males, tall and lean, wears a yellow cape, a domino mask, shorts and some sort of red tunic. The other is more heavyset, in a loose blue cape with a ragged edge, wearing a pointy-eared mask.

The third is a small, older-looking woman, with thin blond hair, lined face and glasses, in uncomfortable-looking leather armour, sitting with a sword across her knees. Both men are bouncing back and forth in their chairs to the tune of tinny explosions.

Cyndra slaps the lean man on the back, triggering a thunderous on-screen blast. 'Shit,' he says, tearing his goggles off. 'Look at what you did!'

The man in the cape leans back in his chair. 'You have much to learn, Boy Wonder.'

Isidore's mouth is dry. He is used to the gevulot handshakes that link names with faces and establish social context. But these are actual *strangers*.

'Has anyone seen Pixil?' Cyndra asks.

'Hey! Stay in character!' growls the pointy-eared man.

'Oh, pshaw,' says Cyndra. 'This is important.'

'She was here a moment ago,' says the lean man, not taking his eyes off the screen, moving a little white device around furiously with his right hand. It makes clicking sounds.

'Who did she come as? We're trying to find her.'

'I don't know.'

'I think she was supposed to be McGonigal,' says the pointy-eared man. 'She was putting together a Werewolf game in the back room. But she hadn't changed her body that much. Lame.'

'All right,' Cyndra tells Isidore. 'You stay here. I'm going to get her. Guys, this is Isidore. He is – ta-da! – Pixil's Significant Other. He's a gamer, too.'

'Oooh,' says the bearded man. The woman in leather gives Isidore an inquisitive look.

'Isidore, these jokers are the zoku elders. They are usually more polite. Drathdor, Sagewyn and,' – Cyndra bows slightly when looking at the woman – 'the Eldest. They will look after you. I'll be right back. I'm so glad you made it!'

'Have a seat. Have a beer,' Sagewyn – the pointy-eared man – says. Isidore sits on one of the baglike chairs on the floor.

'Thanks.' He looks at the can, not quite sure how to open it. 'Looks like a fun party.'

Drathdor snorts.

'It's not a party, it's an age-old ritual!'

'I'm sorry, Pixil didn't tell me much about it. What is it all about?'

'You tell it,' Drathdor says, looking at the Eldest. 'You tell it the best.'

'She was there,' Sagewyn says.

'It's how we honour our heritage,' the Eldest says. She has a powerful voice, like a singer. 'Our zoku is an old one: we can trace our origins back to the pre-Collapse gaming clans.' She smiles. 'Some of us remember those times very well. This was just before the uploads took off, you understand. The competition was fierce, and you would take any chance to get an edge over a rival guild.

'We were among the first who experimented with quantum economic mechanisms for collaboration. In the beginning, it was just two crazy *otaku*, working in a physics lab, stealing entangled ion trap qubits and plugging them into their gaming platforms, coordinating guild raids and making a killing in the auction houses. It turns out that you can do fun things with entanglement. *Games* become strange. Like Prisoner's Dilemma with telepathy. Perfect coordination. New game equilibria. We kicked ass and drowned in piles of gold.'

'We still kick ass,' says Drathdor.

'Ssh. But you need entanglement for the magic. There were no quantum communication satellites, back then. So we threw parties like this one. People carrying their qubits around, entangling them with as many people as possible.' The Eldest smiles. 'And then we realised what you could do if you combined perfect resource planning and coordination and brain-computer interfaces.'

She taps the hilt of her sword gently. It is an egg-sized jewel that looks strange compared to her lacklustre armour, transparent and multifaceted, with a hint of violet.

'We've done a lot of things since. Survived the Collapse. Built a city on Saturn. Lost a war to Sobornost. But every now and then, it is good to remember where we came from.'

'Pixil never told me,' Isidore says.

'Pixil,' says the Eldest, 'is less interested in where she comes from than where she is going.'

'So, you are a gamer?' Drathdor asks. 'Pixil has been talking a lot about the games you play out there, you know, in the Dirt City. She says it's an inspiration on something she's working on, so I'm curious to hear about the source material.'

'Games we play where?'

'Uh, sometimes we call it Dirt City,' Sagewyn says. 'It's a joke.'

'I see. I think you have me confused with someone else, I don't really play games—'

82

The Eldest touches his shoulder. 'I think what young Isidore is trying to say is that he doesn't actually consider what he does a game.'

Isidore frowns. 'Look, I'm not sure what Pixil has told you, but I'm an art history student. People call me a detective, but it is just problem-solving, really.' Saying it makes the tzaddik's rejection sting again.

Sagewyn looks perplexed. 'But how do you keep score? How do you level up?'

'Well, it's not really about that. It's more about ... helping the victim, catching the perpetrator, making sure that they are brought to justice.'

Drathdor snorts into his beer, blowing some of it on his costume. 'That's *disgusting*.' He wipes his mouth with his glove. 'Absolutely disgusting. You mean you are some sort of toxic meme-zombie? Pixil brought you here? She *touches* you?' He gives the Eldest a shocked look. 'I'm amazed you allow this.'

'My daughter can do whatever she wants with her life, with whomever she wants. Besides, I think it would do us some good to acknowledge that there is a human society out there around us and we have to live with them. It's easy to forget in the Realm.' She smiles. 'And it's good for a child to play in the dirt, to build up immunity.'

'Wait,' Isidore says. 'Your daughter?'

'Whatever,' Drathdor says, getting up. 'I'm going before I catch "justice".'

There is an awkward silence as he walks away.

'You know, I still don't understand how you are supposed to keep score—' Sagewyn begins.

The Eldest gives Sagewyn a sharp look. 'Isidore. I would like to talk to you for a moment.' The pointy-eared zoku elder gets up. 'Nice meeting you, Isidore.' He winks. 'Fist bump?' He does a strange gesture in the air, like an aborted punch. 'All right. Take it easy.'

'Apologies for my zoku partners,' the Eldest says. 'They don't really have much contact with the outside world.'

'It's an honour to meet you,' Isidore says. 'She never mentioned you before. Or her father. Is he around?'

'Perhaps she didn't want to confuse you. I like to use the word "mother", but it is a little more complicated than that. Let us say that there was an incident in the Protocol War involving me and a captured Sobornost warmind.' She looks at the entanglement ring in Isidore's hand. 'She gave you that?'

'Yes.'

'Interesting.'

'Excuse me?'

'You poor thing. She should not have brought you here. What a mess you are.' She sighs. 'But perhaps that is what she needs now, to prove something.'

'I don't understand.' He tries to read the woman's expression, but the subtle cues of gevulot are not there. This is one of the things that has always drawn him to Pixil, the riddle. But in her mother it is merely frightening.

'What I wanted to say was that you should not expect too much from my daughter. You understand, she already has a connection to something bigger than herself. That is one reason why I told you the story. She experiments, and that is fine, and so should you. But you two are not entangled. You will never be a part of that. Do you understand?'

Isidore breathes in sharply. 'With all due respect, I would say that our relationship is our business. I'm sure she would agree.'

84

'You don't understand,' the Eldest says.

'If you are saying that I'm not good enough for her—' He crosses his arms. 'My father was a Noble of the Kingdom. And I thought one could join a zoku. What is to say that I don't decide to do that?'

'But you won't.'

'I don't think it is your place to say that.'

'Oh, but it is. This is a zoku. We are one.' Something flashes in her eyes. 'Do not be deceived by this little dress-up. This is not who we really are. You haven't really seen *her*: we made her to go out amongst you and know you. But underneath—'

The Eldest's face ripples, and for a moment, she is a shimmering statue made from a billion dancing dust motes, with a beautiful face floating within, surrounded by dazzling jewels like the one on the sword, arranged about her in complex constellations. And then she is a middle-aged blonde again. 'Underneath we are different.'

She pats Isidore's hand. 'But don't worry. These things will follow their due course.' She gets up. 'I'm sure Cyndra will be back soon. Enjoy the party.' She walks into the crowd, sword swinging at her hip, leaving Isidore staring at the pixel rain on the monitors.

A while after that drinking starts to feel like a good idea, so Isidore tries the beer. It is stale and foul, and he would prefer wine, but he gets two cans down before the effects hit. The day starts to catch up with him, and he almost falls asleep watching the monitors. Two other guests – a young man and a girl wearing makeup that makes her look like a corpse – sit down and play the game. After a while, the man turns around and gives Isidore a sheepish grin.

85

'Hi,' he says. 'Would you like to try? I'm not much of a challenge to Miss Destroyer of Worlds here.' The girl rolls her eyes. 'Lover, not a fighter, huh?' she says.

'Absolutely.' The man looks a little older than Isidore, in his early Martian teens, with Asian features, a pencil moustache, well-tailored suit and slicked-back dark hair. He is carrying a leather shoulder bag. 'So what do you say?'

'I think I'm too drunk,' Isidore says. 'You go ahead.'

'Actually, drinking sounds like an excellent way to save face. Sorry, mistress. You have defeated us.' The girl sighs. 'All right. I'm going to play Werewolf. Puny humans.' She blows Isidore a kiss.

'Enjoying the party?' the man asks.

'Not really.'

'Well, that's a shame.' He picks up one of the beer cans on the table and opens it. 'As you will have discovered, the beer here is absolutely horrible. It's all authentic, you see.'

'Works for me,' Isidore says, opening another one as well. 'I'm Isidore.'

'Adrian.' The man's handshake is clearly from the Oubliette. But it does not seem important, with the odd freedom from gevulot and sweet intoxication.

'So, Isidore, why are you not out there, dancing and entangling and picking up zoku chicks?'

'I've had a very strange day,' Isidore says. 'I nearly got killed. I caught a gogol pirate. Or two. With chocolate. As for zoku chicks, I've already got one. Her mother is a goddess, and she hates me.'

'All right then,' Adrian says. 'I was expecting something along the lines of *I saw a tzaddik*, or *I had somebody else's dream last night*.'

'Oh, there was a tzaddik there too,' Isidore says.

86

'Now, that sounds like a story! Tell me more.'

They keep drinking. It feels right to tell the story of the chocolatier. The words pour out easily. It makes him think of Pixil. *How much did we ever really talk?* And without gevulot restraining his thoughts or tongue, he feels like a stone skipping on water, light and free.

'Who *are* you, Isidore?' Adrian asks, after he is finished. 'How did you get involved in this stuff?'

'I couldn't help it. I have to think about things I don't understand. I used to wander the Maze and break gevulot locks, just for fun.'

'But why? What do you get out of it?'

Isidore sits back, laughing. 'I don't understand people. I need to *deduce* things. I don't know why anyone says or does anything if I don't think about it.'

'That's amazing,' Adrian says when Isidore pauses to sip his beer. Distantly, he notices the man is scribbling on a little notepad, old-fashioned, made from paper. That can only mean one thing, and even through his clouded brain Isidore realises he has made a mistake.

'You are a journalist,' he says. The momentum is gone, and the water swallows the skipping stone. His head feels heavy. In a world of perfect privacy, there are still analog holes, and publishing newspapers is one of the most lucrative tolerated crimes in the Oubliette. They have been after him ever since his first case with the haute couture thieves. But they have never managed to breach his gevulot. Until now.

'Yes, I am. Adrian Wu, from *Ares Herald*.' He takes out an old-fashioned camera from his bag – another trick to get around gevulot. The flash blinds Isidore for a moment.

Isidore hits him. Or tries to: he leaps to his feet and swings wildly, failing to connect. His legs buckle. He grabs the nearest object – the computer monitor on the table – and falls to the floor with it with a crash. He struggles to get up, reaching for Adrian's camera. 'Give me that.'

'Oh, I will. You and fifty thousand other readers, tomorrow. You know, we have been dying to interview you since you were first spotted with the Gentleman. Any chance you'd like to tell us more about her?'

'About *her*?'

'Oh yes.' Adrian grins. 'And you are supposed to be the detective? The word on the street is that the Gentleman is a woman. Speaking of which – here is the lady of the hour.'

'Hi, pumpkin,' Pixil says. Even through the shock, anger and alcohol haze, seeing her makes Isidore feel warm. Her black lipstick makes her lopsided smile look like a comma. Her tiny body is squeezed into a tight tartan-patterned dress with leather straps that highlight her shapely dark-skinned shoulders just right. 'Cyndra told me you made it. I'm so glad.' She gives Isidore a kiss that tastes of punch.

'Hi,' Isidore says. 'I brought you chocolate. The monster ate it.'

'Goodness me. I think you are drunk.'

'Better than that,' says Adrian. 'He's a story.' He gives Isidore a little bow and vanishes into the crowd.

The next hour is a blur, and after a while he forgets about the journalist. It is hot, and absolutely everything everybody says sounds funny. Pixil takes him from one zoku group to another. They talk to quantum gods who sit in circles and argue about which one of them is a werewolf. Pale-skinned super-heroes in ill-fitting latex costumes ask him questions about the tzaddikim. And it is hard to think about anything else except her small hand, warm between his shoulder-blades.

'Can we go and find somewhere quieter?' he finally says.

'Sure. I want to watch the entanglements.'

They find a quiet sofa away from the main area of the party and sit down. The entanglements are spectacular. People attach their qubit containers – jetpacks and rayguns and magic swords – to huge Rube Goldberg devices with optic fibres and cables. With the primitive equipment, the entanglements do not succeed every time, but when they do, there are electric arcs from Tesla coils, thunderous sound effects and loud laughter. The smell of ozone in the air clears Isidore's head a little.

'I think I like you better properly drunk,' Pixil says. 'You just got your *look* back.'

'What look?'

'You are deducing something.'

'I'm not.' He is trying, but it is hard to think. Liquid anger goes round and round in his belly, refusing to settle down.

'Tell me,' Pixil says, tousling his hair. 'I get to guess what you are thinking about. If I get it right, you will be my slave tonight.'

Isidore downs the rest of his drink from a plastic cup – some sort of overly sweet punch thing with guarana in it that they got from the last group, teenage girls in sailor outfits. It takes some of the drowsiness away, but also makes him jittery.

'All right,' he says. 'I'm game.'

'You are thinking about your tzaddik. Are you trying to make me jealous?'

'No. It didn't go well. I'm not going to be a tzaddik. But that's not what I'm thinking about.'

'Oh no.' There is a look of genuine concern on her face. 'What did that bastard want? You are a genius. You solved the ... whatever it was, right?'

'Yeah. But it wasn't enough. Don't worry. I don't want to talk about it. Keep guessing.' The feeling of failure is a yawning pit beneath his denial.

'All right, then.' She caresses his hand, tickling his palm with a forefinger. 'You are trying to work out what is the best way to get me to bed as soon as possible?'

'No.'

'No?' She makes a mock offended sound. 'You might want to call a cab in that case, M. Detective. Why are you *not* thinking about that? I am.'

'You still get a third guess,' Isidore says.

'Well.' Pixil looks serious. She presses her fingers against her temples and closes her eyes. 'You are thinking ...'

'No cheating with qupts or gevulot,' Isidore says.

'Are you kidding? I never cheat.' She purses her lips. 'I'd say you are thinking about Adrian and why I invited him here, and why did I ask Cyndra to parade you in front of the elders and why does my poor old tanglemother hate you?' She gives him a sweet smile. 'Does that sound about right? Do you think I am completely stupid?'

'Yes,' Isidore says. 'I mean, no. You are right. So why did you?' The anger is clotting into a tight clump inside his chest. His temples throb.

'You are cute when you are confused.'

'Tell me.'

'Slaves don't get to make demands. I won,' Pixil says.

'I don't want to play just now. Why?'

'Well, for one thing, I wanted to show you off.' She takes his hand in her lap.

'Show me off? I managed to *offend* them in the first five minutes. And your mother really does hate me.'

'Tanglemother. No, she doesn't. She's just being overprotective. First child created on Mars, you know, gevulot compatibility, bridge between two worlds, blah blah blah. And they are *still* shocked that I end up dating one of you. They *deserve* to be offended a little. They still think that we are going to go back to Jupiter one day, even though there is nothing there except dust and Sobornost drones that eat it. We live here now, and no one else wants to acknowledge it at all.'

'So,' Isidore says. 'You were using me.'

'Of course I was. It's a game. The optimal resource allocation thing is no joke. We are going to do whatever is best for each other, that's the way it works, we can't help it. In this case, rebelling a little is the best thing to do.'

'So it's not really rebelling, is it?'

'Oh, come *on*,' she says. 'You do this stuff with people *all the time*. You're good at it. Why do you think you are with me? Because I'm a *puzzle*. Because you can't figure me out, like you do with *them*. I've seen you talking to people, and you tell them something, and it's not *you*, it's just something you have *deduced*. Don't try to tell me it's not a game to you too.'

'It's not just a game,' Isidore says. 'I almost died today. A girl killed her father in a horrible way. These things happen, and someone has to *solve* them.'

'Solving them makes it better?'

'It does for me,' Isidore says quietly. 'You know that.'

'Yes, I know. And I thought other people should, too. You are doing well, somebody *should* be keeping score. So I invited Adrian, here where he could talk to you without any of that gevulot nonsense. He is going to make you famous.'

'Pixil, that was a bad thing to do. I'm going to be in a lot of trouble because of that. Do you think you can just decide what I need? I'm not part of your zoku. It doesn't work that way with me.'

'No, it doesn't,' Pixil says. 'With the zoku, I don't have a choice.' She touches her zoku jewel, embedded at the base of her throat, where her collar-bones meet. 'With you, it's because I want to.'

A distant part of him knows that she is lying, but somehow it does not matter, and he kisses her anyway.

'You know,' she says, 'you did lose the bet. Come on. I'm going to show you something.'

Pixil takes his hand and leads him to a plain door that was not there a moment before. Entanglement electric arcs flare up again behind them as they walk through together.

For a moment there is another discontinuity.

They emerge into a huge, cavernous space that is full of black cubes of different sizes, ranging from a cubic metre to the size of a house, stacked on top of each other. The walls, floor and the ceiling — somewhere high, high up — are white and faintly luminescent. The illumination makes even Pixil seem pale.

'Where are we?' Isidore asks. His voice has an eerie echo.

'You know we are mercenaries, right? We raid things. Well, this is where we keep the treasure.' Pixil lets go of his hand and runs ahead, touching a cube. It flashes into transparency in an instant. Inside, is a strange, glittering beast, like a feathered serpent, swirling in the air, trapped in a cage of light. A floating spime bubble tells him it is a Langton worm, captured in the wilder virtual reaches of the Realm and given physical form.

Pixil laughs. 'You can find almost *anything* here.' She runs around, touching things. 'Come on, let's explore.'

There are glass eggs and ancient clocks and candy from old Earth. Isidore finds an ancient spacecraft inside one of the larger cubes. It looks like a giant's dirty molar, brown stains marring the white ceramic surfaces. Pixil opens a cube full of theatrical costumes and presses a bowler hat on Isidore's head, laughing.

'Isn't someone going to be upset if they find us here?' Isidore asks.

'Don't worry, slave,' Pixil says, grinning mischievously. She pulls the costumes down and makes a thick pile of them onto the floor, humming to herself. 'I told you. Resource optimisation.' She wraps her arms around his neck and kisses him, hard. Her clothes dissolve under her touch. She pulls him down onto the nest of cloaks and dresses. The anger drains from him, and then he has no room for any shape but hers.

Interlude

GOODNESS

Like every Sol Solis, Xuexue comes to the garden to smile at the red robot.

It stands alone, away from the clusters of fighting machines arranged on the black-and-white marble grid. Its design is a little different, too: sleek crimson lines of a sports car beneath a layer of rust, and a glinting little horse on top of its helmet.

Xuexue sits on a small folding chair in front of it, looks directly at the dark slit in its helmet and smiles, keeping as still as she possibly can. Her record is two hours. The hard part is maintaining the *feeling* of the smile. Today, it is easy: she had a good day with the children in the kindergarten. The little emperors and empresses of the Oubliette – bought dearly with Time by their parents and spoiled accordingly – can be difficult, but they have their moments. Maybe she will break her record today.

'Excuse me?' says a voice.

With some effort, Xuexue fights down a frown and keeps smiling, not turning to look.

A hand touches her shoulder and she flinches. *Damn it.*

She should have closed her gevulot, but it would have spoiled the smile.

'I'm trying to concentrate,' Xuexue says chidingly.

A young man looks at her, amused. He has jet-black hair and a hint of the sun in his skin, dark eyebrows arching above heavy eyelids. He is dressed as if going to a party, sleek jacket and pants, with a pair of blue-tinted glasses against the bright glare of Phobos above.

'I do apologise,' he says with a hint of mirth in his voice. 'What did I interrupt?'

Xuexue sighs. 'You wouldn't understand.'

'Try me.' He removes his glasses and regards Xuexue with a curious expression. His complexion is just a little too perfect, a different style from standard Oubliette bodies. He is smiling, but there is a distracted look in his eyes, as if he were listening to more than one conversation.

'I have been smiling at the red gladiator,' she says. 'For the last year or so. At least an hour every week.'

'Why?'

'Well, there is a theory that there are slow gogols running inside them,' she says. 'An old Kingdom game. For them, this is a fierce battle. They are fighting for their freedom. They move, you know, if you look long enough. So I figured that they must see us, too. If we stand very still. Like ghosts, perhaps.'

'I see.' He squints at the robots. 'I don't think I would have enough patience for that. And why that one in particular?'

'I don't know,' she says. 'It looks lonely.'

The young man touches the robot's breastplate. 'Don't you think it's possible that you'll end up distracting it? So that it loses the fight? Never gets to go free?'

'The Kingdom is gone. They have been free almost a hundred years,' she says. 'I think someone should tell them.'

'It's a nice thought.' He offers her his hand. 'I am Paul. I got a little lost: all those moving streets. I was hoping you could tell me the way out.'

A trickle of emotion bleeds through his rough visitor's gevulot: a sense of unease, a weight, a guilt. Xuexue can imagine the old man of the sea sitting on his back. It feels very familiar. And suddenly it is more important to talk to the stranger than to smile at the robot.

'Sure I can,' she says. 'But why don't you stay for a little while? What brings you to the Oubliette?' As she speaks, she crafts a gevulot contract in her mind and offers it to Paul. He blinks. 'What is that?'

'No one else will remember or know what we are going to say here,' she says. 'Even I will forget, unless you let me remember.' She smiles. 'This is the way things work here. No one has to be a stranger.'

'It's like you have a portable confession booth.'

'Something like that.'

Paul sits down on the ground next to Xuexue, looking up at the robot.

'You know,' he says, 'it is rare to meet a genuinely altruistic person. That is quite admirable.'

Xuexue smiles. 'You don't consider yourself to be one?'

'I took a different turn on the evolutionary highway, quite far back. Somewhere between the dinosaurs and the birds.'

'It's never too late,' she says. 'Especially here.'

'What do you mean?' he says.

'This is the Oubliette. The place of forgetting. Here, you can meet a Kingdom tyrant or a Revolution leader and never know. Or sit next to someone worse, like me.' She sighs.

He looks up at her, eyes wide. She peels her gevulot open like an onion and offers him a memory.

Xuexue sold immortality. She went to towns and villages ravaged by earthquakes or mudslides, to fishing villages by dried-up lakes. She looked at children's brains with the MRI scanner in her phone and talked to their desperate parents about life without flesh. She showed the children videos from Heaven, where gods and goddesses spoke about eternal life as gardeners of code. The children laughed and pointed. In every village, there were a few who wanted to go. She gathered them in automated trucks with the help of company drones and took them to the Iridescent Gateway of Heaven.

The Gateway consisted of hastily erected barracks in the Ordos desert, covered in camouflage cloth. The latrines smelled. The camp beds were dirty.

They did not have a shower for the first two weeks, but Xuexue and the other instructors – most of them faces on the display screens of the teleoperated drone guards – said that it did not matter, that soon they would transcend the needs of the flesh.

The first stage of the transformation took place in the classroom. The children wore itchy skullcaps that told the company machines what they were thinking. Xuexue watched over them through the harsh training: hours and hours of programming, forming code blocks and sequences of symbols in their minds, receiving orgasmic jolts of pleasure through the cap's transcranial magnetic stimulator for every success and experiencing a little hell for being slow or failing. There was no talking in class, only chorused cries of agony and ecstasy.

Usually, they were ready within six weeks, permanent

burns on their shaved, hollow-templed heads, half-closed eyes twitching like in REM sleep. Then she took them to the Celestial Doctor one by one, telling them that they would now get their peach of immortality. No one ever returned from the Doctor's tent. In the evening Xuexue would set up the superdense datalink to the company satellite, sending up the petabytes harvested from young brains, fresh gogols to spin code in the cloud software farms.

Afterwards, she allowed herself a brief oblivion, achieved with cheap rice wine and drugware, before setting out to the world again.

Ten years of work for the company, and she would have true immortality of her own. A high-fidelity Moravec upload, no break in her consciousness, a slow surgery in which her neurons would be replaced by artificial emulations, one by one: a true transformation into something digital. A Realm of her own design, in the cloud.

It was going to be worth it, she told herself.

She had just arrived with a new group of recruits when the Western micro UAVs came down from the sky in angry buzzing clouds, burning everything. For a moment, it felt right, and she just stood there, watching the Gateway die. Then the black terror of death came, and she did the only thing she could: ran into the Doctor's tent.

Her second birth inside is lost to her even now, except for a sea of bright red pinpoints, a clamp around her skull, a grinding sound.

Xuexue opens her eyes. The memory pours off her like cold water. Paul stares at her, eyes wide.

'What happened then?' he whispers.

'Nothing, for a long time,' she says. 'I was brought here

with the King's billion gogols. I woke up as a Quiet. The Revolution was good for me. We really did something new. We made a place without little immortals.' She looks at the robot. 'I suppose I'm still trying to make up for them. It will never be enough, but it's good to try. One thing at a time.'

'Maybe it is,' Paul says. He smiles at her, and there is genuine warmth in his eyes this time. 'Thank you.'

'Don't mention it,' Xuexue says. 'I'm here every week. Come by again if you decide to stay.'

'Thanks,' Paul says. 'Maybe I will.'

They sit together and look at the robot. Slowly, her smile returns. She listens to the young man's breathing. Maybe she will break her record today.

6

THE THIEF AND PAUL SERNINE

'Time, just a little Time, please, miss—'

'I am going to be a Quiet for the third time, I have paid my debts, please help—'

'I am a craftsman, a tailor, you can have my mind for a little Time, it will fetch a good price—'

Mieli is struggling in the crowd of Time beggars. Some are naked like the first one, others look just like everybody else on the Avenue, but they all share a look of hunger and desperation. Some wear masks and hoods. They are pushing at each other to get to her, a tangled ring of heaving bodies tightening around her, and some of her more autonomous defence gogols are waking up. *I need to get out of here before I blow my cover.*

She pushes one beggar aside, rams another with her shoulder: they go down, in a mess of limbs. She rushes past. One of the beggars on the ground grabs her leg. She falls. One of her elbows makes a painful impact with the pavement. An arm tightens around her throat. A voice hisses in her ear.

'Give us Time or we'll see if the Resurrection Men will bring you back, offworld bitch.'

'Help!' she shouts. Her vision goes black, and her temples start pounding. Her metacortex wakes up and muffles the pain, slows time down and starts waking the rest of her systems up. It would be so easy to sweep this rabble aside like so many rag dolls—

A wind rises. The pressure around her throat disappears. Someone screams, and running feet echo in the agora. She opens her eyes.

There is a man in black and silver floating in the air, perfectly polished shoes two metres above the ground, holding a cane. A living wind dances around him, a heat ripple, full of the telltale ozone smell of combat utility fog. *They should not have that here,* she thinks.

Hands made from heat haze hold the masked beggars on the ground – countless nanites, forming invisible structures that are the extensions of the black-clad man's limbs. Other beggars make a run for it past the boundary of the agora and turn into gevulot blurs, disappearing into the crowd.

'Are you all right?' the man says, in a strange rasping voice. He comes down next to Mieli, shoes hitting the marble with a sharp *tap.* He is wearing a polished metal mask that covers his entire head: Mieli is fairly certain it is a q-dot bubble. He holds out a white-gloved hand. Mieli takes it and allows herself to be helped up.

A tzaddik. Great. The Sobornost database she studied during the journey had scant details on the Oubliette vigilantes. They have been active for two decades or so, and clearly have access to technology from outside Mars. Sobornost vasilevs – infiltrator agents – operating with the local gogol pirates, speculate they have something to do with the zoku colony established on the planet after the Protocol War.

'I'm fine,' Mieli says. 'Just a little shaken.'

My, my, Perhonen says. *Who is this? A handsome prince on a white horse?*

Shut up and figure out how I avoid blowing my cover.

'Let's get you away from the agora before the journalists arrive,' the tzaddik says, offering Mieli his arm. To her surprise, her legs are a little shaky, so she takes it and lets him lead her back to the shade of the cherry trees and the noise of the Persistent Avenue. There are people – mainly tourists – watching the scene, but the tzaddik gestures, and Mieli can tell that they are now private again.

'Thank you,' she says. 'Journalists?'

'Yes, they tend to watch agoras very carefully. As do we. As do beggars looking for easy prey, as you found out.' He motions towards the masked attackers on the ground with his cane.

'What is going to happen to them?'

The tzaddik shrugs. 'That will depend on what the Voice decides. An early or extended Quiet, probably: but that's what was waiting for them anyway.' There is a strange, angry note in its chorus voice. 'That is the price we pay for the other good things here, I'm afraid.' Then he takes off his hat and bows. 'But my apologies. The Gentleman – which is the *nom de guerre* I have been given – at your service. I hope your day has not been completely ruined.'

He is flirting with you, Perhonen says. *Oh my god. He so is.*

Of course he isn't. He has no face. Mieli feels a tickle that tells her the tzaddik is scanning her. Nothing that will penetrate the camouflage layers beneath her gevulot, but serves as another reminder that the natives have more than just bows and arrows.

Neither do I, and that has never stopped me.

Never mind. What do I do? I can't tap into the thief's feed with him scanning me.

He's a do-gooder. Ask him for help. Stick to your cover, silly girl. Just try being nice for a change.

Mieli tries to smile, trying to think what her cover identity – a tourist from a mixed asteroid belt habitat – would say. 'You are a policeman, yes? A sysadmin?'

'Something like that.'

'I lost my friend when ... they came. I don't know where he is.' Perhaps the ship is right: the thief is not the only one who can do a little social engineering.

'Ah, I see. And you don't know how to use co-memories to send him a message? You did not share gevulot to know where you are? Of course you didn't. It is really terrible: the customs Quiet are very strict about leaving all your native tech behind, but never really tell you how to use ours.'

'We just wanted to see the sights,' Mieli says. 'The Olympus Palace, maybe go on a phoboi hunt.'

'Here is what we can do,' the Gentleman says. 'Let's have a look at the agora memory – like this.' The sensation is sudden, like finally finding the word that was at the tip of your tongue. Mieli remembers seeing the agora from high up, in incredible detail, knowing that she can recall every face in the crowd. She has a clear memory of the thief running across the agora.

'Oh,' the Gentleman says. There is a sudden gevulot request from him, asking her to forget his reaction. She accepts: the metacortex will store it anyway. She bookmarks it for later perusal. *Curious.*

'What I can do is bend the rules a little to help you find him. We tzaddiks have some ... special resources.' The tzaddik unscrews the top of his cane. A tiny sphere of utility fog bops out, like a soap bubble. It hovers in the air next to Mieli, and starts glowing. 'That should do it: just follow the firefly, and it will take you to him.'

'Thank you.'

'My pleasure. Just stay out of trouble.' The tzaddik tips its hat again, is surrounded by heat haze, and rises up to the air.

See? That wasn't so hard, was it? says *Perhonen*.

'Sorry,' I say. 'I don't know who you are talking about.' I block the gardener's gevulot request, or at least I *think* I do. The gevulot interface they give to visitors is not really meant to deal with all the subtleties of daily Oubliette interactions, but just to provide a few rough settings ranging from full sharing to perfect privacy. I have a vague recollection of an actual privacy sense: compared to it, this is like having a monochrome vision.

'Your body designers must like the same movie star,' the gardener says. 'You look just like a guy who used to come here with his girlfriend. A pretty girl, too.'

I climb down the robot, slowly.

'What were you doing up there, anyway?' he asks, looking puzzled.

'I just wanted to get a better view of the gameboard,' I say. 'You could say I'm something of a games enthusiast.' I dust off dirt from my jacket. 'Is it you who maintains all the flowers here? It's beautiful.'

'That's me.' He hooks his thumbs under the suspenders of his coveralls, grinning. 'Years of work. It's always been a place for lovers. I'm too old for that – a few rounds as a Quiet takes those kinds of thoughts out of you – but I enjoy keeping it nice for the young people. Are you visiting?

'That's right.'

'Well spotted; this is the kind of place most tourists would not find. Your girlfriend seems to like it, too.'

'What do you mean my girlfriend – oh.'

Mieli is standing in the shadow of one of the bigger robots, with a firefly guide hovering above her head. 'Hello, darling,' she says. I tense, expecting to be plunged into an inferno. But she just smiles like an icicle.

'Did you get lost?' I ask her. 'I missed you.' I wink at the gardener.

'I'll give you youngsters some privacy. Nice meeting you,' the gardener says and blurs out, disappearing into the robot ruins.

'You know,' Mieli says, 'a while back you said that we were going to be professionals.'

'I can explain—'

I don't even see the punch coming, just feel a sudden impact on my nose, calculated precisely to cause maximum amount of pain without breaking the bone, that tosses me back against the robot. Then, a series of kicks that hammer me against it and empty my lungs, setting my solar plexus on fire. And finally, light knuckle percussions on my cheekbones and one that rattles my jaw. Ever faithful to its cruel parameters, my body leaves me gasping for breath and feeling oddly disassociated, as if looking at Mieli's impossibly fast movements from the outside.

'*That* is me being professional,' she hisses. 'In my koto in Oort, we never cared that much for explanations.'

'Thanks,' I gasp. 'For not pressing the hell button.'

'That's because you found something.' She gets a distant look that tells me she is going through this body's short-term memories. 'Let's see it.' She holds out a hand.

I pass her the Watch. She tosses it up and down thought-fully. 'All right. Get up. We will talk about this later. Sight-seeing is over.'

'I know you are thinking about stealing it back,' she says as we take a spidercab back to the hotel. She seems to be enjoy-ing the ride as the diamond legs of the carriage-like vehicle telescope out, taking it up to the rooftops of the Maze.

'Oh?'

'Yes. I can recognise the signals now. You caught me twice with that pickpocket trick, but not again.'

'Sorry, it's a reflex. Makes it more of a challenge, I sup-pose,' I say, massaging my smarting face. 'How long does it take for this body to heal?'

'As long as I want it to.' She leans back. 'What is it about it, anyway? Stealing.'

'It's ...' *It's an instinct,* I want to say. *It's like making love. It's becoming more than I am. It's art.* But she would not under-stand, so I merely repeat the old joke. 'It's about respecting other people's property. I make it *my* property so that I can properly respect it.'

She is silent after that, watching the scenery leap past.

The hotel is a massive building near the glider port where we arrived from the beanstalk station. We have a set of large, impressively Time-consuming rooms near the top floor, not decorated opulently enough for my taste (sleek lines and glass surfaces of Xanthean designers), but at least there is a fabber so I can replace my clothes.

Except that I don't get a chance. She points at the small table and chair in front of the balcony. 'Sit.' She places the Watch in front of me. 'Talk to me. What in Dark Man's name happened at the agora?' She clenches and unclenches her fingers. I swallow.

'All right. I saw myself.' She raises her eyebrows.

'It was not another memory, not like on the ship. It must have been a gevulot construct of some kind: somebody else saw it too. It led me to the garden. So clearly, we are getting somewhere.'

'Perhaps. It did not occur to you to fill me in on this? Are there any reasons for me to let you out of my sight again? Or not to recommend to my employer that we should take off the silk gloves and take a more ... direct approach with your brain?'

'It was ... sudden.' I look down at the Watch. The sunlight glints off it, and again, I notice the engravings on the side. 'It felt ... private.'

She grabs my face with impossibly strong fingers and turns it up. Her eyes look unblinking into mine, angry and green.

'As long as we are in this together, *there is no private*. Do you understand? If I need to know, you will tell me your every childhood memory, every masturbation fantasy, every teenage embarrassment. Is that clear?'

'I do wonder,' I say slowly and carefully, 'if there is something affecting *your* professionalism. And I would note that *I'm* not the one who screwed up the Prison exit. I'm just the one who got us out of it.'

She lets go and looks out of the window for a moment. I get up and get a drink from the fabber, Kingdom-era cognac, without offering her a glass. Then I study the Watch again. There are zodiac symbols, in a grid of seven by seven, Mars, Venus, and others I don't recognise. And underneath, cursive script: *To Paul, with love, from Raymonde*. And that word again, Thibermesnil, in copperplate typeface.

Could you have a look at these? I whisper to *Perhonen. You will still talk to me without hitting me, right?*

I don't need to hit you, the ship says. *I have lasers. I'll see what I can find.* Its tone is unusually terse: I'm not surprised. I tell myself it's the cognac alone that makes my face burn.

'All right,' Mieli says. 'Let's talk about this thing you stole.'

'Found.'

'Whatever.' She holds it up. 'Tell me about this. The Oubliette data I have is clearly obsolete.' Her tone is colourless. A part of me wants to break that icy veneer again, dangerous or not, to see how deep it goes.

'It's a Watch. A device that stores Time as quantum cash – unforgeable, uncopyable quantum states that have finite lifetimes, counterfeit-proof, measures the time an Oubliette citizen is allowed in a baseline human body. Also responsible for their encrypted channel to the exomemory. A very personal device.'

'And you think it was yours? Does it have what we need?'

'Maybe. But we are missing something. The Watch is meaningless on its own, without the public keys – gevulot – inside the brain.'

She taps the Watch with a fingernail. 'I see.'

'This is how it works. The exomemory stores data – all data – that the Oubliette gathers, the environment, senses, thoughts, everything. The gevulot keeps track of who can access what, in real time. It's not just one public/private key pair, it's a crazy nested hierarchy, a tree of nodes where each branch can only by unlocked by the root node. You meet someone and agree what you can share, what they can know about you, what you can remember afterwards.'

'Sounds complicated.'

'It is. The Martians have a dedicated *organ* for it.' I tap my head. 'A privacy sense. They *feel* what they are sharing, what is private and what isn't. They also do something called co-remembering, sharing memories with others just by sharing the appropriate key with them. We just have the baby version. They give the visitors a bit of exomemory and an interface to it, reasonably well-defined. But there is no way we can appreciate the subtleties.'

'And *why* would they do this?'

I shrug. 'Historical reasons, mainly: although not much is known about what exactly happened here after the Collapse. The commonly accepted version is that *someone* brought a billion gogols here for a private terraforming project and set themselves up as a King. Until the gogols rebelled. Anyway, the fact that the gevulot system is in place is pretty much why Sobornost has not just eaten this palace yet. It would be too much trouble to decrypt everything.'

All right, you two, says *Perhonen*. *Sorry about the delay, I didn't want to interrupt. The symbols are astrological. The exact sequence only appears in one source, Giulio Camillo's Memory Theatre. It's an occult system from the Renaissance. Thibermesnil is a castle in France. Here are the details.* She sends a spime down our neutrino channel. Mieli looks at it and leaves it hanging in the air, between us.

'Fine,' she says. 'So, what does all that mean?'

I frown. 'I have no idea. But I think everything we need is in my old exomemory. What we need to do is to figure out how to get to it. I think I need to become Paul Sernine again, whoever he was.' I pour myself some more cognac.

'And where do you think your old body is? Did he – you – take it with you when he left? And what is the point of those markings?'

'Could be. And as for the symbols, I don't know – I always had a taste for theatrics. I'm certainly not getting any flashes from them.' I feel slightly disgruntled at my past self. *Why the hell did you have to make this so complicated?* But the answer is obvious: so that secrets would be secrets. And hiding them among other secrets is a textbook way to do it.

'So there is no way we could brute-force this, to get access to your memories through the Watch? We could use *Perhonen* to—'

'No. There are three things they do better than anyone here: wine, chocolate and cryptography. But' – I lift my index finger – 'it is possible to *steal* gevulot. The system is so complex it's not perfect, and sometimes you can trigger whole cascades of gevulot branches by getting a person to share the right thing with you at the right time. Social engineering, if you like.'

'It always comes down to stealing for you, doesn't it?'

'What can I say? It's an obsession.' I frown. 'We even know where to start: I had a significant other here. But we do need some proper gevulot-breaking tools. Maybe more: using this toy gevulot sense they gave us would be like trying to pick a lock with a brick in the dark. So I think it's time you contacted your employer to put us in touch with some gogol pirates.'

'What makes you think that—'

'Oh, come on. Your employer is from Sobornost, clear as day, maybe some powerful copyclan, out to score points with the Founders. He/it/they – whatever pronoun they use these days – will have contacts with the pirates here, the Sobors are their main customers.' I sigh. 'I never cared much for them. But if you want to dig up treasure, you have to be prepared to get your hands dirty.'

She folds her arms. 'All right,' she says. 'I will point out – to deaf ears, I'm sure – that it is not particularly wise or healthy for you to ask questions or make inferences about our mutual … benefactor.' There is a trace of irony in her voice when she says the last word. 'In any case, it seems there are three things we can do. One: figure out why you would leave the Watch to yourself. Two: try to find your old corpse. Three: get in touch with the only people on this planet with less morals than you.'

She gets up. 'I will see what I can do about option three. In the meantime, you and *Perhonen* will work on number one: we will leave option two until we know more. And get yourself cleaned up.' She turns to leave.

'Wait.'

'Look. I'm sorry I escaped. It was a reflex. I haven't forgotten my debt. You have to understand that this is a little strange.'

Mieli looks at me, and smiles cynically, but does not say anything.

'In my profession, the idea is not to get too caught up in the past. If we are going to work together, I hope you can try to do that as well.' I smile. 'I don't apologise to many people. Or get caught by many people. So consider yourself lucky.'

'Do you know,' Mieli says, 'what they do to thieves where I come from?' She smiles. 'We fill their lungs with life-support synthbio. Then we throw them out. Their eyes pop, their blood boils. But they can live for hours.' She takes my glass from the table and walks away with it. 'So consider yourself lucky.'

The anger makes Mieli feel strangely awake. Being angry at the thief is a pure, clean feeling. For a long time, her anger has been wrapped up and locked away, but this is good and straightforward. She takes deep breaths and paces around her room, even enjoying the sense of fighting gravity for a while. Then she swallows the rest of the thief's alcohol. It is a perfect counterpoint to the emotion, a sharpness that turns into warmth. The guilt comes immediately after that. *I'm letting him get to me again. Bastard.*

She leaves the glass hanging in the air and curses when it falls to the floor. The room makes her uncomfortable: it is too two-dimensional, and the gravity reminds her of the Prison. But at least there is a faint scent of roses.

He is going to think about that vacuum line for a long time, Perhonen says. *Good one.*

I don't mind him thinking that I'm some savage barbarian. He certainly makes me feel like one. Mieli sets the glass aside. *Some peace and quiet now, please. I need to talk to the pellegrini.*

Are you sure you'll be all right?

I've done this before, remember? We went to Venus from the other side of the System to see this bitch. I think I can handle a little journey in my head.

You go, girl. And then *Perhonen* is gone.

Mieli lies down on the bed, closes her eyes and imagines the temple. It is in the shadow of Kunapipi Mons, a shield volcano rising from the basalt plain. The surface of the rock is covered in a thin layer of lead and tellurium, condensed from the metal fumes that rise from the canyons and furrows where the temperature exceeds seven hundred Kelvin.

The temple is a stone shadow, a projection of some higher-dimensional object, with strange geometry: the black corridors she walks along suddenly open into vast hollows crisscrossed by stone bridges at impossible angles. But she has been through this labyrinth before, and follows the metal flower markings unerringly.

In the centre, there is the axis, a little trapped singularity, floating in a cylindrical pit, a falling star, suspended. That is where the goddess lives. Even now, Mieli remembers how she felt at the end of her journey here in the physical world, in a thick q-suit, beaten down by the relentless gravity, limbs burning with fatigue.

'Mieli,' the goddess says. 'How nice to see you here.' Strangely, she looks more human here than when she chooses to manifest to her on her own. The lines on her face and neck and the corners of her eyes are visible. 'Let me see where you are. Ah, Mars. Of course. I always loved Mars. I think we will preserve that place, somewhere, once the Great Common Task is done.'

She brushes a lock of hair away from Mieli's forehead. 'You know, I do wish you would come here sometime without having to ask for something. I have time to all those who serve me, and why wouldn't I? I am many.'

'I made a mistake,' says Mieli. 'I let the thief get away from me. I was inattentive. It will not happen again.'

The pellegrini raises her eyebrows. 'Let me see your memories. Ah. But you found him again? And made progress? Child, you don't have to come to me to unburden your soul after every little failure or a bump in the road. I trust you. You have served me well. Now, what is it that you need?'

'The thief wants tools to steal what they call gevulot here. He thinks there are Sobornost agents on Mars who might be able to help, and wants to contact them.'

The pellegrini looks at the bright dot of the axis for a moment. 'A simple enough request, under normal circumstances. They would obey my seal without question. But I cannot be associated with your mission, not directly. I can provide you with information and contacts, but you will have to do your own negotiation with them. It will be vasilevs, they can be troublesome. Such handsome boys, and they know it.'

'I understand.'

'No matter. I will send what you need to that cute little ship of yours. I am satisfied with your progress: do not worry about failures.'

Mieli swallows. The question comes out unbidden.

'Am I being punished?'

'What do you mean? Of course not.'

'Then why am I treating the thief with velvet gloves? In the war, the warminds would take prisoners and find the tiniest things hidden in their minds. Why is the thief any different?'

'He isn't,' the pellegrini says. 'But he will be.'

'I don't understand.'

'You don't have to. Trust me, you were carefully chosen for this task. Carry it out as you have, and both I and your friend will see you here soon, in the flesh.'

Then Mieli is back in the rose-scented room. Slowly, she gets up and makes herself another drink.

While Mieli is away, *Perhonen* and I work on the Watch. Or she does; I mainly act as her hands. Apparently, Mieli has given the ship a degree of access to this body's sensory systems. It is an odd feeling, holding the Watch in my hands while thin q-dot probes crawl from my fingers into it.

'I always liked these,' I say aloud. 'The Watches. Coupling entangled states with oscillators and mechanics. Large and small. Beautiful.'

Hm. Lift it closer to your eye.

While *Perhonen* carries out the analysis, I'm flicking through exomemories of memory palaces, fighting the resulting headache with drink.

'You know, I think I was off my head. Memory palaces?'
An elaborate memory system, based on a technique of impressing places and images on the mind. Imaginary loci where symbols representing memories could be stored. Used by Greek orators, medieval scholars and Renaissance occultists. Made obsolete by the advent of printing.

I wave the Watch in frustration. 'You know, I would have thought that the whole point of hiding things here would have been for *me* to find them easily again. It's almost as if I don't want myself to discover anything.'

Hold still.

'I can't find anything on Paul Sernine, no public exomemories, not that it's surprising. I do wonder what I was doing on Mars, apart from this Raymonde girl.'

Stealing something, probably.

'I love this place, but looking at my previous career, there isn't that much here to steal. And I would not have gone into the gogol piracy business.'

Are you sure? Now put it back on the table.

'Yes, of course I'm sure. What is your problem, anyway?'

The ship sighs, an odd, imaginary sound. *You are. You may think you are charming, but you are causing distress to my friend. She does not do riddles or prison breaks. She is not even a warrior, not really.*

'So why is she doing all this? Serving the Sobornost?'

Why does anyone ever do anything? For someone. Don't ask so many questions, I'm trying to concentrate. The ion traps in these things are delicate.

'All right. Well, the sooner we crack this, the sooner we can all get on with bigger and better things.'

I feel the thing in my hands. The letters on the word Thibermesnil are raised slightly. 'Ah ha.' I suddenly make the connection. When I came back, there was a dream, and there was a book, a book about the flower thief. And a story. *Sherlock Holmes Arrives Too Late.* A secret passage, unlocked by—

I press the letter H with a fingernail. After some pressure, it turns. So do R and L. The cover of the Watch opens. Inside, is a picture of a man and a woman. The man is me, younger, black-haired, smiling. The woman has reddish brown hair and a dash of freckles across her nose.

'Well, hello, Raymonde,' I say.

7

THE DETECTIVE AND HIS FATHER

Isidore blinks at the Phobos-light in the morning. His mouth tastes foul, and his head pounds. For a moment, he buries his face in Pixil's hair, holding on to her warmth. Then he forces himself to open his eyes, slowly easing his hand out from underneath her.

The vault looks different in the morning. The walls and other surfaces let light filter through, and he can see the red line of Hellas Basin's edge in the distance. It feels like waking up outside, in a strange geometric forest.

The previous night is a haphazard jumble of images, and he instinctively reaches out for the exomemory, to remind himself what happened: but of course, here, he only finds a blank wall.

He looks at Pixil's sleeping face. Her lips are curled in a little smile, and her eyes are fluttering beneath the eyelids. The zoku jewel glitters in the morning light at the base of her throat, against her olive skin. *What the hell am I doing?* he thinks. *She is right, it is just a game.*

It takes a while to find his clothes in the pile, and he almost puts on a pair of pantaloons by mistake. Pixil breathes steadily all the way through the operation, and does not wake up even when he tiptoes away.

In daylight, the cubes in the vault resemble a labyrinth, and it is difficult to tell where they entered, even with a sense of direction honed by living in the Maze. As always, the lack of gevulot confuses Isidore, and thus finding the portal comes as a relief. *That must be it.* A silver arch, a perfect semicircle with intricate filigree work along its edge. He takes a deep breath and walks through. The discontinuity is even sharper this time—

'More wine, my lord?'

—and he is in a vast ballroom that cannot be anything else but the Hall of the King in Olympus Palace. Glittering gogol slave dancers with jewelled bodies twist themselves into impossible configurations atop high pillars, performing slow, mechanical acrobatics. A machine servant in red livery is offering him a glass with a mandible-like limb. He realises he is wearing a Martian noble's attire, a living cloak over a dark q-fabric doublet, wearing a sword. Everywhere around him there are people in even more elaborate finery, bathing in Phobos-light from a huge window with a view down the slope of Olympus Mons. The domed ceiling far, far above is like a golden sky.

It all feels completely real, and he accepts the offered glass, dumbfounded.

'Would you care for a dance?'

A tall woman in a Venetian mask, lush body barely contained in a network of straps and jewels, her skin strikingly auburn red, offers him a hand. Still reeling, he allows himself to be led to a clear space in the crowd where a many-handed gogol plays achingly beautiful melodies with brass flutes. She moves lightly, tiptoed, following his lead like a writer's pen; his hand rests on the smooth curve of her hip.

'I want to make my husband jealous,' she whispers, smelling of exotic wine.

'And who is your husband?'

'Up there, on the dais.' Isidore looks up when they swirl around. And there, of course, stands the Martian King, a laughing figure in white and gold, surrounded by a coterie of admirers and courtiers. He turns to tell the red-skinned woman he really should be going, when everything freezes.

'What are you *doing*?' asks Pixil. She is looking at him, arms folded, looking completely awake now, in her plain zoku daysuit.

'Dancing,' he says, disentangling himself from the red woman who has become a statue.

'Silly boy.'

'What is this place?'

'An old Realmspace. Something Drathdor whipped together once, I think. He's a romantic.' Pixil shrugs. 'Not really my kind of thing.' She gestures, and the semicircle is back behind her. 'I was going to make you breakfast. The whole zoku is still asleep.'

'I didn't want to wake you.'

The discontinuity is a relief this time, restoring him and the world to a degree of normalcy.

'All right. What is this about? Sneaking off after last night?'

He says nothing. Shame crawls down his back, leaving cold trails, and he does not entirely know why.

'It's just the tzaddik thing,' he finally says. 'I need to think about it. I'll qupt you.' He looks around. 'How do I get out of here?'

'You know,' Pixil says. 'You just have to *want*. Do qupt me.' She blows him a kiss. But there is disappointment in her eyes.

Another discontinuity, and he is standing outside the colony, blinking at the bright sunlight.

He takes another spidercab and asks it to drop him off near the Maze, asking the driver to go slow this time. His stomach is churning; clearly, whatever ancient abusive chemicals the Elders were drinking are not something the Martian body designers were prepared for.

There is an immediate sense of relief when the cab leaves the Dust District. The gevulot hums in his mind, and things have *texture* again, not just ethereal geometry but stone and wood and metal.

He has breakfast in a small dragon-themed corner café, banishing fatigue with a coffee and a small portion of Chinese rice porridge, but it does not take the guilt away.

And then he sees the newspaper. An aging gentleman with a Watch in a brass chain and a waistcoat is reading the *Ares Herald* at a nearby table. TZADDIK BOY PARTIES HARD, screams the headline. Shaking, he asks his table for a copy, and the waiter drone brings it. It is him, a moving picture on paper, talking about everything, the chocolate case, Pixil.

For a long time now, we have enjoyed the protection of those masked men and women of might, the tzaddikim; and those who follow our publication know that with difficult cases, they, too, need help. We trust the reader does not need to be reminded of the incident of the disappearance of Schiaparelli City, or the disappearing lover of Mlle Lindgren, where an individual, so far unknown, played a key role. Described as a 'pleasant young man', this person worked with the Gentleman on several occasions, unravelling mysteries that perplexed the tzaddik.

The Herald *can now reveal that this unsung hero is no other than Isidore Beautrelet, an architecture student, aged ten. M. Beautrelet gave your humble correspondent an unusually candid interview last night at a sophisticated celebration in the Dust District. The young detective had been invited by a young lady to whom he has been romantically linked to for some time—*

There are pictures; a black-and-white shot of him, mouth open, at the zoku party. He looks pale and wild-eyed, with dishevelled hair. The awareness that people he has not shared gevulot with now know who he is and what he has done makes him feel dirty. The gentleman in the next table is looking at him sharply now. He pays quickly, wraps himself in privacy and makes his way home.

Isidore shares a flat with another student, Lin, in one of the old towers at the edge of the Maze. The place consists of five rooms in two floors, mostly decorated with haphazard tempmatter furniture, with peeling wallpapers that change patterns according to their moods. When he enters, a ripple goes through them, and they adopt an Escheresque pattern of interwoven black-and-white birds.

Isidore showers and makes more coffee. The kitchen – a high-ceilinged room with a fabber and a wobbly table – has a large window with a view of the Maze rooftops and sunlit shafts between buildings. He sits by it for a while, trying to gather his thoughts. Lin is around too. Her animatronic figures all over the kitchen table again. But at least she herself has the decency to stay hidden behind gevulot.

There are already a lot of co-memories tugging his subconscious about the *Herald* article, like a headache. He wants to forget about it all. At least he has no exomemories of the conversation with the reporter, to be prodded and touched like a loose tooth; a small mercy. And then there is the tzaddik. Not thinking about that is harder.

Then there is a gevulot request from Lin. Grudgingly, he accepts it, allowing his flatmate to see him.

'Iz?' she asks. She studies traditional animation and comes from a smalltown in Nanedi Valley. There is a look of concern on her round face, and paint stains in her hair.

'Yes?'

'I saw the paper. I had no idea that it was you who did all that stuff. My cousin was in Schiaparelli.'

Isidore says nothing. He looks at her expression and wonders if he should try to figure out what it means, but there does not seem to be any point.

'Really, I had no idea. I'm sorry you ended up in the paper, though.' She sits down at the table and leans across towards him. 'Are you all right?'

'I'm fine,' he says. 'I have to study.'

'Oh. Well, let me know if you want to go for a drink later.'

'Probably not.'

'Okay.' She picks up something from the table, wrapped in cloth. 'You know, I was thinking about you yesterday, and I made this.' She hands the bundle to him. 'You spend so much time alone, I thought you could use some company.'

Slowly, he unwraps the thing. It is an odd, cartoonish green creature, all head with large eyes and tentacles, the size of his fist. It starts moving in his grip, inquisitive. It smells faintly of wax. It has large white eyes, with two black dots for pupils.

'I found this old chemical bot design and put a syntbio

brain in it. You can give him a name. And let me know about that drink.'

'Thanks,' he says. 'I appreciate it. Really.' *Is this what I have to look forward to? Pity? Misguided gratitude?*

'Don't work too hard.' And then she is gone again, behind her own gevulot wall.

In his room, Isidore sets the creature on the floor and starts thinking about Heian Kyo influences in Kingdom architecture. It is easier to focus surrounded by his own things, a couple of his father's old sculptures, books and the large tempmatter printer. His floor and desk are covered in three-dimensional building sketches, both imaginary and real, dominated by a scale model of the Ares Cathedral. The green creature hides behind it. *Smart move, little fellow. It's a big, bad world out there.*

Many of his fellow students find studying frustrating. As perfect as exomemory is, it only gives you short-term memories. Deep learning still comes from approximately ten thousand hours of work on any given subject. Isidore does not mind: on a good day, he can get lost in the purity of form for hours, exploring tempmatter models of buildings, feeling each detail under his fingertips.

He summons up a text on the Tendai sect and the Daidairi Palace and starts reading, waiting for the contemporary world to fade.

How are you, lover? Pixil's qupt startles him. It comes with an euphoric burst of joy. **Great news. Everybody thought you were adorable. They want you back. I spoke to my mother, and I really think you are just paranoid—**

He yanks the entanglement ring off and throws it away. It ricochets among the Martian model buildings. The green monster scutters away and hides beneath his bed. He kicks at the cathedral. A part of it dissolves into inert tempmatter, and white dust rises into the air. He continues to break the models, until the floor is full of dust and fragments.

He sits among the ruins for a while and tries to figure out how to reassemble them in his head. But his grip keeps slipping, and it feels like no two pieces fit together anymore.

The next day it is Sol Martius, and as always, Isidore goes to see his father in the land of the dead.

He walks down the long, winding steps of the Inverted Tower with the other mourners, in silence, eyes aching from a sleepless night. The Tower hangs from the belly of the city like a crystal teat. They can see the city's shadow for the whole journey, the slow rhythmic rise and fall of the city's legs. Above, the platforms of the city shift and interlock as the city optimises its weight distribution with each step. Everything is tinted with orange dust. The light of Phobos – a former moon, now turned into a star by the tiny singularity inside it – gives the world an odd, timeless, twilight feel.

There are few mourners this morning. Isidore walks behind a black man whose back is bent by the weight of his quicksuit.

Every now and then, they pass a platform manned by a silent, masked Resurrection Man. The movements of the Quiet below are obscured by the dust cloud, but the phoboi walls are visible. The ramparts stretch towards the horizon and define the city's planned route. They contain the trail of new life behind the city, a paintbrush streak of synthbio fields and terraforming machinery. Like its brothers and sisters, the city tries to paint Mars green again. But in the end, the phoboi always come.

At the bottom of the Tower, there are elevators waiting. Resurrection Men give them fireflies to follow, accompanied by stern instructions to make it back by noon. One of them helps Isidore don his quicksuit, Oubliette make, with modern programmable materials but with far too much design effort spent on it, brass and leather, so that it looks like an ancient diving suit. The gloves are clumsy and it is difficult to hold on to the bouquet of flowers he has brought. They crowd into the elevator through an airlock – a simple platform suspended from nanofilament – and descend through the orange mist, swinging back and forth with the city's motion. And then they are on the surface, slow-moving figures in bell-like helmets, each following a firefly.

The vast mass of the city looms above like a second, heavier sky, with fractures and seams where the different platforms meet, moving and shifting slowly like clockwork. From this vantage point, the legs – a forest of multi-jointed shafts – seem too frail to hold it up. The thought of a falling sky makes Isidore uncomfortable, and after a while, he decides to focus his gaze on the firefly.

The sand beneath his feet is beaten hard by legs and tracks and other locomotion methods of the Quiet. They are everywhere here, tiny ones that scatter to make way for his feet, as if he were a giant City striding across their landscape. There are terraforming Quiet, bigger than a man, moving in herds, toiling on the algae and regolith. An Atlas Quiet strides past, making the ground shake, a six-limbed caterpillar larger than a skyscraper, on its way to correct the balance of a city leg or to make sure the ground is safe when it completes its arc. He sees an air factory Quiet in the distance, a plant on tracks that is like a small city in itself, with swarms of flying Quiet around it. But the firefly does not let him linger. It leads him across the shadow of the city at a rapid pace, up and ahead where his father is helping to build phoboi ramparts.

His father is ten metres tall, with an elongated insect body. He burrows into the Martian regolith with a grinding noise, pulling up powdered rock through a chemical processing system, mixing it with synthbio bacteria, turning it into a construction material for the wall. His dozen limbs – spindly and fast-moving – shape the material flow from his beaklike mouth, laying down the wall, layer by layer. His carapace has a metallic hue that looks rusty in the orange light. There is a dent on his side, with another limb bud growing from it; a memory of a recent phoboi battle.

He labours side by side with a hundred others; some of them climb on top of each other, making the wall taller and taller. But his father's section of the wall looks different. It is full of faces, reliefs and shapes. A lot of them are almost immediately shattered by the smaller mechanic Quiet who come and install the wall's weaponry. But Isidore's father does not seem to care.

'Father,' Isidore says.

The Quiet interrupts his work and turns to Isidore slowly. His metal carapace snaps and groans as it cools. The usual fear chills Isidore, the awareness that *he* is going to be inside a body like that one day. His father looms above him in the orange dust like a bladed tree, the mechanisms of his hands slowly spinning down.

'I brought you some flowers,' Isidore says. The bouquet is full of his father's favourites, tall Argyre lilies, and he places it on the ground carefully. His father picks it up gently, with exaggerated care. His blades spin again for an instant, and the spidery shaper limbs dance. The Quiet places a tiny statue in front of Isidore, made from the dark wall material, a man making a bow and smiling.

'You're welcome,' Isidore says.

They stand in silence for a moment. Isidore looks at the crumbling relief on the wall, all the faces and landscapes his father has carved into it. There is a tree lovingly rendered in stone, its branches full of large-eyed owls. *Maybe Élodie was right,* he thinks. *It is all unfair.*

'I have something to tell you,' he says. The guilt clings to his back and shoulders and belly, wet and heavy, like the old man of the sea. It is difficult to speak while in its grip.

'I did something stupid. I talked to a journalist. I was drunk.'

He feels weak and sits down on the sand, taking his father's statuette in his hand. 'It was inexcusable. I'm sorry. I've already had some trouble, and you may have some too.'

Two statuettes this time, the larger holding his hand across the smaller one's back.

'I know you trust me,' Isidore says. 'I just wanted to tell you.' He gets up and looks at the relief: running horses, abstract shapes, faces, Noble, Quiet. The quicksuit lets some of the gunpowder smell of the freshly worked stone through.

'The reporter asked me why I try to solve things. I told him something stupid.' He pauses.

'Do you remember what she looked like? Did she leave you that?'

The Quiet stands up, all angles and metal. It runs its shaper limbs along a row of blank female faces, each subtly different, each an attempt to capture something he has lost.

Isidore remembers the day he stopped remembering his mother, when her gevulot closed. There was sudden awareness of an *absence.* Before, there was always a sense of safety, that someone always knew where he was, always knew what he was thinking.

The Quiet makes another statue in the sand, a female one, faceless, holding an umbrella above the other two.

'I know you think she was trying to protect us. I don't believe that.' He kicks at the statue. It crumbles back to dust. The regret comes immediately.

'I didn't mean to do that. I'm sorry.' He looks back at the wall, at his father's endless labour. *They break it, and he makes it again. Only the phoboi here to see it.* Suddenly, he feels foolish. 'Let's not talk about her.'

The Quiet sways, like a tree in the wind. Then it makes another pair of statues, with familiar features, holding hands. 'Pixil's fine,' Isidore says. 'I ... I don't know where we are going. But once we figure it out, I'll bring her to see you again.'

He sits down again, leaning against the wall. 'Why don't you tell me what you have been up to?'

Back in the city, in the bright daylight, Isidore feels lighter again, and it is not just the lack of the quicksuit's weight. He is carrying the first statue in his pocket: its weight is comforting.

He treats himself to lunch in a fancy Italo-Chinese place along Persistent Avenue. The *Ares Herald* is still running the story, but this time he is able to focus on his food instead.

'Don't worry, M. Beautrelet,' a voice says. 'All publicity is good publicity.'

Startled, Isidore looks up. There is a woman sitting on the other side of the table. He didn't sense even a ripple in the gevulot. She has a tall, young designer body, a face that is beautiful in a carefully unconventional fashion: short-cropped hair, a strong, sweeping nose, full lips and arching eyebrows. She is dressed in white, a Xanthean jacket over an expensive variant of the Revolution uniform. Two tiny jewels wink at him from her earlobes.

She lays two slender hands on top of the newspaper, long fingers arcing like the back of a cat.

'What does fame feel like, M. Beautrelet?'

'I'm sorry, I haven't had the pleasure—' Again, he makes a gevulot offer, at least to learn her name; he's not even sure she should be able to know his, or to see his face. But it is as if there was a solid wall of privacy around her, a one-way mirror.

She waves a hand. 'This is not a social call, M. Beautrelet. Just answer my question.'

Isidore looks at her hands, resting on the black-and-white picture. He can see his own drowsy eyes from the reporter's picture between her fingers.

'Why do you care?'

'How would you like to solve a case that would give you *real* fame?' There is something childlike about her smile. 'My employer has been watching you for some time. He never fails to notice talent.'

Isidore is awake enough now to deduce, to access exo-memory. She is comfortable in her body, which means she has spent a lot of time as a Noble, too long perhaps to look so young. She has the slightest hint of a slowtown accent, but carefully hidden. Or perhaps hidden just enough for him to notice.

'Who are you?'

She folds the newspaper in two. 'You will find out if you accept our offer.' She gives it to him, and with it, a tiny comemory. 'Have a pleasant day, M. Beautrelet.' Then she gets up slowly, flashes that smile at him again and walks away, becoming a gevulot blur in the crowd.

Isidore opens the memory, something just at the tip of his tongue flashing into his consciousness. A place, a time. And a name.

Jean le Flambeur.

Interlude

WILL

It is Isaac's idea to break into the synagogue. But it is Paul who gets them in, of course, whispering to the clamshell-shaped white building's gevulot until it shows them one of its doors, beneath a high arch embellished with intricate plasterwork.

'After you, rabbi,' Paul says, almost stumbling when he makes an exaggerated bow, face burning.

'No, no, after you,' Isaac insists. 'Or what the hell, let's go in together.' He flings an arm around the young man's shoulders, and they stumble into the place of worship, side by side.

They have been drinking for fourteen hours. Isaac loves the crude sensation of alcohol buzzing in his brain: so much better than sophisticated drugware. The increasingly small sober part of his mind recognises it as a meme rather than a physical thing: thousand years of a culture of intoxication, worship of Bacchus built into his Oubliette-made body.

In any case, what is important is that the world around them has an odd, twisted logic, that his heart pounds in his chest in a way that makes him ready to stand on one of the phoboi walls and roar a challenge to all the dark creatures of the Martian desert. Or to take on God himself, which is what he originally had in mind.

But as always, the quiet sanctuary of the synagogue makes him feel small. The eternal light – a bright q-dot sphere – burns above the doors of the Ark, its glow mixing with the first beams of the dawn, filtering through the through the blue-and-gold patterns of the high stained-glass windows.

Isaac sits down on the chairs facing the reader's platform, takes his metallic field flask from his jacket pocket and shakes it. It sounds half-empty. 'Well, here we are,' he tells Paul. 'What's on your mind? Start talking. Otherwise, we'll have wasted a lot of good booze for nothing.'

'All right. But first, tell me: why religion?' Paul asks.

Isaac laughs. 'Why alcohol? Once you try it, it's hard to give it up.' He opens his flask and takes a swig. The vodka burns on his tongue. 'Besides, this is the faith of champions, my friend: a thousand arbitrary rules you just have to accept, all completely irrational. None of this baby stuff about being saved if you just believe. You should try it sometime.'

'Thanks, but no thanks.' Paul walks to the Ark doors, an odd look on his face. 'The musical sound of breaking the law,' he mutters. Then he turns around. 'Isaac, do you know why we are friends?'

'Because I hate you a little bit less than all the other idiots that this Martian gnat town carries on its back,' Isaac says.

'Because you have nothing that I want.'

Isaac looks at Paul. In the stained-glass light and through the vodka haze, he looks very young. He remembers how they met: an argument in an offworlder bar that got out of hand, Isaac's old anger came out of him in spurts like a cough, bloomed into a fight in which he was delighted to find that the young man did not hide behind gevulot.

Isaac is silent for a moment. 'I beg to differ,' he says, holding up the flask. 'Come and get it.' He laughs, long and hard. 'Seriously, what is eating you? I know what these intoxication marathons lead up to. Don't tell me it's about that girl again.'

'Maybe,' Paul says. 'I did something very stupid.'

'I'd expect no less,' Isaac says. 'Want me to punish you? Want God to punish you? I'll gladly oblige. Come here so I can smack you.'

He tries to get up, but his legs refuse to cooperate. 'Look, you daft bastard. One reason I did not smash your face in the first time we met was that I saw the addiction. I don't know what it is that you crave, but you can't hide from it. For me, it's memes: brain worms, religion, poetry, Kabbalah, revolutions, Fedorovist philosophy, booze. For you, it's something else.' Isaac looks for the flask in his jacket pocket, but his hands feel clumsy and large, like mittens. 'Whatever it is, you are about to throw away a good thing because of it. Get rid of it. Don't do what I did. Cut it out.'

'I can't,' Paul says.

'Why not?' Isaac says. 'It'll only hurt once.'

Paul closes his eyes. 'There is this ... *thing*. I made it. It's bigger than me. It grew around me. I thought I could get away from it but I can't: whenever I want something, it tells me to take it. And I can. It's easy. Especially here.'

Isaac laughs. 'I don't pretend to understand any of that,' he says. 'This is some offworld nonsense, isn't it? Embodied cognition. Many minds and bodies and all that crap. Well, to me you sound like a whiny little boy with too many toys. Put them away. If you can't destroy them, lock them away somewhere where it'll really hurt to touch them again. Back on Earth, that's how I was taught to stop biting my fingernails.' Isaac leans back in his seat and finds that he is slowly sliding on the wooden bench. He looks at the lion carvings in the ceiling. 'Be a man,' he says. 'You're bigger than the toys. We are always bigger than the things we make. Put them away. Make something new with your life, with your own mind and hands.'

Paul sits next to him and stares at the doors of the Ark. Then he takes Isaac's metal flask from his pocket and drinks. 'And how did that work out for you?' he asks.

Isaac slaps him. To his surprise, he actually connects. Paul drops the flask and stares at him, one hand on his stinging ear and cheek. The flask clatters to the floor, spilling its remaining contents.

'Now look what you made me do,' Isaac says.

8

THE THIEF AND THE
PIRATES

The Museum of Contemporary Art is hidden below the street level, a series of transparent tubes, balconies and galleries snaking around the city's hips like an elaborate glass girdle. The arrangement offers abundant light to the exhibits and amazing views of the legs of the city below, drawing slow arcs in the Hellas Basin.

We wander from one gallery to the next, carrying coffee in tempmatter cups. I'm enjoying it; I've always found art calming, even though much of the latest work on display here has a violent, aggressive undercurrent, explosions of colour and sharp edges. But Mieli looks bored. Studying a series of watercolours, she makes a strange, humming sound.

'Not much of an art enthusiast, are you?'

She laughs softly. 'Art should not be *flat*, or dead, like this,' she says. 'It should be *sung*.'

'I believe they call that music around here.'

She gives me a withering look, and I stay quiet after that, content to look at the older, abstract works and the art student girls.

After a while, we start noticing the gogol pirates.

Mieli got the public keys of the Soborost agents from her employer and sent them co-memories. The museum as a meeting place was my idea. The gevulot here is well-structured, enough agora spaces around the exhibits to discourage violence, but allowing perfect privacy for quiet conversations. But I did not expect them to come in such numbers.

A little girl looking at a painting of a herd of gracile elephants grazing in the Nanedi Valley touches the tip of her nose exactly the same way as a passing couple, holding hands. And their gait is identical to that of a tall female art student in a revealing top, who I can't help staring at for a moment. An entire family of them goes past, a father with thinning red hair laughing in odd synchrony with his son. And many more, everywhere in the crowd, all around us. I realise they are opening small parts of their gevulot to us to highlight where they are. Strangely, the mannerisms are familiar to me, from a long time ago, from my human days on Earth.

'They are herding us,' Mieli whispers to me. 'This way.'

We end up on a large balcony separated from the main part of the museum by glass doors. There are three fountain sculptures, standing in a large shallow pool of water. They look like totems, made from jagged metallic and organic shapes that – I learn from the little co-memory attached to them – are discarded Quiet body parts. Water trickles from between the seams: the sound would be soothing if it didn't make me think of blood.

The balcony fills with the pod people, perhaps twenty of them. A group of them position themselves in front of the glass doors firmly, preventing all possibility of escape.

To my surprise, Mieli seems to like the sculptures, standing there for a while, until I touch her arm. 'I think it's time.'

'All right,' she says. 'And remember, I'll do the talking.'

'Be my guest.'

A little black girl, perhaps six years old, walks up to us. She is wearing a startlingly blue dress, and has pigtails that stick out to both sides of her head. She touches her nub of a nose in a way that is now all too familiar. 'Are you offworlders?' she asks. 'Where are you from? My name is Anne.'

'Hello, Anne,' Mieli says. 'No need to stay in character. We are all friends here.'

'You can't be too careful,' says the leggy art student standing behind us, not looking up from her sketchbook.

'You have,' says a woman in a kaleidoscopic dress, holding hands with a young man by the railing of the balcony, 'one minute to explain how you found us.'

'After that we find out ourselves,' finishes Anne.

'I'm sure you would not want to start anything here,' Mieli says. 'This place is full of agoras.'

Anne smiles. 'We deal with agoras all the time,' she says. 'Fifty seconds.'

'I serve one who serves your copyfather,' Mieli says. 'We require assistance.'

'Show us a seal,' says the young, red-haired father, trying to calm down his crying baby. 'We are delighted to serve,' says the art student. 'But show us a seal.' There is a sudden hush in the balcony. Some of them are still carrying on normal conversations, pointing at the statues, laughing. But all their eyes are on us.

'The Great Common Task requires secrecy, as you know better than I,' Mieli says. 'We found you. Is that not proof enough?'

'Darling, we are going to need a little more than that. We are *vasilevs*. Few carry out the Great Common Task with more passion than we do.' Anne grabs the hem of Mieli's toga with a tiny hand. 'And we are not going to jump just because a singleton servant of some puny non-Founder clan tells us to.' She smiles, displaying an uneven row of sugar cube teeth. 'Time is running out. Perhaps we should have a look inside that pretty head of yours.'

'We do not need much,' Mieli says. 'Merely tools. For gevulot emulation, a Martian identity—'

'Are you a *competitor*?' asks the red-haired father. 'Why would we do that?'

Mieli tenses. This is about to turn ugly. The Sobornost are not great negotiators: having all your behaviours dictated by your copyclan template does not leave a lot of room for creativity. That's why I love them, of course. I think about where I last saw the smile, the gestures, the tone of voice. On Earth, centuries ago, in a bar, getting drunk with hackers arguing about politics. Who else was there? *Ah, yes.* Matjek, short and angry. Matjek, who became a Sobornost god.

I shift my posture, like I was a short man wanting to be taller. I pull my shoulders back. I twist my face into a scowl of righteous anger.

'Do you know who I am?'

A ripple of fear runs across the vasilevs' faces. The art student drops her sketchbook into the pool with a splash. *Gotcha.*

'My servant does not need to explain herself. I trust I do not have to explain myself. The Great Common Task requires *faith.* You have been found wanting.' Mieli stares at me, wide-eyed. *Just play along,* I whisper in my feed. *I'll explain later.*

'Do you need seals and symbols to know that a Founder walks among you? I need tools. I have a mission here. The

Task takes us to unexpected places, so I did not come pre-pared. You will give me what I need, immediately.'

'But—' Anne pipes.

'I have a fragment of a Dragon with me,' I hiss. 'Perhaps you would like to be a part of it?'

The vasilevs are silent for a moment. Then a burst of data hits me. I can feel the Sobornost body recognising it, cata-loguing it. Personality templates, gevulot sense emulators, the works: everything you need to maintain a false identity in the Oubliette. *Goodness me, it actually worked—*

Suddenly, Anne shudders and her eyes go blank. The data stream stops, as abruptly as it began. Maintaining my posture, I let my gaze wander around the room, trying to project regal displeasure. 'What is the meaning of this? Did I not make myself clear?'

'Perfectly, M. le Flambeur,' the vasilevs say in unison. 'Now please stay still. Our friends would like to talk to you.'

Crap.

I turn to look at Mieli to tell her that I've got what we need and that she needs to get us out of here, but before I can complete the thought, the fireworks begin.

Mieli watches the thief's gambit with a mixture of shock and astonishment. She has met Matjek Chen, and the thief imi-tates his voice and body language perfectly. To the Sobornost minds inside the stolen Martian bodies, it is quite literally like standing in the presence of a divine being. And when they attack, it is with the ferocity of true believers faced with a blasphemer. *To hell with subtlety. I'm taking them down.*

Her metacortex online, she slows time to give herself time to think, pulling down the veil of combat autism.

Perhonen. *Sweep.*

Far above, the ship sends down a burst of exotic weakly interacting particles through the room. The skeletons of the vasilevs ghost in her vision. Her metacortex matches patterns, classifies hidden weapons. Ghostguns. Sobornost weapons, with bullets that take over your mind. *Damn it.* With a thought, she brings her own systems online.

Her right hand contains a q-dot gun, a linear accelerator firing semi-autonomous coherent payloads. Her left has a ghostgun with an array of nanomissiles: each has a war gogol ready to invade enemy systems, to flood them with copies of itself. The programmable matter layer under her epidermis becomes armour, her fingernails harder than diamond. The fusion reactor in her right thighbone spins up. The metacortex Nash engine chooses a set of optimal targets and a cover position for the thief.

Fire support. On my mark, she tells *Perhonen.*

I'm going to have to change orbits, the ship says. *There will be trouble with the orbital Quiet.*

Do it.

Mieli feels the knife edge of nearby death. She is a singleton, truly finite: anything else would be betraying her ancestors. She won't get a second chance if she fails. And sometimes, that edge makes all the difference, especially against the Sobornost.

The gogol pirates are speeding up too, but they are infiltrators. Their synthbio bodies do not have the same level of military enhancements. Still, they have ghostguns, implanted in eyes, hands and torsos. After ten milliseconds they fire the first volley, stars of infrared playing across their faces like glittering makeup as the nanomissiles are launched. The room explodes into a deadly spiderweb of vectors and trajectories in Mieli's vision.

She grabs the thief and throws him against the base of the middle statue, into a gap in the web. At the same time, she fires a burst of q-dots. It feels like fingerpainting in the air, each stroke leaving a glowing trace. The dots – each a Bose-Einstein condensate, charged with energy and quantum logic – become extensions of her mind, like disembodied limbs. She uses three of them as a flail to swat missiles out of the air, tearing the deadly web to give herself room to manoeuvre. The other two flash towards the vasilev crowd, ready to explode into bursts of coherent light.

The vasilev missiles respond, targeting her. Others shift their trajectories to curve towards the thief. The vasilev crowd splits, trying to avoid the incoming q-dots, but too slowly. The dots blossom into white laser suns that light up the interior of the gallery, melting glass, synthbio bodies and priceless art.

She leaps forward. The air feels like greasy water. Even through combat autism, the freedom of movement is exhilarating. She weaves her way through the missiles, leaving frozen footprints in the water, punching through the art student's abdomen as an afterthought.

Then they are upon her, Anne, the family, the woman in the garish dress, three others. Disassembler tendrils shoot out of their fingers, lines of vibrating destruction. One lashes across her back. Her armour reacts, burning away the infected layer, giving her wings of flame for an instant.

She programs a simple defence routine into her ghostgun and fires it at them, one, two, three: the thief will need more protection. She gets two. The ghost gogols take over the vasilevs' brains and hurl their bodies at the paths of missiles aimed at the thief.

She tears off the caleidoscope's disassembler arm, swinging

it at Anne. The girl's torso explodes into dust as the molecular fingers tear her cells apart. She fires her last q-dot into the red-haired man's eye. Several vasilevs return fire. Ghostgun impacts make her armour scream. Gritting her teeth, she grabs one of the bullets in her fist. It will contain a copy of a vasilev mind – time to ask it questions later.

They rush her, all at once. There is a mass of bodies on top of her, a coordinated mountain of synthflesh, ignoring her punches and kicks that tear into it as if it were mist. Her skull presses against floor. She sends *Perhonen* a set of coordinates. *Mark.*

Fire from the sky cuts the balcony from the hip of the city like a surgeon's knife. Metal groans. Somewhere above, *Perhonen*'s wings rain hard hot light.

The sudden freefall feels like home. She navigates through a bloody mist and tangled bodies, finds the thief and seizes him. Then she opens her wings. As always, the sensation – like flower buds opening in her shoulders – brings back her childhood, flying in her koto's forests in the ice, racing paraspiders. But her wings are stronger now, remade, strong enough to carry both her and the thief, even in this heavy city.

Together they burst through the ceiling of the gallery. The twisted, burning remains of the balcony and the vasilevs plummet towards the city legs below.

Shame about the statues, she thinks.

The world is a chaos of bodies, explosions and the smell of burning flesh. I blink, and my body is hurled against stone. Staccato thunderclaps rock my skull. I am crashing through glass, Mieli is holding me and we are *flying* and there are flames below us and a whooshing sound of air as if in a wind tunnel that empties my lungs—

I scream. And then I fall. For about a metre. In Martian gravity. I land on my back, ears ringing, colours flashing in front of my eyes, mouth still open after the air in my lungs runs out.

'Stop that,' Mieli says. She is kneeling, a few metres away, and a pair of *wings* are slowly retracting into her back, two delicate trees of silver with gossamer-thin tracery, separated by a transparent, shimmering film, like *Perhonen*'s wing fabric. In a moment, they are gone.

'Fuck,' I say, when I catch my breath. We are on a gently sloping rooftop, somewhere near the edge of the city. The conflagration and a column of smoke in the horizon clearly shows where we were mere seconds ago. A flock of tzaddikim descend towards the battlefield, like crows. 'Fuck, fuck, fuck.'

'I told you to stop that,' Mieli says, standing up. Her toga is in tatters, showing expanses of smooth brown skin. She notices my gaze and turns her back as her garment starts knitting itself back together.

'F—' I take a deep wheezing breath, cutting myself short. 'The bastards. Somebody told them. Who we were. Somebody knew.'

Darling doves, says *Perhonen. I'm glad you are okay, but don't expect to hear from me for a few hours. I had to flee my holding position in stealth mode: the orbital Quiet might as well be blind and deaf, but even they have noticed me firing lasers down at their planet. I'll let you know when I get back. Be safe.*

'What happened back there?' I ask Mieli.

'They attacked. I had to ask *Perhonen* to take them out, with extreme prejudice. Protocol.'

'So, they are – all dead?'

'Destroyed. No possibility of an exomemory sync; if they get resurrected, they won't remember us. They were stealth vasilevs, they would not have had neutrino comms equipment.'

'Jesus. Any collateral damage?'

'Just art,' Mieli says, and for the life of me I can't figure out if she is making a joke. 'But you got what we came for, yes?'

I touch the data the little pirate girl dumped on me. Parts are missing, but the important bits are intact.

'Yes. I'm going to have to study this.' I massage my temples. 'Look, something is going on. Clearly, somebody tipped them off. Is there some twisted Sobornost power game going on with your employer? Is there something I should know about?'

'No.' Her answer does not leave any room for argument.

'All right, then we have to assume it's local. We are going to have to look into it.'

'*I* am going to look into it. *You* are going to get on with the mission.'

I get up, slowly. My body is undamaged – no broken bones – but it *pretends* that it is. Everything tingles as if covered by one massive bruise. 'Yes, about that.'

'What?'

'You do realise that you are going to have to give me more than just hurt privileges for this body? If I'm going to create a new identity, I'm going to need some flexibility. Even hunting this Raymonde girl down is going to involve more than just eyes and ears. Not to mention emulating the gevulot sense or *surviving* if we ever happen to encounter our many-voiced friend there again.'

She studies me carefully, massaging her hands together. A

thin layer of dried gore is peeling off them, falling down in flakes as her skin cleans itself.

'Oh, and thank you for saving my ass, by the way,' I tell her. I know the effort is wasted, but I summon some warmth – most of it genuine – into my eyes and give her my best smile. 'You have to let me repay the favour.'

Mieli frowns. 'All right. Once we get back, I'll see what I can do. Now, let's get out of here. I don't think we left any public trails outside gevulot, but the same rules don't seem to apply to the tzaddikim. I don't want to fight *them* on top of that.'

'Are we flying?'

She grabs my shoulder firmly and drags me to the edge. The street is almost a hundred metres down. 'You can try if you want,' she says. 'But that body does *not* have wings.'

That night, at the hotel, I make myself a new face.

We sneaked back a roundabout route, under full gevulot cover, covering half the sights of the city – somewhat excessively paranoid as under full gevulot we should not be recognisable by anyone – but Mieli insists. She also sets up a defence grid of some kind; little dots of light come out from her hands and start patrolling the doors and windows.

'Don't touch them,' she says, unnecessarily. And then she does something magical, something that almost makes me kiss her. And I would, too, if I didn't have flashing images of her tearing a young girl's arm off and beating three people to death with it. In any case, she closes her eyes for a moment and there is a *click* inside my head. Nothing excessive, nothing like the complete freedom I briefly felt when we fought the Archons, but it is something. An increased awareness of myself, a sense of control. I now know there is a network of q-dots – artificial atoms capable of assuming any range of physical properties – under the skin of this body, able to simulate an epidermis of any colour, shape or appearance.

Mieli claims that her systems need to recharge and that she has some damage to regenerate, so she goes to bed early. *Perhonen* is quiet as well, dodging the orbital sentinels, no doubt; or hacking into their systems and manufacturing convincing excuses about why they lost her for a moment. So I am as alone as I have been since the escape from the Prison.

It feels good: I spend some time simply watching the night view of the city, on my balcony and drinking, single malt this time. Whisky has always tasted like introspection to me, a quiet moment after taking a sip, the lingering aftertaste, inviting you to ponder upon the flavours on your tongue.

I lay out the tools in my mind, one by one.

Gevulot is not perfect. There are *loops* in it, places where a node – representing a memory, an event, a person – has more than one parent. That means that sometimes, sharing gevulot about an innocuous memory, a taste or an intimate moment, can unlock whole swathes of a person's exomemory. The gogol pirates have software that tries to map out a person's gevulot tree, tries to scan for the key nodes in conversation.

There is a man-in-the-middle attack software that attempts to intercept the quantum communications between a Watch and the exomemory. That will require a lot more brute force, and quantum computation capability besides: I will have to talk to *Perhonen* about that. A perfect emulation of the privacy sense organ which I want to start running immediately. And finally, a set of public/private keys and blank exomemories to choose from. I don't want to think about how those have been obtained, but at least the dirty work has been done for us. Some of them are fragmented from the interruption of the transfer, but what is there will do, for now.

Being about to become someone else is a thrilling feeling, a tickle of possibility in my gut. There must have been times when I flicked from one identity to another, posthuman, zoku, baseline, Sobornost. And that makes me want to be the god of thieves again, more than anything.

I flick the Watch open and look at the picture again. *Who should I become for you, Raymonde? Who was I for you before?* Her smile has no answers, so I close the lid, finish my drink and look at myself in the bathroom mirror.

The face – heavy-lidded eyes, a tinge of grey in the hair – makes me wonder about Mieli's employer again. She must have known me, a long time ago. But whoever she is, she belongs to the things that the Prison took away from me. I relish the image for a moment. I'm not narcissistic, but I like mirrors, the way they let your define yourself through some-thing external. And at last, I test how this body responds. *Become a little younger*, I tell it. *A little taller, higher cheekbones, longer hair.* The image in the mirror starts flowing like water, and my belly thrill becomes glee.

'You are enjoying this, aren't you?' says a voice. I look away from the mirror and around the room, but there is no one there. And the voice feels awfully familiar.

'Over here,' says my mirror image. It is the young me from the picture, dashing and dark-haired, grinning. He tilts his head slightly, studying me across the glass. I stretch my hand and touch it, but the image does not move. The same sense of unreality as with the boy at the agora is there.

'You are thinking about her,' he says. 'Which means you are about to go to talk to her again.' He sighs a little wistfully. 'There are a few things you should know.'

'Yes!' I shout at him. 'Where are my memories? Why are we playing games? What are those symbols—'

He ignores me. 'We really thought she was the one. The redemption. And for a while, she was.' He touches the glass surface from the other side, a reflection of my earlier gesture. 'I really envy you, you know. You get to try again. But remember that we treated her very badly last time. We don't deserve a second chance. So don't break her heart, or if you do, make sure there is someone to put it back together.'

Then the grin is back. 'I'm sure you hate me now, a little. This is not meant to be easy. I made finding things difficult, not for you, but for *myself*. Like an alcoholic who locks the booze in the basement and throws away the key.'

'But you are here, so it wasn't enough. There we are. Give her my best.'

He takes out a Watch, the one I'm holding as well, and looks at it. 'Well, got to go. Have fun. And remember, she likes balloon rides.'

Then he is gone, replaced my own new reflection.

I sit back and start making a new one, for a first date.

9

THE DETECTIVE AND THE LETTER

Later that evening, Isidore lets the co-memory take him to the Tortoise Park. It leads him down a narrow sandy path, through a grove of pine and elm. Beyond the trees, he finds the chateau.

It is the largest restored Kingdom building Isidore has ever seen apart from the Olympus Palace; it is astonishing that it is hidden from public view by gevulot. The last sunbeams of the day glance off two towers that weave left and right as they rise towards the sky, like Oriental daggers. The chateau casts long blue shadows on a field of flowers, laid out with geo-metrical precision. The flowers form triangles and polygons of many colours, as if the gardener was proving Euclidean theorems. It takes Isidore a moment to realise that they are laid out in the shape of a Darian solar clock, with the shadow of the taller tower as the dial.

There is a tall iron fence with a gate. A Quiet is stand-ing behind it, waiting. It is an unusual creature: a sculpted humanoid, no larger than a man, a golden mask and gloves hiding the angles and edges beneath, wearing blue silver-embroidered livery. It reminds him of the jewelled mannikins in the Kingdom simulation. Naturally, it gives him no greeting, but he feels it is polite to say something.

'I'm Isidore Beautrelet,' he says. 'I'm expected.'

Silently, it opens the gate for him and leads him towards the chateau. They walk through fields of roses, lilies and more exotic flowers he needs to 'blink to recognise. The smell is intoxicating.

The evening sun casts a golden pool in a clearing where a small pagoda-like pavilion stands. A pale-haired young man – barely more than a boy, perhaps six or eight Martian years old – sits inside, reading a book, an empty teacup next to him. He is wearing a plain Revolution uniform that hangs loose on his frame. His thin eyebrows are squeezed together in concentration in a delicate face, rounded by baby fat. The Quiet servant stops and rings a small silver bell. The man looks up slowly and gets up with exaggerated care.

'Dear boy,' he says, offering a hand. His fingerbones feel like porcelain in Isidore's grip. He is taller than Isidore, but almost painfully thin, the elongated Martian bodymorph taken to the extreme. 'How delightful that you could come. Would you like some refreshments?'

'No, thank you.'

'Sit, sit. What do you think of my garden?'

'Impressive.'

'Yes, my gardener is a genius. A very modest man, but a genius. And that, of course, often applies to other individuals possessing rare talent, such as yourself.'

Isidore watches him quietly for a moment and tries to shake away the disturbance in gevulot. It is not *absence* of privacy like in the Dust District, but uncertain, as if it could tear any moment.

150

The young man smiles. 'And are you genius enough to know who I am?'

'You are Christian Unruh,' Isidore says. 'The millenniaire.'

Finding that out was not difficult, but it occupied him for the other half of the afternoon, going through public exomemories and comparing them to the co-memory the woman in white gave him. Unruh – if that is his name – is a private person even by Oubliette standards: apart from his youth, it is difficult to find out anything about his background. His name comes up mainly in the context of society events and business deals in newspapers. It is obvious that he has more Time than God.

'You have a personal Time fortune based on gevulot brokering, something the Voice only made possible a few years ago. And clearly, you are worried about something. Gogol piracy?'

'Oh no. I have been careful to be perfectly ordinary in everything else except making Time. A defence mechanism, you might say. No, what concerns me is this.'

Unruh hands Isidore a note, fine, linen, unmarked paper, with a few words written on it in an elegant, flowing hand.

Dear M. Unruh, it says,

In response to your unsent invitation – I will be delighted to attend your carpe diem party on the 28th sol of Vrishika, 24**. I will bring one guest.

Your obedient servant, Jean le Flambeur.

Isidore has been thinking about le Flambeur all afternoon. The Oubliette exomemory does not have much on him. In the end, he spent Time on an expensive data agent that ventured into the Realm outside the Oubliette noosphere. What it brought back was a mixture of fact and legend. No actual memories or lifecasts, not even video or audio. Fragments from before the Collapse, online speculation about a criminal mastermind operating in Fast London and Paris. Fanciful tales of a sunlifting factory stolen from the Sobornost, a *guberniya* brain that was broken into; dirty dealings in Realm unreal estate.

It can't all possibly refer to the same individual, a copy-family perhaps. Or maybe it is a meme, an idea for criminals – whatever that word may mean in different parts of the System – to sign their felonies with. So whatever this is, it must be a prank of some sort. Isidore hands the note back.

'Your carpe diem party?' he asks. 'That's in a week.'

Unruh smiles. 'Yes. A millennium of Time goes quickly, these days. I'm giving most of it away, and some of it will be managed by my associate – Odette, whom you already met.'

'I understand it is rare among our generation – not to rail against the injustice of it all – but I'm something of an ideal-ist. I believe in the Oubliette. I have had a rich eight years in this body; I'm ready to do my part as a Quiet. But of course, I want to conclude things with style, before the next time. To seize the day, for one night.' There is an odd bitterness in his voice.

The Quiet servant hands them both fine porcelain cups of tea: Unruh tastes his with relish. 'Also, finiteness gives everything such an edge, don't you think? I think that's what our founding fathers and mothers had in mind. Experiencing that is all I wanted. Until the note came along.'

'How did it arrive?'

'I found it in my library,' Unruh says. 'In my library!' Hard anger lines look strange on his childlike face. His cup rattles when he sets it down. 'I don't let *anyone* in my library, M.

Beautrelet. It is my inner sanctum. And no one outside my immediate circle of friends even has the gevulot to come to this castle. As I'm sure you can understand given your recent experiences with the press, I feel … violated.'

Isidore shudders. The thought of someone coming to his personal space, unannounced, without access to his gevulot makes his skin crawl. 'You don't think it is possible that this is a prank of some kind?'

Unruh presses his palms together. 'I have considered the possibility, of course,' he says. 'As you can imagine, I went through the castle exomemory thoroughly. I found nothing. Sometime last night, between seven and eight thirty, the letter simply appeared. I don't recognise the handwriting. The paper is from a stationery shop on the Avenue. There are no obvious DNA traces, apart from mine. That is as far as Odette got. I am convinced that offworld technology is involved. The *modus operandi* would certainly fit with what we know about this character – announcing a date and time for his crime.

'In some way, I'm not surprised. The offworlders think that we are a backwater, a playground. And for some reason, this … thief has chosen me as his plaything. But if I went to the Voice or the tzaddikim, they would tell me the same thing: it is a prank. And that's why you are here, M. Beautrelet.' Unruh smiles. 'I want you to help me. I want you to find out how the letter got into my library. I want you to figure out what he is going to do, and stop it. Or if he succeeds, recover what is mine.'

Isidore takes a deep breath. 'I think you may have a somewhat exaggerated view of my abilities,' he says. 'I'm not convinced that this is the real le Flambeur by any means.

But if it is, why do you think I will be a match for such a creature?'

'As I said, I'm an idealist,' Unruh says. 'I am familiar with your work. Indeed, I consider myself to be something of a fan. And, while I am deeply insulted by the thief's actions, I do find the thought of having my demise accompanied by a battle of wits amusing. Naturally, we can find a suitable compensation for your efforts, if that is an issue. What do you say?'

To catch a thief, Isidore thinks. Something pure. Something simple. Something clean. Even if it turns out to be a joke.

'All right,' he says. 'I accept.'

Unruh slaps his hands together. 'Excellent! You know, M. Beautrelet, you are not going to regret your decision.' He gets up. 'Now, let's find Odette and visit the scene of the crime.'

The chateau is built with the same grandeur as the Kingdom simulation at the zoku colony: high ceilings, marble floors, matte black suits of robotic armour lining the corridors along with large landscape paintings of old Mars: red cliffs, Valles Marineris, the grinning visage of the King in white and gold.

Odette – the woman in white – is waiting for them in the library, and gives Isidore a curt nod when they enter.

'Well done,' Unruh tells her. 'It appears that your charms persuaded young M. Beautrelet to assist us with our little dilemma.'

'I thought he might,' she says. 'I think you will find this interesting, M. Beautrelet.'

The library is a high room, well-lit by a skylight, with large windows to the garden. There are comfortable-looking leather couches. And books, both analog and spime, thousands of them in neat rows in dark oak shelves, attended to by a treelike synthbio drone. A large brass orrery – metal casing containing a real-time image of Mars and the surrounding space – sits in the centre of the room on a dark wine-coloured rug.

Unruh holds out a hand, and the drone hands him a tome, black branch limb snaking up to one of the higher shelves. 'This is the lifecast of the Count of Isidis. He belonged to a little cabal that tried to oust the King a few years before the Revolution. Naturally, they failed. But it is a fascinating period, the pre-Revolution years; when things could have gone very differently indeed. Full of gaps left by the Spike, of course. As I'm sure you can tell, I had something of a Kingdom enthusiasm phase a while back.' There is a hollow note in his voice.

'In any case, this is the volume I was studying when I noticed the letter. It was over here.' The millenniaire points to a small reading desk. 'Carefully placed so that I would see it when sitting in my favourite chair.' He leaves the book on the table, walks over to one of the chairs and sits down. 'Only I, my three Quiet servants and Odette – and now you – have gevulot to this place.'

'Any other security measures?'

'Not yet; but I am happy to give you free rein to put anything you like in place, up to and including black market tech. Odette will see to the details, just let her know.' Unruh looks at Isidore and grins. 'And I'd also visit Persistent Avenue with her. You will need something to wear for the party.'

Isidore coughs, suddenly self-conscious in his rumpled old Revolution uniform replica. 'Do you mind if I take a look around?'

'Of course not. I would imagine that you will be spending

a considerable amount of time here over the next few days. I have given you access to the exomemory – apart from certain private portions – so you should feel free to explore.'

Isidore picks up the volume that Unruh set down and opens it. A dazzling display of images, video and text spills out, floating around him. Point-of-view video, sound and noise, glimpses of elegant faces and great halls—

Unruh yanks the book from his hands with a sudden violence. His eyes are bulging, and there are little patches of red on his pale cheeks. 'I would prefer it,' he hisses, 'if you stayed away from the contents of the library. Many of these were … difficult to acquire, and I am somewhat jealous of them.' He hands the book back to the library drone, who returns it to the shelves.

Isidore's expression must betray his shock and rapid pulse: Unruh shakes his head and then gives him a shy smile. 'I apologise. You have to understand a collector's passion. And as I said, this is a very private place for me. I would be much obliged if you could carry out your investigations without … academic pursuits.'

Isidore blinks the images away and nods, heart pounding. There is a sudden hard look on Odette's face. 'I was never that interested in history,' he says quietly.

Unruh laughs, an odd, coughing sound. 'And perhaps it would be best for all of us if we spent more time in the present, hmm? In fact, that is very much what I intend to do for the next few days. I have some last-minute … human things to attend to.' He takes Isidore's hand again. 'I have faith in you, M. Beautrelet. I hope I am not disappointed.'

'I hope so too,' Isidore says.

*

After Unruh is gone, Isidore takes out his magnifying glass and starts studying the room. It overlays the room with information: DNA traces, patterns of wear in the carpet, fingerprints and grease stains, molecules and trace elements. At the same time, he reaches for the room's exomemory. An infinite tower of past instants opens in his head. A brief 'blink tells him that the letter is there at 8.35pm the previous night, but not a few seconds before. And there is no one in the room, either before or after. He expands the memory through the castle: a servant standing in eternal silence *here*, another *there* – and a block, hiding Unruh's private quarters from view.

He looks at the letter again. There is no sign of self-assembly: it is actual handmade paper, or a perfect nanotech replica. Even with advanced offworld tech, it is hard to imagine a cloud of nanites constructing it out of nowhere in a matter of seconds; the energy required for such an operation would have left many other traces in the castle's exomemory.

'We tried all the obvious things,' Odette says, perched on one of the armrests of Unruh's chair, looking at Isidore, smiling her little girl's smile. 'I doubt your zoku toy will discover anything I didn't.'

Isidore barely hears her: he is too focused on examining the floor and the walls of the library. As might be expected, they are solid, quickstone-laced basalt. He sits down and closes his eyes for a moment. There are fleeting images from the book that obscure the shape of the mystery, although a part of him wants to fit them in too. He brushes them aside and focuses on the letter itself. A locked room, a mysterious object; there is something almost too clean about it.

'When was the last time you acquired something for M. Unruh?' he asks Odette.

She touches her lips with a fingertip. 'Perhaps three weeks ago. Why?'

'I was wondering about Trojan horses,' Isidore says. 'Is it possible that he could have bought a disguised device, something containing a microdrone or something that could have placed the letter where M. Unruh found it? For that matter, the device could have been purchased a long time ago, sitting here until it was activated.'

'I find that unlikely,' Odette says. 'Christian reviews every item he buys very carefully with the help of experts. And even if there had been a device of some sort, it would have shown up in the exomemory.'

'True.' Isidore looks at her curiously. 'And do you have a theory of your own?'

'That's not what I'm paid for,' Odette says. 'But if I had to offer one ... well, let us just say that during my employ I have seen dear Christian do more eccentric things than writing letters to himself.' She smiles, something much older and wicked this time. 'He gets bored easily. For your sake, M. Beautrelet, I hope you are as good at creating mysteries as you are solving them. And a better detective than you are a dresser. Your wardrobe *definitely* needs some improvement.'

Isidore is still thinking about the letter when he returns home that evening. He realises how much he has missed it, the slowly unfolding map of a new mystery inside his head.

Lin must still be awake: the lights are on in the kitchen. He realises he has not eaten since lunch, and tells the kitchen fabber to whip up some risotto.

As he watches the fabber arm dance over the plate, painting rice grains into being with its atom beam, he thinks about Unruh. There is something about him that does not quite fit.

Odette's suggestion that he has been invited to play along in some elaborate charade seems to fit all the facts. But its shape is too awkward to be acceptable.

He stares at the steaming plate, decides he wants to hang on to the sharpness of hunger and thought, leaves it on the kitchen table and goes to his room.

'Long day?'

Pixil is sitting on his bed, legs crossed, playing with the green creature.

'What are you doing here? How did you get in?' He has deliberately excluded Pixil from his gevulot for the past few days. It has felt like a local anaesthetic, covering up something raw with numbness.

Pixil holds up the entanglement ring. There is a blurry granularity in her features, and he realises she is a utility fog image. 'It's not just a communication device, you know,' she says. 'I got tired of playing the *guess what your boyfriend is thinking* game. I suppose you showed initiative in coming up with that one.'

'Are you—'

'Serious? No. Most people in the zoku would be, no question about it. I like this guy. Does he have a name?'

'No.'

'Shame. He could use one. Something from Lovecraft perhaps. Although there are bigger slimy and tentacled beings around here.'

Isidore says nothing.

'I suppose you are too busy to talk?' Pixil says.

'Maybe I'm just tired of the *let's talk about our feelings* game.'

Pixil looks at him for a while. 'I see. And here I was coming up with a new scoring system for that. One point every time you say a true thing, with achievements unlocked by actual emotional revelations. But I see I wasted my time.' She crosses her arms. 'You know, if I asked Drathdor, he could set up a little emotional response model that would tell me exactly what makes you tick.'

A horrible thought strikes Isidore. 'You don't have anything to do with this le Flambeur thing, do you?' He hits the boundaries of what the gevulot allows him to share about Unruh's assignment, and his tongue freezes. But it *does* feel exactly the kind of thing Pixil would do. Setting up an elaborate puzzle to restore his confidence. With some horror, he realises it is not a hypothesis he can discard outright.

'I have no idea what you are talking about,' she says. 'Clearly, you are busy focusing on *important* things. I came to say that no matter *what* game you want to play with me – and believe me, I play better than you – *it's your move.*'

She disappears. The entanglement ring and the green thing fall to the bed with a thump. The creature lands on its back and waves its tentacles in the air helplessly.

'I know exactly how you feel,' Isidore says.

He picks the creature up and turns it upright. It gives him a large-eyed thankful look. He lies down next to it and stares at the ceiling. He should be thinking about Pixil, and ways to make it up to her, he knows. But his thoughts keep returning to the letter. The letter is a physical object. It has an origin. Somebody wrote it. It is impossible for exomemory not to have recorded where it came from. Therefore, one must be able to find its origin in the exomemory. Unless—

Unless exomemory itself is flawed.

The thought makes him blink. It is like saying that gravity might not be a constant 0.6g, or that the sun might not come up tomorrow. But the thought, wrong as it is, fits. And not only that, it feels like it is only a part of some larger shape, looming in the darkness, just beyond his grasp. *When you eliminate the impossible, whatever remains, however improbable, must be the truth.*

Something chilly touches his toes, and he lets out a small yelp. It is the creature, exploring the world under his blanket. He picks it up again and gives it an angry look. It flutters its tentacles innocently.

'You know,' Isidore says, 'I think I'm going to call you Sherlock.'

As promised, she assists him in choosing an outfit for the carpe diem party. They spend half a day on Persistent Avenue. The celebration is going to be Time-themed, and a deft-fingered outfitter measures him up for a costume based around Sol Lunae, the second day of the Darian week: black and silver.

'Isn't the Moon supposed to be feminine?' he protests when Odette informs him of the theme.

'Christian has thought about this very carefully,' Odette says, frowning as the shop projects various designs on Isidore's lean frame. 'I wouldn't argue with him: I've never managed to change his mind. I think we are going to try another fabric, possibly velvet.' She smiles. 'The Moon also symbolises mystery, and intuition. Perhaps that is what you represent to him. Or perhaps not.'

Isidore stays quiet after that and submits to the gentle torture of the tailor without complaint.

After the shopping trip, he returns to the chateau and starts to eliminate the impossible, coming up with a series of hypotheses to explain the appearance of the letter, each more elaborate than the last. They range from self-assembling paper to an invisibility fog sophisticated enough to fool the ubiquitous exomemory sensors. But everything brings him back to the improbable conclusion: something is wrong with exomemory itself.

One of the Quiet servants brings him a light lunch, which he eats alone. Apparently, the millenniaire is too occupied with his last week in a Noble body to spend much Time on something already set in motion.

In the afternoon, Isidore considers the possibility of exo-memory manipulation. He 'blinks until his head pounds with technical information about distributed ubiquitous communication and quantum public key cryptography, Byzantine general problems and shared secret protocols. The exomemory is everywhere. Its tiny distributed sensors – in every piece of smart- and dumbmatter – record everything, from events to temperature fluctuations to object movements to thoughts, with access to it controlled only by gevulot. But it has been designed to be write-only, with massive redundancy. Hacking into it and editing it would mean nanotechnological and computational resources far beyond the reach of any Oubliette citizen.

The realisation sends a chill down Isidore's spine. Perhaps some otherworldly force has indeed chosen Unruh as its target.

After a walk in the garden – where a white-haired man in blue coveralls is working on Unruh's flowers with the help of a Quiet servant – he goes through all of the castle exomemory he has access to, looking for other gaps. He sits in one of the library chairs, remembering. Unruh has had a regular life for the past year, almost hermit-like, apart from the occasional small party. There are times when exotic courtesans from Serpent Street pass through the memories, making Isidore wonder what Adrian Wu would make of his new patron. But mostly Unruh spends his time in solitude, receiving antique dealers, eating alone, and spending endless hours immersed in study in the library.

He is almost ready to give up – the amount of detail is too much to absorb on one sitting – when he decides to cross-reference the memory with the book Unruh was reading, the lifecast of Count Isidis. The last time Unruh read it was four weeks ago. And in the memory—

It takes a few moments to take in. Then he leaps to his feet and goes to find Odette. She is overseeing preparations for the party in a small office in the eastern wing of the chateau, surrounded by floating spime invitations, like a flock of birds frozen in time.

'I want to see M. Unruh.'

'I'm afraid that is not possible,' she says. 'Christian has only a few days left, and unless he tells me otherwise, he is going to spend them how he pleases.'

'I have some questions for him.'

'If I were you, M. Beautrelet,' Odette says, 'I would be content to play your part in this little drama of his.' She touches a virtual sheet in the air. It becomes a young woman's face: she studies it, touching her lips lightly with the tip of her pen. 'A lifecast artist,' she says. 'I don't think she would fit. Sometimes I think I should have been a musician. Organising a party is much like composition: considering how different instruments complement each other. For me, you are another instrument, M. Beautrelet. Christian trusts me to be the conductor of his final day. So please, save your dramatic revelations for the party. Comedy is all about timing, I've always been told.'

Isidore folds his arms. 'I heard a quote once,' he says.

'Tragedy is when I slip on a banana peel. Comedy is when you fall into a hole and die. I do wonder what I would find if I spent more time investigating *you*.'

She holds Isidore's gaze for a long time. 'I have nothing to hide,' she finally says.

Isidore smiles, saying nothing. She is the first to look away.

'All right,' Odette says. 'I suppose he could use some light entertainment.'

Unruh greets him at one of the galleries of the chateau, wearing a dressing gown and a chilly expression. Isidore sees someone walk past along a corridor, blurred by gevulot, wondering what activity the millenniaire interrupted to see him.

'M. Beautrelet. I am told that you have discovered something.'

'Yes. I am convinced that your concern is real, and there is an offworld force of some sort at work here. I will help you to make appropriate preparations for the party.'

'I suppose I should thank you for not agreeing with Odette and claiming I wrote the letter myself,' Unruh says. 'And?'

'Nothing. The local exomemory has been manipulated in some fashion, but I cannot determine how or by who. But that is not what I wanted to talk to you about.'

'Oh?' Unruh raises his eyebrows.

'When going through the exomemory and looking for gaps, I noticed you had frequently studied the Isidis lifecast, and went back to its first appearance. I realise that I was, perhaps, abusing the powers that you had given me, but I felt it was important to study all the elements of the case from all possible angles.'

'Indeed.'

'I could not help noticing your … reaction to the text.' Unruh had screamed, thrown the book across the room, flung other books from their shelves, toppled the orrery with violence that seemed to overflow his thin frame, before collapsing into a heap in his reading chair. 'If I'm correct, soon after that you made up your mind to enter Quiet early. What was it that you saw?'

Unruh sighs. 'M. Beautrelet, I should perhaps clarify that it is not a generic investigation you are carrying out here. I did not empower you to pry into my private life, or the reasons to my actions: merely to protect my property and my person from what I felt was a threat.'

'You hired me because you wanted to solve a mystery,' Isidore says. 'And I think it was not just the mystery of the letter. I also 'blinked Count Isidis.'

'And what did you discover?'

'Nothing. I can't find any references to a Count Isidis in the public exomemories. As far as the general public is aware, he never existed.'

Unruh walks to one of the gallery's large windows and looks out. 'M. Beautrelet, I admit I have not been entirely honest with you. A part of me was hoping you would spot certain things on your own as you have done.' He presses a pale hand against the glass. 'A strange thing happens when you are very rich, even when one's wealth is as artificial as in our society. You develop a solipsism of sorts. The world yields itself to your will. Everything becomes your reflection, and after a while looking into your own eyes is dull.'

He sighs. 'So I sought to find more solid ground in the past, in our origins, our history. I doubt there are many of our generation who have put as much effort into the study of the Kingdom and the Revolution as I have.

'At first it was the perfect escape. So much richer than our bland existence, with real struggle, real evil, ideas triumphing over oppression, despair and hope. Count Isidis, plotting against a tyrant. Drama. Intrigue. And the Revolution! I bought memories from Time beggars. I remember being there, in Harmakis Valley, tearing Noble bodies with diamond claws.

'But after a while I realised that something was wrong. The deeper I delved, the more inconsistencies there were. People who appeared in lifecasts I bought from black market dealers, memories that contradicted each other. The Isidis lifecast was when I had the first revelation, and you ... saw how I reacted.'

Unruh clenches his hands into fists.

'I lost my faith in the past. Something is wrong with it. Something is wrong with what we know. That is why I didn't want you to study the texts in the library. I would not wish this feeling on anyone. Perhaps the old philosophers were right, and we are living in a simulation, playthings of some transhuman gods; perhaps the Sobornost has already won, Fedorov's dreams are true and we are merely memories.

'And if you can't trust history, what should you care of the present? I don't want any of it anymore. Merely Quiet.'

'Surely, there is a rational explanation,' Isidore says. 'Perhaps you have been a victim of forgery; perhaps we should investigate the sources of your library texts—'

Unruh waves a hand in dismissal. 'It does not matter anymore. You may do what you want with this knowledge, once I am gone. One perfect moment for me, and then I'm done.' He smiles. 'I'm glad I was right about le Flambeur, though. That encounter should be entertaining.' He touches Isidore's shoulder.

'I am grateful, M. Beautrelet. I wanted to discuss this with someone. Odette is many things to me, but she would not understand. She is a creature of the moment, as I should try to be.'

'I appreciate your confidence,' Isidore says, 'but I still think—'

'We will say no more about it,' Unruh says firmly. 'The only thing you need to worry about now is the party, and our thief. Speaking of which – any security arrangements I should ask Odette to make?'

'We could demand full gevulot disclosure at the entrance, or set up a series of agoras in the garden—'

'How gauche! Absolutely not!' Unruh frowns. 'Being robbed is one thing, lack of manners another.'

10

THE THIEF AND THE SECOND FIRST DATE

Raymonde is having her lunch near the playground when we meet again for the first time. She has sheets of music in her lap and spread across the bench and studies them while eating an apple with a kind of ferocity.

'Excuse me,' I say.

She comes here every day and eats from a small tempmatter bag, in a hurry, as if she feels guilty about allowing herself a moment of peace. She watches the children in the high elaborate climbing racks where they move like monkeys, the toddlers playing with the round and colourful synthbio toys in the sandpits. She sits on the edge of the bench, graceful long limbs folded uncomfortably, ready to spring away.

She looks at me, frowning. Her gevulot is open just a little, showing the forbidding expression on her proud, angular face. Somehow that makes her even more beautiful.

'Yes?' We exchange a gevulot greeting, brief and sparse. The gogol pirate engine is scanning for gaps, but there aren't any, not yet.

Perhonen and I looked for her in agoras and public exomemories, and after hours of work, there she was: a sudden vivid memory of a girl in a neat cream-coloured skirt and a blouse, passing through an agora, her stride purposeful. She did not wear the mask-like expression that Martians so often do in public places, but looked serious, lost in thought.

The day before I stole a sheet of music from her, wearing a different face. Now I hold it up.

'I believe this is yours.'

She accepts it hesitantly. 'Thank you.'

'You must have dropped it yesterday. I found it on the ground.'

'That's handy,' she says. She is still suspicious: her gevulot withholds even her name, and if I did not know her face already, I would forget it after our conversation.

She lives somewhere near the edge of the Dust District. She does something involving music. Her life is regular. Her wardrobe is modest and conservative. Somehow, that feels strange to me: it is at odds with the smile in her picture. But a lot can happen in twenty years. I wonder if she has been a Quiet recently; it usually causes young Martians to hoard Time with excessive care.

'It's very good, you know.'

'Excuse me?'

'The music. The sheet is analog, so I couldn't resist reading it.' I offer her a little gevulot. She accepts. *Yes.*

'I'm Raoul. I'm sorry about the intrusion, but I have wanted an excuse to talk to you for a long time.'

It's not going to work, whispers *Perhonen.*

Of course it is. A woman can never resist a good narrative. A mysterious stranger on a park bench? She is loving it.

'Well, I'm glad you found one,' she says. A little more gevulot: she has a boyfriend. Damn; but we'll see how much of an obstacle that one is.

'Is someone patroning you?' Another gevulot block. 'Apologies for prying, I'm just interested. What is it about?'

'An opera. About the Revolution.'

'Ah. That makes sense.'

She gets up. 'I'm meeting a student. Nice meeting you.'

There you go, Perhonen says. *Down in flames.*

Her perfume – a hint of pine – goes right to my amygdala, triggering a memory of a memory. Dancing with her in a glass-floored club in the Belly, until dawn. Was that when I met her the first time?

'You have a problem with the *a cappella* bit,' I say. She hesitates. 'I can tell you how to fix it if you meet me for dinner.'

'Why should I take your advice?' she asks, taking the music sheet from my hand.

'Not advice, merely suggestions.'

She studies me, and I give her my best new smile. I spent a long time practising it in front of the mirror, fitting it to this new face.

She flicks a lock of her black hair over a pale earlobe. 'All right. You'll have to convince me. But I'll decide where we are going.' She passes me a co-memory, indicating a place near the Revolution memorial. 'Wait for me there, at seven.'

'Deal. What did you say your name was?'

'I didn't,' she says, gets up and walks away past the playground, heels clicking on the pavement.

While the thief is out in the city looking for love, Mieli tries to force herself to interrogate the vasilev.

The ghostgun bullet – barely the size of a pinhead – has just enough computational power to run a human-level mind. She weighs it in the sapphire casing that keeps it dormant, tossing it up and down, still unused to the novelty of gravity. Even the tiny thing feels heavy, like failure; small impacts on her hand, again and again.

This is war, she tells herself. *They started it. What else can I do?*

The hotel room feels too small, too confined. She finds herself walking out to the city, the bullet still clutched in her hand, wandering the now-familiar Persistent Avenue in the afternoon lull.

Perhaps the restlessness comes from the thief's biot feed. She has not dared to suppress it after the thief's escape attempt – especially now, with his reluctantly granted permission to change his face and mental makeup. So she is painfully aware of his excitement, a constant phantom itch.

She stops to eat some of the rich, flavoured food here, served by a young man who keeps smiling at her, throwing suggestive co-memories at her, until she wraps herself in gevulot and eats in silence. The dish is called *cassoulet* and leaves her feeling bloated and heavy.

'How is it going in there?' she asks *Perhonen.*

He just got her to agree to a first date, the ship says.

'Great.'

You don't sound enthusiastic. Not very professional.

'I need to be alone for a while. Keep an eye on him for me.'

Of course. You should follow him yourself, though. It's sort of entertaining.

Mieli cuts the link. *Entertaining.* She walks, trying to emulate the light stride of the white-clad Martians, wishing she could fly again. After a while, the sky feels too big. The nearest building is a church of some kind, and she walks in, trying to find shelter.

She does not know the god they worship there, and has no wish to find out. But the high arches of the ceiling remind her of the open spaces of the temples of Ilmatar in Oort, ice caverns of the goddess of the air and space. So somehow it seems appropriate to sing a quiet prayer.

Air mother, grant me wisdom,
daughter of sky, strength provide
help an orphan to find a way home,
guide a lost bird to the land of south

Forgive a child with bloody hands
a poor shaper who mars your work
with ugly deeds, and uglier thoughts
with cuts and scars befouls your song

Repeating the apology makes her think of home, and of Sydän, and that makes it easier. After sitting quietly for a while, she returns to the hotel, darkens the windows and takes out the ghost bullet.

'Wake up,' she tells the vasilev mind.

Where? Ah.

'Hello, Anne.'

You.

'Yes. The servant of the Founder.'

The vasilev mind laughs. Mieli gives it a voice, not a child's voice but a vasilev voice, male, smooth and low. Somehow, that makes it easier, 'He was no Founder. Clever enough to deceive us. But no chen, no chitragupta,' the mind says.

'I'm not talking about him,' Mieli whispers. 'You are *done*,' she says. 'You have hindered the Great Common Task. But out of mercy, I give you one opportunity to speak out of your free will before oblivion, to redeem yourself.'

The vasilev laughs again. 'I don't care who you serve; you are a poor servant. Why waste words to find what is in my mind? Get it over with, and don't waste a Founder's time with your prattle.'

Disgusted, Mieli shuts the thing up. Then she pulls the surgeon gogol from her metacortex and tells it to begin. It traps the vasilev into a sandbox and starts cutting; separating higher conscious functions, rewarding and punishing. It is like some perversion of sculpting, not trying to find the shape hiding in a stone but breaking it to pieces and reassembling them into something else.

The surgeon gogol's outputs are cold readouts of associative learning in simulated neuron populations. After a while she shuts them down. She barely makes it to the bathroom before the sick comes, the remains of her lunch, stinking and undigested.

She returns to the vasilev with an acid taste in her mouth.

'Hello, darling,' it says, in an odd, euphoric tone. 'What can I do for you?'

'You can start by telling me everything you know about Jean le Flambeur,' Mieli says.

Raymonde arrives late, taking care to walk across the small agora, hand in hand with a tall, handsome man with leonine hair, younger than her. He gives her a goodbye kiss. Then she waves at me. I get up and hold the chair for her as she sits down. She accepts the gesture, slightly cockily.

I have been sitting at the small restaurant she chose, outside by the heater. It is a strange little place, with plain glass doors and a blank sign; but the inside is a riot of colour and exotica, jars filled with exotic taxidermy, glass eyes and lush paintings. I have been replaying our first meeting, thinking about what she reacted to – not the mystery, but the banter. I have even altered my appearance subtly, nothing that could not be expected with more revealing gevulot, but appearing ever so slightly more mischievous. It is enough to warm her smile a degree.

'How was the class?'

'Good. A young couple's daughter. Lots of potential.'

'Potential is what it's all about. Like your music.'

'Not really,' she says. 'I've been thinking. You are *bluffing*. There is nothing wrong with that piece. I'll have you know that this is the Oubliette, and I am a beautiful girl. That means this stuff happens *all the time*.' She cocks her head, letting her hair hang loose. 'A mysterious stranger. Serendipity. Seriously? Old hat.'

She rattles off two orders to the waiter drone.

'I wasn't really done looking at the menu,' I say.

'Rubbish. You are going to have the teriyaki zebra. It's excellent.'

I spread my hands. 'All right. I thought that is the way things are done here. So why did you agree to meet with me?'

'Maybe it's me who has been stalking you.'

'Maybe.'

She eats an olive from the starter bowl, and brandishes the pick at me. 'You were polite about it. You didn't do a great job with your gevulot. Clearly, you are from somewhere else. That is always interesting. And now you owe me something. That is always handy.'

Damn. I query the pirate engine. It is still trying to find openings in her gevulot, without much success. But obviously she is doing a better job than it is.

'Guilty as charged. I bought a citizenship. I'm from Ceres, in the Belt.' She raises her eyebrows. It is not easy to buy a Martian citizenship; usually, it involves a ruling by the Voice. But the gogol pirates seem to have done an airtight job of establishing the backstory of this particular identity, carefully planting things in public exomemories here and there.

'Interesting. So why here?'

I gesture at our surroundings. 'You have a *sky*. You have a whole planet. You have done something with it. You have a *dream*.'

She looks at me with the same curious intensity she gave her lunchtime apple, and for a moment I wait for the bite. 'A lot of people think that. But of course, we did have a horrible civil war first that unleashed self-replicating killing machines that undid the terraforming our slaver overlords managed to do before we killed them.' She smiles. 'But yes, there is a dream in there, somewhere.'

'You know, no one has yet told me how often they—'

'Attack? The phoboi? It depends. Most of the time you don't even notice, or if you do, it's this rumble in the distance. The Quiet handle all that. There are kids who go up in gliders to watch, of course. I used to do it when I was younger. It's spectacular.'

The co-memory she gives me catches me by surprise. A smartmatter glider, white wings; a landscape of thunder and fire below, a dazzling laser tracery inside orange dust, a black avalanche of *things* breaking against the Quiet troops; a blinding explosion. And someone in there with her, touching her, kissing her neck—

I take a deep breath. The pirate engine seizes the flirtatious memory and starts churning through it.

'What's wrong? You look confused,' she says.

175

I notice that the food has arrived; the delicious smell pulls me out of the memory, leaving me gasping with a sensory overload. The waiter – a dark-skinned man with flashy white teeth – grins at me. Raymonde nods at him.

'This is a confusing place,' I say.

'All interesting places are. That's what I'm trying to do with the music you had so many ideas about.'

'You are trying to give your listeners a heart attack?'

She laughs. 'No, I mean, we are confused too. It's nice to talk about the Revolution dream, recreating an Earth, a promised land and all that, but really, it is not that simple. There is a lot of guilt mixed with the dream, too. And the younger generations don't think the same way. I have been Quiet once, and I don't want to do it again. And people younger than me, they see zokus coming here, and people like you. They don't know what to think.'

'What was it like? Being Quiet?' I try my food. The zebra is indeed excellent, dark and juicy: she has good taste. Perhaps she picked it up from me.

She crumbles a piece of bread on her plate, lost in thought. 'It's difficult to explain. It's very abrupt: when your Time runs out, the transition happens. The Resurrection Men just come to pick your body up, but you are already there. It's like having a stroke. Suddenly, your brain works differently, in a different body, with different senses.

'But after the shock passes, it's not so bad. You become very focused in your work, and the concentration is quite pleasing. You are wired differently. You can't speak, but you have these very vivid waking dreams you can share with others. And you are *powerful*, depending on what kind of body you end up in. That can be ... exhilarating.'

'So there is some sort of Quiet sex life?'

'Perhaps one day you will find out, offworld boy.'

'Anyway, it does not sound so bad,' I say.

'There have been endless arguments about it. A lot of the kids think it's just a guilt thing. But the Voice has never had any proposals about overturning the system. You can ask why: could we not do it differently? Could we not use synthbio drones to do it all?

'But it's not that simple. When you come back, you are a mess for a while. You look into a mirror and see your *other* self. And you miss it. It's like having a conjoined twin. You'll never really be apart.'

She raises her glass – she also chose the wine, Dao Valley Sauvignon. I distantly recall it is supposed to have aphrodisiac effects. 'Here's to confusion,' she says.

We drink. The wine is rich, brawny, with traces of peach and honeysuckle. With it comes a strange feeling, a mixture of nostalgia and the first flush of fresh infatuation. In a mirror somewhere, my old self must be smiling.

'They wanted him,' the vasilev says, eagerly. Every time it answers a question, the surgeon gogol stimulates its pleasure centres. The flipside is that it takes its time answering.

'Who?'

'The hidden ones. They rule here. They promised us souls for him, as many as we wanted.'

'Who are they?'

'They spoke to us through other mouths, like the Founders sometimes do. We said yes, and why not, why not work with them, the Task will swallow them all in the end, all will be brought down before the altar of Fedorov and can we go back to the museum and look at the elephants?'

'Show me.'

But the coherence of the vasilev is breaking down. Gritting her teeth, Mieli restores a previous version and tells the surgeon to begin again.

The dinner turns into a dessert and then a walk around the Tortoise Park. We talk, and little by little, her gevulot opens to me.

She is from a Kasei slowtown. She had a wild, Time-wasting youth, then settled down (with an older man, apparently). She does not forget debts: she makes me buy her ice cream from a girl in a white apron, and chooses us flavours; odd synthetic taste symphonies that I can't even name, a little like honey and melon. I try to hold on to the little things she shares for a moment before throwing them into the pirate engine's hungry maw.

'The reason I want to do an opera,' she says, when we sit down by a Kingdom-style fountain with our cones, 'is that I want to do something *big*. The Revolution was big. The Oubliette is big. No one tackles it head on. Something grand, something with gogol pirates and zokus and rebellion and noise.'

'Oubliettepunk,' I say. She gives me an odd look, then shakes her head. 'Anyway, that's what I want to do.' We can see Montgolfiersville from here, across the park, tethered balloon residences strewn across the horizon like many-coloured fruit. She watches them with an expression of yearning.

'Have you ever thought about leaving?' I ask.

'To go where? I know, there is an infinity of possibilities. Of course I have. But I'm a big fish in a small world, and I sort of prefer it that way. I can make a little bit of difference here, I think. Out there – I don't know.'

'I know the feeling.' And, to my surprise, I do. It is

tempting to stay here, to do something on a human scale, to build something. That must be what *he* felt when he came here. Or maybe that's how *she* made him feel.

'That doesn't mean I'm not curious, of course,' she says. 'Maybe you could show me what it's like, where you come from.'

'I'm not sure it's that interesting.'

'Come on. I want to see.' She takes my hand and squeezes it. Her fingers are warm, and a little sticky from the ice cream. I scan my fragmented memory for images. An ice castle in Oort, comets and fusion reactors tethered together into a glittering orrery, winged people chasing them. Supra City, where buildings are the size of planets, domes and towers and arcs rising up to meet Saturn's ring. The Beltworlds and wild synthbio covering them in coral and autumn colours. The *guberniya* brains of the Inner System, diamond spheres adorned with the faces of the Founders, filled with undeath and intrigue.

The odd thing is that all that feels less real than sitting in the sun with her, pretending to be human and small.

She closes her eyes for a moment, savouring the memory. 'I don't know if you just made that up,' she says. 'But you deserve a little reward.'

She kisses me. For a moment, I try to figure out what her ice cream tastes like. Then I'm lost in the sensation of her lips, her tongue flicking against mine. She passes me a flirtatious co-memory, the kiss from her perspective, a reversal of viewpoints.

In my head the pirate engine lets out a shout of joy: it has found a loop, a memory of *me*, a hole in her gevulot that opens into a yawning chasm of *déjà vu*. Another kiss, a long time ago, superimposed with this one; a chimera of present and past. I ignore the pirate engine's roar of triumph and return the kiss, then and now.

'Tell me about the tzaddikim,' Mieli says. She could let the gogol surgeon do this. But this is dishonourable enough as it is. At least she is prepared to carry the burden herself.

'Anomalies,' the vasilev says, wistfully. 'Our worst enemy. Zoku technology. There are power struggles here, unseen, between the hidden ones and the zoku colony. The tzaddikim are a weapon. Quantum technology. Theatrics. The people here trust them. We try to assassinate them when we can, but they guard their identities well.'

'Who are they?'

'The Silence. Brutal. Efficient. The Futurist. Fast. Playful.' The vasilev juggles colourful names and images with apparent glee. A blue-cloaked, masked figure; a red blur that moves like the Quick Ones on Venus. Hypothetical identities, possible targets; agora views and cracked exomemories.

'The Gentleman.' The man in the silver mask. And behind it—

'No, no, no,' whispers Mieli. 'Dark Man take me.'

She tries to reach for the thief, but the biot link is silent.

Much later, we make it to her apartment, laughing, stumbling and stopping to make out surrounded by gevulot blur – and wide in the open, sometimes. I feel drunk on an emotional cocktail: lust mixed with guilt mixed with nostalgia, propelling me on a trajectory that leads to a collision with the hard, unforgiving surface of the present.

Her place is in one of the inverted towers, beneath the city. As we take the elevator down, I kiss her neck, hands wandering under her blouse, across her silky belly. She laughs. The pirate engine is seizing every touch, every shared caress that we allow each other to remember, digging mercilessly into her gevulot.

Inside, she disentangles herself from my grip, pressing a finger against my lips. 'If we are going to remember this,' she says, 'it might as well be *memorable*. Make yourself comfortable. I'll be back in a moment.'

I sit on her couch and wait. The apartment has high ceilings, with shelves that display both Martian art and old Earth artefacts. They look familiar. There is an old gun, a revolver, in a glass casing. It reminds me uncomfortably of the Prison. There are books and an old piano. The mahogany surface is a sharp contrast to all the glass and metal. She is letting me see and remember all this, and I can feel the gogol pirate engine approaching critical mass, almost ready to leech out all her memories.

Music starts, almost a whisper at first, then louder; a piano piece, a beautiful melody broken by occasional, achingly deliberate discord.

'So, tell me, Raoul,' she says, sitting next to me in a black silk gown, holding two champagne glasses, 'what exactly is wrong with it?' The soft lights of the Quiet move below us in the blue night, thousands of them, large and small, like a starry sky inverted.

'Absolutely nothing,' I say. We clink glasses. Her fingers brush mine. She kisses me again, slowly, deliberately, with one hand touching my temple lightly. 'I want to remember this,' she says. 'I want *you* to remember this.'

Her warm soft weight is on me, her perfume a pine forest, her hair tickling my face like

rain, getting drunk with Isaac the rabbi in the rain and singing, wandering home late at night and dragging her outside with

*me to see the clouds under the dome of the angelnet and her hair
getting wet*

as the music swells around us I remember

*when she played for me for the first time, after we made love,
naked, fingers light and slow on the black and ivory keys*

her hands trace lines on my chest

*maps and drawings, architecture, shapes fitting together, long
hours; and she picks up one of the sketches and tells me they look
like musical scores*

'Tell me,' she says

*and I do, about being a thief, about the boy in the desert who
wanted to be a gardener, about wanting to make a new life, and
to my surprise she does not run away but just laughs*

softly

*like the paws of a dancing cat in a flamboyant hat, a puss-in-
boots, like something out of a dream, in the corridor of a castle—*

'You fucking bastard. You unbelievable fucking bastard,'
Raymonde screams.

The present is a champagne bottle, breaking across my
head. I black out a moment, and when my vision returns,
I am lying on the floor and she is standing over me, an old
cane in her hand.

'Have you. Any idea. What you did?'

Her face is a silver mask. Her voice is a chorus rasp. *Just
when I was wondering where the police are on this world,* I wonder weakly, just before Mieli crashes through the window.

Mieli shatters the pseudoglass with her wings. The shards
billow across the room in slow motion like snow. The
metacortex floods her with information. The thief is *here*,
the tzaddik *there*, a fleshy human core surrounded by a cloud
of combat utility fog.

She dropped all subtlety hunting the thief down, telling *Perhonen* to risk its cover again and run WIMP scans, to find the spot where the biot feed signal was lost. Then she took to the skies in a gevulot blur, flicking through the ship's dossier on the woman. Putting the pieces together seemed to take forever, but she is not surprised to find the tzaddik has taken the thief to her home.

She tries to grab the thief and leave as quickly as she came, but the fog is faster, surrounding her wings in a layer of thick gel, trying to force itself down into her lungs, blocking her ghostgun ports. She fires a q-dot, in blind/stun mode. It goes off like a miniature sun. But the fog stays ahead. It turns into a white opaque cloud around the pinpoint of brightness, not letting out much more than a lava lamp. Then her wings' waste-heat radiators are blocked too, and she has to drop back to slowtime.

The tzaddik's foglet-enhanced blow is like colliding with an Oortian comet. It takes her through a glass shelving unit and the wall behind it. The plaster and ceramics feels like wet sand when she passes through it. Her armour screams and a quickstone-enhanced rib actually snaps. Her metacortex muffles the pain; she gets up in a cloud of debris. She is in the bathroom. A monster angel stares at her in the bathroom mirror.

More blows. She tries to block them, but they flow and snake around her arms. The tzaddik is out of reach, the foglets forming amorphous extensions of her will. Mieli is fighting a ghost. She needs space. She channels power from the fusion reactor in her thigh into the microfans of the wings. A mighty wind howls. The foglets scatter. She grabs a handful, swallows, sets a gogol to work on them. *There.* Outdated Protocol War combat fog. It will take the gogol a few moments to find the right countermeasures.

Wings clear, she dumps enough waste heat to go into quicktime. Now approaching the tzaddik is a leisurely walk, ducking beneath static foglet tendrils, hanging in the air in her enhanced vision like frozen soap bubble streams. The tzaddik is a silver-masked statue. Mieli hits her, a carefully placed blow on a soft, human, base of her neck, just enough to take her out—

—and her hand passes through a foglet image.

The Gödel attack is a 120-decibel speaker pressed to her eardrum. Genetic algorithm viruses flood her systems, trying to get past the machines and into her human brain. The countermeasure gogol's whiny voice says something. She launches it at the fog and shuts all her systems down.

The sudden humanity feels like a bad cold. For a moment, she is helpless in the grip of the foglet tendrils, her wings hanging limply down her back. Then the countermeasures bite and the fog explodes into inert white powder. She falls to the floor, gasping, coughing, flesh and blood.

Complete destruction reigns in the room: shattered furniture, glass and dead fog. The tzaddik stands in the middle of it, holding her cane. But she, too, is merely human now. To her credit, she reacts quickly, and comes at Mieli fast, with a kendo fighter's shuffling steps, cane raised high.

Without getting up, she tries to sweep the silver-masked woman's legs from under her. But she just leaps up, lightly, impossibly high in the low gravity, and aims a blow right at Mieli. She rolls aside, follows through with a somersault that takes her upright, aims a blow at the tzaddik, only to find it painfully blocked by the cane—

'Stop it. Both of you,' the thief says.

He is holding a weapon, a primitive metal thing that looks

ridiculously large in his grip. But it is clearly dangerous, and his aim does not waver. *Of course. He spent a lot of time with firearms in the Prison.* And the remote control of his Sobornost body is just as dead as the rest of her systems after the tzaddik's attack. *Typical.*

'I suggest we all sit down – if you can find somewhere to sit – so we can all have a chat about this like civilised people,' he says.

'The others will be here soon,' Raymonde says.

My head is ringing and I'm trying not to cough at the dust in the apartment. But I can recognise a bluff when I hear one. 'No, they aren't. I'm guessing Mieli took your cute fog stuff out. And vice versa, given that I am still walking and talking. Actually, that would be my cue to escape, if it weren't for my damn honour.' Mieli snorts. I gesture with the gun. 'Find somewhere to sit.'

Keeping an eye on Mieli, I take a sip from the one champagne glass that has miraculously survived the destruction. It helps my throat a little. Then I sit down on a wall fragment. Mieli and my ex-girlfriend look at each other, then slowly position themselves so that they can keep an eye on both each other and me.

'Now, it is flattering to have women fight over me, but trust me, I'm not really worth it.'

'At least we agree on *something*,' Raymonde says.

You know, says *Perhonen, I'm about four hundred ks up, but I can still burn your hand off if you don't drop that gun.*

Ouch.

Please. It's an antique. It probably doesn't even work. I'm bluffing. Please don't tell Mieli. I'm trying to resolve this without anyone getting hurt. Pretty please?

For such a fast-thinking gogol, the ship considers its response for an uncomfortably long time. *All right*, it finally says. *One minute.*

Time constraints again. You are worse than she is.

'Raymonde, meet Mieli. Mieli, meet Raymonde. Raymonde and I used to be an item; Mieli, on the other hand, tends to treat me like an item. But I have something of a debt of honour to discharge to her, so I don't complain. Much.' I take a deep breath. 'Raymonde, it was nothing personal. I just need to have my old self back.' She rolls her eyes. She looks achingly familiar now.

I turn to Mieli. 'And seriously, *was this really necessary?* I had things under control.'

'I was about to tear your head off,' Raymonde says.

'I suppose the safe word is one of the many things I don't remember,' I say and sigh. 'Look. Forget about you and me. I am looking for something. You can help me. You are a tzaddik – very cool, by the way – so I'm betting there is something we can help you with in turn. For example, gogol pirates. Lots of them. On a platter.' They both look at me for a moment, and I'm certain the fighting is about to start again.

'All right,' Raymonde says. 'Let's talk.'

Breathing a sigh of relief, I toss the gun to the floor with a clatter, and thank Hermes that it doesn't go off.

'I don't suppose we could have some privacy?' I say, looking at Mieli. She looks like a wreck: her toga is in tatters again, and her wings look like a pair of ragged, bare tree branches. But she still looks threatening enough to tell me what she thinks without words. 'Forget I asked.'

Raymonde stands in front of the shattered window, hands shoved in the sleeves of her gown. 'What happened?' I ask her. 'Who was I here? Where did I go?'

'You really don't remember?'

'I really don't.' Not yet, anyway. The new memories are still reassembling themselves in my head, too much to take in at a moment's notice; I can feel a strange headache coming on with them.

She shrugs. 'It doesn't matter.'

'I left something here. Secrets. Tools. Memories. Not just the exomemory, but something else, bigger. Do you know where?'

'No.' She frowns. 'But I have an idea. It's going to take something bigger than just gogol pirates to get me to help you, though. And your new girlfriend owes me a new apartment.'

Interlude

WISDOM

It is only a few steps from death back to life. There is light ahead: but every step is like being immersed in water, slow and heavy, and Bathilde feels herself floating upwards, rising out of her quicksuited body. She sees herself struggling forward below, brass helmet gleaming in the light. It seems right, for some reason. She lets her body fall away and rises towards the light above. *Finally,* she thinks—

—only to step into Martian twilight, almost falling down, but supported by a pair of strong arms. She gasps for breath, blinking. Then she looks back at the Hallway of Birth and Death; a low, long, rectangular structure printed by builder Quiet. It sits in a low ditch a mile away from the city's path, in Martian desert proper. It is nothing but gravel and sand glued together with bacterial paste, with thin slits and peepholes on its sides. Close to the hulking phoboi wall of the Quiet, it looks like a child's construction block. But inside—

'Oh my,' Bathilde says, drawing a deep breath.

'So, what did you think?' asks Paul Sernine, the architect of her brief death. He supports her gently, guiding her away from the exit as other dazed guests emerge. Her protégé is grinning triumphantly behind the glass of his helmet. 'You look like you could use a drink.'

'Oh yes,' says Bathilde. Paul offers her a champagne glass in a little q-dot bubble. She takes it and drinks, glad of the clear taste in the dry air of the helmet. 'Paul, you are a genius.'

'You don't regret your patronage, then?'

Bathilde smiles. All around, the party is getting started. She is glad that the publicity campaign was successful; viral co-memories of the intense moments in the Hallway. And it was a nice symbolic gesture to have it outside the Wall, to add a tiny bit of danger to the proceedings.

'Not in the slightest. We'll have to get the Voice to incorporate something like this in the city permanently. It would do us a world of good. Whatever gave you the idea?'

Paul arches his dark eyebrows. 'You know how much I hate being asked that.'

'Oh, please,' Bathilde says. 'You love talking about yourself.'

'Well, if you must know – I took inspiration from Noguchi's Hiroshima piece. Birth and death. Something we've forgotten how to face.'

'Curious,' Bathilde says. 'That is not that different from something that Marcel over there' – she points at a young black man looking at the Hallway's yawning black exit with a disdainful look – 'proposed to the Voice a few months ago.'

'Ideas are cheap,' Paul says. 'It's all in the execution.'

'Indeed,' Bathilde says. 'Or perhaps your new muse helped.' A red-haired woman in a dark quicksuit is standing a short distance away, touching the rough surface of the Hallway.

'Something like that,' Paul says, looking down.

'Don't waste more time talking to an old woman,' Bathilde says. 'Go and celebrate.'

Paul grins at her again, and for a moment she almost regrets that she decided to be professional with him. 'I'll see you later,' he says, gives her a slight bow and vanishes into the quicksuited crowd, an instant centre of attention.

Bathilde looks at the Hallway again. Such an innocent thing from the outside, but, inside, the angles and lights and shapes resonate in the design of any human-derived brain, triggering cortical mechanisms that simulate a near-death experience. An architectural magic trick. She thinks back to her many deaths and births and realises that she has never experienced that before. A genuinely new experience. She smiles to herself: how long has it been since *that*? She touches the bracelet Watch that Paul gave her, tracing the word *Sapientia* engraved in it.

'Hi,' says the red-haired girl. There, at least, is genuine youth, untouched by death, temporary or otherwise.

'Hello, Raymonde,' Bathilde says. 'Proud of your boy-friend?'

The girl smiles shyly. 'You can't imagine,' she says.

'Oh, but I can,' Bathilde says. 'It is a difficult thing: you watch them do something like *that* and then you start wondering if you are good enough for them. Am I right?'

The girl stares at her mutely. Bathilde shakes her head. 'My apologies. I am a bitter old woman. I am happy for you, of course.' She touches the girl's gloved hand. 'What were you going to say? Interrupting is a problem we old people have, we think we have heard it many times before. I'm looking forward to being a Quiet again soon. It will force me to listen.'

Raymonde bites her lip. 'I wanted to ask you for … advice.'

Bathilde laughs. 'Well, if you want to hear bitter truths

about life filtered through a few centuries of experience, you've come to the right place. What do you want to know?'

'It's about children.'

'What is there to know? I've had them myself: troublesome, but can be worth it if you are careful. Exomemory tells you all you need to know. Get a Resurrection Man to help you with genome splicing, or go to the black market for offworld designs if you are feeling ambitious. Just add water. And poof.' Bathilde chides herself for enjoying Raymonde's expression when she makes an expansive gesture with her hands.

'That's not what I was going to ask,' Raymonde says. 'I meant ... about him. Paul.' She closes her eyes. 'I can't read him. I don't know if he is ready.'

'Walk with me,' Bathilde says. She leads them around the Hallway, towards the phoboi walls. Above, the sky is getting dark.

'I know this much,' Bathilde says. 'When I speak to Paul, he reminds me of someone I knew a long time ago, someone who gave me a little bit of a heartbreak.' She laughs. 'I gave as well as I got, to be sure.' She touches the already crumbling wall of the Hallway. 'There are those of us who live a really long time,' she says. 'We are the ones who learn not to change, no matter what happens. Bodies, gogols, transformations, there is something about us that stays the same. It's an evolutionary thing; otherwise we would effectively die by metamorphosis, never a light at the end of the tunnel, just time chipping away at us.

'Whatever Paul has told you, he is one of us, I can tell that much. So you have to decide if the *real* him – not this smiling architect – is someone you want as the father of your children.

'But he is trying, and he is trying for you.'

'Here you are,' Paul says. 'My two favourite ladies.' He embraces Raymonde. 'Did you go inside yet?'

Raymonde shakes her head.

'You should go,' Bathilde says. 'It's not as bad as it seems at first. Have fun.'

The two enter the Hallway from the other end. As Bathilde watches, she thinks of that time in the Olympus Palace, a running watercolour of a memory: the time she danced with the King. She wonders if her eyes looked like Raymonde's then.

11

THE THIEF AND THE TZADDIKIM

The tzaddikim are not what I expect. I imagined a secret lair of some kind, with trophies of past victories, perhaps; a council room with a round table, with high chairs, each customised with each tzaddik's personal iconography.

Instead, we meet in the Silence's kitchen.

The Futurist fidgets with her glass impatiently, rolling its base around on the wooden table. She is a red, sleek creature, a cross between a human being and an ancient automobile, unable to stay still.

'All right,' she says. 'Would somebody please tell me what we are doing here?'

The Silence lives in a little zeppelin house in Montgolfiersville: a gondola suspended from a teardrop-shaped bag of gas, tethered to the city. The kitchen is small but has a high-tech look to it. In addition to the fabber, it has traditional cooking implements, knives, pots and pans and other chrome and metal instruments I do not recognise: clearly, the Silence is someone who cares about food. Between the two of us and the six tzaddikim, things are somewhat intimate; I'm squeezed between Mieli and a skull-faced tall man in black

– the Bishop. His bony knee presses against my thigh.

Our host opens a bottle of wine with a deft motion of his wrist. Like the Gentleman, he wears a faceless mask, but of dark blue, along with a utility fog cloak that makes him look like a living blot of ink. He is tall and even though he hasn't said anything so far, there is a gravitas about him. He fills our glasses quickly and efficiently, then nods towards Raymonde.

'Thank you for coming,' she says, with the rasping voice of her tzaddik persona. 'I have here two offworld visitors with whom I had a little … misunderstanding two nights ago. I have reason to believe that they might be sympathetic to our cause. Perhaps you can explain it yourself, Jean.'

'Thanks,' I say. Mieli agreed to let me do the talking, with the understanding that if things go south, I will be shut down with extreme prejudice. 'My name is Jean le Flambeur,' I say. 'You can 'blink that if you wish.' I pause for a moment for effect, but it is hard to read an audience wearing masks.

'I used to be a citizen of the Oubliette, in a past life. My associate here and I are looking for some property that I left here. Your tzaddik colleague, whom I have some previous … familiarity with has assured me that she can help me. In return, we are offering to help *you*.' I try the wine. Old Badeker Solarancio. The Silence has good taste.

'I'm not sure we should be having this conversation,' the Futurist says. 'Why would we involve third parties in anything? And for God's sake – am I the only one who is smelling the Sobornost tech this bitch here is stuffed full of?' She whips her gaze from Raymonde to the Silence. 'If anything, we should be *interrogating* them. At the very least. If you have some personal history with these creatures, deal with it yourself. There is no need to compromise the rest of us.'

'I take full responsibility for everything, of course,' Raymonde says. 'But I believe that what they can do could help us to finally get to grips with the cryptarchs.'

'I thought you were training your little pet detective for that,' Cockatrice says. Her outfit is somewhat more revealing than those of the others, a red leotard, a Venetian-style mask that leaves her blond locks free and shows a sensual, large mouth. Under other circumstances, I would be focusing all my attention on her.

Raymonde is quiet for a moment. 'That is a different discussion, and does not concern us here,' Raymonde says. 'In any case, we have to pursue more than one option at a time. What I've been trying to say is we are treating the *symptoms*. Offworld tech. Gogol pirates. But we are just as affected by the underlying infection as the people we are trying to protect.' She leans across the table. 'So when I see an opportunity to work with an outside agent who can help us with that, I bring it to your attention.'

'And the price?' the Rat King asks. He has a young, high voice and a thick body. His comical-looking rodent mask leaves his chin bare, showing a rough five o'clock shadow.

'Let me worry about the price,' Raymonde says.

'So what exactly can they do that we can't?' The Futurist looks at me suspiciously.

I give her a sweet smile. 'We can come to that in a moment, Mme Diaz.' I can't see her face, but a satisfying shudder of shock goes through her, turning her into a red blur for a moment.

I haven't been idle for the two days it has taken Raymonde to set the meeting up. Mieli gave me a database whose source I did not dare to ask about, containing fairly solid leads to the identities of all the tzaddikim. I was able to confirm most of it with a little footwork and gevulot pilfering. As a result, I don't know the names of their pets or favourite sexual positions, but I know *enough*.

'But before we come to that, it might be useful for us to understand what exactly it is that you people are trying to do.'

'Three things,' Raymonde says. 'To uphold the ideals of the Oubliette. To protect its people from gogol pirates and other outside forces. And to find out who really rules it, and destroy them.'

'It started with the Voice,' Raymonde says. A quick 'blink fills me in on the details of the Oubliette e-democracy system; specialised co-memories serving as votes and public policy decisions, implemented by the office of the Mayor and the public Quiet servants. 'There were ... strange patterns in the decisions. Opening up to the outside world. Granting citizenship to offworlders. Weakening tech restrictions.

'Soon after that, the first gogol pirates started appearing. The Silence was among the first who suffered.' She touches the tall tzaddik's hand. 'Our system is not stable if you introduce outside forces. The Quiet could not deal with technology disruptions. So we decided to. We have backers. With their own interests, of course. But aligned with those of the Oubliette.

'We were able to do good. But whenever we saw a pattern, a way to fix things more permanently – to shut down a pirate radio transmitting stolen uploads, or excise a polluted gevulot network – things tended to disappear. The pirates *know* how to choose their targets and how to get close to them. They are good at what they do, but it is clear that they have help.

'For some time now we have known that exomemory has been compromised. There are people, one or more, who are manipulating it. To what extent, how or why, we don't know. We call them cryptarchs. The hidden rulers. Or, as the Futurist puts it, fucking bastards.

'We believe in what the Revolution stood for. A human Mars. A place where everyone owns their own minds, a place where we belong to ourselves. And that is not possible when someone behind the curtain is pulling our strings.'

Raymonde looks at me. 'So that's our price. Give us a way to find the cryptarchs, and we will give you what is yours.'

'Of course,' says the Bishop, 'that assumes that the Gentleman's high opinion of you is in any way justified.'

'M. Reverte.' I give him my most sharklike grin. 'It took me two days to find out who you are. These cryptarchs – they *know* you. In fact, I think they *keep you around.* You fit the system they have created. You keep it stable. And that's exactly what they want.'

I drain my glass and lean back in my chair. 'You never play dirty. You are glorified cops, when you need to be revolutionaries. *Criminals.* And that's definitely something I can help you with. Is there any wine left?'

'Frankly,' says the Futurist, 'this is exactly what we should be fighting. Offworld influences who think they are better than us.' She looks around the room. 'I vote we kick them off the planet and get back to the real business. And the Gentleman should be reprimanded for her behaviour.'

There are nods around the table, and I curse myself for not reading them right; I'm still not quite as good with gevulot as a native Martian, in spite of the gogol pirate engines. *This is not going to end well.*

That's when Mieli speaks.

*

'We are not your enemy,' Mieli says.

She stands up and looks at the tzaddikim. 'I come from far away. I believe in different things than you. But trust me when I say this: what the thief says he can do, whatever agreement we make, I will make sure it is honoured. I am Mieli, of the Hiljainen Koto, daughter of Karhu. And I do not lie.'

Strangely, there is something more familiar about the people in the room than in anything she has seen on this world so far. There is a dream burning on their masked faces, something bigger than themselves. She remembers seeing the same thing in the young warriors of her koto. The thief will never understand it: he speaks a different language, of games and tricks.

'Look into my thoughts.' She opens her gevulot to them, completely, as far as she can. They can read her surface thoughts now, see all her memories of this world so far. It is like casting off a heavy cloak, and suddenly she feels light.

'If you find any deceit there, banish us here and now. Will you accept our help?'

For a moment there is a complete silence around the table. Then the Silence speaks one word.

'Yes,' he says.

Raymonde leads us through Montgolfiersville, through the small fenced gardens where the balloon homes are tethered. The sunlight filtering through the many-coloured gas sacks and the vertigo sensation caused by gevulot – not being allowed to remember where the meeting place was – keeps me quiet for a while. But after we enter the more familiar, wide streets of the Edge and Raymonde reverts from the Gentleman to her elegant female self, I feel compelled to speak.

'Thank you,' I tell her. 'That was a big risk you took. I'll try to make sure you won't regret it.'

'Well, there is a strong chance that you will get hurt doing this,' she says. 'So don't thank me yet.'

'Was it really that bad?'

'Yes. Yes, it was. I thought I had made a mistake until your friend spoke.' Raymonde looks at Mieli with respect. 'That was a ... noble thing to do,' she tells her. 'I apologise for the circumstances of our first meeting, and I hope we can work together.'

Mieli nods quietly.

I look at Raymonde. It is only now that I realise she looks different from my memories. Less vulnerable. Older. In fact, I'm not sure I know this new, strange woman at all.

'This is really important to you, isn't it?' I say.

'Yes,' she says. 'Yes, it is. I'm sure it is a completely alien sensation to you. Doing something for other people.'

'I'm sorry,' I say. 'It has been a ... confusing time for me too. I was in a very nasty place for a very long time.'

Raymonde gives me a cool look. 'You were always very good at coming up with excuses. And there is no need to apologise, it won't help. In case it is not completely clear, there are few people in the universe who repulse me more. So, if I were you, I'd go and find them, as discussed. Perhaps then we can at least make a favourable comparison.'

She stops. 'Your hotel is that way. I have a music class to teach.' She smiles at Mieli. 'We'll be in touch soon.'

I open my mouth, but something tells me it is wiser to let it go this time.

That afternoon, I sit down to make plans.

Mieli is turning our quarters into a small fortress – q-dots are now patrolling the windows – and is still regenerating some of the damage from the tussle with Raymonde. So once again I can indulge in relative solitude – apart from the awareness of our biot link. I sit down on the balcony with a pile of newspapers, coffee and croissants, put on my sunglasses, sit back start going through the society pages.

As with everything here, they do not skimp on craftsmanship, and I find myself enjoying the exaggerated reality drama of the stories quite a lot. The tzaddikim feature heavily, tone depending on the publication; some outright worship them. I note a story about a kid working on a gogol pirate case with the Gentleman and wonder if this is the detective the Cockatrice mentioned.

But the real meat is the list of upcoming carpe diem parties; supposedly secret, of course, but the journalists put an admirable effort into finding things out.

That looks like too much fun to be called work, Perhonen says.

'Oh, but it is: serious business. I'm coming up with a plan.'

Care to explain it to me?

'What, you are not just a pretty face?'

I look up at the clear sky. The commlink shows me the ship a dot, invisible to the bare eye, somewhere above the horizon. I blow a kiss at it.

Flattery will get you nowhere.

'I never explain my plans before they are fully hatched. It's a creative process. The criminal is a creative artist; detectives are just critics.'

We are in high spirits today, I see.

'You know, I'm finally starting to feel myself again. Fighting a cabal of planetary mind-controlling masterminds with a group of masked vigilantes – that's what life should be all about.'

200

Is that right? the ship says. *And how is the path to self-discovery going?*

'That's private.'

To quote Mieli—

'Yes, yes, I know. Raymonde caught me too early. I didn't get anything except flashes. Nothing that useful.'

Are you sure?

'What do you mean?'

Someone suspicious might think that you already know how to find what we are looking for. That you are just stringing us along to amuse yourself, to get into that flamboyant thief persona of yours.

'I'm insulted. Would I really do something like that?' The ship does have a point. I have been stepping around the memories like they were eggshells, and yes, perhaps a part of that is because in spite of myself, I'm having fun.

I have another theory, too. You are trying your damnedest to impress this Raymonde girl.

'That, my friend, is in the past. Allowing such things to cloud my thinking would be more than dangerous in this profession.'

Uh huh.

'As much as I enjoy your company, the sooner I can get back to the things I do best, the happier I'll be. Speaking of which – I could use some peace and quiet. I'm trying to think about breaking into the land of the dead.' I lean back in my chair, close my eyes and cover my face with the newspaper to hide from the sun and the ship.

See? That's exactly what I mean, Perhonen says. *You have been waiting to say that all day.*

*

Mieli feels tired. Her body is in the process of checking and rebooting its systems. She hasn't had her period for years, but vaguely remembers that this is what it felt like. When they return from the meeting with the tzaddikim, all she wants is to lie down in her room, play gentle Oortian songs and drift to sleep. But the pellegrini is waiting for her. The goddess is wearing a deep blue evening gown. Her hair is done up, and she is wearing long black silk gloves.

'Dear child,' she says, planting a scented kiss on Mieli's cheek. 'That was *delightful*. Drama. Action. And such passionate conviction on your part: convincing the people in their funny costumes that they need you. A custom-made gogol persona would not have done a better job. I'm almost sorry that you will receive your reward so soon.'

Mieli blinks. 'I thought we were going to let the thief—'

'Of course, but there are limits. A few vasilevs here and there, that is one thing, but there are aspects of this place that we do have to consider in the context of the Great Common Task. The cryptarchs are one of them: a balance that we do not want to upset just now, for a variety of reasons.'

'We are not going to ... destroy them?'

'Of course not. You are going to *meet* with them. And coordinate activities. You are going to give the tzaddikim precisely enough to get what we need. And then – well, we are going to give the tzaddikim to the cryptarchs. Everybody wins.' The pellegrini smiles.

'Now, child, I think our thief is going to talk to you about his new ideas. Do humour him. Ciao.'

Mieli touches Sydän's jewel, just to remember why she is doing this. Then she lies down to wait for the knock on the door.

12

THE DETECTIVE AND CARPE DIEM

On the evening of the carpe diem party, the garden has the hushed tone of a performer holding his breath, muttering his lines.

There are tables with champagne glasses in orderly rows, little pavilions for more exotic offworld vices, and foglet fireflies still unlit. A Quiet orchestra test their instruments – parts of their body – creating a gentle brass cacophony. A fireworks expert, wearing a tall hat, is laying out multicoloured rockets in a device that looks like a miniature pipe organ.

'So, what do you think, M. Detective?' Unruh asks. He is dressed as Sol Jovis, the last day of the Darian calendar week. The colours of the long-lost gas giant blaze across the fabric of his tunic. In the shadows of the trees, it glows faintly in hues of bright red and white.

'It looks like one of the old Kingdom parties,' Isidore says.

'Ha. Yes. Not a bad way to spend a few hundred mega-seconds, in any case,' Unruh says. He holds up his Watch, attached with a chain to his waistcoat, surprisingly plain: a black disc with a single golden dial. 'When do you think I will be robbed?'

'We are as prepared as we can be. Le Flambeur or not, we will make him work hard for his loot.'

In the end, the security arrangements consist of a few carefully placed agoras and additional Quiet servants hired from the Voice by Odette – assault anti-phoboi Quiet with a variety of specialised sensors and weapons. Isidore hopes it will be enough. He considered a variety of more elaborate options involving black market tech, but in the end, he concluded that they would introduce more vulnerabilities than strengths.

'That's the spirit,' Unruh says, patting Isidore on the shoulder. 'You know, we never discussed the matter of your fee.'

'M. Unruh, I assure you that—'

'Yes, yes, very noble of you. I want you to have the library. Perhaps you will be able to make sense of it. Or burn the whole thing down. Odette has already drawn up the contract; I will be sure to transfer the gevulot to you before the end of the night.'

Isidore stares at the millenniaire blankly. 'Thank you.'

'No need to thank me. Just give our uninvited guest a run for his money. Are you bringing a date tonight, by any chance?'

Isidore shakes his head.

'A pity. Now, I have some debauchery to engage in before I die. Excuse me.'

Isidore watches the preparations for a while and instructs the Quiet – low, panther-like creatures with sleek, black carapaces – on their patrol routes on the grounds. Then he goes to one of the guest rooms where his Sol Lunae costume has been laid out. It still looks a little feminine, too tight in the wrong places. He puts it on anyway. It feels like something is missing, and realises that the entanglement ring is in his trouser pocket. He takes it out and hangs it on his Watch chain.

So this is what stage fever feels like, he thinks.

Raymonde and I arrive at the party fashionably late, and so does everyone else. Around us, spidercabs disgorge men and women in elaborate costumes, Xanthean dreams of silk, lace and smartmatter. *Time* is the theme, so there are Indian gods and goddesses of the Darian calendar, planets and stars, and, of course, prominently displayed Watches.

'I can't believe I let you talk me into this,' Raymonde says. A humanoid Quiet servant in dazzling livery, sculpted face covered by a mask, checks our invitation co-memories and guides us along with the flow of the crowd that is slowly filling the sundial garden, pooling into small groups. The tinkle of glasses, aching ares nova music and the voices of the guests all merge into an intoxicating symphony of its own.

I smile at Raymonde. She is a seductive Phobos, in a deep-cut dress that includes white gloves and a glowing sphere of light in her abdomen, bright enough to cover strategic areas with luminescence. I am content to be a modest peacock next to her, in white tie, with several ornamental Watch replicas and a flower in my lapel.

'I assure you, this is one of the least immoral jobs I've ever been involved in,' I say. 'Robbing from the rich and giving to the poor. After a fashion.'

'Still.' She nods to a passing couple dressed as Venus and Mars whose gevulot reveals just enough to ensure that they are seen. 'This is not what we do. Quite the opposite of what we do, in fact.' The glow of the little Phobos in her belly highlights the elegant bone structure of her face: she reminds me of a sculpture of some Greek goddess.

'Your masked friends need proof. We'll give them proof.'
I pick up a champagne glass from a passing Quiet servant. I
brush a dust particle away from the front of its coat, giving it
an invisible dose of Part A of the plan from my flower. Potent
stuff, but it is good to release it early: it will take some time
for it to do its work. 'Don't worry. Provided that your friend
can get us an introduction, everything will be as smooth as
silk.'

How are we doing on security? I whisper to Mieli. She is
our backup in the hotel, coordinating things with *Perhonen*.
Minimal, she says. *Still, more than you expected. War Quiet
concern me: they actually have pretty decent sensors.*

'Do me a favour,' Raymonde says. 'Don't try to put me at
ease. Come on, let's mingle.'

Raymonde got us invitations with surprising ease.
Apparently, Christian Unruh is a patron of the arts *and*
a Kingdom enthusiast, so a friend of Raymonde's at the
Academy of Music thought it would be an excellent idea if
she could discuss her opera concept with him. Of course,
the party is full of would-be artists seeking patronage, but
her contact promised to get us a personal introduction. And
that's all I need.

'Raymonde!' A short older woman waves at us. She is wearing a smartmatter dress that is like an hourglass without the
glass: there is no fabric, just red Martian sand that runs down
her generous figure. The effect is hypnotic. 'How wonderful
to see you here! And who is this handsome gentleman?'

I bow and open my gevulot a little as common courtesy dictates, but take care not to allow her any permanent
memories of my appearance. 'Raoul d'Andrezy, at your
service.' Raymonde introduces my cover identity, the emigré
from Ceres. The hourglass lady's gevulot reveals that she is

Sofia dell'Angelo, a lecturer in the Academy of Music and Drama.

'Oh, I'm sure we can think of something,' Sofia says. 'Now, what happened to poor Anthony? I *loved* his hair.'

Raymonde blushes a little, but does not reply. Sofia winks at me. 'You should watch out, young man. She is going to steal your heart and keep it.'

'Hush, I don't want you to scare him away. It took a lot of effort to catch him,' Raymonde says. 'Any sign of our host yet?'

Sofia looks crestfallen, plump cheeks flushed. 'No, I'm afraid not. I have spent almost an hour trying to find him. I absolutely think he should hear about your new piece. But apparently he is only going to show himself to a close circle of friends tonight. Do you know, I think he is actually afraid of that le Flambeur character? Terrible,' she says in a hushed tone.

'Le what?' Raymonde asks.

'Haven't you heard?' Sofia says. 'The rumour has it that some sort of offworld criminal invited himself here – even sent a letter announcing himself. It is all terribly exciting. Christian actually hired a detective, you know, the young boy who was in all the papers.'

Raymonde's eyes widen. *Announced himself?* hisses Mieli in my mind. *Announced?*

I have no idea what she is talking about, I protest. *That would be terribly unprofessional.* It's true: the preparations over the past few days have kept me too busy to incorporate additional flourishes. I feel a sudden twinge of regret: sending a RSVP would have played exactly the right note. *I'm innocent, I swear. It is the same thing as with the gogol pirates. Somebody knows too much.*

We are going to abort, Mieli says. *If they are expecting you, the risk is too great.*

Don't be ridiculous. We are not going to get an opportunity like this anytime soon. It's just going to make this a little more exciting. Besides, I have an idea.

We are not going to argue about this, Mieli says.

Are you telling me that we are going to run away with our tails between our legs? What kind of warrior are you? I trust you to deal with the violence, all right? Let me make this call. This is what I do. Any sign of trouble, and we are gone.

Mieli hesitates. *Fine. But I'll be watching you,* she says.

I know you will be.

Raymonde thanks Sofia for the attempt and we excuse ourselves, finding a little pavilion near the clearing where a group of acrobats perform with a pair of gracile elephants – trunks weaving intricate patterns with torches – and a flock of trained megaparrots, a riot of screeching colour.

'I knew this was a bad idea,' Raymonde says. 'We are not going to get close to Unruh. And – why does *he* have to be here?' She stares at a young man across the clearing, tall and lanky with tousled hair, dressed in an ill-fitting black and silver outfit. He is wandering through the crowd with a distracted, daydreaming look on his face.

'Is that the detective?'

'Isidore Beautrelet, yes.'

'Interesting. Close to Unruh, apparently.'

Raymonde gives me a flinty look. 'Don't get him involved.'

'Why not?' I feel the gogol pirate tools in my mind. The identity theft engine is something I have not tried yet, but it is there, waiting to be used. 'You know him, right? Any gevulot access you could share?'

She takes a deep breath.

'Come on, don't be such a goody-two-shoes,' I say. 'We are trying to commit a crime here. We have to use all the tools we have.'

'Yes, I have a lot of his gevulot,' she says. 'So what?'

'Oh? Is he a former lover? Another one whose heart you stole?'

'None of your business.'

'Help me out. Give me his gevulot, and we can do what we came here for.'

'No.'

I fold my arms. 'All right, then. Let's go home, and let your hidden puppeteers continue pulling your strings. Their strings. His strings.' I gesture at the detective and the crowd. 'This is exactly what I was talking about. You have to compromise to win.'

She turns away from me. Her face is hard. I try to take her hand, but she does not open her fingers. 'Look at me. Let me do this. So you won't have to.'

'Damn you.' She grabs my wrist. 'But whatever I give you, you'll give back, after it's over. Swear it.'

'I swear.'

'And I swear too,' she says. 'If you hurt him, you'll wish you were still in your Prison.'

I look at the young man. He is leaning on a tree, eyes half-closed, almost as if asleep.

'Raymonde, I'm not planning on hurting him. Well, perhaps his ego, a little bit. It'll do him good.'

'You were never much good at doing good,' she says.

I spread my hands, give her a small bow and go to meet the detective.

*

Isidore is alert, walking around, observing, deducing; it is not hard to see social patterns below the flow of gevulot. Here is the composer responsible for the music the Quiet will play later tonight, fishing for compliments; here, a Quiet resurrection activist trying to get a donation from Unruh for their cause. He tries to *feel* more than look, brushing a mental fingertip over his surroundings, reading a Braille of reality that has always been there for him, looking for things that do not belong.

'Good evening.'

Isidore looks up, his concentration interrupted. A dark-skinned man in a white tie stands in front of him. He is of indeterminate age, a little shorter than Isidore. The stranger's waistcoat glitters with golden ornamental Watches – ostentatiously, in Isidore's opinion – and in spite of the dim firefly lighting, he is wearing blue-tinted glasses. There is a strikingly red flower in his lapel. He brings with him the faintest whiff of a feminine perfume, a fine scent of pine.

The man removes his glasses and gives Isidore a smile made world-weary by his heavy eyelids. His eyebrows are very dark, almost as if sketched with a sharp pen. His gevulot is carefully closed.

'Yes?'

'I am sorry, I am looking for … how do you say, a private place?'

Isidore frowns. 'I'm sorry?'

'For … bodily functions, you understand?'

'Oh. Are you an offworlder?'

'Yes. Jim Barnett. I'm afraid I find it difficult to navigate here.' The man taps his temple. 'My brain, it hasn't yet adjusted, yes? Can you help?'

'Of course.' Isidore passes the man a little co-memory,

indicating the restrooms in the castle. He feels a quick twinge of a beginning headache as he does so. *Perhaps I have been working too hard.*

The man grins and pats him on the shoulder. 'Ah! So convenient. Thank you very much. Have a nice time.' Then he disappears into the crowd.

Isidore wonders if he should direct a guard Quiet to keep an eye on him. But an anomaly catches his eye from a nearby agora. There is something familiar about a short man dressed as Sol Mercurii, all blazing silver and heat and wearing a winged helmet, having a conversation with a young woman in a Gemini costume – a foglet image of herself shadowing her every move. The man's eyes are fixed on something far away.

Isidore whispers to one of the Quiet, approaches the pair and touches the man on the shoulder.

'Adrian Wu.'

The journalist jumps.

'Let's talk,' Isidore says.

'But I have an invitation,' Wu protests. 'Unruh has been handing them out right and left. I need to cover this. I'm surprised to see *you* here, though. Is there something my readers should know?'

'No.' Isidore frowns. 'Have you been taking analog photographs?'

'Well—'

One of the assault Quiet pads soundlessly next to Isidore. Its faceless head stares at the journalist. There is a silent, subsonic hum around it that echoes in Isidore's lungs. Wu stares at it.

'You know, I'm in charge of security around here,' Isidore says.

'But—'

'Give them to me, and I'll let you stay.'

Wu takes off his helmet, unscrews a cylinder-like object from it and hands it to Isidore. It is an analog camera, apparently triggered by his chin strap, a primitive device with light-sensitive film, far too simple to be affected by gevulot.

'Thank you,' Isidore says. He nods to the Gemini woman. 'I would be very careful what you say around this man. Let me know if he causes any problems.' He smiles at Wu. 'You can thank me later.'

The first dance has started. Isidore decides he deserves a drink and finds a glass of white wine. Then he checks the time: Unruh still has an hour left until his Timely demise.

That is when he realises his entanglement ring is gone from its chain. His heart pounds. He 'blinks at his encounter with the man with the blue-tinted glasses and sees the stranger steal it, with an almost imperceptible motion, separating his Watch from the chain and then putting it back, removing the ring, in a matter of seconds, talking to Isidore all the while, masking what can be masked with gevulot.

Isidore takes a deep breath. Then his mind is racing through the agoras of the party, sending the co-memory of the man to Odette and the Quiet guards. But he is nowhere to be seen, either gone or masked by gevulot. He walks around frantically, trying to locate all the gevulot blurs that could be hiding the uninvited guest that he has no doubt was no other than Jean le Flambeur. But the man seems to have vanished. *Why did he come to talk to me? Just to taunt me? Or* – He feels the odd headache again and a bizarre sense of *déjà vu*, flashes of faces, as if he was in two places at once.

He takes out his magnifying glass and Wu's camera and looks at the film. Without effort, the zoku device translates the grains on the film into full-colour images. He flips through them, tapping the glass disc. Society women. Performers. And there – Unruh. A picture taken only minutes ago, according to the timestamp, showing the millenniaire laughing with a group of friends, among whom there is a familiar figure in black and silver, with tousled hair—

Isidore drops the camera and starts running.

Duplicating the detective's physical appearance takes only a moment. I do it in one of the full privacy pavilions our host has considerately provided for his guests' carnal and other clandestine activities: imprinting his three-dimensional image to my own flesh and reprogramming my clothes to resemble his. The match does not have to be absolute: a lot can be hidden with gevulot.

Absently, I look at the ring I stole from him: zoku tech, clearly. Deciding to investigate it later, I put it in my pocket.

The real problem is his identity signature, and that's what I need the gevulot Raymonde provided for. And I need *Perhonen*'s quantum computation capability as well, to approximate the quantum state his Watch uses to identify itself.

I thought being a thief was easy, the ship says, as we bounce information back and forth. *This is hard work.*

'Waiting and sheer terror, as I said.' I try to ignore the memories that scroll through my mind as the ship and the identity theft engine work on them, to keep my promise to Raymonde. There are flashes of blank faces sculpted on a wall, and a girl with a zoku jewel at her throat. There is a strange innocence about the memories, and briefly I wonder what this boy is doing chasing gogol pirates and criminals like me.

I brush them aside: it is not the detective's past I'm here to steal, but Time. The gogol engine chimes, announcing success, talking to my hacked Watch and making the world think I'm Isidore Beautrelet. Only a few moments before his Watch renews his identity signature with the ambient gevulot, so I have no time to waste. I check my remaining equipment – the q-spider and the trigger in my mind – and decide it is time for the main event of the night.

I approach Unruh's group – the borrowed gevulot now allows me to see them – and imitate the detective's distracted, meandering walk. My mark is talking to a tall woman in icy white, and looks cheerfully drunk.

'M. Beautrelet!' he shouts when he sees me. 'How goes the villain hunt?'

'There are too many to choose from,' I say. Unruh bursts out laughing, but the woman in white looks at me curiously. Better make this quick.

'You are in a festive mood, I see,' Unruh says. 'Good for you! Here's to that.' He drains his glass.

I hand Unruh another glass from a passing Quiet waiter. As he takes it, I give the q-spider a quick instruction. It runs up my arm, leaps to his palm and vanishes into his gas-giant-coloured sleeve. Then it goes looking for his Watch.

The spider took three days to grow and another protracted argument with Mieli to play with the Sobornost body. *Perhonen* and I came up with the design, and it grew in the crook of my arm, a little many-legged lump, storing inside it some of the EPR states that both Mieli and I use for our superdense communication link with the ship. I smile at Unruh and guide it with my mind.

'It's hard not to be,' I say, 'when the fireworks are about to start.'

There. The spider nestles on his Watch and crawls inside it, connecting little q-dot threads to the ion traps that store Unruh's personalised, unforgeable units of Time, quantum states that his Watch sends to the resurrection system one by one, counting down his lifetime as a human. Then it shoots a little signal up at *Perhonen.* One, two, three, ten, sixty seconds of Time, quantum teleported away, transformed into quantum states up in the sky, stored in *Perhonen*'s wings. *Yes.*

Unruh frowns. 'I was saving the fireworks for my big moment tonight,' he says.

I smile. 'Shouldn't every moment be a big moment?'

Unruh laughs again. 'M. Beautrelet, I don't know where you found your wit – at the bottom of a glass or on a pretty girl's lips – but I'm glad you did!'

'M. le Flambeur, I presume?'

The detective stands in front of me flanked by two of the Quiet guards, two sleek black creatures made of sheer power and ferocity. I raise my eyebrows. Faster than I expected, much faster. He deserves the bow I give him.

'At your service.' I let my features revert to my own. I grin at Unruh. 'You have been a gracious host, but I'm afraid I must take my leave now.'

'M. le Flambeur, I must ask you not to move.'

I throw my flower into the air and form the mental image of pressing a large red button.

The fireworks go off all at once. The sky is full of trails of fire, weaving double and triple spirals, stars bursting into flakes of silver and sudden thunderclaps. After a cascade of bright purple confetti, two blue rockets draw a sign of infinity. There is a smell of gunpowder.

Around me, the party stops. The Quiet guards are statues. The music dies. Unruh drops his glass, but remains upright, eyes glazed. There are a few slow collapses, but overall, almost everyone at the party remains standing, gazes fixed on something far, far away, but unseeing, as the fireworks fizzle and die above us.

Another trick from the gogol pirate handbook: an optogenetic virus that makes brain cells hypersensitive to certain wavelengths of light. It was not hard to customise it not for the purposes of uploads, but for creating a period of inactivity. It looks like the infection from my flower spread even faster than I thought. And there are only so many fireworks manufacturers in the Moving City: bribing them with the pretence of a little innocent surprise for M. Unruh was the easy part.

I wrap myself in gevulot and make my way past the stunned, silent, thoughtless crowd. Raymonde is waiting for me at the garden gate, also wrapped in full privacy.

'Are you sure you don't want to stay for one more dance?' I ask her. I close my eyes and wait for the slap. It doesn't come. When I open my eyes, she is looking at me, face unreadable.

'Give it back. His gevulot. Now.'

And I do, returning all the rights to the detective's memories she gave me, purging all of him out of myself, becoming just Jean le Flambeur again.

She sighs. 'That's better. Thank you.'

'I take it that your crowd will cover our tracks here?'

'Don't worry,' she says. 'Just go and do your part.'

'In case it makes you feel any better,' I say, 'the next part involves me dying.'

We are in the public park. It is dark. Raymonde becomes the Gentleman and floats into the air. The dying fireworks reflect from her silver mask. 'I never wanted you to die,' she says. 'It was always about something else.'

'What? Revenge?'

'Let me know when you figure it out,' she says and is gone.

Amazingly, the party continues after the period of stolen time expires. Ten minutes have passed. The band picks up the tune, and the conversations begin again. And of course, there is only one topic.

Isidore's temples throb. With the Quiet guards and Odette, he searches the grounds and the garden's exomemory, over and over. But there is no sign of le Flambeur. The sense of failure and disappointment is a leaden weight in his belly. When the hour approaches midnight, he finally returns to the party.

Unruh has opened his gevulot to the public. He is the centre of attention and loving it, complimented on his bravery facing the thief. But eventually he waves his hand. 'My friends, it is time for me to leave you,' he says. 'Thank you for your patience with our unplanned entertainment number.' Laughter. 'But at least – and thanks to the bravery of our very own M. Beautrelet – he went away empty-handed.

'It was my intention to do this in bed between my lovely ladies here,' he says, clutching two Serpent Street courtesans, 'and possibly while being crushed by an elephant.' He raises his glass to the gracile pachyderm looming behind the crowd. 'But perhaps it is better to do it here, with friends. Time is what we make of it; relative, absolute, finite, infinite. I choose to let this moment last forever so that when I toil to clean *your* sewers and protect *you* from phoboi and carry *your* city on my back – I can remember what it is like to have such friends.'

'And so, with a drink, and a kiss,' Unruh kisses both girls – 'or two' – laughter – 'I die. See you in the—'

He falls to the ground, dropping his glass. Blinking, staring at the still form of the millenniaire, Isidore looks at his Watch. It shows one minute to midnight. *But how? He planned it so carefully, to the last word.* But his thoughts are drowned by cheers and popping champagne bottles, all around.

As the Resurrection Men come to take the body away and the wake part of the celebrations begins, Isidore sits down with a glass of wine and begins to deduce.

Interlude

TRUTH

On the night of the Spike, Marcel and Owl Boy go out over Noctis Labyrinthus in a glider.

It is Owl Boy's idea, of course. Everybody knows the Labyrinthus canyons are full of phoboi and deceptive thermals. Marcel cannot exactly afford the Time for the glider either, but there is no arguing with his lover.

'You have become an old man,' he says. 'You will never be an artist if you don't court death every now and then.' The barb about the concept he had been working on so long only to see it realised by someone else stings: and he can't live that down. And so he ends up in the sky, looking down at the dark chasms and up at the stars, and, in spite of everything, enjoying himself.

Above Ius Chasma, Owl Boy suddenly steers the glider down until they almost scrape the dark pseudotrees that grow there, then pulls sharply up. They veer close to the canyon's rim and the bottom of Marcel's stomach goes down to his toes. Seeing his expression, Owl Boy whoops with laughter.

'You are crazy,' Marcel tells Owl Boy, and kisses him.

'I thought you were never going to do that,' Owl Boy says, smiling.

'That was fun,' Marcel says. 'But could we go higher and just look at the sky, for a while?'

'Anything for you, my love. Besides, we have all night for acrobatics.'

Marcel ignores his wink, swings his seat back and looks at the sky. He 'blinks the constellations and planets into being.

'I've been thinking about going away,' Marcel says.

'Leaving?' Owl Boy says. 'Where would you go?'

Marcel gestures. 'You know. Up. Out there.' He presses his palm against the smooth, transparent skin of the glider. A bright Jupiter winks at him between his fingers. 'It's a stupid cycle here, don't you think? And it doesn't feel *real* here anymore.'

'Isn't that supposed to be your job? Feeling unreal?' There is a hint of anger in his voice. Owl Boy is an engineering student, and he would never have gone for him if not for the physical attraction; but every now and then he says things that make Marcel's heart jump. Many times during the course of their two-year partnership, Marcel has thought about leaving him. But moments like this always pull him back in.

'No,' Marcel says. 'It's about making unreal things real, or real things more real. It would be easier, up there. The zokus have machines that turn thoughts into things. The Sobornost say that they are going to preserve every thought ever thought. But here—'

Beneath his fingers, Jupiter explodes. For a moment, his hand is a red silhouette against bright whiteness. He blinks, feels the glider shudder around them, its wings curling into strange shapes like paper twisted by flame. He feels Owl Boy's cold hand in his own. Then his lover is shouting, words that do not make sense, larynx-tearing glossolalia. All around, the sky is burning. And then they fall.

It is not until much later that Marcel hears the word *Spike*, after the Quiet have brought their bodies from the desert and the Resurrection Men have put them back together.

The cities have suffered. There is damage in the exo-memory itself. Beyond the sky, things are worse: Jupiter is gone, eaten by a singularity, gravitational or technological or both, no one knows. The Sobornost claim to be containing a cosmic threat and offer an upload asylum to all citizens of the Oubliette. The remaining zokus out in Supra City are moving in response. There is talk of war.

Marcel cares little about any of it.

'Well, this is an unexpected pleasure,' says Paul Sernine, sitting in Marcel's studio. Perhaps Marcel only imagines it, but his rival's gevulot betrays a hint of silent envy as he looks at the claytronic models and sketches and found objects. 'I really did not expect to be the first point of a social call after such a long absence. How are things?'

'Well,' Marcel says. 'Come see for yourself.'

Owl Boy is in the nicest room in Marcel's Edge house, looking away from the city. Most of the time he sits by the window quietly in his medfoam cocoon, eyes blank. But every now and then he speaks, long strings of rough throat-tearing clicks and metallic sounds.

'The Resurrection Men don't understand it,' Marcel says. 'There is a permanent coherent state in his brain, like one of the old quantum theories of consciousness: a condensate in the microtubules of his neurons, entangled with his exo-memory. He may recover if it collapses, or he may not.'

'I am very sorry to hear that,' Sernine says. To Marcel's surprise, the concern in his voice sounds genuine. 'I wish there is something I could do.'

'There is,' Marcel says.

'I don't understand.'

'I'm giving up,' Marcel says. 'You have obviously found my ideas worth emulating in the past. So I'm going to sell them to you.' He gestures at the studio. 'All of them. I know you can afford it.'

Sernine blinks. 'Why?'

'It's not worth it,' Marcel says. 'There are giants out there. We do not matter. Someone can step on us without noticing. There is no point in making pretty pictures. It's all been done, anyway. We are ants. The only thing that matters is looking after each other.'

Marcel touches Owl Boy's hand. 'I can do that for him,' he says. 'It is my responsibility. I can wait for him until he gets better. But I need Time to do that.'

Sernine looks at them for a long time. 'You are wrong,' he says. 'We are just as big as they are. Somebody needs to show them that.'

'By building toy houses? If you wish.' Marcel waves a hand, thinks a gevulot contract at Sernine. 'It's all yours. You won.'

'Thank you,' Sernine says quietly. Then he stands still and listens to the Owl Boy's sounds. Finally, he clears his throat. 'If we do this,' he says slowly, 'could I visit, from time to time?'

'If you wish,' Marcel says. 'It makes a little difference to me.'

They shake hands on the agreement. Out of courtesy,

Marcel offers him cognac, but they drink quietly and after they are finished, Sernine leaves.

Owl Boy is quieter after Marcel feeds him. He sits with him for a long time, telling the house to play ares nova. But when the stars come out, Marcel closes the curtains.

13

THE THIEF IN THE UNDERWORLD

We stage my death the next morning, at the Place of Lost Time. This is where the Time beggars come to draw their last breath. It is an agora, with dark bronze statues of death and bones and suffering. And it is a show, meant to win the performers a few more precious seconds.

'Time, Time, Time is running out,' I shout at a passing couple, shaking a musical instrument made from fabber-printed bones. Behind me, two beggars make desperate love in the shadow of the statues. A group of nude *morituri* with painted faces dance a wild dance, pale bodies twisting and shaking.

My throat is hoarse from shouting at tourists from other worlds who form the majority of our audience. A puzzled-looking Ganymedean in a willowy exoskeleton keeps throwing us slivers of Time as if feeding pigeons, seemingly missing the point.

Don't overdo it, Mieli says in my head. She is observing in the crowd, looking at the *danse macabre* of the square.

It has to be believable I tell her.

Of course you are. Anytime you are ready.

All right. Go.

'Time is the great Destroyer,' I yell. 'I could be Thor the God of Thunder and the Old Age would still wrestle me to the ground.' I take a bow. 'Ladies and gentlemen, behold – Death!'

Mieli shuts me down remotely. My legs give away. My lungs stop working, and there is a terrible sense of drowning. Absurdly, the world remains as crisp and sharp as ever. My mind is still running inside the Sobornost body, but in stealth mode, while the rest of the body shuts down. My view lurches and I fall to the ground, as part of the Danse Macabre pattern I have been practising with my fellow soon-dead for the last couple of days. Our fallen bodies form words on the square: MEMENTO MORI.

A ragged cheer goes up from the watching crowd, a note that is a mixture of guilt and fascination. There is a moment's silence. The square resonates to the sound of heavy footsteps, approaching in unison. The Resurrection Men are coming.

The crowd parts to let them pass. Over the years, the whole thing has been turned into a ritual, and even the Resurrection Men have accepted it. They walk to the square in rows of three, perhaps thirty of them, red-robed, with very tight gevulot hiding their faces and gait, Decanters hanging from their belts. A group of Resurrection Quiet follow them. They are vaguely humanoid but huge, three or four metres in height, with blank slabs of black shiny carapace for faces and a cluster of arms from their torso. I can feel their footsteps in the ground below me.

A red-hooded figure appears above me, and holds a Decanter above my hacked Watch. For a moment, I feel irrational fear: surely these grim reapers have seen every possible attempt to cheat Death. But the brass device makes whirring sounds and then chimes, once. Gently, the Resurrection Man bends over and closes my eyes with one flick of his fingertips, a quick, professional movement. A Quiet lifts me up, and the slow drumming of the footsteps begins again, carrying me to the underworld.

I can't see anything, I tell Mieli. *Any other senses you could turn on for me?*

I don't want them noticing anything. And besides, you are supposed to play your part properly.

It is an odd feeling, being carried through the tunnels into the underworld, listening to the echoes of footsteps in the city beneath the city and smelling the odd seaweed smell of the Quiet. The movement lulls me into a strange melancholy. I've never died, not in all my centuries. Perhaps the Oubliette has it right, the right approach to immortality; die every now and then and appreciate life.

Still having fun? Perhonen asks.

Hell, yes.

I find that worrying. Time to wake up.

I am back from the dead a second time, but without transition dreams. My eyes feel like they are covered in a layer of dust. I float in a clammy gel in a small space. It takes only a moment to regurgitate the little q-stone tool I brought and open the coffin door. It is not sealed with gevulot, simply with a mechanical lock: it is amazing how traditionalist the Resurrection Men are. The door slides aside, and I crawl out.

I almost fall down: I am high up on the wall of a huge cylindrical chamber with metal walls, covered by a grid of little hatches. It makes me think of a filing cabinet. Vertical cables run through it. Below, a Quiet – an octopus-like cluster of machinery and arms – hangs from them. It is placing fresh bodies into storage. I close the hatch, leaving a small opening to see through, and wait for it to leave. It zooms up past me, climbing up the cables like a spider. Then I venture out again. Gel dripping from my skin, I look for handholds.

All right, Perhonen says. *I'm getting some imagery now. There are some maintenance shafts below: you can get Mieli in through there.*

I reconfigure the q-dot layer under my skin to grab the material on the wall and climb down the coffins of the sleeping dead.

There is a constant background noise, a mix of distant and nearby hisses, rumbles and thumps. This is where the organs of the city are, pistons and engines and tubes where the synthbio repair organisms circulate, and the vast artificial muscles that move the city's legs.

A splay of transparent tubes snakes down a series of shafts along the edges of the chamber, with rungs along them clearly designed for smaller Quiet. They are just big enough for me to squeeze in. *Perhonen* is feeding me ghost images she can get from my WIMP beacon: around me there is a chaotic anatomy of chambers, tunnels and machines.

I climb downward for more than fifty metres, skin scraping against the tubes and the walls of the shaft, stopping whenever I hear the scuttling of a Quiet. Once, a swarm of beetle-sized Quiet swarms past me, ignoring me, climbing all over me, tiny eyes aglow in the dark, and it is hard to keep from screaming.

Finally, there is another horizontal tunnel, this one made from some ceramic material, slick with bitter-smelling slippery fluids that drip from the porous walls. It is completely dark, and I switch to infrared, trying to ignore the ghost world of giants moving at the edge of my vision, focusing on the destination.

After a dark eternity of crawling, the tunnel widens and slopes down: I have to struggle to keep from sliding. Finally, there is some light, an orange dusk in the distance, and I can feel a freezing cold wind. In the light, I can see that the tunnel widens into a sloping shaft, ending in a fine mesh that lets the light from the outside through.

Tell Mieli I'm ready when she is, I tell *Perhonen.*

She's following your beacon. Should be there any moment.

Getting to this point involved a lot of planning. The gevulot around the base of the city is incredibly thick: the Oubliette does not want to make the lives of gogol pirates any easier. So the only way to get in was from the inside.

I take out the q-tool again and cut a hole in the mesh. It eats through the material smoothly. I feel a moment of vertigo, looking down. Then there is a gust of hot wind, and Mieli is there, hovering beneath the opening, wings extended.

'What took you so long?' I ask.

She looks at me disapprovingly.

'I know, I know,' I say. 'I should put some clothes on when I come back from the dead.'

Mieli leads us through the tunnels towards the q-spider's beacon that tells us where Unruh's body is kept. I'm glad she is here: the tunnels and corridors are a blur. A few times she surrounds us with stealth fog as bigger Quiet pass us, wheezing and rumbling, carrying a stench of the sea.

Then there are the crypt chambers, cylindrical rooms a hundred metres in diameter, surgically clean and chromed in contrast to the dark tunnels, coffin hatches engraved with names and codes. We find Unruh in the third one.

As I enter, there is a hissing sound above: the mortician octopod Quiet has spotted us. It plummets down the cables towards me.

Mieli shoves me aside and fires her ghostgun at it. There is a grinding sound as it brings itself to a stop, metres above me, hanging from the cables like a puppet, swaying back and forth. I look at its mandibled non-face and swallow.

'Don't worry,' Mieli says. 'My gogol just took over its motor functions. The mind inside is going to be fine. We wouldn't want to violate your professional ethics.'

'I'm not so worried about that,' I say. Mieli brought smart-fabric overalls for me, but I still feel cold. She gestures, and obediently the Quiet climbs up to fetch Unruh's body. In a few moments, the coffin is on the floor in front of us. I open it with the q-tool.

'Like I told Raymonde,' I say, 'we take from the rich and give to the poor.'

The former millenniaire is pale, white and naked apart from the black disc of his Watch. *Go on*, I tell *Perhonen*. Its particle beam shows up in my augmented vision, a white pencil of light playing on the Watch, quantum teleporting the minute we stole back. The augmented view explodes into white noise as the ambient resurrection system starts working, dumping the latest synchronised version of Unruh's mind back into his body from exomemory.

Unruh's body shudders. He draws a deep, wet, ragged breath. He coughs, and his eyes fly open.

'What – where—'

'I'm sorry, M. Unruh, this will only take a moment.' Mieli hands me the upload helmet, a featureless black cap. I place it onto his head, and it sticks to his skull eagerly.

Unruh laughs, only to be broken by a cough. 'You again?'

He shakes his head. 'I am disappointed. I did not expect you to be some common gogol pirate.'

I smile. 'I assure you that I don't have a sliver of your gevulot, and I have returned all I stole from you. This is about something else. Hold still.'

It was the obvious thing to do. How do you find out if there are shadowy forces manipulating people's minds? You find a clean template, and make a before-and-after comparison. Unruh was young, with no previous resurrections or Quiet time: his mind as a whole had never passed through the resurrection system. Now it has, and if someone has done something to it, we will find out. If not – well, I have been to worse parties.

'If I must.' Unruh sighs. 'I see. You stole a minute of my Time, and gave it back? To get access to my mind here? Interesting. I can't imagine why. This is a very strange crime, M. le Flambeur. I wish I could stay and watch young M. Beautrelet catch you.'

'I will pass him your regards,' I say. 'And by the way, I apologise for the surroundings. I wish we could have at least arranged a drink.'

'It's fine. I have recently experienced much more discomfort.'

'While we wait,' I say, 'I wonder if you mind me asking how you knew we were going to be at your party?'

'The letter.' He waves a hand.

'A letter?'

He looks at me curiously. 'It wasn't from you? Oh, this is even richer than I imagined. Such a shame that I have to miss all this. A letter in my library, from you. We could not figure out how it got there. M. Beautrelet thought there was something wrong with the exomemory—'

We are getting the data now, Perhonen says. *It does indeed look like there have been some changes, especially in the—*

Unruh's features twist into a snarl. He goes for my throat, white fingers digging into my flesh. He screams, a terrible, tearing sound, slamming his forehead against my face. My vision goes red in a haze of pain.

Mieli pulls him off me, twisting his arms behind his back. 'Le Flambeur!' he shouts, in a different voice. 'He will come for you. Le Roi will come for you!'

Then he goes limp in Mieli's grip as his Time runs out again.

I massage my throat. 'Well,' I say. 'I'd say that if further proof of manipulation of Oubliette minds is required, we've got it.'

We got the data, Perhonen says. *It is very strange.*

Mieli cocks her head, listening. 'Someone is coming,' she says. And then I hear it too, distant footsteps and approaching Quiet.

'Oh my,' I say. 'I think the teen sleuth actually worked out what we were going to do.'

Mieli grabs my arm. 'You can play games later,' she says. 'We need to go.'

Mieli studies the three-dimensional map *Perhonen* has been compiling from their sensor data, looking for escape routes.

'Shouldn't we be running?' the thief asks.

'Ssh.' The metacortex suggests ways out, computing paths with minimal probability of a hostile encounter. She has no desire to fight their way out. *There*: a possible path, up this chamber and then through—

The ground and the walls shake. There is a groaning sound, and the map *changes*. She realises what the large clumps of artificial muscle, heat and energy in the map are: Atlas Quiet. They balance the city platforms and its internal structure. They must be directly below the Maze, where the things change the most. The Resurrection Men are using the Quiet to corner them, blocking escape routes. That means a fight. Unless—

'This way,' she snaps at the thief and starts running down the tunnel, towards the voices.

'More to the point,' says the thief, 'shouldn't we be running *away* from them?' Not wanting to argue, Mieli gives him a little jolt through their biot link.

'There was absolutely no need for that!'

The tunnel running through the crypt chamber is wide and cylindrical, widening as they go. Her metacortex spots the echoes of the Quiet and Resurrection Men ahead. But they are not what she is interested in.

They enter a wide, low chamber a hundred metres in diameter. It is lit dimly by fluorescence from synthbio tubes. One of the walls is rough and organic, moving and pulsing, a scaled carapace of something alive: the side of an Atlas Quiet. Mieli summons her combat autism, mapping the geometry of the underworld around them, the platforms, the seams, how the pieces fit together.

'Stop!' shouts a voice. On the other side of the chamber, a group of hooded Resurrection Men enter, flanked by hulking war Quiet.

Mieli fires her ghostgun at the Atlas Quiet's side, loading it with a simple slave gogol that will self-destruct after a few iterations. The walls and the floor begin to shake. The Quiet wall spasms. Its scales break. With a tremendous crack, the chamber splits open in the middle. Daylight shoots up from the yawning chasm. Mieli grabs hold of the thief and jumps.

They fall through the wound in the flesh of the city. Synthbio solutions rain around them like blood. And then they are outside, in the middle of the forest of the city legs, blinking at the bright daylight.

Mieli opens her wings to catch their fall, wraps them in gevulot and starts the flight back to the city of the living.

My spirits are high when we return to the hotel.

Under my gevulot, I'm covered in dirt and grime, shaky from yet another Mieli-powered flight, but elated. A part of me is thinking about whatever took over Unruh. But it is overruled by the majority that wants to celebrate.

'Come on,' I tell Mieli. 'We have to celebrate. It's traditional. And you are an honorary thief now. This is when one traditionally gets caught, by the way; arguing over loot, or bungling the getaway. But we did it. I can't believe it.'

My head is buzzing. In the last few hours, I have been a Belt emigré, a detective, a Time beggar and a corpse. *This is what it must have felt like before.* It is difficult to stay still.

'You did good. Like an Amazon.' I am babbling, but I don't care. 'You know, when this is over, I might just come and settle here again. Do something modest. Grow roses. Steal girls' hearts and some other things every now and then.'

I order the most expensive beverage the hotel fabber can make, virtually grown Kingdom wine, and offer Mieli a glass. 'And you, ship! Well done with the quantum magic.'

I believe I should think of myself as the loony expert type who likes blowing things up, Perhonen says.

I laugh. 'She knows pop culture references! I'm in love!'

I'm finding interesting things in the data, by the way.

'Later! Save it for later. We are busy getting drunk now.'

Mieli looks at me oddly. Again, I wish I could read her,

but the biot link only goes one way. But to my surprise, she accepts the offered glass.

'Is it like this for you every time?' she asks.

'My dear, wait until we spend months planning a *guberniya* brain break-in. This is nothing. Just sparkles. That's the real fireworks. But I am a thirsty man in a desert. This is good.' I clink my glass against hers. 'Here's to crime.'

The thief's elation is infectious. Mieli finds herself getting happily drunk. She has carried out operations involving elaborate preparation and planning before – getting the thief out of the Prison, among other things – but there has never been an illicit thrill like the one that radiates from the thief. And he did play his part well, like a *koto* brother, without any sign of rebellion, a different kind of creature entirely, in his element.

'I still don't get it,' she says, sitting back on the couch, letting herself coast on the bubbling feeling. 'Why is it fun?'

'It's a game. Did you never play games back in Oort?'

'We race. And compete in craft and *väki* song.' She misses it, suddenly. 'I used to like it, crafting, making things out of the coral. You visualise a thing. You find the words that it *is*. And you sing them to *väki*; it grows and makes it. And in the end you have something that is truly yours, a new thing in the world.' She looks away. 'That's how I made *Perhonen*. That was a long time ago.'

'You see,' the thief says, 'for me, stealing is exactly the same.' He looks serious, suddenly.

'What are you doing here?' he asks. 'Why are you not back there, making things?'

'I'm just doing what I have to,' Mieli says. 'That's what

I've always done.' But she does not want to let the darkness well up.

'Well, not tonight,' says the thief. 'Tonight, we are doing what we *want* to. We're going to have fun. What do you want to do?'

'Sing,' Mieli says. 'I would like to sing.'

'I know just the place,' the thief says.

The Belly: underground streets and walkways between the inverted towers. Pinpoints of Quiet lights below, newspaper drones selling stories of the city quake earlier during the day and the strange goings-on at the carpe diem party the night before.

The tiny bar is called the Red Silk Scarf. It has a small stage; the walls are covered in feed posters of musician lifecasts that throw flickering lights across a group of small round tables. They do open mike nights. The audience consists of a few young Martians who have seen everything, wearing perpetual expressions of being unimpressed. But the thief ushers them in, getting her into the program, talking to the landlord in hushed whispers while she waits at the bar, drinking more strange-flavoured alcoholic drinks from tiny glasses.

The thief insisted she spend time getting dressed, and with *Perhonen*'s assistance she obliged, fabbing a dark pantsuit with platform shoes and an umbrella. The thief quipped that she looked like she was going to a funeral. He flinched when she said it could be his. That actually made her laugh. The strange clothes feel like armour, letting her feel like someone else, someone reckless. It is all a little fake, she knows: her metacortex will flush out all the intoxication and unnecessary emotions at the first sign of trouble. But it feels good to pretend.

How's it going? she whispers to *Perhonen. You should come and join us. I'm going to sing.*

On stage, a girl in oversized sunglasses is doing something that combines poetry with abstract tempmatter images and the sound of her heartbeats. Mieli can see the thief cringing.

I'm sorry, the ship says. *Busy solving a high-dimensional lattice cryptography problem with a thousand mathematics gogols. But I'm glad you're having fun.*

I miss her.

I know. We'll get her back.

'Mieli? You're up.' Mieli flinches. *Got to go. Got to sing.* She suppresses a burp.

'I can't believe you talked me into this,' she says.

'I get that a lot,' the thief says. 'You know, you are the only person I can really trust here. So don't worry. I've got your back.' She nods, feeling a lump in her throat, or his, perhaps. A little unsteadily, she gets on stage.

The songs come out of her in a flood. She sings of ice. She sings of the long journey of Ilmatar from the burning world, of the joy of wings and the ancestors in the *alinen*. She sings the song that makes ships. She sings the song that seals a *koto's* doors against the Dark Man. She sings of home.

When she is done, the audience is quiet. Then the handclaps start, one by one.

Much later, they walk back together. The thief has her arm, but it does not feel wrong, somehow.

Back in the hotel, when it is time to say good night, the thief does not let go of her hand. She can feel his arousal and tension through the biot link. She touches his cheek and pulls his face closer to hers.

Then the laughter comes, bubbling up from her like the

song earlier, and the hurt look on his face makes it impossible to stop.

'I'm sorry,' she says, doubled up, tears in her eyes. 'I can't help it.'

'I apologise,' says the thief, 'for not seeing the humour.' His face is so full of hurt pride that Mieli thinks she's going to die. 'Fine. I'm going to get myself a drink.' He turns to leave with an abrupt twist on his heel.

'Wait,' she says, sniffing and wiping her eyes. 'I'm sorry. Thank you for the thought. It's just ... funny. But really. Thank you for tonight.'

He smiles, a little.

'You're welcome. See, sometimes it is good to do what you want.'

'But not all the time,' she says.

'No.' The thief sighs. 'Maybe not all the time. Good night.'

'Good night,' Mieli says, suppressing one more giggle, turning to go.

There is a sudden lurch in her gevulot, a sudden recollection that there is someone else in the room.

'Oh my,' says a voice. 'I hope I am not interrupting anything.'

There is a man sitting in the thief's usual balcony seat, smoking a small cigar. The sudden pungent smell is like a bad memory. He is young, with black, swept-back hair. He has draped his coat over the chair, and his shirtsleeves are rolled up. He grins, showing a row of sharp, white teeth.

'I thought it was time that we had a little chat,' he says.

14

THE DETECTIVE AND THE ARCHITECT

Isidore looks at Unruh's dead body for the second time. The millenniaire looks less peaceful in death than the previous night: his pale face is twisted in a hideous grimace, and there are red marks on his forehead and temples. His fingers are curled into claws.

It is cold in the crypt chamber and Isidore's breath steams. The locked-up gevulot here makes everything feel unreal and slippery, and the silence of the three Resurrection Men who escorted him here does not help. The red-robed figures, faces hidden by gevulot and darkness, stand unnaturally still, without fidgeting or, it seems, breathing.

'I appreciate you letting me come down here,' he says, addressing the one with the golden infinity symbol at his (or her?) breast. 'I realise that this is somewhat ... unusual.'

There is no reply. He is almost certain that the Resurrection Man is the same one he spoke to earlier at the Resurrection House, after realising what the thief was planning to do. After the city quake, they brought him here, to show him what had happened, but so far no one has spoken a word.

It was the only logical conclusion: the only reason to steal such a small amount of Time was to give it back, to carry out something criminal in the underworld. *Poor Unruh.* The pieces do not fit, and it makes him uncomfortable.

He studies the scene with his magnifying glass. There are two different types of body preservation gel on the floor, in different states of coagulation: Unruh's and someone else's. That fits with his theory of how the thief got in: by somehow pretending to be dead, then opening an entrance to a heavily armed accomplice. He makes a mental note to check the exomemories of all the *memento mori* agoras where the Time beggars go to die.

There are also traces of bizarre artificial cells – far more complex than anything from an Oubliette synthbio body – under Unruh's fingernails, clear signs of a struggle. And the marks on his head and the trace damage in his dead brain indicate a forced upload.

'Would it be possible to bring him back, just for a minute?' Isidore asks the Resurrection Men. 'We could use his testimony, to figure out exactly what happened here.' He is unsurprised that the red-robed underworld guardians only reply with silence: they are not willing to compromise the resurrection laws for any purpose, even to solve crimes.

He walks around the room, thinking. One of the Resurrection Men is treating the damaged Quiet the thief's accomplice attacked. Isidore has already inspected the bullet, a little sliver of diamond. Whatever internal structure it once had, it has fused into a solid mass.

The thing that bothers him is the lack of motive. The incident at the party, and now this: it has nothing in common with the gogol pirate cases he has either read about or been involved in. By all accounts, the thief made no attempt whatsoever to gain access to Unruh's gevulot. It is a non-crime. Some Time was stolen, and returned, with two separate copies of Unruh's mind – which, of course, are completely useless without his gevulot keys to decrypt them. And how was the Time stolen in the first place?

'Do you mind if I have a look at this?' He picks up Unruh's Watch, carefully disentangling its chain from the millenniaire's hand. 'I want to have this investigated.'

The Resurrection Man with the infinity sign nods slowly, takes a little unadorned Watch from his pocket and touches it and Unruh's Watch with a Decanter. Then he places the new Watch exactly where the old one was and gives Unruh's sleek black timepiece to Isidore.

'Thank you,' Isidore says.

The Resurrection Man shoves his hood back and opens his gevulot a little, revealing a round, friendly face. He clears his throat.

'Apologies ... we spend so much time with ... our Quiet brothers, that it is hard to ...'

'That's all right,' Isidore says. 'You have been very kind.'

The man takes something from his pocket. 'My partner ... down there ...' He points at the floor. 'When un-Quiet ... he was a ... fan.' He coughs. 'So I was wondering ... could you ... perhaps ... an autograph?'

He holds out a newspaper clip covered in tempmatter film. Adrian Wu's article.

Sighing, Isidore takes it and digs out a pen from his pocket.

Isidore blinks at the daylight, glad to leave the dark facade of the Resurrection House behind. The wind on Persistent Avenue feels hot after the chill of the underworld, but the sound of human voices is refreshing.

The optogenetic attack at the party left him feeling disoriented, with a mild headache. A med-Quiet inspected him along with the rest of the guests, but found no permanent traces of an infection. It was able to isolate the virus, and when Isidore and Odette searched the grounds, they found the discarded flower that had been used to spread it. Isidore carries it with him in his shoulder bag, safely wrapped in a smartmatter bubble.

He has not slept, but the thoughts racing through his head won't let him rest. And whenever he thinks about the thief, there is a tingle of shame in his belly. They were so close, face to face – and he stole both Isidore's countenance and the entanglement ring. How the identity theft was accomplished is yet another mystery. As far as Isidore knows, there is no way the thief should have been able to gain any access to his gevulot.

Not that the thief left any traces of himself in the garden exomemory either: the only time he appears without a gevulot mask is when he speaks to Isidore. And it is clear that he is able to alter his appearance at will. Distantly, he wonders if a part of the unease he feels is fear: perhaps le Flambeur is out of his league.

He stops for a moment under one of the Avenue's cherry trees and breathes in the smell of the blossoms to clear his head. Nothing but reputation and a certain flair separate his enemy from any common gogol pirate. Somewhere, le Flambeur will have made a mistake, and Isidore is going to find it.

Gritting his teeth, he heads for the side alleys of the Avenue, to find a Watchmaker's shop.

*

'Interesting,' says the Watchmaker, squinting at Unruh's Watch through a massive brass eyepiece. 'Yes, I think I can tell you how it was done.'

The eyepiece lens flickers with digital information. The Watchmaker is a lanky, middle-aged man in a black T-shirt with ripped sleeves, blue hair, a scraggly moustache and ears stretched by implants and earrings. His workshop is a cross between a quantum physics laboratory and a horologist's workspace, full of sleek humming boxes with holodisplays hovering around them and neatly sorted piles of tiny gears and tools on wooden work surfaces. Violent music plays in the background, and the Watchmaker bops his head up and down frantically to its rhythm as he works. After Isidore told him the story of Unruh, he was more than happy to help, although it takes some effort to ignore the occasional lewd glance he casts at the young man.

He pulls something out of the Watch with the pincers that the fingers of his gloves end in, miniature hands with fingers extending to the molecular level. He holds it up against a light. It is barely visible, a tiny flesh-coloured spider. He places it into a tiny tempmatter bubble and magnifies it: it becomes an insectoid monster the size of a hand. Isidore takes out his magnifying glass, prompting a curious glance from the Watchmaker.

'This baby here has EPR states in its belly,' the Watchmaker says. 'It wormed its way into the ion traps of the Watch where the Time credits are stored, got the stuff in its stomach entangled with the trap quantum states, sent out a signal of some kind – and bamf, the states got teleported away. Almost the oldest trick in the quantum mechanic's handbook, although this is the first time I've seen it used to steal Time.'

'Where would the receiver be?' Isidore asks.

The Watchmaker spreads his hands. 'Could be anywhere. Qupting does not need a strong signal. Could be in space, for all I know. This little bug is definitely not from around here, by the way. Sobornost, for my money.' He spits to the floor. 'I hope you catch 'em.'

'Me too,' Isidore says. 'Thank you.' He looks around the shop. There is something familiar about the Watches under the glass counter, something that tickles his mind—

A Watch. A heavy brass face. A silver band. The word Thibermesnil—

Where does the memory come from?

'Are you all right, son?' asks the Watchmaker.

'Yes, I'm fine. I just need to sit down for a moment.' Isidore sits down on the chair the quantum horologist offers. Closing his eyes, he revisits the exomemories from the party. *There:* a bizarre sense of seeing double, just after he spoke to the thief, just before he stole Time from Unruh. Of course: if the thief used Isidore's own identity key to pretend to be him, he has access to the exomemories created during those moments.

'Could you turn the music down, please?'

'Sure. Sure. Would you like a glass of water?'

He massages his temples, carefully sifting through the memories, separating the ones that are his from the ones that should not be. *He looked at his Watch. That is his Watch.* And there are other thoughts there too, glimpses of architectural drawings, a beautiful woman with a scar on her face, and a butterfly-like spaceship with glittering wings. Emotion, too: arrogance and self-confidence and bravado that make him angry. *I'm going to get you,* he thinks. *See if I don't.*

He opens his eyes, head pounding, accepts the offered

glass and drinks deep. 'Thank you.' He takes a deep breath. 'One more question, and then I'll stop bothering you. Have you ever seen this Watch?' He passes a co-memory of the Watch he just saw to the Watchmaker.

The man considers it for a moment. 'Can't say I have. But this looks like something that old Antonia would have made, two streets down. Tell her Justin sent you.' He winks at Isidore.

'Thank you again,' Isidore says. 'You have been a big help.'

'Don't mention it. It's difficult to meet young people who appreciate Watches these days.' He grins, putting his glove-less hand on Isidore's thigh. 'Although if you really want to show your appreciation, I'm sure there's something we can come up with—'

Isidore flees. As he hurries down the street, the roar of the music starts again, mixed with laughter.

'Yes, I remember this,' says Antonia. She is not old at all, at least not in appearance: in her third or fourth body, perhaps, a petite dark-skinned woman with Indian features. Her shop is bright and orderly, with Xanthean designer jewellery displayed alongside the timepieces. She immediately printed out a tempmatter instantiation of the co-memory, weighing it in her hands, tapping it with a bright red fingernail.

'It would have been years ago,' she says, 'twenty Earth years maybe, judging by the design. The customer wanted a special little mechanism, you could hide something inside it and open it by pressing a combination of letters. A gift to a lover, probably.'

'Do you, by any chance, remember anything about the person who bought it?' Isidore asks.

The woman shakes her head.

'It's shop gevulot, you know – we rarely get to keep that sort of thing. I'm afraid not. People tend to be very private about their Watches.' She frowns. 'However – I'm pretty sure there was a whole series of these. Nine of them. Very similar designs, all for the same customer. I can give you the schematics, if you like.'

'That would be wonderful,' Isidore says. Antonia nods, and suddenly his head is full of complex mechanical and quantum computing design diagrams, along with another headache jolt. As he blinks at the pain, Antonia smiles at him. 'I hope Justin did not scare you,' she says. 'This is a lonely profession – long hours, not much appreciation – sometimes he gets a little carried away, especially with young men like you.'

'Sounds like being a detective,' Isidore says.

Isidore has lunch at a small floating restaurant in Montgolfiersville and gathers his thoughts. Even here, he is recognised – apparently his involvement in Unruh's carpe diem party has been prominently reported by the *Herald* – but he is too preoccupied with the Watches to hide from every curious glance with gevulot. Hardly tasting his pumpkin quiche, he goes through the designs in his mind.

They are all identical, except for the engravings. *Bonitas. Magnitudo. Eternitas. Potestas. Sapientia. Voluntas. Virtus. Veritas. Gloria.* Goodness, Greatness, Eternity, Power, Wisdom, Will, Virtue, Truth, Glory. None of them qualities he would immediately associate with Jean le Flambeur. But they do suggest that the Unruh affair was not some random impulse to play games with Oubliette barbarians, as the millenniaire suspected. Clearly, le Flambeur has some connection to Mars, one stretching back twenty years at least.

Drinking coffee and looking at the view of the city below, he spends an hour 'blinking at the words. In combination, they appear in medieval texts, Raymond Lull's Dignities of God from the 13th century, with some connections to the sephiroths of Kabbalistic tradition and the lost art of ... memory. One of Lull's followers was Giordano Bruno, who perfected the art of memory palaces, of storing mental images in physical locations, as if outside the mind. That, at least, is a connection that resonates. The Oubliette exomemory does the same thing, stores everything thought, experienced and sensed in a location in the ubiquitous computing machinery around it.

The shape of it feels right, but he is not sure if it is just pattern matching, like seeing faces in the clouds. Then the memory fragment about the architectural drawings comes back.

Another 'blink – looking for memory palaces – reveals that there was a series of architectural pieces commissioned by the Voice twenty years ago. *Nine reflections on memory*, by an architect called Paul Sernine.

All the palaces are located in the Maze, relatively close to each other, but the public exomemories about them are old, and Isidore is forced to do some footwork to find them.

The first piece he comes across is near a Maze marketplace, squeezed between a synagogue and a small public fabber centre. It is completely bizarre. The size of a small house, it is made from some black, smooth material. It consists of geometric surfaces, planes, cubes, stuck together in a seemingly haphazard fashion: still, he can sense that there is some order to its structure. And the surfaces do form spaces resembling rooms and hallways, only oddly distorted as if by a funhouse mirror. A plaque near what could be called an entrance has a small plaque that says *Eternitas*.

The structure looks like something designed by an algorithmic process, rather than a human being. And parts of it look fuzzy, as if the surfaces continued to fork and divide fractally beyond the human range of vision. On the whole, it looks rather forbidding. Someone local has made the black interior slightly less sinister and tomblike by placing a few flower-pots inside: vines have grown to curl around the jutting spikes and surfaces to find light.

There is a little local exomemory that opens up while Isidore studies the structure. It describes *Eternitas* as an 'experiment in transforming exomemory data directly into architecture and livable spaces.' The Oubliette is full of similar art projects – indeed, many of Isidore's fellow students work on considerably stranger things – but clearly there is something deeper here, something that is or has been important to the thief.

On impulse, he takes out his magnifying glass. He gasps. When he zooms in, the surface reveals immense complexity, black leaves and spikes and pyramids, whole architectures with alarming regularity that go all the way down to the molecular level. And the material is something the glass does not even recognise, something resembling what it calls zoku q-matter, but denser: in spite of its relatively small size, the structure must be immensely heavy. Underneath, it looks less like a piece of architecture than a part of some unimaginably complex machine, frozen in time.

And there are nine of these? Isidore takes a deep breath. *Maybe I really am out of my depth.*

*

Deep in thought, he starts walking towards the next Reflection piece, only a few hundred metres away, trusting his sense of direction to guide him through the Maze.

How is all this related to Unruh? he thinks. *Time,* memory castles, *Dignities of God? Maybe it doesn't make sense: maybe le Flambeur is insane.* But his every instinct tells him there is a logic here; that everything so far is a sliver of some larger iceberg.

He jumps at a sudden noise. There is the silhouette of a parkrouller on a nearby rooftop. This is one of the parts of the Maze where construction was started and then stopped when the drifting of the city platforms moved it to an unfavourable position: everything here is half-finished and deserted. The buildings lining the narrow streets look like decayed teeth. As he watches, the parkrouller disappears, becoming a gevulot blur. He quickens his pace and keeps walking.

After a minute, he hears the footsteps, following him. At first, he thinks the sound belongs to one person. But when he stops to listen, it is clear from their echo that there are several followers, marching in perfect synchrony, like soldiers. He walks briskly and turns away from the main street, into a small alley, only to see the slow drift of the Maze close the other end and turn it into a dead end. When he turns around, he sees the four Sebastians.

They all look like Élodie's boyfriend: sixteen, perfect features, blond hair, a young Martian's zoku-influenced, tight-fitting clothes. At first their faces are expressionless. Then they all smile in unison, mouths twisting into cruel, mirthless lines.

'Hello, copykiller,' one of them says.

'We recognise you now,' says the second.

'You should have—'

'—minded your own business,' finishes the last.

'Foolish to come to our domain, smelling of the underworld.'

'Foolish to come near the places the hidden ones have told us to guard.'

Like trained soldiers, they take a single step forward, and draw out small knives.

Isidore turns and runs, as fast as he can, looking for handholds to climb up the obstacle that has closed the alley.

The parkroulling Sebastian takes him down in a flying tackle. Air escapes his lungs, and he slams both elbows at the pavement, followed by his nose. The world goes red for a second. When his vision returns, he is prone on his back, and four perfect porcelain faces loom in a circle above him. There is something cold and sharp, pressing against his throat. Hands hold his limbs down. Desperately, he opens his gevulot, reaching for the police Quiet's emergency feed. But it feels distant and slippery: the gogol pirates are doing something to stop it.

Upload tendrils dance above his face like the firework snakes at the party: he imagines them hissing. He feels a little pinprick of pain at his throat. One of the Sebastians lifts up a small injection needle. 'We are going to have your mind, copykiller,' he says. 'It was such a blessing to find out what you looked like. We praised Fedorov when we saw the paper. You are going to scream now, just like the chocolatier in my brother's memories. Pray that the Founders in their wisdom give you a part of the Great Common Task. As a missile guidance system. Or food for the Dragons, perhaps.' The tips of the tendrils feel like sharp, electric kisses on his scalp.

'Let him go,' says a rasping chorus voice.

The Gentleman stands at the other end of the alley, just at the limit of Isidore's blurring vision, a black shape with a glint of silver.

'I don't think so,' the first Sebastian says. Some of the tendrils peek out of his mouth like a bouquet of glowing snakes. 'I am touching his brain. Even your witch fog is not faster than light, bitch.'

Light. The Sebastians are looking at the Gentleman now. With a thought, he dissolves the q-bubble that holds the thief's rose in his bag. *I hope it works fast enough. I hope it works on them.* He opens his gevulot to the Gentleman, enough to show his surface thoughts. *Fireworks,* he thinks at the tzaddik. *Light.*

'In fact, you can listen to his screams—'

There is a flash of light, and then a long fall, down somewhere dark.

Eventually, the light comes back. Something soft cradles Isidore. The faces of the Sebastians still flicker in his vision, but after a moment he realises it is his own, reflecting from the Gentleman's mask.

'Don't try to talk,' says the tzaddik. 'Help is on its way.' Isidore is floating in the air, on a soft cushion of *something*: it feels nicer than his bed.

'Let me guess,' Isidore says. 'That was the *second* stupidest thing you have ever seen?'

'Not exactly.'

'That was good timing,' Isidore says. 'We could have used you at the party last night.'

'We cannot be everywhere. I take it that this foolish pursuit of yours involves the infamous uninvited guest?'

Isidore nods.

'Isidore, I have been meaning to talk to you. To apologise. My judgement after our last case was … harsh. I do feel that you have what it takes to be one of us. I never had any doubts about that. But that does not mean that you *have* to be. You are young. There are other things you can do with your life. Study. Work. Create. Live.'

'Why are we talking about this now?' Isidore asks. He closes his eyes. His head is throbbing: a double dose of the optogenetic weapon in less than a day. The tzaddik's voice sounds hollow and far away.

'Because of this,' the tzaddik says. 'Because you keep getting hurt. And there are more dangerous things than vasilevs out there. Leave the thief to us. Go home. Sort things out with that zoku girl of yours. There is more to life than chasing phantoms and gogol pirates.'

'And why … should I listen to you?'

The tzaddik does not reply. But there is a gentle touch on his cheek, and, suddenly, a light kiss on his forehead, accompanied by an odd sensation of a silver mask flowing aside. The touch is so light and smooth that, for once, Isidore is prepared to admit that Adrian Wu was right. And there is a perfume, smelling faintly of pine—

'I'm not asking you to listen,' the tzaddik says. 'Just be careful.'

The kiss burns on his forehead when he opens his eyes. Suddenly, there is a bustle of activity and voices around him: Resurrection Men and red-and-white medical Quiet. But the tzaddik is gone. Lights flash in Isidore's eyes again, and he closes his eyes. *Like fireworks,* he thinks. And with that, just before the dark, comes a question.

How did the tzaddik know about the fireworks?

15

THE THIEF AND THE GODDESS

Mieli and I stare at the stranger. He gets up, putting on his jacket. 'Would either of you like a drink?' He walks to the fabber and fills his glass. 'I'm afraid I went ahead and helped myself while I was waiting. I understand you are celebrating, and no wonder.' He takes a sip. 'That was quite a little coup you pulled. We followed it with interest.'

Come on, I nudge Mieli. *You can take this guy. Let's make him talk.*

Mieli gives me a strange look.

The man nods at Mieli. 'Thank you for the invitation, by the way. My associates and I appreciate directness.' He drops his cigar into his glass: it goes out with a hiss. 'But where are my manners? Please.' He gestures at the couch. 'Do have a seat.'

I grab Mieli's shoulder. *Invitation?* She shakes me off. *Later.* The Oortian singer from the Red Silk Scarf is gone, and her features are flint-hard again. Recognising that she is not in the mood to argue, I sit next to her. The man perches on the edge of the table, raising his eyebrows.

'By the way, Jean, I'm surprised. Back in the old days, you

would have been much more direct. You would not have waited for someone to die voluntarily, you would have made bodies where you needed them. You must be getting soft.'

'I'm an artist,' I say. 'Bodies do not make good art. I'm sure I would have told you that even in the old days, M.?'

'My apologies,' he says. 'I'm not wearing my own body. This young man came back from Quiet earlier this morning, and I appropriated it for the purpose of having this meeting to avoid any ... temptations to cause me harm.' He takes out another cigar, wets its tip in his mouth and smells it. 'Besides, it is nice to try on something new every once in a while. You can call me Robert. We have met before, although I understand you may not recall it. And we have both moved on in our careers since. I have become ... one of the enlightened individuals your friends the tzaddikim call cryptarchs, whereas you, apparently, became a prisoner.'

Robert the cryptarch lights the cigar and puffs on it. The tip glows red. 'Makes you wonder about karma, doesn't it? I'm thinking that should be a feature in the next-generation resurrection system.'

'What do you want?' I ask.

He raises his eyebrows. 'Well, now. Your associate here had a very interesting proposition. Perhaps the lady wants to repeat it for your benefit.'

Mieli looks at me. The light makeup she is wearing looks odd in the harsh light of the room: it makes her look like a corpse.

'You stop interfering with our work,' Mieli says, 'and we give you the tzaddikim.'

'It's tempting, isn't it?' says Robert.

The rage wells up in my chest, hot bile and brimstone. The alcohol does not help. I take a deep breath and squeeze it in, making a mental fist to hold it, saving it for later. I smile at the cryptarch.

'You know, Jean, we have been watching you since you came. For a professional, you were quite conspicuous. We still remember the last time. You did not make any friends here. Such a shame: we go back such a long way. But then loyalty was never one of your strong points. Just look at what happened with that Raymonde girl.'

I stop myself from rising to the bait. 'So why all the pussyfooting around? Gogol pirates, the Unruh letter—' Something flashes in his eyes: he tries to hide it with gevulot hastily, but it fails. *He does not know about the letter.* He waves his cigar dismissively.

'Just a little game to spice things up. We are old and get bored easily. But now it is time to get down to business. The answer to your offer is no.'

Mieli frowns. 'Why?'

I answer for him. 'Because you already know who the tzaddikim are. One of them is yours, maybe more. They have all been Quiet. And they are convenient. They keep the streets clean.'

'They are flashy and ineffectual and sometimes a little annoying, but yes, they help us to deal with the small problems. But that is not the point. Jean, I always loved the way you are so quick to see everybody else as monsters. We *agree* with the tzaddikim. We *want* this place to be free and special and safe, a good place to live free from the burden of past sins.' He shakes his head. 'It's not the tzaddikim we have a problem with, it's who's behind them. And we want to feed them a little misinformation.'

'The zoku colony,' I say.

'I'm glad you take an interest in our local politics.' He

takes a small object from his pocket: a round, egglike thing that looks like a zoku jewel. 'There is a little co-memory that comes with it, prepared for your tzaddikim friends – something that you could have plausibly discovered in your little exercise with M. Unruh, but more useful to our purposes.'

'That's it?' Mieli asks.

'Of course not.' The cryptarch grins again, teeth stained by cigar juices, an old man's grimace in a young man's face. 'Of course it's not enough. Jean, we want *our share*.'

'What?'

'We let you leave here all those years ago. You were going to come back. You were going to share all your offworld treasures with us. Remember that? Of course you don't.' Robert shakes his head. 'You really should not have come back. We have had a long time to think about the bad old days.'

He gets up. 'Here is our offer. One: you deliver this to the tzaddikim, with conviction. Two: whatever data crumbs you dug out from that poor boy's mind, you share with us and destroy – we can make arrangements about that later. And three: when you find what you are looking for, we get our cut. With interest. Come on, Jean, don't be greedy. Surely your fabled treasure has enough for all of us.'

'You know what I think?' I say. 'I think you are *bluffing*. I don't think you are nearly as powerful as you claim. I think you are *scared* of what we found. And you should be. The answer is—'

Mieli freezes my body. It feels like a cold hammer blow to the head.

'Yes,' Mieli says. I want to throw my hands up and scream and jump up and down, but I can't shake her mental kung fu grip. I can only watch helplessly when the cryptarch bows to Mieli.

'My employer recognises you as valuable allies,' she says. 'We will share some of our … findings with you, as a token of good faith. And she will consider what she can do to help with your zoku issue.'

'Delightful,' Robert says. 'I'm glad we understand each other. A pleasure doing business with you.' He leans on his knees and pats me on the cheek, sharply. 'Looks like the lady has you under her heel, Jean. But then, that was always the way with you and women, wasn't it?'

Mieli escorts him out while I sit still like a statue, pounding my temples with imaginary fists of rage.

'I can't believe we are doing this!' I shout at Mieli. 'You want to *work* with them? What happened to vows? Your *koto's* honour? The tzaddikim are the *good guys*.'

'He did have a point,' Mieli says. 'It's not our place to judge.'

'Hell it isn't.' I pace around, stop and press my forehead against the window to cool it. 'And you forget something. They know *me*. That makes them bad guys *by definition*. We can't trust them.'

'It's not about trust,' Mieli says. 'We will wait until we recover your memories before doing anything.'

'And what if something goes wrong with that? What if the tzaddikim won't buy it? What if Raymonde—' I grit my teeth. 'This is a huge mistake.'

'It is not your call to make,' Mieli says. 'We have a job to do, and it's my job to decide what the best way to do it is.'

'You know,' I say, 'for a moment back there I thought you actually had some *humanity*.' I try to stop the words but they come out like bullets from a machine gun. 'But the Sobornost got into you. They have turned you into a robot. That singing – that was just the tune in a music box. A recording. A gogol.' I clench my hands into fists. 'I was in the Prison for an eternity. But they never broke me. What did whatever bastard it is you serve do to you?'

I take the half-empty glass that the cryptarch left, with the cigar stub floating in it. 'Here. This is what it tastes like.' I take a swig and spit it out to the floor. 'Like ashes.'

Mieli's expression does not change. She turns to leave. 'I have work to do,' she says. 'I am going to study the Unruh data. We need insurance in case there is a problem.'

'There *is* a problem,' I say. 'My glass is empty. I'm going to get drunk.'

'Enjoy,' Mieli says coolly. 'If you try to contact your tzaddik friend, I will know. It will not go well for you.'

Bitch. Everything feels heavy. I am trapped. I curse my old self for the hundredth time, for making such a mess of things when there are perfectly straightforward ways to hide treasure, like burying it in a hole in the ground. Bastard.

Idiot, says a voice in my head. *There is always a way out. No prison, except in your mind.*

'Wait,' I tell Mieli. She looks at me like she looked at me on the ship on the first day after the Prison, full of disgust.

'Let me talk to him. Her. It,' I say.

'What?'

'Let me talk to your employer. I know you are in touch. Let's settle this. If we are going to do things your way, I want to hear it from the organ-grinder and not the monkey.'

Her eyes flash. 'You dare to—'

'Go ahead. Shut me down. Send me back to hell. I don't care. I've been there already. I just want to say my piece. And then I'll be a good boy.' I swallow the rest of the foul, ashy liquid. 'I promise.'

We stare at each other. Her pale green gaze does not flinch. But after a moment, she brushes her scar. 'Fine,' she says. 'You asked for it.'

She sits down on the couch and closes her eyes. When she opens them, she is someone else.

It is like she is wearing a mask. She looks older, and composed, not the warrior-like ascetic stillness, but someone who is used to being looked at and in control. And there is a serpent in her smile.

'Jean, Jean, Jean,' she says, in a musical voice that is hauntingly familiar. 'What are we going to do with you, my little flower prince?'

Then she gets up, wraps her arms around my neck and kisses me.

Mieli is a prisoner in her own body. She wants to close her eyes, but can't; wants to pull away from the thief, but can't. She can smell the foul liquor in his breath. She can see where this is going to go, and suddenly there is nothing funny about it.

'Help me,' she tells *Perhonen* soundlessly. 'Get me out of here.'

Poor baby. Here. Suddenly, comforting, cool blackness surrounds her. Whatever subroutine her mind has been demoted to, at least the ship still has access to it.

'What is she *doing*?'

Mysterious ways and all that, the ship says. *Are you all right?*

'No.' Bodiless, voiceless, Mieli wants to cry. 'He was right, I was wrong. But there was no choice, was there?'

No, there wasn't. What the goddess there says, goes, and that's the way it is, for now. I'm so sorry.

'And I broke vows. I need to beg Ilmatar's forgiveness.'

I'm sure she is understanding, as goddesses go. I'm sure you'll do better with her than with the other one. Don't worry. She and the thief deserve each other.

The voice of the ship is soothing and calm. 'That's right,' Mieli says. 'Besides, don't we have work to do?'

Indeed.

Suddenly, the blackness around Mieli is no longer empty. She is in a datascape, vast and complex. It whispers to her, explaining itself: two vast trees of nodes and lines, superimposed, representing the two versions of Christian Unruh's encrypted mind and memory.

Kissing Mieli's body is like finally kissing that old friend you have always had sexual tension with. Except the kiss is nothing like I imagined: there is a ferocity and strength to it that takes my breath away. And, of course, she is much stronger than I am: I have to turn my head away to come up for air.

'Who are you?' I manage, out of breath.

She lets herself fall back onto the couch pillows, laughing like a little girl. Then she spreads her arms along the back and crosses her legs.

'Your benefactor. Your liberator. Your goddess. Your mother.' She sees my horrified expression and laughs even louder. 'I am *joking*, darling. Although you could call me your *spiritual* mother. I taught you a lot of things a long time ago.' She pats the pillow next to her. 'Now sit down.'

Somewhat gingerly, I obey.

She runs her fingers down my cheek and to my open shirt collar, sending cold waves through me. 'In fact, we should find out if you still remember them.' She kisses my neck, hard, nibbling at my skin, and I find it difficult to focus on my rage. I tense.

'Relax. You like this body, I know you do. And I made sure yours is ... receptive.' She whispers the last words, and her hot breath on my skin turns the anger into something else. 'When you live a very long time, you become a connoisseur in all things. Especially those you get to sample seldom. Sometime, when this is over, I will show you how to live. These things are so heavy and clumsy: we can do better in the *guberniyas*. But it's fun, don't you think?' She bites my earlobe, hard, and flinches.

'Oh, this silly biot feed. Poor Mieli, so paranoid. I am going to turn it off. You are not going to go anywhere, are you?'

'No,' I breathe. 'But we need to talk.'

'Talk can come after. Don't you think so too?'

And, God help me, I do.

Bear in mind I don't understand all of this, Perhonen says. *But the mathematics gogols do. This is one of the root nodes of his gevulot tree.* To Mieli, the complex data structures look like the incomprehensible visions one has in the *alinen*. Her viewpoint hovers over an intersection of innumerable lines, connecting in a sphere full of symbols and three-dimensional sections of a brain. *The changes took place here, here and here.* The objects inside the sphere change colour. Mieli touches the sphere to absorb the information and considers it for a moment.

'It's his procedural memory,' she says. 'So in a certain situation, it would trigger him to act in a certain way. For example, voting for the Voice.'

Yes. There are other changes too, here and there, but nothing major. Now, the interesting thing is that we can actually trace where the edit came from.

260

The ship highlights one of the lines connecting to the node they are viewing. There is additional information attached to it as well: complex mathematical formulae. *The way gevulot works is by generating a tree of public and private key pairs: a new pair is generated whenever the user has a new memory, domain or experience they want to specify gevulot rights for. They are also encrypted with the pair above them in the hierarchy. The point is that only the individual is supposed to have access to the root.*

'Except that—'

Except that it looks like all the roots are also generated from another pair. A master key, if you like. Whoever holds those is able to access every exomemory in the Oubliette, and to rewrite them. For people who pass through Quiet, that means their entire mind. That's where these new edits to Unruh's mind came from. The cryptarchs must have some sort of automated system that modifies everybody who passes through the Quiet.

'Mother Ilmatar,' Mieli breathes. 'So potentially—'

—if they want, they can view and change every memory and thought of anyone who has been a Quiet. Of course, that is too much information for any one person to keep track of, so I assume they have some mechanical ways of augmenting it. Given the minor edits they have made to Unruh's mind, I would imagine that they only have limited resources to do this.

But the bottom line is, the Oubliette is not a place of forgetting. It's not a privacy heaven. It's a panopticon.

It has been a long time. So at first, everything is a hot fast blur of flesh and skin and mouths and touches and bites. She is much stronger than me, and not afraid to show it. She plays with Mieli's enhancements too, teasing me with a hot q-dot at her fingertip, grinning like a cat.

By the third time, we discover that her wings are touch-sensitive, and that's when things get really interesting.

'So what can we do with this?'

Well, we can't do anything about the root access. But — the gogols say — we can put another encryption layer on top of all that. With the pirate engines, we can make fake Oubliette identities. We made a few of those with keys that did not come from the Oubliette key generator interface.

'And?'

Well, that allowed us to make co-memories that the cryptarchs will never have access to. Anyone we share those with will be inoculated against any manipulation by the cryptarchs, passing through Quiet or otherwise. It's viral: you can pass it on to as many people as you want. And we made another that makes you forget the edits that have already been made. In fact, the thief suggested publishing them through a newspaper—

'Wait. The thief suggested what?'

Yes, we had this conversation already. While you were singing. It really did not take that long for the maths gogols to come up with all this.

'He knows about this already? Does he have the co-memories?'

Yes. The ship pauses. *He played me, didn't he? Bastard.*

Mieli lets it sink in. 'Yes. Yes, he did. And I think someone else is about to be played too.'

It is early morning before we stop to rest. At some point, we made it to my bedroom. I lean back on the pillows, eyes half-closed, and look at her, reclining on the other side of the bed, naked apart from her temporary Watch, wings still half-open, catching the light of the dawn.

'I *did* teach you well, didn't I?' she says.

'You did. Were we ... you know, alone?'

'Oh, you are worried about hurting poor little Mieli's feelings? How nice of you to get attached to her. I admit I'm a little sentimental about her as well. It's like having a favourite pen or a lucky charm.' She stretches. Even the scar looks different on her face, more mischievous. 'But don't worry, she is with the ship. We are all alone. I have you all to myself. I should have done this sooner, but there are only so many of me, you know.'

'It's hard to believe that I don't remember you,' I say. 'Except – when I came out from the Prison, there was a flash. Another prison, on Earth. I was reading a book—'

'That was the first time we met,' she says. 'You were a street apache, back then, in the big city, with desert sand between your toes. So rough, so brave. And look at you now. A diamond. Or you will be one again soon. And then—' she smiles – 'and then you can thank me properly.'

'You heard what I told Mieli, right?' I say. 'I don't approve of what you are doing with the cryptarchs.'

She waves her hand. 'Nonsense. Jean, you don't know *anything* about what is really going on here. They have done a good job with this place. The Oubliette *works*. They are happy here. Even *you* thought you were happy here when you came here, last time.' She looks at me, with a hint of poison in her eyes. 'I think your idealism has less to do with politics than with a desire to impress that freckle-faced little bitch.'

'A prison is a prison even if you don't know it is one,' I say. 'And I have a problem with prisons.'

'Poor baby. I know you do.'

'And do you know what else I have a problem with?

Breaking promises.' I swallow. 'I know I owe you. And I will pay my debt no matter what. But I'm not going to go back on my word, not even for you.'

'And how are you going to keep your promises, my little flower prince?'

'Well,' I say. 'I promised to be a good boy. So I'm going to start by getting arrested.'

'What?'

'You know that q-spider I made? The time-stealing trick? Well, I made two.' I look at my Watch. 'This would never have worked on Mieli: I have to say it seems she knows me much better than you do. And you were much more susceptible to certain ... distractions: you should have seen the charm I turned on her last night, with no results. But you? You are about to run out of Time.'

She moves, faster than I can see. Her knee presses painfully in my stomach. Her hands are around my throat. Her face is a mask of rage. I can't breathe. I can see the dial of her Watch, ticking towards zero—

'I'm – going to—' she screams.

There is a little brass *ting* from her Watch. She becomes a black, still statue. Whatever you say about Oubliette technology, the temporary gevulot system they give visitors is pretty good, almost like military-grade utility fog. You don't go to the Quiet, but it cuts you off from the rest of the world, shuts your vital functions down. Her grip on my throat loosens and she topples off the bed, a winged statue of black marble, unmoving.

I shower and get dressed, whistling to myself. Down at the hotel lobby, I tip my hat to the white-uniformed immigration official and the two large Quiet with him: I love it when civil servants do their jobs efficiently.

Outside, it is going to be a beautiful day. I put on my blue-tinted glasses and go looking for Raymonde.

16

THE THIEF AND MEMORY

I send Raymonde a co-memory to meet me at the park, on our vantage point near Montgolfiersville. The reply comes quickly: I remember she will be there. I make my way through the Maze in a full gevulot wrapping, hoping that *Perhonen*'s new anti-cryptarch co-memory will do its job according to plan.

She is there before me, sitting on our bench with a temp-matter coffee cup, watching the balloons. She raises her eyebrows when she sees I'm alone.

'Where is your Oortian chaperone? If you think this is going to be another one of your romantic encounters—'

'Ssh.' I flick the viral co-memory at her. She accepts it and wrinkles her nose. Her expression changes from a frown to pain to astonishment. *Good. It worked.* The only side effect I noticed was the lingering bad smell.

'What the *hell* was that?' She blinks. 'I have a headache now.'

In words and co-memories, I fill her in on the results of the Unruh operation, the visit from the cryptarchs and my disagreement with Mieli's employer – although I leave out a few more intimate details about the latter.

'You did this?' she says. 'I never thought you would—'

'You can do whatever you want with it,' I say. 'Stage a revolution. Give them to the other tzaddikim as a weapon. I don't care. We don't have a lot of time. When Mieli comes back online, she is going to shut me down: if you have any pull with the immigration Quiet, please try to get them to slow the process down. I need to find my secrets before that.'

She looks down. 'I don't know where they are.'

'Oh.'

'I was bluffing. I was angry. I wanted to show you … what I had become. That I had moved on. And I wanted some leverage.'

'I understand.'

'Jean, you are a bastard. You will always be a bastard. But you did good this time. I don't know what else to say.'

'You can let me remember being a bastard,' I say. 'All of it.'

She takes my hand. 'Yes,' she says.

They are her memories, not mine. But when she opens her gevulot, something *clicks*. It is as if a flower opens in my head, fed by what she is giving, blooming, growing; parts of me joining with parts of her, making something more. A shared secret, hidden from the Archons.

Mars, twenty years ago. I am tired. There is a weight that comes from years and transformations, from being a man and a gogol and a zoku member and a copyfamily, from living in one body, many bodies, in particles of thinking dust; from stealing jewels and minds and quantum states and worlds from diamond brains. I am a shadow, thin, faded, stretched.

The Oubliette body I wear makes things simpler, a

heartbeat in unison with the ticking of a Watch, making things delightfully finite. I walk along Persistent Avenue and listen to human voices. Everything feels new again.

A girl sits on a park bench, looking at light dancing among the balloons of Montgolfiersville. She is young, and has a look of wonder on her face. It looks like a reflection. I smile at her. And, for some reason, she smiles back.

It is hard to forget what you are, even with Raymonde. Her friend Gilbertine gives her lover a look that I want to steal. Raymonde finds out. She leaves me, and goes back to her slowtown.

I follow her, to Nanedi City, where white houses climb up the sides of the valley like a smile. I ask for forgiveness. I beg. She doesn't listen.

So I tell her about the secrets. Not all of them, just enough that she understands the weight. I tell her I don't want them anymore.

And she forgives.

But it still isn't enough. The temptation is there, always, to take on a different form, to escape.

My friend Isaac tells me about memory palaces and the nine Dignities of God.

I make a memory palace of my own. It is not just a mental space to store memorised images. My secrets are heavier than that. Hundreds of years of life. Artifacts stolen from the Sobornost and the zokus, minds and lies and bodies and tricks.

I craft it from buildings and human beings and entangled qubits; out of the fabric of the City itself. And most of all, my friends. They are all so trusting, so open, so accepting. They suspect nothing, not even when I give them custom-made Watches, my nine Dignities. I fill their exomemories with things that belong to me. I put picotech assemblers stolen from Sobornost in nine buildings, to remake it all if I need to.

I lock the palace behind me, thinking I will never visit it again. I lock it twice: once with a key, once with a price.

I give the key to Raymonde. And for a time, I am light and free and young again. Raymonde and I build a life. I design buildings. I grow flowers. I am happy. We are happy. We make plans.

Until the Box.

I sit down. I touch my face. It feels wrong, like a mask: there is another countenance underneath, another life. For a moment, I want to scratch it until the false layer falls away.

Raymonde looks different too. Not just the freckled girl with music sheets, not the Gentleman. There is a halo of memories around her, ghosts of a thousand moments. And awareness that she is not mine anymore.

'What happened?' I ask. 'To you, to them?'

'What happens to people? They live. They move on. They go to the Quiet. They come back. They make themselves into something new.'

'I didn't remember any of them. Isaac. Bathilde. Gilbertine. Marcel. Everyone else,' I say. 'I didn't remember you. I made myself forget. So if I get caught, no one would ever find you.'

'I like to think that's why you did it,' Raymonde says. 'But I know you too well. Don't try to fool yourself. You escaped. You saw something you wanted more than you wanted us.'

She smiles, sadly. 'Were we really such a bear trap that you had to cut us all off?'

'I don't know. I really don't.'

Raymonde sits down next to me. 'For what it's worth, I believe you.' She looks at the balloon houses. 'It was difficult after you left. I found someone else, for a while. That didn't help. I went to an early Quiet, for a while. That helped, a little. But when I came back, I was still angry. The Silence showed me I could be angry at something useful.'

She covers her mouth with a hand, eyes closed. 'I don't care what your Oort woman wants you to steal for her,' she says. 'You already did you worst. You stole what could have been. From me and from yourself. And you can never have it back.'

'You didn't tell me what happened to—' I begin.

'Don't,' she says. 'Just don't.'

We sit quietly for a while, watching the balloon houses. I have a crazy thought about cutting their tethers so they could float up to the pale Martian sky. *But you can't live in the sky.*

'I have your key,' Raymonde says. 'Do you still want it?'

I laugh. 'I can't believe I already held it in my hands.' I close my eyes. 'I don't know. I need it. I have a debt to pay.'

A part of me wants it more than anything. But there is the price. *Lives of half-remembered strangers. Why should I care?*

'You said something when you gave it to me. "Tell me to go see Isaac." So I'm telling you.'

'Thank you.' I get up. 'I'm going to go and do that.'

'All right. I'm going to go and talk to the Silence and the others. Let me know what you decide when you're done. If you still want it, you only have to ask.'

'You might have to rewrite that opera when you're done,' I say.

She kisses me on the cheek. 'I'll see you soon.'

Isaac lives alone in a small Maze tower apartment. I send him an anonymous co-memory to expect a visitor, and get an answer that he is home. When he opens the door, he frowns: but as I open my gevulot, his bearded face lights up.

'Paul!' He grabs me in a rib-crushing bear hug. Then he grabs the front of my coat and shakes me, up and down. 'Where have you been?' he bellows. I can feel the rumble inside his broad chest.

He drags me bodily inside and tosses me onto a couch like a rat. 'What the hell are you doing here? I thought you were Quiet, or eaten by the damn Sobornost!'

He rolls up the sleeves of his flannel shirt, revealing thick hairy arms, puffing. There is a thick brass Watch around one massive wrist. Seeing it makes me flinch, even if the word engraved on it is hidden.

'If you are here to mess with Raymonde again—' he says.

I lift my hands up. 'I'm innocent. I'm here on … business. But I wanted to see you.'

'Hrmph.' He grunts, looking at me suspiciously from beneath thick eyebrows. Then he grins, slowly. 'All right. Let's drink.'

He marches across the room, kicking at some of the debris on the floor – books, clothes, tempmatter sheets, notepads – and makes his way to his small kitchen. The fabber begins to gurgle. I look around the apartment. A guitar hanging from the wall, animated wallpapers with children's cartoon characters in them, high bookshelves, a desk covered in a perpetual snowfall of e-paper.

'This place hasn't changed at all,' I say.

Isaac returns with a tempmatter bottle of vodka. 'Are you

kidding? It's only been *twenty years*. Spring cleaning is every forty.' He takes a swig from the bottle, then pours each of us two fingers in two glasses. 'And I've only been married twice in that time.' He holds up his glass. 'Here's to women. Don't talk to me about business. It's women who brought you here.'

I say nothing and clink my glass against his. We both drink. I cough. He laughs, a rough, booming sound.

'So, am I going to have to kick your ass or did Raymonde do it already?' he asks.

'Over the last few days, people have been queueing for the position.'

'Well, that's as it should be.' He pours more vodka into the glasses in a liberal waterfall that doesn't spare the floor. 'Anyway, I should have known that you were coming when the dreams started again.'

'The dreams?'

'Puss-in-boots. Castles. I always suspected you had something to do with them.' He folds his arms. 'Anyway, it doesn't matter. Have you come back to find true happiness with your true love?'

'No.'

'Well, that's good, because it's *too late*. Idiot. I could see it coming, I have to say. You were always restless. Never happy with anything. Even Raymonde.' He squints at me. 'You are not going to tell me where you went, are you?'

'No.'

'Doesn't matter. It's good to see you. It's been a dull world without you.' Our glasses clink again.

'Isaac—'

'Are you going to say something mushy?'

'No.' I can't help laughing. I feel like I haven't been away at all. I can imagine the afternoon running down a stream of vodka, sitting here and talking and drinking until Isaac starts reading his poetry and arguing about theology and talking endlessly about women, daring me to interrupt. I can't think of anything I'd rather do.

And that, of course, is the price.

'I'm sorry,' I say and put my glass down. 'I really have to go.'

He looks at me. 'Is everything all right? That's a queer look you've got.'

'It's fine. Thanks for the drink. I'd stay longer, but—'

'Phh. So it *is* a woman. It's nothing. I'll have this place tidied up by the time you come next time.'

'I'm sorry,' I say.

'About what? It's not my business to judge what you do. Enough people around throwing stones.' He claps my shoulder. 'Go on. Bring me an offworld girl next time. Green skin would be good. I like green.'

'Doesn't it say something about that in the Torah?' I say.

'I'll take my chances,' Isaac says. '*Shalom.*'

I feel mildly drunk when I find my way to Raymonde's apartment.

'I wasn't expecting you until much, much later,' she says, when she lets me in. I squeeze past the inert synthbio drones that have been fixing the place. Tempmatter coverings hang everywhere, like spiderwebs.

'I'm sorry about the mess,' she says, 'but it's your fault.'

'I know.'

She looks at me sharply. 'So?'

'Let me see it.'

I sit down on a freshly printed, flimsy-looking chair and

wait. Raymonde returns and hands me an object, wrapped in a cloth.

'You never told me what it actually does,' she says. 'I hope you know what you're doing.'

I take the gun out and look at it. It feels heavier than the last time I held it, ugly with its snub barrel and bulbous chamber with the nine bullets, nine dignities of God. I put it in my pocket. 'I need to go and do some thinking,' I tell Raymonde. 'And if I don't see you again – thank you.'

She does not say anything and looks away.

I close the door behind me and take the elevator back to the street level. I feel an odd tingling in my gevulot, and suddenly there is someone walking with me down the Avenue, a dark-haired young man wearing a dashing suit, matching my step. His face is mine, but his easy smile is not. I gesture him to lead on and follow.

Interlude
VIRTUE

Gilbertine dreams about the puss-in-boots again. It is a streaky tom on two legs, wearing a flamboyant hat and heavy boots. It leads her through marble-and-gold corridors of a palace, with rows of doors on both sides. One door is open.

'What is in there?' she asks the cat. It looks up at her with strange, glittering eyes. 'You will know,' it says, in a high-pitched quivering voice, 'when the master comes back.'

She wakes up in her Montgolfiersville apartment, next to the warm, snoring body of her latest lover, whose name is already fading from her memory. Her gevulot contracts are always well-crafted, a minimum of disruption for everybody, leaving only pleasing memories of flesh here and there, hot flushes of emotion associated with tastes and places.

The dreams have been more frequent lately. And her own memories feel loose, uncomfortable. She wonders if she is getting old, not in the old-fashioned way but developing the malady of immortals that Bathilde talks about, being erased and rewritten too many times.

The co-memory message comes when she is in the shower

with her lover, his nameless fingers lathering her back. It is full of sudden anxiety and urgency. *Raymonde.*

She disappears from beneath his touch into a gevulot blur. That was always the plan anyway. She stops only to pick up her Watch from her night table: she hates wearing it when making love. The word *Virtus* engraved on it has always felt too much like a bad joke.

Raymonde waits for her in her Belly apartment. Her face is pale and drawn, and her freckles stand out against her skin.

'What's wrong?' Gilbertine asks.

'Paul. He is gone.'

'What?'

'He is gone. I don't know where he is. I don't know what to do.'

Gilbertine embraces her friend, anger rising inside her. 'Sssh. Don't worry. It's going to be fine.'

'Is it?' Raymonde's shoulders shake. 'How is it going to be fine?'

Because I'm going to find him and make him pay, Gilbertine thinks.

Her gevulot contracts are always well-crafted, even the old ones. And they always have emergency clauses.

To her satisfaction, she actually surprises him. He is in the strange robot garden of the Maze, sitting on a small luggage pod, smiling at empty space. He wears a sleek dark blue full-body garment, zoku style, not quite matter, not quite light. He holds a small box that he keeps turning in his hands, round and round.

When she lets him see her, for a fleeting moment he looks like a frightened little boy. Then he smiles.

'Ah, there you are.' Paul says. But he does not look like

the Paul that Gilbertine remembers, the sometimes foolish, self-centred architect hopelessly in love with her friend. His eyes are clear and emotionless, and the smile playing on his lips is cold. 'Can you remind me what your name is?'

'Don't you remember?'

He spreads his hands. 'I made myself forget,' he says.

Gilbertine takes a deep breath. 'I am Gilbertine Shalbatana. You are Paul Sernine. You loved my friend Raymonde. She is hurting. You need to go back. Or at least have the guts to say goodbye. She already forgave you once.'

She hurls the memory at him, opening her gevulot.

Raymonde introduced them. Raymonde, Gilbertine's comrade-in-arms ever since she came from Nanedi; a slow-town girl in the big city, wanting to make music. Secretly, Gilbertine hated her easy grace, the way things fell into place for her, seemingly without effort. He was one of those things. So of course she wanted him. And making him want things he did not have was not difficult.

But it did not last. He went back to her, content not to even remember who Gilbertine was, chased after Raymonde to Nanedi and back. She accepted it as the way of things. But this, this she won't accept.

Paul looks at her with a detached look on his face. 'Thank you,' he says. 'I didn't have enough from you before.' To her horror, she can feel *something* eating through her gevulot.

'But you are quite right,' Paul says quietly. 'Paul Sernine could never leave. But he is staying here, you see, inside you and the others. Whereas me – there is somewhere else I need to be. Stealing the fire of the gods. Being Prometheus. That sort of thing.'

'I don't care,' Gilbertine says. 'You have a child with that girl.'

He flinches. 'I would have remembered *that*,' he says. 'No, that does not seem right.'

'Damn right it doesn't,' Gilbertine says, filling her voice with as much venom as she can draw from the old hurt.

'You don't understand. I would have not forgotten that.' He shakes his head. 'In any case, it doesn't matter. We are not here to talk about me. This is all about you.'

Gilbertine pulls her shoulders back, reaching for the exomemory. 'You are insane.' A tingling sensation crawls across her scalp, and suddenly there is just a wall where the part of her that is connected to everything else should be. It is like having a phantom limb, trying to convince you that it is not gone, only inside her mind.

Paul stands up. 'I'm afraid I've cut off your exomemory link. Don't worry, you'll get it back in a moment.'

Gilbertine takes a step back. 'What are you?' she hisses. 'A vampire?'

'Not at all,' Paul says. 'Now stay still. This will hurt a little.'

Gilbertine runs. It is hard to think, with the hole inside her head. *The Watch. Whatever he is doing, it must be through the Watch.* She claws at her wrist, to get it off—

—but she is not really running, it's just a *memory* of running, and she is still standing in front of Paul whose eyes look a lot like those of the puss-in-boots—

He holds up the box. 'See? I found out about this from the dreams of a poor boy hurt in the Spike. I took it from the zoku: they will never miss it.'

'What is it?' Gilbertine whispers.

'A trapped god,' Paul says. 'I need to put it somewhere. That's why you are here.'

278

The box starts to glow. It disappears from Paul's hand. And then it is inside her head.

She *remembers* abstract shapes, a data structure like a vast metallic snowflake, sharp edges pressing against the soft parts of her mind. A flood of alien sensations passes through her exomemory. For a moment it is like a hot metal rod being pushed through her temples. Then the pain is gone, but a sense of weight remains.

'What did you do to me?'

'The same thing I did to all of you. Put things in a place where no one will look for them. In your exomemories, protected by the best cryptography in the System. In a place that will claim a price if I want them back. That was the last thing I had to dispose of. I am sorry about the discomfort. I hope you can forgive me.' The not-Paul sighs. 'For what it's worth, your Paul had nothing to do with this.'

'I don't believe you,' Gilbertine says. 'It's not all about memory. A part of you is Paul, no matter who you think you are, no matter what you have done to your brain, no matter if he was just a mask you wore. And I hope he burns in hell.' She wants to claw at his face. But the faint foglet halo around whatever the creature wearing Paul's shape tells her that violence would be useless.

'I'm sorry you feel that way,' he says. 'I can't let you remember any of this, of course. I hope you can comfort Raymonde in some way.'

'Do what you want to my memory,' she says. 'I'm going to make sure she hates you forever.'

'Perhaps I deserve that,' he says. 'Goodbye.'

He touches her forehead, and a wind blows through her mind—

*

Gilbertine blinks at the bright Phobos light. She is standing alone in the robot garden. She feels disoriented, and it takes a few moments to remember meeting Raymonde. What did she do after that? She 'blinks at the last few minutes, but finds them empty. *Damn. Must be another Spike legacy glitch.*

For some reason, she remembers the dream she had last night: a puss-in-boots, a closed door. Did she have a dream?

For a moment, she considers 'blinking the dream, too, but decides against it. There is too much to do in the waking world.

17

THE DETECTIVE AND THE GORDIAN KNOT

It takes Isidore the rest of the day to recover. The Quiet medics refuse to let him go before he is pumped full of synth-bio nanodocs. His thoughts are a confused jumble, racing in all directions at once: but when he gets home, the exhaustion takes over and he collapses in his bed. He wakes up late after a long, dreamless sleep.

Frustratingly, rest does not offer any solutions, so he sits at the breakfast table for a long time, staring at the world through the kitchen window, trying to grasp where everything belongs, where the seams are, where everything fits together: the tzaddik, the thief, Time, the memory palaces. The wallpapers are a complex Escheresque jungle again, garish in the bright, mixed daylight. His thoughts are interrupted by a cheerful gevulot request.

'Good morning,' Lin says.

'Hnnh,' Isidore grunts. His roommate is wearing a more careful attire than usual, jewellery glinting in her ears. She smiles at Isidore and starts making breakfast with the fabber, a Spanish omelette.

'Coffee and sustenance?' she asks.

'Yes, please.' Isidore realises that he is starving. The hot food restores some of his fortitude. 'Thank you.'

'Don't mention it. You look like you need it.'

'You know, I gave your creature a name,' Isidore says, between mouthfuls.

'What did you call him?'

'Sherlock.'

She laughs. 'That's a good name. Do I dare to ask how the detective business is going? You were in the *Herald* again. Parties, thieves and death. You have an exciting life, M. Beautrelet.'

'Well.' Isidore massages his temples. 'It has its ups and downs. Right now, I don't really know what I'm doing. It is all very confusing. I can't figure out what this thief is doing, or if he is really a thief in the first place.'

Lin gives his arm a little squeeze. 'You'll figure it out, I'm sure.'

'What about you? Did something happen? You look … different.'

'Well,' Lin says, running a finger along the wood grains of the table surface. 'I met someone.'

'Oh.' There is an odd twinge of disappointment that should not be there. He ignores it. 'That's great.'

'Who knows? We'll see how it goes. It's kind of been there for a while, you know, and we just … decided to stop stepping around it.' She grins. 'But I'm hoping it'll last long enough that we can have some sort of party here. If you could bring your girlfriend over, we could all cook together. Or do zoku people eat? Just a thought.'

'It's a little bit complicated at the moment,' Isidore says. 'I'm not sure I can exactly call her my girlfriend anymore.'

'I'm sorry to hear that,' Lin says. 'It's funny, no matter how smart you are, these things always get so tangled. I think after a while you just have to treat it like a Gordian knot. One cut, that's it, and it's open. Not so complicated anymore.'

Isidore looks up and stops chewing. 'You know what? You are a genius.' He swallows, gulps down the rest of his coffee and runs to his room, grabbing his coat. He pats Sherlock on the head and rushes to the door.

'Where are you going?' Lin shouts.

'To find somebody with a sword,' Isidore says.

The zoku colony is strangely forbidding this time. The glass cathedral's points, edges and protrusions look sharp. Isidore stands at the gates, trying to decide what to do.

'Hello?' he says. But nothing happens. *How is this supposed to work again? Just think, Pixil said.*

He touches the cold surface of the door and imagines Pixil's face. His fingers tingle. The reply is sudden and violent, much harsher than ever with the entanglement ring.

Go away. It comes with a sensation that is like a physical blow, a stinging slap on the cheek.

'Pixil.'

I don't want to talk to you right now.

'Pixil, can we meet? It's important.'

Important things have an expiry date. Like me. I have things to do.

'I'm sorry I haven't been in touch. Things have been a little insane. Can you let me in or come out and meet me? It won't take long, I promise.'

I'm supposed to go on a raid in twenty minutes. I'll give you ten. Now get out of the way.

'What?'

Get out of the way!

Something big comes through the door. The surface shimmers and ripples. Pixil is astride a massive black creature, like a six-legged horse but larger, covered in gold and silver plates, with bloodshot eyes and white, sharp teeth. She is wearing elaborate armour with wide shoulderplates like a samurai's, and a ferocious mask pushed up to her forehead. A sword hangs at her side.

The creature snorts and snaps at Isidore, sending him scrambling backwards. He backs up against a pillar. Pixil dismounts and pats the creature's neck. 'It's all right,' she says. 'You have met Cyndra already.'

The epic mount lets out a bellow that stinks of rotting meat and rings in Isidore's eardrums.

'I know we are in a hurry,' Pixil tells the creature, 'but you don't have to eat him. I can handle him all by myself.' It turns around and vanishes through the doors.

'Sorry about that,' Pixil says. 'Cyndra wanted to come along to tell you what she thought of you.'

'I see,' Isidore says. His knees feel weak, and he sits down on the steps. Pixil crouches down next to him, armour clinking.

'So, what is this about?' she asks.

'I have been thinking,' Isidore says.

'Really?'

He gives her a reproachful look.

'I'm allowed to tease you,' she says. 'That's how these things work.'

'All right.' He swallows. It is difficult to say the words. They are jagged, awkwardly shaped things in his mouth. He remembers reading about Demosthenes, the great orator who practised speaking while chewing on small rocks. He bites down on them and speaks.

'It's not going to work. Us,' he says, and pauses for a moment. She says nothing.

'I've been with you because you are different,' he says. 'I couldn't read you. I couldn't understand you. It was fun for a while. But it was never going to be any different.

'And I never put you first. You were always just ... the other thing. The distracting voice in my head. And I don't want to think of you like that. You deserve better.'

She looks at him, face grim, but then he realises it is just mock seriousness. 'That's what you came to tell me? That's what it took you all this time to figure out? All by yourself?'

'Actually,' he says, 'Sherlock helped.' She gives him a curious look. 'Never mind.'

Pixil sits down next to Isidore, rests her sword on one of the steps and leans on it.

'I have been thinking too,' she says. 'I think the thing I like best about you is that you drive the elders up the wall. It's fun to watch. And not having any entanglement between us, no strings. And being with someone who is a little slow, like you.' She sticks her tongue out at him and brushes a lock of hair off his forehead. 'Dim but pretty.'

Isidore takes a short, sharp breath.

'I'm kidding about that last part,' Pixil says. 'Sort of.'

They sit still for a while, side by side.

'See, this wasn't hard,' Pixil says. 'We should have done this ages ago.' She looks at Isidore. 'Are you sad?'

Isidore nods. 'A little bit.'

She hugs him, hard. The armour plates press into Isidore's chest painfully, but he hugs her back anyway.

'All right,' she says and gets up in a clatter of metal. 'There are monsters I need to go and kill. And you have a thief to catch, or so I hear.'

'Yes, about that.'

'Uh huh?'

'Remember when you said that you could tell me who the Gentleman was? Were you kidding about that too?'

'I never kid,' Pixil says, brandishing her sword, 'about matters of love and war.'

Isidore walks to the edge of the Dust District and sends a co-memory to the tzaddik. *I know who you are,* it says. Then he sits on a deck chair in a small square, just near the boundary where the colony begins, where stone becomes diamond.

He closes his eyes and listens to the water. He lets his mind drift with the sound. And suddenly, he feels like the water, flowing over a rock, feeling the shape that has been eluding him. It unfolds in his head like a giant snowflake. And it makes him angry.

There is a gust of wind. He opens his eyes. The Gentleman steps from a heat ripple. For a moment, her foglet aura is visible in the spray of water from the fountain. Her mask glitters in the sun.

'This had better be important,' she says. 'I am very busy.'

Isidore smiles. 'Mme Raymonde, I apologise. But there are things I need to talk to you about.'

The silver mask melts into the freckled face of a red-haired woman as she locks them within a tight gevulot contract. She looks tired. 'All right,' she says, folding her arms. Her real voice is like the ringing of a bell, deep and musical. 'I'm listening. How did you—'

'I cheated,' Isidore says. 'I called in a favour.'

'Pixil, of course. That girl could never keep her mouth shut. I was counting on the fact that you would be too proud to ever ask.'

'There are things more important than pride,' Isidore says. 'Perhaps you don't know me as well as you think.'

'I take it we are not here to admire your cleverness. Nor, apparently, to hear thanks for saving your mind. You are welcome, by the way.' Her voice is cold, and she does not meet his gaze.

'No,' he says. 'We are here to solve a mystery. But I need your help for that.'

'Wait.' She passes him a co-memory. He accepts it, and suddenly remembers a pungent smell that makes him think of the rotten food that his father once left in his studio.

'What was that?' he asks.

'Something that the whole Oubliette will have soon,' she says. 'Continue.'

'I've been thinking about the word *cryptarch* ever since you mentioned it,' Isidore says. 'They manipulate the exomemory, am I right?'

'Yes. We know how it works now: they have a master key of some sort that lets them read anyone who has been a Quiet.'

'And you fight them.'

'Yes.'

'And you have been working with the thief. Jean le Flambeur. Whoever he really is.'

She looks surprised, but nods. 'Yes. But—'

'I'll come to that. What he did to Unruh was *obtaining evidence*, wasn't it? Comparing his mind before and after the resurrection system, to see if it had been changed. You got him to do your dirty work for you. An offworld criminal.'

Raymonde covers her mouth with a fist. 'Yes, yes we did. But you don't understand—'

'Make me understand,' Isidore says. 'Because I know what

he wants. And I can make sure he never gets it. I can let everyone know what you did. So much for trust in the tzaddikim then.'

'Trust,' she says. 'It's not about *trust* anymore. It's about *justice*. We can *beat* them. We finally have a weapon to beat them. All those cases we worked on, gogol pirates, offworld tech – it was all *them*. And they have done worse things, things we don't even know about. Every decision of the Voice. It's not the Revolution dream. We are still slaves.'

She walks to the steps and stands over Isidore. 'It is *still* a game to you. No wonder you got along with the zoku girl so well. Wake up. Yes, you won, you beat me; you worked it out. But the rest of us, we have bigger things to do. Not just another case, but justice, for everyone.'

Her eyes are hard. 'You have never had to fight. You have always been protected. I started to work with you to show you that—' She bites her lip.

'To show me what?' Isidore asks. 'What did you want to show me, mother?'

She still looks like a complete stranger to him. The memories she denied him remain closed.

'I wanted to show you that there were bad people in the world,' she says. 'And to make sure you did not turn out like—' Her voice breaks. 'But in the end, I couldn't see you hurt. So I called it off.'

'I think that people who keep the truth from other people,' Isidore says, 'are no better than the cryptarchs.'

He smiles bitterly. 'You don't know everything about them either. It's not just the Voice they have been manipulating. It's *everything*. It's history. You talk about the Revolution? I think they made it up. Unruh saw it. If you look at it all in detail, it's all fake. He gathered enough to see it. Anyone who remembers the Revolution – it's all from exomemory. You can't trust it, any of it.'

Isidore takes a deep breath. 'I have seen the Kingdom. It took me a long time to realise it, but it's inside a box in the zoku colony. It's a simulation. That's where all the Kingdom memories come from. The buildings, the artifacts – that's all just dressing. So there you go. You work for the zoku; they work for the cryptarchs. So whatever it is you are planning, you are doing it for them.'

He looks at her and thinks about the row of faces on his father's wall. 'So I'm sorry if I take anything you say about the past – or the future, for that matter – with a grain of salt.'

'I was—'

'Protecting me?' Isidore almost spits the word out. 'That's what father wants to believe. Protecting us from what?'

'From your father,' Raymonde says. 'Your real father.' She squeezes her eyes shut. 'Isidore, you said that you know what the thief wants. What is it?'

'You don't know?'

'Tell me.'

'There are nine buildings in the Maze. He designed them, when he was Paul Sernine. They link up to the Atlas Quiet somehow: there is a mechanism that brings them together. He had nine Watches made, they have something to do with it. Like what he did in the underworld, making the Quiet move. The buildings are parts of a machine. I don't know what it does. I think it has something to do with the exomemory—'

'Nine buildings. Oh God.' She grabs Isidore by the shoulders. 'When did you work this out?'

'Just before the gogol pirates attacked—'

'That means,' she says, 'that the cryptarchs know about it too. Something terrible is about to happen. I have to go. We will continue this conversation later. You have to go somewhere safe. The zoku colony is the safest place. Stay there, with Pixil. Things are going to get very ugly here.'

'But—'

'We are not going to argue about this. Go, right now, or I will take you there myself.'

She becomes the Gentleman again and takes to the air before Isidore can answer.

Isidore stares after her for a moment. Then he sits down again. He is used to the ground moving beneath his feet – the constant, gentle sway of the city – but this is like teetering on the brink of a vast chasm that has suddenly opened. He tries to hold on to the shape in his mind, but his heart beats so fast that it is hard to focus—

The earth shakes. There is a terrible grinding sound. The cobblestones in the small square buckle. He falls to the ground, shielding his face with his arms. Vast machines in the underworld are rumbling, and for a moment it feels like the city is a thin layer of life on the rough skin of some huge creature, stirred by a bee sting, shaking itself. Then it is over, as quickly as it began. *The thief's machine.*

Still shaking, Isidore gets up, blinking away the head rush. Then he starts running towards the Maze.

The aftershock echoes through the city. Most of the damage has been cosmetic – the buildings in the city have smart-matter skeletons – but the city has stopped moving. Persistent Avenue is filling with a noisy crowd: the air is full of the restless murmur of thousands of human voices. Something has happened in the Maze: a cloud of dust swirls to the sky above the rooftops. And behind it looms a new structure, a black needle, hundreds of metres high.

Isidore tries to make his way through the throng of the crowd. Gevulot shields are open in the confusion. Everywhere, there are wide-eyed faces, nervous laughter and quiet fear.

'Another damn art project,' says a rough-faced man in a cobweb mask, leaning on his grounded spidercab. 'If you ask me, it's another damn art project.'

'Could you take me up there?' Isidore asks him.

'Not a chance,' the man says. 'The tzaddikim are blocking it off. Look.'

Isidore follows his gaze, and sees a cloud of tzaddikim hovering over the Maze, surrounded by heat haze, creating a shield of some kind.

'They've all gone mad,' the cab driver says. 'Did you see what they did earlier? I got that co-memory of theirs. Tasted foul. And there's another one.'

One of the tzaddikim – the Cockatrice – is hovering above a nearby agora. Her voice seems to come from everywhere, from the air itself.

'Don't trust the Voice!' she says. 'We have been lied to!'

She talks about the cryptarchs, and how the Voice has been manipulated, about the secret rulers. She offers a co-memory that will protect against them. She talks about gogol pirates, evidence of mind manipulation, about the data from Unruh's mind. She says that the tzaddikim will make sure the exomemory remains intact, that the cryptarchs will be found and brought to justice. There are angry mutters in the crowd.

As she talks, Isidore 'blinks at the public exomemory feeds from the Avenue. She is not there in them, just a crowd, listening to empty space.

'Shit,' he says. *They are trying to block it.*

The sudden Voice memory comes with a crushing force and emotion and almost makes him fall to his knees. He remembers that the *tzaddikim are spreading lies* and that *they are agents of the zoku*, and that *the zoku wants to destroy the Oubliette way of life.* The Voice has always been just a suggestion, just a nagging little voice of remembering a to-do list, but this – it's direct, violent, a memory branded into his mind, impossible to ignore. He remembers that *he should go home and use full gevulot privacy until things are back to normal*, and that *any disruption in the city machinery has to do with a mild phoboi infection that is being dealt with.*

He shakes his head. The memories are full of guilt: he wrenches himself away from them as if from quicksand.

'This isn't right,' the cab driver says, massaging his temples. 'This isn't right. I heard what she just said.'

There are shouts. A fight has started on the edge of the agora, a young man in zoku-style clothing being pushed around by a group of men and women in Revolution uniforms. 'Dust-kisser,' they shout. 'Quantum whore.' Ripples of anger and violence are spreading through the crowd. And there is another movement, too, a slow flow of people moving in unison, in silence. A couple with middle-aged bodies passes Isidore. They have a strange, glassy look in their eyes. *She was right*, Isidore thinks. *It is not just a game.*

He shakes the cab driver. 'A megasecond if you get us to the Dust District right now,' he says.

The man blinks. 'Are you crazy? These people are going to go there and tear it apart.'

'Then you better get us there first,' Isidore says.

Then he looks at Isidore, squinting. 'Hey, you are that

tzaddik's sidekick boy, aren't you? Do you know what the hell is going on?'

Isidore takes a deep breath. 'An interplanetary thief is building a picotech machine out of the city itself while the cryptarchs take over people's minds to try to destroy the zoku colony in order to stop the tzaddikim from breaking their power,' he says. 'I want to stop them both.' He pauses. 'Also, I think the thief is my real father.'

The driver stares at him blankly for a second.

'Right on,' he says. 'Get in!'

The spidercab moves like a possessed insect, scampering away from the Avenue and cutting through a part of the Maze, crossing the streets with crazy leaps. The black needle looms over the Maze, and a few tzaddikim still hover around it. The Maze itself has been seized by vast hands and moved around like a child's puzzle: there are collapsed buildings and broken streets. Yellow rescue and medic Quiet are everywhere, but their movements are uncoordinated and confused. There are strange ripples going through the whole exomemory, flashes of *déjà vu*.

The Dust District looks like a snowglobe. It is surrounded by a q-dot bubble that distorts everything inside, making the zoku buildings look elongated and surreal. And everything inside is moving, folding, changing shape.

The mob is marching towards it in the streets below, but it seems likely that their efforts are going to be frustrated. *This can't be what the cryptarchs are planning*, Isidore thinks. *They are not going to get rid of them with just a mob—*

'Well, that's it,' says the driver. 'Do you want me to turn back? We are not going to go through that.'

'Just get me somewhere close.'

The driver sets him down in a side alley, just outside the q-dot field. It looks like a soap bubble, thin but impossibly huge, curving towards the sky like a vertical, iridescent horizon.

'Good luck,' says the driver. 'I hope you know what you are doing.' The cab takes off again, legs striking sparks from the pavement as it leaps up.

Isidore touches the bubble. It feels insubstantial and slick, but the harder he pushes against it, the harder it pushes back. Every push he makes just ends up sliding along its surface. He thinks about Pixil. *Let me in.* But there is no response. 'I want to talk to the Eldest,' he says aloud. 'I know about the Kingdom.'

For a moment, nothing happens. Then the bubble yields under his hand and he almost falls down. He walks through it: it passes over his skin exactly like a soap bubble, wet and tickling.

In the zoku colony, everything is in motion. The diamond buildings are *folding*, becoming smaller, changing shape, as if they were papercraft castles being disassembled and put away. There are zoku creatures everywhere, in a variety of shapes from faces in foglet clouds to green monsters, manipulating matter with gestures.

A man-sized q-dot sphere appears in front of him, like the inverse of a soap bubble popping. Pixil steps out, still wearing her armour and sword. Her face is grim.

'What is happening out there?' she asks. 'Our raid got cancelled. And the whole zoku is getting ready to *leave*. I would have told you, but—' She touches her zoku jewel helplessly.

'I know, I know. Resource optimisation. I think we are about to have a revolution,' Isidore says. 'I need to talk to the Eldest.'

'Oh, good,' Pixil says. 'Perhaps this time you can *really* make her mad.'

The q-dot bubble takes Isidore and Pixil into the treasure cave. It, too, is full of activity: the black cubes rise off the ground and vanish into the portals of silver. The Eldest is in the middle of it, a giant, shimmering female form, serene face surrounded by a circle of floating jewels.

'Young man,' she says. 'You are always welcome to visit us, but I must say you have chosen a particularly bad time.' Her voice is the same as that of the blonde woman Isidore met, deep and warm.

Isidore looks up at the Eldest, summoning all the anger and defiance he can before the posthuman. 'Why did you do it? Why did you help the cryptarchs?'

Pixil stares at him incredulously. 'Isidore, what are you talking about?'

'You know the cryptarchs that the tzaddikim out there have been talking about today? Do you remember that Realm that you said Drathdor whipped up? Well, that *is* the Kingdom. That's where all the memories anyone in the Oubliette has about the Revolution and before come from. Your zoku made that possible.'

'That's not true!' She stares at Isidore, eyes blazing. 'That does not even make sense!' She turns to the Eldest. 'Tell him!'

But the Eldest says nothing.

'You have got to be kidding,' Pixil says.

'We had no choice,' the Eldest says. 'After the Protocol War, we were broken. We needed a place where we could hide from the Sobornost while we healed. We made a deal. It seemed like a small thing: we rewrite our pasts and memories all the time. So we gave them what they wanted.'

Pixil takes Isidore's hand. 'Isidore, I swear I didn't know about this.'

'We made you to be like them, to go among them,' the Eldest says. 'So we couldn't let you know any more than they did.'

'And you just *let them do what they wanted*?' Isidore asks.

'No,' the Eldest says. 'We had some … regrets after we saw what happened. So we created the tzaddikim – gave technology and assistance to young Oubliette idealists. We hoped that they would act as a counterweight. Clearly, we were wrong, and this thief of yours has disrupted things.'

'Tell me one thing,' Isidore says. 'What was this place before?'

The Eldest pauses. An expression of sadness flickers across her serene face.

'Isn't that obvious?' she says. 'The Oubliette was a prison.'

18

THE THIEF AND THE KING

I stand in the robot garden with my old self, weighing the gun in my hand. He is holding it too, or a dream reflection of it. It's strange how it always comes down to two men with guns, real or imaginary. Around us, the slow war of the ancient machines goes on.

'I'm glad you made it,' he says. 'I don't know where you have been. I don't know where you are going. But I know you are here to make a choice. Pull the trigger, and you get to be who we were. Do nothing and – well, you will go on with your life, doing smaller things, dreaming smaller dreams. Or you can go back to listening to the music of the spheres, and the musical sound of breaking their laws. I know what I would do if I were you.'

I open the gun and look at the nine bullets. Each has a name on it, holding a quantum state, entangled with the Time in a person's Watch. Isaac's. Marcel's. Gilbertine's. The others. If I pull the trigger nine times, their Time will run out. The engine will start. Nine people will become Quiet, Atlas Quiet, beneath the city. They will make my memory palace. And I will never see them again.

I close it and spin the chamber, like in Russian roulette. The young me grins. 'Go on,' he says. 'What are you waiting for?'

I throw the gun away. It lands in a rosebush. I look at the empty space where my young self stood. 'Bastard,' I say. 'You knew I'd never do it.'

'That's all right,' says a voice. 'I will.'

The gardener discards his gevulot, holding the gun in his hand. His hair is white, his features carefully aged, but there is something awfully familiar about them. I take a step forward, but a sleek, egg-shaped device – a zoku q-gun – is hovering above his right shoulder, looking at me with a bright quantum eye.

'I wouldn't move,' he says. 'This thing will make a mess of even that fancy Sobornost body of yours.'

I raise my hands slowly.

'Le Roi, I presume?' I say. He smiles, the same smile I saw on the cryptarch in the hotel. 'So, you are the King here?' I calculate my chances of survival if I were to rush him. They are not very high. My body is still locked in its human state, and the five metres between us might as well be a lightyear.

'I prefer to think of myself as just a gardener,' he says. 'Remember Sante Prison, on Earth? What you told your cellmate? That the thing you'd really like to steal was a Kingdom of your own. But ruling it would be too much trouble, much better have someone else be the figurehead, watch its people prosper and be happy, while you weed the garden and give flowers to young girls and give things a little nudge every now and then.' He moves his free hand in a wide arc, encompassing the garden and the city around us. 'Well,

I'm living the dream.' He sighs. 'And like all dreams do, it's getting a little old.'

'Yes, it is,' I say. 'The tzaddikim are about to end it and wake the people up.' I frown. 'We were cellmates?'

He laughs. 'After a fashion. If you want, you can call me le Roi. Jean le Roi, that's what they called me here, although I don't much care for the name anymore.'

I stare at him. Now that his gevulot is open, the resemblance is there.

'What happened?'

'We were careless before the Collapse,' he says. 'And why not? We worked with the Founders. We cracked our cognitive rights management software as soon as Chitragupta came up with it. There were lots of us. And some of us got caught. Like me.'

'How did you end up here?' I ask. Then it hits me. 'This was never a Kingdom, was it?' I say. 'It was a prison.'

'This was supposed to be a new Australia,' he says. 'A typical pre-Collapse idea: put criminals inside terraforming machines, get them to pay their debts to society. And we worked hard, believe me, processed regolith and lit up Phobos and melted the ice cap with nukes, all just to be human for a little while again.

'Of course, they made sure we were safely locked up here. Even now, if I even *think* about leaving Mars, it hurts like hell. But then the Collapse happened, and the lunatics took over the asylum. We hacked the panopticon system. Turned it into the exomemory. Used it to give the power to *us*.'

He shakes his head.

'And we decided to tell the others a nicer story. The Spike was a blessing, wiped out all the traces we left – not that there were many. It was only after the zoku came that we were really able to flesh it out, of course. In retrospect, we should never have let them in here. At the time, we needed something to keep the Sobornost off our backs. Much good that turned out to do. But at least they gave us tools to make pretty dreams.'

'We? Who else is there?' I ask.

'No one,' he says. 'Well, not anymore. I took care of the others a long time ago. A garden only needs one gardener.' He reaches out with his free hand and touches the stem of a flower.

'I was content here, for a while,' he says. Then his face twists in a grimace. 'And then *you* had to come here. You had done so much better than I. All that power, all that freedom. All that, and you went native. You can't believe how angry that made me.'

Le Roi laughs. 'You know the feeling as well as I do, wanting something someone else has. So you can imagine how much I wanted what was *yours*. So after you left, I had what I could. Your woman, for example. She will never be yours again. She thinks you left her with the child you made together and disappeared. I never understood what you saw in her. At least you hid your traces well there, with that memory you split with her: I never knew what *this* was.'

He holds up the revolver with nine bullets. 'You thought you were so clever. Hiding your treasure in your little friends' exomemories. Great minds think alike, so much so I admit I could not find it. But I knew you would come back, and so I laid out a trail for you. The gevulot images came from me. Still, it was the detective who finally put the pieces together for me. Very appropriate.' He points the gun at me. 'I even gave you a chance to go through with it: fair is fair, after all. But you didn't. So now it's my turn.'

With a shout of red fury, I lunge towards him. The q-gun flashes. I fall to the ground, face hitting the marble hard. The Sobornost body screams for a moment, then applies some merciful anaesthesia, numbing the pain. I roll over and try to get up, only to realise my right leg is a blackened stump, gone from the knee down.

Le Roi looks down at me and smiles. Then he lifts the revolver into the air and starts firing. I try to claw at his legs but he kicks me in the face. I try to count the shots, but lose track.

The ground shudders. Deep beneath the city, the Atlas Quiet who once were my friends awaken with new minds and a new purpose. The memory palaces are parts of them, and with the force of a natural disaster, they want to be together again. A storm of stone rages around us. The buildings around the robot gardens collapse. The palaces loom above them like black sails, ploughing through everything in their way, bearing down on us.

They come together on top of us like the templed fingers of two hands made of black geometry. Then all is dark, and the pins and needles come, taking me and the King apart.

19

THE DETECTIVE AND THE RING

Mieli's skin tingles from the gevulot locks. But she feels light and weightless again, and *Perhonen*'s cockpit is the closest thing to a home she has left. The sense of safety and comfort is almost enough to drown out the raging voice of the pellegrini inside her head.

It's good to have you back, Perhonen says. The ship's butterfly avatars dancing around Mieli's head. *I felt like a piece of me was missing.*

'Me too,' Mieli says, delighting in the familiar tickle of wings fluttering against her skin. 'A big piece.'

'How soon can you get back down there?' demands the pellegrini. The goddess has been Mieli's constant companion ever since the immigration Quiet delivered her back to the ship and woke her up. Her mouth is a cold red line. 'This is intolerable. He will have to be punished. Punished.' She seems to taste the word. 'Yes, punished.'

'There is a problem with his biot feed,' Mieli says. She feels an odd sensation of *absence. Can I actually be missing his feed? The poisons you get addicted to.*

Just go ahead and admit that you are actually worried, Perhonen says. *Don't tell anyone, but so am I.*

'The last thing that registered is severe damage. And we can't go down for thirty days, not legally at least.'

'What is that boy *doing?*' the pellegrini mutters.

The Oubliette orbital control is telling us to get a Highway approach vector, Perhonen says. *And they are turning all visitors away from the beanstalk station. There is something happening down in the city.*

'Can we see anything?' Mieli asks.

The ship's butterfly avatars open a fan of moving images across various wavelengths in front of her. They show the city, a dark lenticular shape in the orange bowl of the Hellas Basin, blurred by its gevulot cloud.

Something is seriously wrong down there, Perhonen says. *It has stopped moving.*

There is something else in the images as well. A black fuzzy mass, pouring down from the rims of the impact crater towards the city.

Perhonen ramps up the magnification, and Mieli finds herself looking at a vision from hell.

Those? the ship says. *Those are phoboi.*

'What should we do?' Mieli asks the pellegrini.

'Nothing,' the goddess says. 'We wait. Jean wanted to play games down there: let him play. We wait until he is done.'

'With all due respect,' Mieli says, 'that means the mission is a failure. Are there any remaining agents on the ground who could be used? Gogol pirates?'

'Do you presume to tell me what to do?'

Mieli flinches.

'The answer is no. I cannot leave any signs of my presence here. It is time to cut our losses.'

'We are going to abandon him?'

'It is a pity, of course. I was a little sentimental about him: it has been a pleasant experience, for the most part. His little betrayal even added some spice. But nothing is irreplaceable. If the cryptarch emerges victorious, perhaps he will be easier to bargain with.' The pellegrini smiles wistfully. 'Perhaps not as entertaining, though.'

Whatever problems the city is having, I think they are spreading, Perhonen says. The Quiet fleet is in disorder. In case you are interested, the phoboi will hit the city's ramparts in approximately thirty minutes.

'Mistress,' Mieli says. 'I have given up everything to serve you. My mind, my body; much of my honour. But the thief has been my koto brother these last few weeks, however reluctantly. I cannot leave him behind and face my ancestors. Let me have that much.'

The pellegrini raises her eyebrows. 'So, he got through to you in the end, did he? But no, you are far too valuable to risk. We will wait.'

Mieli pauses, looking at the unmoving city in the images. *He is not worth it,* she thinks. *He is a thief, a liar.*

But he made me sing again. Even if it was a trick.

'Mistress,' Mieli says. 'Grant me this, and I'm willing to renegotiate our bargain. You can have a gogol of me. If I don't return, you can resurrect me as you wish.'

Mieli, don't do this, the ship whispers. *You can never go back on that.*

That's the only thing I have left, apart from honour, Mieli says. *And it is worth less.*

The pellegrini narrows her eyes. 'Well, that *is* interesting. All that for him?'

Mieli nods.

'Very well,' the goddess says. 'I accept your offer. With the condition that if anything goes wrong, *Perhonen* will use the strangelet device on the city: you still carry me inside you, and I cannot be found.' She smiles. 'Now, close your eyes and pray to me.'

It only takes minutes to get past the disorganised Quiet sentry fleet. Mieli does not feel like being subtle and burns the ship's antimatter engines hard. The ship is a sleek diamond dart, slicing through the troposphere, down towards the Hellas Basin.

Show me the phoboi.

Nightmare things race across the Basin. There are millions of them, in endless variations, all packed closely together in a mass that moves like a coherent organism. Swarms of transparent insects that form hulking, walking shapes. Clumps of bulbous sacks full of chemicals that move by pulsing and flowing. Humanoids with glasslike bodies and disturbingly realistic faces – apparently some of their ancestors have found that human countenances slow the reflexes of the warrior Quiet a small fraction.

The phoboi are hybrid biot/biological weapons, breeding themselves through billions of virtual generations and then modifying their own design accordingly. The Oubliette has been at war with them for centuries. And when the Moving City does not move, they can smell blood.

Mieli assesses their weaponry. Her countermeasure gogols are tailored to be used against zokus, not likely to do well against the phoboi's simple chemical brains. So brute force appears to be a more realistic option: q-dots, antimatter, lasers, and – if it comes to that – the remaining strangelet:

305

although she is worried about what the latter would do to Mars itself.

All right, Mieli says. *The plan is simple. You slow them down. I go get the thief. You pick us up. Just like last time.*

Understood, the ship says. *Be careful.*

You always say that, Mieli says. *Even when you are about to drop me on a dying city.*

I mean it every time, the ship says. Then it wraps Mieli in a q-dot bubble, grabs her with an EM field and fires her at Mars.

Metacortex fully active, Mieli steers with her wings, aiming towards one of the Persistent Avenue agoras. She fires nano-missiles at the city at a considerable fraction of *c.* She wears armour and carries an external weapon this time, a Sobornost multipurpose cannon – a sleek cylinder full of destruction. The missiles send back fragmented imagery before evaporating: the gevulot system is not fast enough to stop them from transmitting. Her metacortex pieces them together into a coherent picture of the city below.

Bloody faces, stains on white uniforms. Gogol pirates with their upload tendrils out, attacking anything that moves. Young and old Martians locked in battle, wielding makeshift weapons. Military Quiet, cordoning off streets. Tzaddikim, fighting Quiet and humans both, blocking gunfire with utility fog shields. The zoku colony under a q-dot bubble, surrounded by particularly heavy fighting. There, in the centre of the Maze, a black needle that was not there before. And almost directly below her—

The Gentleman is fighting in the Place of Lost Time, harried by a flock of assault Quiet. Her foglet shapes crackle under heavy fire.

Mieli takes the Quiet out with autonomous missiles with a quark-gluon plasma payload. They sweep half the square in an arc of nova-bright flame, illuminating the invisible foglet shapes momentarily: they look like exotic coral, blooming out from the Gentleman.

Phoboi report? Mieli asks *Perhonen*. The ship shares its senses with her. It is dancing above the seething mass, lobbing microton AM warheads at the phoboi. The sky of the city blinks in synchrony with them, like impossibly bright lightning flashes; the booms follow seconds later.

Not good, the ship says. *We really need a viral weapon of some kind. I'm slowing them down, but pincer number two is going to hit the city any minute now.*

Mieli slows the descent with her wings but still hits the ground hard. Stone cracks beneath her q-armoured feet. As she gets up from the small crater, she sees Raymonde. A cloud of foglet blades hovers around her, ready to strike.

'Which one are you?' she asks. 'Mieli or the other one?'

'The one who tells you that you are going to have a phoboi problem in a few minutes,' Mieli says.

'Oh, hell,' Raymonde mutters.

Mieli looks around at the destruction. There is more gunfire down the Avenue, and a distant explosion. 'Is this supposed to be a revolution?'

'It went bad an hour ago,' Raymonde says. 'The cryptarch-controlled started executing everyone who had the co-memory infection, and then they brought in the military Quiet as well from the ramparts. We have been arming the survivors. As long as the resurrection system survives, we can bring everybody back. But at the moment we are losing. And the real problem is *that*.' She points at the needle above the Maze.

'What is it?'

'That's what Jean made,' Raymonde says. 'He is inside. With the cryptarch.'

'The phoboi are coming,' Mieli says. 'We need to get this under control now or you are *all* going to find out what permanent death feels like. You need to get the city moving again. I take it the zoku is not doing anything?'

'No,' Raymonde says. 'I can't reach them anymore.'

'Typical,' Mieli says. 'All right. *You* need to get inside that thing, get the cryptarch out and make him stop the fighting so we can deal with the phoboi. *I* am coming to get the thief out. So it looks like we are going to the same direction.'

Mieli spreads her wings. The tzaddik takes to the air next to her. They fly over the burning city, towards the black needle.

'*You* were the ones who disrupted things,' Isidore says. 'You have to help us. We are going to have a civil war unless the cryptarch is stopped. The tzaddikim cannot do it alone.'

'No. Our first loyalty is to ourselves. We have healed; we are strong again. It is time for us to go.' Around them, the treasure chamber is almost empty: only the silver portals remain.

'You are running away,' Isidore says.

'Merely optimising the use of resources,' the Eldest says. 'You are free to come with us, although you will find that your current form will not be appropriate.'

'I'm staying here,' Isidore says. 'This is my home.'

A part of the Eldest's shimmer forms a miniature city. The streets are full of tiny people. There are flashes of light and flames. Isidore sees the conflict between the cryptarch-controlled and the memory-inoculated. He tastes blood and realises he is biting his tongue. And near the ramparts, white waves, crashing against them, lapping at the legs of the city. *Phoboi.*

'You may wish to reconsider your decision,' the Eldest says.

Isidore closes his eyes. It is a shape that is different from a mystery, rapidly changing, shifting, not static like a snowflake that can be examined from different angles and understood.

'The cryptarchs,' he says. 'The cryptarchs could still end this. They could get the city moving again, stop the fighting. Raymonde thought they were going to go there, with the thief—' He points at the needle in the miniature city, sticking up like an arrow in its heart.

'The ring,' he says. 'The thief stole my entanglement ring. Pixil, that ghost thing you did, would it work inside *that*?'

'Maybe, depending on what *that* is,' Pixil says. 'We just need a Realmgate to find out.' She starts towards the nearest silver arc.

'The zoku will not allow this,' the Eldest says.

'Just get me through it,' Isidore says. 'That's all I ask. I can't just stand here and watch.'

Pixil touches the zoku jewel at the base of her throat. She squeezes her eyes shut. For a moment, her face twists in pain. The jewel comes off, like a small creature being born. She holds it up with bloody fingers. 'The freedom we always have left,' she says, 'is the freedom to leave. I'm out. I was born here. I'm staying.'

She takes Isidore's hand. 'Let's go.'

'What are you doing?' the Eldest says.

Pixil touches the gate. Honey-coloured daylight pours out. 'The right thing,' she says. Then she steps through, pulling Isidore in after her.

20

TWO THIEVES AND A DETECTIVE

The darkness rebuilds us. For a moment, I feel like I'm being sketched by a pen, feeling returning to my flesh and skin and limbs, one by one. And then I can see again.

A cat stares at me. It is standing on its hind legs, wearing boots and a hat. A tiny sword hangs from a broad belt. Its eyes look glassy and dead, and I realise they *are* glass, glinting golden and bright. Then the cat moves jerkily, takes off its hat and bows with mechanical flourish.

'Good afternoon, master,' it says with a whirring, high-pitched voice. 'Welcome back.'

We are in the grand gallery of a palace. Paintings hang on the gilded walls, and crystal chandeliers glitter in the ceiling. There are wide windows opening to an Italian terrace, with golden, late afternoon sunlight pouring in, giving everything an amber glow. I am on the same level as the cat, hunched on the floor. A small mercy, my leg is no longer a stump. Like le Roi, I'm dressed in a costume of some ancient courtier, with coattails, brass buttons, ridiculously tight hose and a ruffled shirt. But it is to him that the cat is bowing. And he still holds the revolver in his hand.

I tense to leap, but he is faster. He strikes me across the face with the butt of the gun, and bizarrely, the pain is more real here than in the real world. I feel the metal digging into my flesh and cheekbone, and I almost pass out. My mouth fills with blood.

Le Roi gives me a nudge with his foot. 'Take this creature away,' he says. 'And find me something to wear.'

The cat bows again and claps its paws together. The tap is barely audible, but there are distant foosteps, and a door opens.

I struggle up to a sitting position and spit blood at le Roi's feet. 'Bastard,' I say. 'I was prepared for you. There are traps here you don't know about. You'll see.'

'Now, that is a pathetic attempt, not worthy of either of us,' says le Roi. 'Be grateful that I find it amusing to keep you around. As a distant memory, perhaps.'

He gestures with the gun, and strong, unyielding hands lift me off the floor and start dragging me away. Wax figures: a man in an early twentieth-century suit, with a thick moustache, and a woman I don't recognise, dressed as a maid. Both have glass eyes and yellow, clumsily sculpted wax faces. I try to struggle, but I am no match for their mechanical strength.

'Let me go!' I shout. 'He is not your master, I am!' But clearly, the gun grants le Roi more authority than I can muster here. 'Bastard!' I shout. 'Come back and fight!'

The creatures drag me down a corridor with open doors. There seem to be hundreds of them: inside, silent wax figures enact scenes in slow motion. They strike a chord: a young man in a prison cell, reading a book. A dark tent, with a woman sitting in a corner, humming to herself, preparing food over a pitiful fire. I glimpse a wax-faced nude Raymonde, playing the piano with slow, clumsy fingers. They are all dead and mechanical, and suddenly I realise what a *distant memory* could mean.

But it is not until they take me to the workshop, with the moulds and the pool of hot wax and the sharp instrument that I start screaming.

There is a discontinuity. When it ends, Isidore is still holding Pixil's hand. He blinks. The air smells of dust and wax. They are in what looks like a torturer's workshop, but with high, ornate windows opening to a garden. The thief is strapped to a long table, with fairy tale creatures looming above him: a wolf in the clothes of a woman, a moustached man and a maid in costumes from ancient Earth history. They are holding sharp, curving knives in paws and waxy hands.

Pixil leaps forward. Her sword comes out of its scabbard with a *zing* and slices left and right, through wax and brass. A furry head flies into the air; cogs and metal spill out of the back of the man's pierced cranium. The wax creatures fall to the floor in pieces. Then she places the tip of the blade gently on the thief's throat.

'Don't move,' she says. 'This is a Realmspace sword. As you can see, it adapts to this place quite nicely.'

'I was just going to say *thank you*,' the thief wheezes. Then he grins at Isidore. 'M. Beautrelet. Delighted to see you here. We have met before. Jean le Flambeur, at your service. But – obviously – your lady friend has the, uh, advantage of me.'

'What is happening here?' Isidore asks.

'The cryptarch – le Roi – controls this place, I'm sorry to say.' He blinks. 'But how did you get here? Of course, your zoku ring,' he says. 'It is amazing how useful kleptomaniac habits can be, sometimes – watch out!'

Isidore turns. He catches a glimpse of a furry creature,

darting across the floor. 'Catch it!' the thief shouts. 'It has your ring!'

Here they come, Perhonen says. *I can't hold them anymore.*

She can feel the impacts of the flying phoboi on the ship's skin, draining its armour. 'Get out of there.' The ship rises up, and Mieli sees the phoboi tide hit the disorganised Quiet wall like a scythe, pouring over it. She blinks the ship's view away and returns her attention to firing at the cryptarch-controlled assault Quiet.

A yellow constructor Quiet brought her down by filling the air with fabbed construction dust, temporarily blocking her wings' microfans. The Quiet keep throwing themselves at her and Raymonde stubbornly, turning their advance towards the black needle into a crawl.

'The phoboi are getting through,' Mieli shouts at the tzaddik. Even through the dust and the silver mask, Mieli can see the despair on her face.

Mieli! Something is happening! She slows time and sees through the ship's eyes again.

The bubble around the zoku colony disappears. Howling ghosts made from shimmer and diamond and jewels ride out, raining coherent light on the phoboi horde, cutting through it as if it wasn't there, moving faster than human eye can see. Wildfires start in their wake – self-replicating nanotech weaponry – and circles of flame spread through the seething mass. *What made them change their minds?* Mieli wonders. But there is no time to reflect.

'Come on!' she tells Raymonde. 'There is still time!' Gritting her teeth, she extends a q-blade from the cannon and rushes the mass of Quiet ahead.

*

The zoku girl cuts me free. The detective is already running after the cat, and I race after him. The creature is no longer in sight, and I dash madly onwards in the direction I think it went, passing more memory automata.

And then I see it, in a small gallery, sitting on a one-legged table made of dark wood: a black, unadorned object that could hold a wedding ring. The Schrödinger Box. It is just as tempting as it was twenty years ago, when I found out that the zoku colony had it, and I can't resist. Warily, I enter and grab it, expecting a trap. But nothing happens. I squeeze it in my fist and return to the corridor.

The detective and the zoku girl are running back.

'I'm sorry,' the detective says. 'It got away.'

'Are you looking for this?' says Jean le Roi. He looks different now, younger, much more like me. His face is smooth, his hair black, and he has a pencil moustache. He is wearing a black tie, white gloves, and an opera cloak draped over his shoulders, as if before a night out on the town. He carries a cane. A cluster of zoku jewels floats around his head, flashing in hues of green and blue. But the sneer is still there.

He holds up the ring, a silver band with a blue stone. 'Don't worry, you won't be needing it anymore.' He waves his hand like a conjuror and the ring vanishes in a puff of flash powder. 'You can all stay here, as my guests.' He brushes invisible dust away from his lapels. 'I have found a body I'm going to wear, I think. It's time to leave all this strife behind.'

The zoku girl lets out a wild cry, and before I can stop her, she swings her sword in a wide arc at le Roi. With a movement too fast to follow, he twists the head of his cane, and a blade comes out in a bright flash. He parries her blow, then drops and lunges. The swordcane's tip blooms out of her back, an evil, sharp flower. He pulls it out in one smooth movement. She falls to her knees. The detective rushes to her side, holding her up. But I can tell it is already too late.

Le Roi nudges her fallen sword with his own. 'A nice toy,' he says. 'But mine are much nicer.' He seems to notice the detective for the first time. His eyes widen.

'You are not supposed to be here,' he says quietly. 'What are you doing here?'

The detective stares up at him. There are tears on his cheeks, but his eyes are brimming with anger. 'M. le Roi,' he says with a steady voice. 'I am here to arrest you for crimes against the Oubliette, and in the name of the Revolution order you to turn your exomemory key over to me immediately—'

'No, no.' He kneels next to the boy. 'You have it all wrong. I thought you were a memory he turned against me. I didn't mean for this to happen.' He looks at the girl. 'We can bring her back if you want. And my key, here it is, if you want.' He drops his cane and fumbles for something in his pocket. 'Here. You have it.' He presses something in the detective's hand. 'Take it. I'll send you back. It is only right that the prince will inherit the kingdom—'

The detective strikes him across the face. He leaps up and picks up his swordcane, pointing at him. Then he shakes his head. 'Enough.' He gestures with the weapon, and the detective is gone, in a flash of light.

'You are breaking all your toys,' I say, holding up the Realmspace sword. 'Want to try me as well?'

The sword is talking to me, showing the underlying structure of everything around us. This is a little Realm, a virtual world that serves as an interface for the picotech machine around us. I am a software entity, containing all the information of the matter of my body the palace disassembled. And there is something blue inside my belly, like a ghost—

Le Roi's eyes narrow. 'The boy is not broken,' he says. 'He turned out well. He outsmarted you. I will come and visit him in a hundred years.'

'No thanks to you,' I say. 'And he is right. You have to pay for what you have done.'

He salutes me with the swordcane, sneering. 'Then carry out the sentence, if you can. Let's finish this.' He assumes a fencer's stance, his eyes a reflection of my own.

I raise the Realmspace sword with both hands and plunge the point into my stomach. The pain is blinding. The sword cuts through the software construct that is me.

And lets the Archon loose.

It comes out with my blood and guts, spilling out in a flood of data. It spreads into the walls and the floor of the palace. They start turning into glass. The walls of the cells come down between me and Jean le Roi, and as I give birth to a Dilemma Prison, I start laughing.

Mieli almost shoots the detective when the needle spits him out. A part of its jagged dark side turns into a naked body of a young man and falls forward. And then Raymonde is next to him, holding him up.

'He got Pixil,' the boy mutters.

They made it to the base of the needle minutes ago. It looks like the pseudomatter Mieli has only seen near Spike remnants, not made from atoms and molecules but something more subtle, quark matter or spacetime foam.

Mieli, says *Perhonen, I'm not sure it's safe to be there. There is something happening inside that thing. Gamma rays, exotic WIMPs, it's like a fountain—*

A ripple goes through the structure. And suddenly it is

like smoked glass, dark, cold and dense. *Like the Prison. He released the Archon.*

Mieli lowers her weapon and touches the wall of the needle. It opens and accepts her like a lover.

The Archon is happy. New thieves, new things to make, new games to grow, in dense soil that makes its mind expand a thousandfold. Someone touches it: the Oort woman, the fugitive, returning to its embrace. It lets her in. She tastes of cinnamon.

Isidore aches. His body is new and raw, and inside, Pixil's death is a fire. But there is no time to think about that, because suddenly he knows everything.

The exomemory is a sea around him, clear like a tropical ocean. Quiet, Nobles, tzaddikim: every thought ever thought, every memory. They are all his. It is the most beautiful and the most terrible shape he has ever seen or felt. The history. The present: rage, blood and fire. Atlas Quiet, going mad, labouring to keep the city standing. People fighting like puppets, the triggers and knobs and dials in their heads that his father put there turned to madness.

He speaks to them with the Voice and reminds them of who they are. The Quiet return to man the phoboi walls. The fighting stops.

And slowly, step by step, the city starts to move again.

So, here we are again. Doing time.

I am naked. I keep my eyes closed. On the floor in front of me is a gun. And soon, I am going to pick it up and decide to shoot or not to shoot.

The sound of shattering glass sounds like music, or like

breaking the law. A wind blows through the cell, carrying tiny shards. I open my eyes and see Mieli, wings outspread, a scarred angel in black.

'I was hoping you would come,' I say.

'Is this the part,' she says, 'where you tell me that you are Jean le Flambeur and that you only leave this place when you choose?'

'No,' I say. 'It's not that part.'

I take her hand. She embraces me. She beats her wings and we rise up, through the glass sky, away from guns, memories and kings.

21

THE THIEF AND THE STOLEN GOODBYE

I say goodbye to the detective – Isidore – in his kitchen, the day after the zoku brings Pixil back.

'She is different now,' he says. 'I don't know why, but she is different.'

We sit around his kitchen table, and I try to avoid looking at the sombre, dirty brown wallpaper.

'Sometimes,' I say, 'it only takes a few moments to make you a different person. Sometimes it takes centuries.' I try to shake off the green creature that has been wandering around the table. It seems to regard me as a natural enemy, and keeps chewing on my sleeve. 'But of course, you should not really listen to anything I say. Especially about women.'

I look at him: a bony nose, high cheekbones. The resemblance is there, around the mouth and the jaw and the eyes. I wonder what Raymonde and le Roi would have left to chance. I hope there is more of her in him than me.

'You have changed a lot too,' I continue. 'Isidore Beautrelet, Cryptarch of the Oubliette. Or perhaps *king* would be a better word. What are you going to do next?'

'I don't know,' he says. 'I can't make every decision. I have to give the Voice back to the people. There has to be a better way to make this work. I'm going to give it up as soon as I can. And I have to figure out if ... if I'm going to let everyone remember where the Oubliette really came from.'

'Well, a revolution is always a beautiful dream,' I say. 'And you have just had a real one. Whatever you do, be careful. The Sobornost is going to come after you, hard and fast. The zoku will help now, I think: but it won't be easy.' I smile. 'It'll be exciting, too. Big and confusing. Like an opera, someone told me once.'

He looks out through the window. The city is still healing: it must be a different view than before. And the Prison is visible from here, a diamond needle above the Maze roof-tops.

'What about you?' he asks. 'Are you going to go off and do something ... criminal?'

'Almost certainly. I still have a debt to pay, I'm afraid.' I grin. 'You are welcome to catch me if you can. But I think you are going to be too busy.' I give the green creature a dark look. It is now trying to get into my lap. 'Of course, others here don't seem to have that problem.'

I get up. 'I'd better get going. Mieli hasn't killed any-thing for a few days now, and that always puts her in a bad mood.'

I shake his hand. 'I'm not your father,' I say, 'but you are a better man than I am. Keep it that way. But if you are ever tempted by the other path, let me know.'

To my surprise, he hugs me, hard.

'No thanks,' he says. 'Be seeing you.'

Can we go yet? Perhonen asks. *Do we have to wait for him?*

The ship sits in the walled trail of the city, near the battered and scorched Quiet wall. Mieli is outside in a quicksuit, walking her restlessness away. There are are reliefs on the wall that remind her of Oort, landscapes and rows upon rows of blank faces. She touches them and hears the faint song carved in them, inside her mind.

'Hi,' says Raymonde. She is wearing her Gentleman outfit, but without a mask, and instead of a suit she wears a faint foglet halo. She notices the reliefs and a look of sadness and guilt passes across her face.

'Is everything all right?' Mieli asks.

'Just remembering that there is someone I need to see.' Raymonde looks at *Perhonen*. 'That's a beautiful ship.'

Thank you, Perhonen says. *But I'm not just a pretty face.* Raymonde gives the ship a bow. 'You too, have our gratitude,' she says. 'You didn't have to do what you did.'

You can't see it, the ship says, sapphire shell gleaming, *but I'm blushing.*

Raymonde looks around. 'He isn't here yet? No surprise there.' She kisses Mieli on both cheeks. 'Good luck, and safe journey. And thank you.' She pauses. 'When you opened your gevulot, you showed us your thoughts. I saw why you are doing this. For what it's worth, I hope you find her.'

'It's not a matter of hope,' Mieli says, 'but will.'

'Good answer,' Raymonde says. 'And – don't be hard on him. I mean – be hard, but not too hard. He can't help what he is. But he is not as bad as he could be.'

'Are you talking about me?' the thief says, stepping out of a zoku transport bubble. 'I knew you would talk about me behind my back.'

'I'll wait in the ship,' Mieli says. 'We are leaving in five minutes.'

*

In the end, I don't know what to say to her. So we stand in silence, on the red sand. The shadows the city casts flicker all around us, wings of light and dark, beating.

After a while, I kiss her hand. If she has tears in her eyes, the shadows hide them. She kisses me lightly, on the mouth. She stands there, watching, as I walk to the ship. I turn to wave as the ship's skin opens, and blow her a kiss.

Inside the ship, I weigh the Box in my hand.

'Are you going to open that thing or not?' Mieli asks. 'I'd like to know where we are going.'

But I already know.

'Earth,' I say. 'But can you ask *Perhonen* to take her time? I'd like to watch the scenery.'

To my surprise, she does not object. *Perhonen* rises slowly and makes a turn above the Moving City, over the vein of Persistent Avenue, the green expanse of the Tortoise Park, the papercraft castles of the Dust District. The city wears a different face now, but I smile it at nevertheless. It ignores me and keeps moving.

We are halfway to the Highway before I realise that the detective stole my Watch.

Interlude

THE HUNTER

It is springtime, and the Engineer-of-Souls is happy.

His *guberniya* virscape is a machine garden, vast and blooming. The seeds he planted during the long Dyson winter when the *guberniya* slowed itself down to shed its waste heat have blossomed, and now there is variety, variety everywhere.

His gogols swarm around him like a flock of white-coated birds as he plumbs its depths: plunging a billion pairs of hands into black soil where each particle is a cogwheel that fits together with its neighbours perfectly, to feel the seeds of new composite minds about to bloom. Engineer-Prime himself is everywhere, directing the culling of this memetic tree, watching that flock of genetic algorithms alight into a new parameter space from a branching process.

With infinite gentleness he pulls up a freshly bloomed shoot of a newly made gogol, one with a rare disorder that makes it think its body would be made of glass, easily shattered: something he thought lost centuries ago. Combined with an exquisite schizophrenia, it will result in a mind that can divide and recombine itself at will, integrating memories: something Matjek's warminds will love. He splits off a gogol to carry on the mundane details of the work, and returns his attention to the big picture, letting Engineer-Prime shoot upwards to the sky, white lab coat flapping in the fresh breeze. Yes, that patch there will yield a good harvest of Dragonspeakers. In that vast labyrinth, single-minded Pursuers are already gestating: soon they will be ready to explore parameter spaces larger than worlds, mathematical ants, combing the vast Gödel universe for unproven theorems.

It occurs to the Engineer that he has never been happier: a quick search through his gogol library verifies the fact. He is more content than any Engineer has ever been, since his earliest days as a student in the University of Minsk – although one moment in time, with someone special, comes close. That, in itself, is worth splitting off a gogol and storing it into his Library, frozen in time.

So of course, it cannot last.

There is a ripple in the virscape as no less than two other Founders arrive, unannounced: waves of religious terror spread through the lesser gardener gogols, who prostrate themselves among the growing machines. A gestating warmind escapes its suddenly distracted handlers, a metallic spider of controlled poisonous aggression, demolishing a promising patch of Dreamers until the Engineer can stretch out one of his billion hands to unmake it. *What a waste.* Oblivious to the destruction they are causing, the two strangers stride towards the main concourse of the Garden. One of them is a small, unassuming Chinese man with grey hair in sober monkish robes. At least Matjek Chen, the most powerful Founder in all of Sobornost, has the courtesy not to appear in his full Founder form here.

But the other, a tall woman in a white summer dress, holding a delicate parasol, hiding her face—

Filled with sudden haste, the Engineer works quickly to contain the visitors in a subvirtual – no mean task, given that with their Founder powers, they could easily rip such illusions apart – and sends Engineer-Prime down to meet them.

The Garden becomes a true garden, with cherry trees in full bloom. There is a stone fountain in the Fedorovist style, heroic figures of a man and a woman holding a cup aloft. Lesser Engineer gogols arrange refreshments as Engineer-Prime goes to meet his visitors.

'Welcome,' he says, stroking his beard – a royal gesture, he thinks. He gives the two a slight bow. Chen acknowledges him with a barely perceptible nod. The Engineer tries to judge the seniority of this gogol: not the Prime, certainly, but enough of the Founder aura to hold true power.

The woman folds her parasol and smiles at him, diamonds glittering around her swanlike neck. 'Hello, Sasha,' she says.

He holds out a chair for her. 'Joséphine.'

She sits down gracefully, crossing her legs, leaning delicately on the folded parasol. 'It is such a lovely garden you have here, Sasha,' she says. 'It is no wonder that we never see you anymore. Why, if I lived in a place like this, I would not want to leave.'

'Sometimes it is tempting,' says Chen, 'to ignore the realities of the world at large. Unfortunately, not all of us have such luxury.'

The Engineer gives the old Founder a curt smile. 'The

work I do here is of benefit to all of Sobornost, and the Great Common Task.'

'Of course,' Chen says. 'You are uniquely qualified for that work. Indeed, that is why we are here.' He sits down to the edge of the fountain, touching the water. 'This is all a little excessive, don't you think?' The Engineer remembers that Chen's own realms tend to be abstract, Spartan places, with bared-down physics and barely enough detail to stay out of the valleys of the uncanny.

'Oh, please, Matjek,' says Joséphine. 'Don't be such a bore. It is beautiful here. And can't you see that Sasha is busy? He always strokes his beard when he is eager to get back to work but is too polite to say so.'

'He has gogols aplenty to do his work,' Chen says, 'but very well.' He crosses his hands and leans across the table.

'Brother, we have a slight problem with one of your creations. The Dilemma Prison has been breached.'

'Impossible.'

'See for yourself.' The virscape wavers as Chen passes the Engineer a memory: for a moment, he sees the Founder gogol as he truly is, the voice of trillions of Chens, stretching across all the vast *guberniyas* and *oblasts* and *raions* of the Sobornost, not so much a person but a limb. Then he is holding a frozen gogol that he recognises as his own handiwork instantly, a little experiment with games and obsessions he had almost forgotten about. An Archon, he called it, made to hold the mad ones and bad ones of Sobornost somewhere far away. He peels it open like an orange, and absorbs its memories.

'How strange,' he says, watching the Prison spit out three minds into a fragile matter shell. He feels a sting of admiration for the little thing in the Oortian ship that manages to fool his own creation, and makes a note to make sure that the

326

next Archon generation has the ability to distinguish between different layers of reality.

'We would not have even noticed,' says Chen, 'if they had not made a mistake. But they did: they were supposed to take out two gogols, not three. The third one is quite interesting, as you can see.'

'Ah yes,' says the Engineer, feeling grandparental pride at the Archons' creation. 'The defector. Fascinating.'

'Founder codes. Somebody opened the Prison with Founder codes. We need to know why.' Chen slams a fist against the table. 'We are at war, all of us, between ourselves, some of us even against ourselves. But there are some things we agreed not to do.'

'Perhaps you did, Matjek,' says Joséphine, running a finger along the rim of her glass of water. 'Somebody else clearly did not.'

'We need those gogols back: we – I – need to know what they know.'

'And have you not gogols aplenty of your own to accomplish that?' asks the Engineer, feeling satisfied that he can hold the older Founder's gaze for a moment. 'There are greater works to be begun and completed.' He can feel Chen's irritation gathering behind the gogol's calm veneer, like static electricity in the air.

'Sasha,' Joséphine says. 'We are not children. We – I – would not come to ask if we did not need you.' She touches his hand, and smiles: and even after three centuries and billions of branchings, the Engineer finds it difficult not to smile back. 'Matjek, perhaps you should let me talk to Sasha alone.' She holds the old Founder's gaze for a moment. To the Engineer's surprise, he looks away. 'All right,' Chen says. 'Perhaps a child can talk some sense to another child. I will be back soon.' He leaves the virscape ungracefully, pulling the gogol avatar into a rupture in space so violently that the Engineer has to struggle to smooth it out.

Joséphine shakes her head. 'We all talk about change,' she says. 'There are some things that do not change.' Then she looks at him, luminous eyes aglow. 'But you have. I love all these things you have built. It's amazing. I wonder – did you always have it in you, even back then? Or did you grow up?'

'Joséphine,' he says. 'Just tell me what it is that you want.'

She pouts. 'I'm not sure I like this grown-up Sasha. You are not even blushing.'

'Please.'

'All right.' She looks up and takes a deep breath. 'They are killing me. The others. Things have changed during your last Winter, changed a lot. Anton and Hsien are together now. Chitragupta is ... well, it is itself. But me – they never liked me. And I am weak, weaker than you can believe.'

The Engineer stares at her in disbelief. 'Gogolcide? Have we come that far?'

'Not yet, but that is what they intend. Matjek is my only hope, and he knows that you will listen to me. It is not *really* about the Prison, you understand: he just wants a weapon against the others. And your support.'

'I could ...' He hesitates. 'I could protect you.'

'You are sweet, but we both know you could not. This place is something that the others give you because you are useful. If that ceases, so will this. Help Matjek, and he will help us both. Make something that will catch the little runaways. It is a small thing, but it will show him that you listen to me. And that will make *me* valuable to him.'

The Engineer closes his eyes. He can feel his Garden, alive and growing, his billion hands in its soil: all inside a mighty *guberniya* brain, eating matter and energy from the sun itself, a diamond sphere the size of old Earth, containing his trillion gogols and the Dragons within. And yet he feels small.

'All right,' he says. 'Just this once. For old times' sake.'

'Thank you.' She kisses his cheek. 'I knew I could count on you.'

'Don't let it get too far, with him,' he says.

'I know Matjek, as much as it is possible to know him. I can handle him, for now. I may have … other options, but those will take time. So I thank you for this gift.'

'It is nothing.' He smiles. 'I will make you a hunter. Would you like to watch?'

'I always love to watch you work.'

He lets the garden vir dissolve around them. In her Founder form, she is equally beautiful, a creature of spun silver woven from many gogols. He guides her through the Factory to the Orchard, where his favourite things grow. Taking quiet pleasure in the astonishment she radiates, he loses himself in the work. This is a task for a different scale, no longer supervision but craftsmanship: the cognitive modules of the new thing he is making are vast atlases around them, symphonies of neural pathways and thoughts.

With some pleasure he is able to incorporate his new discovery in the design. This Hunter will not be one, but many: able to split itself into many parts and become one again. He gives it a single-mindedness he found in an Oortian sculptor, and the coordination ability of a concert pianist, seasoned with more primitive animal forms from the older libraries: shark and feline. He gives it enough cognitive rights to be intelligent, but not enough to have latency, and allocates a fragment of the *guberniya* smartmatter to it, so it is ready to be launched when its new mistress commands.

The finished thing does not speak, but regards them both silently, observing, waiting for a target. It has the kind of beauty that weapons often have, the kind that lures you to touch it even though you know that its sharp edges will cut.

'It's yours,' he says. 'Not Matjek's. Yours. Just tell it what you want to be found.'

Joséphine Pellegrini smiles, and whispers a name in the Hunter's ear.